Also by Cathryn Grant

Cathryn Grant

SHE'S LISTENING

A Novel

D2C
D2C Perspectives

1

Ann

They call an orgasm the little death — *la petite mort*.

Each time a man is satisfied, he dies for a moment in a woman's arms.

When I was a teenager, learning more about sex through books and magazines, blogs and girlfriends than I did from hands-on experience, I was informed that when a man has an orgasm, he belongs to you more than he will in any other moment.

I don't know if that's true. I never asked a man whether it was true. Depending on the man who's asked, how would I know whether or not the answer was truthful? People lie about sex all the time. A therapist is in a position to know this. Often, the lies are exposed when my patients recount their dreams. As they begin to describe the dream, they don't immediately realize they're telling the truth for the first time.

A female patient retells a dream that makes clear the cousin she believed was her closest friend, with whom she's had a bitter falling out, put his hand down her pants when she was four. Partway through the telling of her dream, I've seen a woman stop speaking. Her gaze holds mine for a few seconds, then darts toward the door, looking for escape, terrified as she uncovers the lie she's told herself for so many years.

Some of my patients are pleased when they realize they've finally said something real. Others are shocked and ashamed that anyone, even the therapist who keeps their secrets under lock and key, has seen their naked soul.

Other times, the lies about sex are finally cast away when a patient admits the truth to herself, or himself, without the accusing finger of a dream. Therapy has a way of backing people into a corner. If it's done correctly, they come face to face with the many ways they lie to themselves. After that, they experience intense freedom. There's a rawness in their psyche, but overall, they're free. The truth does indeed set you free.

Of course, la petite mort isn't just about a man dying in a woman's arms. The term applies equally to women.

And the little death also more broadly refers to a period of melancholy or transcendence that follows the release of the life force. The little death is an experience that pre-figures death itself.

Death is the farthest thing from a patient's mind when she, or he, enters my office for the first time. Very few people start seeing a therapist to talk about the bigger questions of life. There's a presenting issue — divorce, a rebellious child, a controlling mother, a cold father, betrayal, compulsive eating or drinking or gambling or sex, career frustration, crushing guilt, and yes, grief. But the grief that drives a person to a therapist is more about their own life and loss, not death per se.

Gemma Hughes was the first patient who sought me out through an ad I'd placed on Facebook. It's an unorthodox way to acquire new therapy patients, but my referral channels had dried up slightly. Too many people are looking for quick-fix behavioral counseling — *help me stop uncontrolled snacking in eight sessions, provide techniques for moderating my short temper in six weeks*, that sort of thing. It took a while for the ad to attract new patients, but eventually, it did. Facebook allows very granular targeting, which helps. For example, women bereft after the end of a love affair. I had to turn away a few who responded, but not all, and not Gemma. She fit the ad profile perfectly.

Therapy takes at least a year, often more, if it's done correctly.

Right from the start, Gemma told me she had no intention of spending a year with me, but she'd been gripped by the teaser in my ad. The text asserted my ability to help women who'd been dumped, abandoned, cheated on, or betrayed, to regain their sense of self and heal the pain.

Can you really make the pain go away?

That was the first question out of her mouth. She slid right past the promise of regaining a sense of her self.

Studying her parted lips, her dilated pupils, the chewed-off fingernails, my heart ached, feeling the pain that was written across every feature of her very pretty face. She looked like her heart had truly been cleaved in two. "I believe I can."

"That doesn't sound as guaranteed as your ad."

It was advertising, what did she expect?

I needed to see a woman, or man, in person to establish that heartfelt connection that would assure them they were in good hands with me. To help them believe I could help, that I wanted to help, that I would feel every step of the process with them.

Therapists are trained to avoid shouldering a patient's

feelings, but that can be taken to the extreme. Patients know when you're too detached, and they read it as insincerity. They know when you *get it* and when you're keeping your distance — simply asking questions, taking notes, nodding and looking empathetic, pretending to care.

I truly cared. I *do* care. Deeply.

"You have to truly want to be free of the pain," I said.

"I do."

"Then, yes. I can help. If you're willing to work hard."

"Work hard?"

"Explore the difficult questions. Refuse to lie to yourself."

"I never lie to myself." She smiled.

That, of course, was a lie. We all lie to ourselves. And each lie is a little death of our true selves.

"Tell me why you're here," I said.

She looked confused. She was quiet for several minutes. "He doesn't love me anymore." She gasped for air. "It feels like something's squeezing my heart all the time. I can't breathe." Her eyes filled with tears.

I thought again about the little death. The way a man dies, for a moment, a fraction of second, after the satisfaction of making love.

The man that would soon die in my arms would not be taken by the little death. He would be a victim of the big death, *la grande mort*, if you will.

Blood would seep across his chest, soaking his shirt as he exhaled his final breath. I would be relieved to see him go. I would be satisfied, but he would not.

2

Gemma

When a man breaks your heart, it's the worst pain imaginable.

I know many people would disagree with that. They would say the worst pain is losing a child. But I don't know about that. The moment a child exits a woman's body, she knows that child will be walking away from her every day of her life. First, the baby will crawl and resist her mother's effort to restrain her scrambling to another room. Then she'll toddle, shrieking with laughter as she eludes her mother's hands. In the blink of an eye, she's off to elementary school, and then she's closing her bedroom door to keep her mother out. She prefers her friends, and then she leaves for college, an apartment, a career, a man.

Obviously, the loss of a man is nothing like the death of a child, but you expected separation from the beginning. You knew you were opening yourself up to a world of pain.

Knowing that you're going to face overwhelming loss prepares you.

Once you connect with a man, once you start falling in love, and you see that he's doing the same, you believe it's forever. When you feel him empty his body into yours, you know his heart belongs to you. When he collapses across you, and you feel the weight of him, his skin melting against yours, you know it will never end, never change. There's no question even at the furthest corner of your mind.

It's real. It feels like you've become a single entity, hearts beating with the same rhythm.

The pain of losing him is literally like having your skin torn off your flesh. No, that's not right. It's deeper than that. It's a squeezing of your organs, a pressure so tight it's impossible to breathe. When you wake in the morning, the pain is a razor across your heart, and then it settles back to that constant ache, accompanied by tears that come when you least expect them.

Going to therapy seemed like a good idea. It was that or slicing my wrists or taking pills. And maybe she would give me pills, so I'd always have that option if Dr. Wilcox didn't live up to her promise to make the pain go away.

Walking into her office was like entering a spa. The waiting area was small, but the soft edges of the pale yellow walls and the dark green fabric of the armchairs gave it a spacious air. The color made the walls seem almost permeable. Two large leafy plants in the corners made me feel as if I were in a private garden. There was no need for more square footage, the mental expanse was enough. I was the only one waiting.

This was my second appointment. At the first session, she'd asked why I wanted therapy. She asked me to give a brief outline of my childhood. She spent the final minutes helping me fill out forms for insurance.

In response to her first question, I told her my heart was literally broken.

She tucked her dark silky hair behind one ear, making her seem almost vulnerable, which made me relax. Slightly.

She gave me a kind smile. It was a soft, genuine smile that filled her eyes as much as her mouth. A smile that looked warm against her milky skin. She promised she could make the pain go away. I hoped so. I wanted to believe her, but it had been a month since he'd left me and the pain was worse than ever.

She wanted to know about my childhood because that was where everything began. We would talk about the rest of my background in future sessions. I should say *I* would talk...

Therapy, the kind she practices, involved me doing all the talking. She would ask questions. She would not give advice, and she would not comment on my experiences or offer judgement of any kind. I said it sounded like I could sit at home and talk to myself with the same results. She said absolutely not because her expertise would guide the areas we explored. I would be startled by the transformation.

I was born in 1984. It seemed like that should mean something. Dr. Wilcox asked why it should mean something. I couldn't answer because my first thought was — *No wonder therapy takes a year or more, if she was going to question every word I said*. I smiled but couldn't find any explanation. She said if I wasn't sure, it was something to consider when I was alone with my thoughts. She suggested I keep a journal to help me remember my insights and to guide my thoughts, as well as for recording my dreams.

Being born in 1984 should mean something because it's the title of a classic novel. That's all. Everyone thinks the number is a little bit scary, ominous, so that's why I'd always thought being born in that year should mean *something*.

During the summary of my childhood, she didn't ask any more questions.

I told her I was born in Southern California. Our parents moved to San Jose when I was eleven and Geoff was ten. My dad was a high school history teacher, and my mother was a stay-at-home mom.

I went to a public school where I had normal experiences — I made friends, got picked on once or twice, picked on others a few times, had crushes on boys, and did my homework. I took ballet lessons, had sleepovers, and loved and hated my brother — sometimes both in a single afternoon.

All of those things were normal, but it seemed to me that all of them could have layers of secrets and forgotten events beneath them, which is what Dr. Wilcox had said about the psyche, so I expected her to ask for more details.

Still, she didn't say a word. It made me wonder if my childhood was boring. Maybe any secrets I harbored weren't all that interesting. Maybe *I* wasn't all that interesting.

Maybe that was why David didn't want me anymore. The thought made tears rush into my eyes.

Dr. Wilcox handed me a box of tissues. She asked whether I considered my childhood a happy one.

"I don't know. I never thought about it, until now." My voice was a rough whisper.

I pulled two more tissues out of the box and started bawling like a baby.

She told me I was doing a good job, to be sure to purchase a notebook dedicated to therapy. At our next session, I would tell her about my high school years where many seeds for adult relationships take root.

I didn't see the point, not really. And I certainly wasn't going to tell her everything that happened in high school and college. Those stories were all a distraction from the pain throbbing inside my chest twenty-four hours a day.

I wanted her to make me stop hurting, not dredge up more pain.

3

Ann

Many therapists create audio recordings of their sessions. It helps them remember every nuance of their patients' histories, the stories and subterfuges, and the breakthroughs. A recording provides a detailed recollection of things that might be forgotten if they aren't precisely captured in handwritten notes. Sometimes, in the moment of listening and making notes, the important things aren't always obvious. It's only when listening to previous sessions that patterns and themes emerge.

That's the belief, anyway.

I don't agree. I understand the concern, but I think it's too easy to get lost in minutiae. I don't need to sit through every pregnant pause, every emotional breakdown, every off-topic stream-of-consciousness avenue of thought. Even though I believe every thought has meaning, it's not possible to deconstruct them all.

In my view, written notes are far more valuable. It allows me to insert the thoughts I was having as a patient is revealing a particular piece of information, including visible signs of lying or distress. It allows the things she's saying to flow through me a second time and with a different set of filters — first through my ears, and half a moment later, through the fine motor muscles of my hand.

My peers have suggested recordings supplemented with notes so I can comment on particular topics as the patient is speaking, but still retain every moment of each session. That never worked for me. Trying to connect those notes to a recording was cumbersome and ultimately prevented me from gaining clarity.

Because I do need clarity in treating a patient. Some people who are reluctant to undertake therapy have the impression the therapist is just a dummy for another part of the patient's psyche. But the questions that are asked are critical, it's not just a casual conversation with mundane lines of inquiry. Neither are the questions always leading. And I must have clarity with a patient in order to formulate the timing and the content of my questions. It's not as simple as it looks to a layperson.

Only a trained therapist knows where to inquire further, and how to pose the right question in order to nudge the patient toward *self*-discovery.

When I look at my notes, having trusted my instinct in what to record and what to leave for burial by the sands of time and imperfect memory, I get a concise picture of each patient.

Maybe this works for me because I have an excellent memory. I can write a two-word sentence and recall the essential events of Gemma's childhood. I can sketch her expression and have a perfect record of what pieces of her history were particularly meaningful to her.

I like having a blue, fine-point rollerball pen and acid-free paper. I use a large leather-bound notebook, one for each patient. The patients see my leather notebooks, and it makes them feel valued. They *are* valued.

I assure them the notes are well-secured. If they're concerned, I show them the good-sized safe in the closet beside my office bathroom. The enormous combination dial is enough to convince them it's a serious safe. I've even gone so far as to tell them there are instructions in my will to destroy all notes following my death. Instructions have been given to my attorney, not to a family member, which is proof of my serious attention to this.

And it's the truth. Their life stories and secrets are safe with me. I want to help them, not betray them. I want to see people made whole and in control of their lives and living up to their potential.

It would take something criminal to make me reveal anything in my session notes. And even then, it would depend on the situation. It would have to be a crime involving bodily harm, not even embezzlement or insurance fraud would move me to expose a patient to law enforcement.

Crimes are confessed to therapists. More crimes than most people can imagine. But our job is to heal the individual, not society. It's not the therapist's job to deliver punishment.

4

Gemma

As instructed, I bought a notebook. I also bought a red ballpoint pen. Red seemed fitting, since I imagined I'd be pouring out blood as I re-lived the months I'd been with David. They were the four most incredible months of my life. When I allowed myself to sink into those memories, the ache in my heart eased slightly. I indulged those memories often, with a glass of wine in my hand as I looked out over the county park behind my condo. It was almost as if I were still with him, living it again. I felt every stroke of his hands, the taste of his lips, and the warmth of his body. I heard his easy voice and the echo of his laughter. David liked to laugh, and he made me laugh. Then, my thoughts would shift, and the pain crashed into me as brutally as ever.

I was looking forward to telling Dr. Wilcox all the details, re-living all of it through the filter of another person. No one else knew how we'd met and fallen in love. They didn't know about the magic of those thirteen weeks. My mother had heard bits and pieces of it. Geoff knew I was *smitten*, as he called it, which made it sound childish, so I'd told him hardly anything. My girlfriend Sara knew a little more.

Mostly, it was all between David and me. Our private world where no one else existed.

Dr. Wilcox had suggested I invest in a beautiful notebook to symbolize the importance I placed on exploring my inner world. Maybe even leather. She'd smiled, giving me that warm, welcoming look she had. Her expression relaxed me and reassured me all of this talking would get my life back on track.

I chose a cheap spiral notebook with a bright turquoise cover. When I was finished with therapy, it would be easily burned. I didn't want anyone seeing the things I might write. Ever.

I stood in the checkout line waiting to pay for my notebook and pen.

The clerk eyed my purchase as if I'd come to the wrong store. It was a big box store that offered low prices and large quantities for stocking up. Everyone else in line had carts stuffed with packages of office supplies — ten notebooks wrapped in cellophane, packets of twenty pens, cases of printer paper.

He rang up my notebook and pen. "Anything else?"

"Nope."

He smirked. "Four-thirty-nine."

I paid in cash — four ones, a quarter, a dime, and four pennies. He eyed the coins on the counter as if he wasn't quite sure what to do with them. Then, he plucked them up, dropped them into the cash tray, tore off my receipt, and ordered me to have a nice day.

At home, I wrote the date at the top of the first page in my notebook. Below it, I wrote this —

I have no idea whether therapy actually works…

But I have to do something. I can't live like this. The

main thing I'm not going to mention, ever, is that I still hope David will come back. Sara said this is unrealistic and it's keeping me from moving forward. I've stopped telling her how I'm feeling. She's been replaced. Now, it's just me and Dr. Wilcox. I won't make the same mistake with the doctor, baring my soul so she can tell me I'm deluded and weak and not valuing myself. Those are all the things Sara said, as if she thinks she's a therapist. I didn't ask for her *opinion* about how to live my life, I wanted her to understand how empty I am without him. I wanted her to be a friend, that's all.

This will be an equal friendship. I will not let the doctor push me into saying things I don't want to. It's impossible to tell her every detail of my entire life. It would take the rest of my life to tell her everything. Besides, she can't fix what happened a long time ago.

For my third therapy session, I wore the same navy blue dress I'd worn to work that day. I slipped on flip-flops because it was hot, and I couldn't see the need for professional shoes when all I'd be doing was sitting in an armchair cradling a box of tissues.

Dr. Wilcox opened the door to her office before I had a chance to settle into the waiting room. Her office was even more spa-like than the waiting area.

There was no desk. I'm not sure why I'd expected a desk. They can be off-putting, and she obviously was trying to create a welcoming, peaceful, safe atmosphere. One wall had a large picture window that looked out on a tiny park. The window was covered with sheer curtains. Toward the center of the room were two armchairs, both upholstered with pale blue fabric. Beside the doctor's chair was a table with a drawer and a cabinet below. On the table was a chocolate brown leather notebook and a red Mont Blanc pen. The tissues were tucked out of sight, so you weren't immediately thinking about the possibility of dissolving in a flood of tears.

A spindly table stood beside the patient's chair. On it was a small bottle of Fiji water.

The ceiling was painted a soft, very light blue with fluffy white clouds. The walls were white. On the wall opposite the window was a series of black and white photographs of waterfalls, trees, and mountains.

Each print was about eighteen-by-twenty-four inches with a thin black metal frame. They were hung in a single row — nine photographs in all. The carpet was the same shade of blue as the ceiling.

Comparing her office to a spa wasn't quite accurate. It was more like sinking into the sky.

In the corner behind the doctor's chair, hanging from the ceiling, was a figurine of a girl with a kite. She wore a green dress with white polka dots. The kite was attached below her body — the kite flying the girl. Her brown hair was fanned out behind her head, and her dress billowed around her legs. Her feet were bare. Her expression was blissful.

Dr. Wilcox saw me studying it.

"What do you think of it?"

"It's upsetting."

"Why?"

"She looks like she's out of control."

"None of us are in control of our environment or the events in our lives. But therapy can help you understand yourself, and enable you to better manage your thoughts and the resulting feelings. It's the only thing we truly control.

That, and our behavior." She smiled.

I turned my attention away from the flying girl and waited for the first question.

5

Gemma

"**W**hat was the most significant event in your life between the ages of thirteen and eighteen?" Dr. Wilcox picked up her pen, which I thought was a rather intimidating move. It made me want to be extra careful with what I said. I hadn't wanted to start so soon with a lie, but the real answer was fast and urgent in my mind, and it wasn't the answer I wished to give the doctor. It had nothing to do with David and the hole he'd left in my heart.

I must have hesitated too long before answering because she spoke again.

"Therapy is only successful if you're honest…if you say whatever comes to mind first, even if it occasionally doesn't seem to make sense, or if it causes shame, or regret, or any other emotion you'd rather avoid. It's the only way to move forward."

"I guess there were a few significant events and I can't make up my mind which one to talk about. It's not that I'm not being honest."

She wrote something in her notebook, a single word, from what I could see.

She saw me watching. My face must have said something.

"Don't worry about the notes," she said.

"I'm not."

"You looked anxious."

"Sorry."

She smiled. "Don't apologize, just shift your focus to your memories. What was the most significant event?"

"I fell in love for the first time. I had sex. So that's two things, but they're sort of the same."

"Is sex the same as love?"

"No, but they're hard to separate."

She nodded. "Does falling in love define your life more than other things — career, friendships?"

"No. I don't think so." I felt my heart tighten as David filled my thoughts.

"Tell me how that was — your first love, and the other highlights of your high school experience."

"High school was mostly normal. I got good grades, I had friends. I was a little different from most girls maybe because I didn't play soccer, which nearly every girl in California seems to do.

"I was really into dance. I'd taken ballet all through elementary and junior high school. I branched out to modern dance in high school. I performed in a recital every spring. Our dance school was large enough that the recitals were held in the De Anza Junior College auditorium. It made me feel important, like I was a professional dancer. It was a real theater with nice seats and velvet curtains. I wanted to be a professional dancer, but my parents said that was ridiculous. My father said it was no way to make a living, and my mother said it was a hard life.

"Aidan was in my Geometry class. I got A's in Geometry. I liked how everything fit together, how the interior angles of a triangle always added up to one-hundred-eighty degrees. Aidan sat behind me. He tried to cheat off my test once, but I wouldn't let him. After that, he asked me to help him with his homework.

"At the beginning of October, when it was as hot as summer in the afternoons, we would sit on the front lawn of the high school under this enormous oak tree. Our math books and binders were spread open around us like little islands in a green sea. At first, there was always a foot of grassy space between our legs, and then six or seven inches, and then our ankles were almost touching. I would take off my sandals so I could feel the grass on my bare feet. He wore flip-flops and cargo shorts. His legs were tan. The hair on his legs was like tiny gold threads.

"The first time he kissed me, it was almost five in the afternoon, and we thought no one else was around. But one of his friends was cutting across the lawn behind us. His friend whistled. It didn't bother Aidan at all, he kept his mouth on mine, his tongue digging deeper until I thought he was going to turn everything inside of me into hot syrup.

"Still, we moved our study sessions to a grove of trees that was more secluded. After about a month or two of serious making out that moved from kissing to his hands inside my bra, to my bra unhooked, to him placing my hand on his fly so I could feel how hard he was, to him unzipping his fly, to his hands down my pants, he got his driver's license. It was good timing because now we could take off our clothes and make love. It was as amazing as movies made it appear.

"My grades started going down — from a three-point-eight GPA to three-point-five and then, finally, by the end of my Junior year, to three-point-two. My father threatened to stop paying for dance classes if I didn't improve my grades. We fought every time I brought home a test or a paper that had a C or even a B-minus, but he never followed through on his threats. He never did anything but complain and sometimes shout at me, and my mother."

"Why did he shout at your mother?"

"He thought she wasn't on the same team with him — putting schoolwork first."

Dr. Wilcox nodded.

"Should I keep going?"

She nodded again.

"Aidan and I were together all of our Sophomore and Junior years. We broke up the summer after Junior year. Mostly because I changed schools. We moved to Fresno, and I had to start all over for my last year — no Aidan, no friends, no more dance classes.

"Obviously, my grades shot up, and I finished high school on the honor roll. I missed my chance at Salutatorian by two other kids. I was glad my grades improved so I could get into a decent college. I couldn't wait to get out of there. I was so angry with my parents. I took dance classes in college, but my major had to be something *serious*, something *solid*. I picked education. If I couldn't be a dancer, I wanted to do something useful in the world. Children are...if you can influence a child's life, turn a child in the right direction, that's the most important and satisfying job in the world."

As I told her these things, Dr. Wilcox remained silent. She made notes, hardly looking at the page in front of her, just jotting a word or two in most cases. Every so often, she looked down and wrote something more lengthy. It was strange, but the more she wrote, the less I cared what she was writing. She'd said no one would ever see what she wrote, and besides, she couldn't possibly write down every detail, so even if someone did read her notes, they wouldn't really know much about my life.

6

Dr. Ann Wilcox: Notes on Gemma Hughes

There's a jaded quality to Gemma Hughes, despite her obvious effort to appear sweet. There's a hardness under the surface of that smile. It's not clear what she's hiding...maybe a lot of things. I don't have specifics I can point to, but my instinct says it's there.

Despite a passion for ballet that appears to have started early and retained its importance in her life, her first love affair dominates her memories of high school. Understandable. Not atypical, but suggests inner conflict.

She avoided eye contact when she talked about her first sexual experience...suggests she's either uncomfortable with the subject or leaving out part of the story. Is this because of the family move immediately after? ...or simultaneous with? ...the breakup? I believe my second instinct is correct: part of the story is missing.

My figurine of the girl being flown by her kite upset her. She seemed almost angry that the figure was hanging in my office. Without reading too much into it, I had the sense she hated that figure. She resented the fact that such happiness and freedom is possible. She's so involved with her own misery, she wants to inflict that on others. The mobile brings a smile to the face of almost every patient I've treated. There's something about it that makes a person feel light and free. It evokes a sense of joy and a childlike approach to life, not taking oneself too seriously. Not to belabor the point, but Gemma was visibly disturbed.

Grief over the loss of her first love seems to have an undercurrent of rage.

The missing pieces in the story of her high school breakup possibly include more extreme emotional trauma. Was she put on any kind of medication? Teenagers take breakups with such ferocity. Her relationship was all-consuming, demonstrated by her falling grades. It's strange that even a threat to take away her dance classes didn't cause her to give more attention to her schoolwork. To have a relationship of that intensity come to an end, and brush it off as the result of a move to a new location doesn't ring true.

The remainder of my initial thoughts are focused on her physical appearance —

She wears a lot of unnecessary makeup. She has clear, smooth skin and obviously does not need the heavy foundation and shading products she uses. It struck me odd that someone going through the emotional pain she described at our first session would go to so much trouble to apply makeup. Normally people who are battling emotional upset neglect their appearance. Gemma is the opposite.

Her legs were tanned and freshly shaved. Her hair had a healthy shine, her bangs were neatly trimmed and the layers expertly styled.

She sits with her legs crossed and never adjusted them during the entire fifty minutes. She's comfortable with her body, which is another factor in favor of my view that the reporting of her first love affair was edited to conceal an important point, not that she was avoiding a discussion of sex.

She keeps her hands in her lap and doesn't fidget with them or constantly touch her hair or face in an effort to control anxiety.

Concluding thoughts: Anger. Danger of self-harm? Lying to me, which is indicative of lying to herself.

7

Gemma

During the week following my third therapy session, I didn't write a single word in my notebook or journal or dream diary or whatever it's supposed to be. Dr. Wilcox hadn't told me to write anything in my notebook, so I didn't think I was supposed to. I had a lot of crazy dreams that week, but there was nothing new about that. I'd had weird, confusing dreams for a long time.

There wasn't much to write about the therapy session. I spent the whole hour answering questions about being a first-grade teacher.

Then, at my next session, as if she wanted to trick me, as if she wanted to imply that I wasn't taking therapy seriously, Dr. Wilcox settled in the chair across from me and asked what insights I'd had from writing in my journal.

"I didn't write in my journal."

"Most of my patients find it useful. It will help you reflect on what came up during the session you just completed."

"You didn't tell me to write in it."

"Do you think it's important to wait for specific instructions?"

"No."

She didn't say anything more, just let my answer hang in

the air. A moment later, she smiled and wrote a few words in her own notebook. It was obvious I was supposed to be thinking something, but I wasn't sure what, and it made me nervous. I knew this kind of therapy wasn't an actual conversation, but I also kept wondering how it was going to help if she just sat there and waited for my thoughts to wander all over the place.

After the silence had grown into something that felt almost physical, a pressure inside my ears, a swelling in my throat, Dr. Wilcox laid down her pen and smiled. "I think we've covered enough of your earlier history…for now. Why don't you tell me how you met the man whose absence you're grieving."

"What do you want to know?"

"What would you like to tell me?"

I didn't know where to start. Our actual meeting? Or how we got together? It was like any random person you meet — nothing too unusual. There was nothing that told me we'd end up having sex that was far beyond anything I'd imagined was possible, except in books and movies. There was nothing that told me he was my soul mate.

I thought about that moment David looked up from the reading rack on the elliptical trainer just as I was bending over to re-tie my shoe.

The gym had been almost empty that day. It was always less crowded on Monday mornings. I'd seen him a few times before, but we'd never talked to each other. I hadn't felt any interest from him, and I hadn't felt that buzz you sometimes do with a guy who's super good-looking, or turns you on, or who just has an aura about him that pulls you toward him.

I wasn't looking for a relationship. I was sort of seeing

another guy. Nothing amazing, but we had fun together. Maybe that was part of why I hadn't thought about the guy on the elliptical very much.

That morning, I felt his eyes on the top edge of my shirt as it dipped down when I bent over. It wasn't a dramatic revelation of my breasts, but I'm sure he saw a little more than usual.

What I loved about him from that first look was the smile he gave me. He stared right into my eyes and gave me the tiniest curve of his lips, a smile that admitted he'd been caught and he wasn't going to pretend he wasn't looking, and that I should be flattered, not pissed off. The smile said he was a nice guy and not a creep staring at any pair of tits he could find.

I *was* flattered. I smiled back.

I finished tying my laces and walked to the treadmill. I had that feeling when every inch of your body tingles and hums because you know someone is watching you. I was hyper-aware of the movement of my legs and the way I held my arms, and how my ponytail brushed between my shoulder blades. Even the loose pieces of hair that didn't fit in the elastic touched the sides of my face in a way that drew my attention to them. It seemed as if every part of me was coming to life.

"Why do you think you're hesitating?"

"I'm not."

"You haven't spoken. Were you thinking about the first time you met?"

"I wasn't sure if you meant when we met or when we got together."

"Which event is more clear in your memory?"

I shrugged.

"What was the first thing that came to mind?"

"When we met."

"So tell me about that."

"I don't remember everything exactly."

"Tell me what you do remember. Try to relax and not over-think. Whatever stands out is more important than a detailed account."

I closed my eyes for a minute. I felt like she could see inside my head. I didn't want to tell her about him looking down my shirt. I'm not sure why. It just seemed...personal, or something. I didn't want her to assume he was a creep, to not believe that we really did love each other. I wasn't sure how to explain it without sounding cheap.

"I met him at my gym. He always worked out on the elliptical trainer, and I used the treadmill." I squeezed my hands in my lap. I felt like crying. It was so stupid. Why would I cry over that? I suppose because I cried all the time lately. The hurt came rushing back like a huge wave that wanted to knock me over and pull me under the water, dragging my face through the sand, filling my lungs and nose with burning salt water.

"Go on..."

I took a deep breath, and the tears slid to the back of my skull. "I don't remember how we first started talking. I think he said I was in good shape and we talked about how cardio makes you feel so much better, like you can start the day at the top of your game. He said that — *the top of your game.*"

Dr. Wilcox nodded. She didn't write anything in her book.

"We usually got to the gym around the same time and finished our cardio at the same time. After a few weeks, he asked if I wanted to get coffee. It wasn't a typical first date, but then I realized he was just a nice guy. He was interested in me as a person, not just for sex. And I liked that. We started having coffee when we ran into each other at the gym. We talked about everything. Just everything in our whole lives."

"You considered him a friend?"

"Yes. He's easy...was easy...to talk to." My throat tightened. I swallowed more tears. "I felt like he understood me. I felt like he was interested in me as a person, not just as someone for sex."

"So you said. Do you think most men have been interested in you only for sex?"

I slid my fingers under the gold snake bracelet I wear on my left wrist. It felt cool against my fingers, which seemed hot and a little swollen. Maybe all of my body was feeling hot, but the room was a comfortable temperature, so I wasn't sure why I suddenly felt my skin was steamy and soft. "No, not really."

"Then why do you think it struck you that this man..." She glanced at her notebook. She flipped back a page. "I don't think you've told me his name."

"David."

"David what?"

"Does that matter?"

She laughed. "Not really. It's a question I'm used to asking." She smiled and went smoothly back to what she was saying. "Why did it strike you that David wasn't simply looking for sex?"

Dr. Wilcox never seems to forget anything, which means

I'll have to remember what I say. Not that I plan to lie about a lot of things. I just don't want her knowing everything about me, all my bad points, thinking she's better than me because she knows everything about my life and I don't know a single thing about hers. "His last name is Graves. It's not like I'm trying to hide it. And I don't know why it struck me. Maybe because everyone knows men pick up women in gyms or bars for casual sex. Maybe because I wasn't expecting a relationship? I really don't know."

"It's something to think about."

"Aren't all men wanting sex?"

"It might seem that way, but you should try to understand why you're so convinced that's *all* they want."

I swallowed.

"How did you move into a relationship?"

"After the coffees, we met for lunch a few times. And one time, when we walked out of the restaurant, it was raining. It was weird because it was summer. And it never rains in the summer, right? We stood under the overhang. It was narrow, and the wind was blowing a bit, so we had to press ourselves against the side of the building to not get wet. And he just…we started kissing." I laughed. I wanted to cry, remembering that kiss. It was the most fantastic thing I'd ever felt. It ran right through me. His mouth filled my body with something soft and creamy. I collapsed into him, and I felt him do the same. I couldn't tell the doctor that. It was too amazing. It was too impossible to describe. And it wasn't going to take away this pain.

I started crying.

She didn't make any notes. She didn't say anything. A few minutes later, she said in a very soft voice. "This is a good place to stop."

I couldn't wait to get out of there. I didn't know if this was going to help me at all. It hurt so bad.

8

Dr. Ann Wilcox: Notes on Gemma Hughes

The story Gemma told of how she met the man who wounded her was unremarkable in every way. A cliché, really.

It's even more clear that she's withholding information. I can't get a good read on what's driving that. Possibly it's a trust issue…we are still in the early stages. But it doesn't fit my experience with women who have been jilted, dumped, abandoned, whatever you want to call it. Usually, they can't wait to re-live every bit of minutiae. The amount of detail I'm usually given is enough to put me to sleep.

I've provided therapy for a lot of women, and men, who are recovering from broken relationships. They want to flood me with details, they can't stop talking, and they almost always share very intimate thoughts and experiences. I have seen a fair amount of lying about sex, especially when the relationship involved sexual situations they're either ashamed of or fear I'll judge them for, that they don't want to admit they enjoy. I've also heard minute-by-minute descriptions of sexual encounters.

Other than the obvious withholding of things they're ashamed of, the stream of consciousness is nearly unbroken. The talking alone is helpful. It's really the point of therapy, even if during those initial weeks and months the talking lacks insight. Eventually, they get there. Telling me about their love affairs is often the first time they can really let loose and verbalize how deeply they feel, how significant every moment of the relationship was to them. They want to verbally deconstruct every conversation, every email and text message, and every disagreement. They want to delve into the timeline, looking for that precise moment where things began to fail. And Gemma may still get to that point, but her approach is definitely not the norm.

What makes me think she's holding back is that most of my patients dissect the first moments of the relationship, looking for clues, even where none exist, as to why it ended.

Patients fall into two camps — those who want to paint themselves in a good light, who can't fathom why the relationship ended because they see themselves as undeniably lovable, blind to their own flaws; and those who want to berate themselves for all their failures, real and imagined, believing wholeheartedly they're not worthy of love.

Gemma doesn't do either. She almost seems not to want to talk about it at all, which makes me wonder why she chose therapy. She wants me to "fix her", mend those wounds, but she doesn't want to commit to the process. I'm perplexed, but also challenged, which I'm enjoying. I'm looking forward to finding the way into her thoughts, the right question or series of questions that will finally crack that facade.

It's worth noting that she found it surprising he wasn't just looking for sex. When I questioned her on that, she dodged the truth, I think. She insisted she didn't view all men that way, and yet his friendship was a key point in her story. She was adamant that her earlier relationships hadn't been that way, and yet it was stated as the primary reason she was drawn to this man.

Their conversation about working out doesn't ring true. Of course, that's normal gym chatter, but in my experience, those conversations are between women or men exclusively, not cross-gender. And she was vague about what initiated the conversation.

It's starting to eat at me that she's crafting stories that leave out those telling details. She needs to open up and let her thoughts flow in a more unfiltered fashion.

Gemma shapes her behavior around the influence of external authority, failing to write in a journal as suggested unless I gave her explicit instructions. I didn't give that instruction at the end of this session either, I'll see what she does with it.

Concluding thoughts: Dig deeper into parental relationships, her relationship to authority as a child and as an adult. I have her release form, but consider getting explicit permission to talk to her parents.

9

Gemma

My dreams have always been beyond crazy. But that's how everyone's dreams are, I think. Isn't that the point? I'm not sure if mine are crazier than other people's because I've never asked anyone, except Geoff. When we were kids, Geoff and I told each other our dreams. We'd laugh about how freakish they were. Geoff would tease me about my nightmares. He never had nightmares, and he wondered what lived inside my head that I was so afraid of.

When I turned twelve, I stopped telling him my dreams. I didn't like him laughing. It felt like he was laughing at me, instead of at the crazy places our heads go when we're not paying attention.

Dreams take such weird directions. I've always wondered where all that stuff comes from. Sometimes, it's obvious why certain things took place in a dream, like when I was learning to dance on point, and I kept dreaming that my feet were made of modeling clay and every time I rose to my toes, they'd collapse under me. You don't need a dream interpretation book to figure that out, or a therapist.

The really intense nightmares are impossible to figure out. Especially when they're filled with people I've never met and places I don't recognize.

So Dr. Wilcox wanted me to write in my journal. I didn't

want to write about David. I didn't want to write about the
end of my relationship with Aidan. I wasn't even sure I
wanted to write about how I felt after four therapy sessions,
but writing down my dreams…that could be interesting.
Maybe I'd figure out something. If nothing else, it would
distract me from the pain for a few minutes.

The dream I wrote about was so vivid, I remembered
the entire scene a week later. It had fuzzy, foggy snippets of
events leading up to the main dream. That happens a lot. It
also happens that the dream crumbles near the end and all
these unmatched, confusing experiences fall into each other,
turning even more senseless. But the middle section is what I
remembered.

I was sitting in the therapist's office. Instead of the
armchair, I was sitting on a wooden side chair. Instead of
those clouds painted on the ceiling, the chair was in the
middle of a field, and the clouds were real, drifting above me,
fluffy and white and soft. The kind of clouds that when you
see them from an airplane, you have this insane urge to yank
that huge lever, open the door, and leap out into the soft
comfort, like falling into an endless pile of the best feather
pillows you can buy.

The therapist wasn't seated in her chair. And her chair
wasn't her chair either. It was a throne. The back was about
six feet tall with a gold frame. The back and seat were
upholstered with gold lamé.

Dr. Wilcox was floating above the chair, sitting in the
clouds. She wore a white robe and a gold crown studded with
emeralds, sapphires, and rubies. Her legs were crossed at the
ankles, and she was holding out her hands with the palms
facing down as if she were placing a blessing on me. A bright

light surrounded her, coming through the clouds in streaks, like they do after a storm. The light was so intense it was impossible to see the features of her face, but her dark hair was soft and long, framing the face I couldn't make out.

Instead of feeling awe in her god-like presence, or experiencing the healing warmth dripping from her fingers like honey, I was terrified. I began crying. I twisted in my chair, trying to break free. It felt like I'd been tied there with thick ropes, but I wasn't. Still, I couldn't get out of the chair, couldn't leave the room that wasn't really a room, but a vast open space with no walls and no floor, and the pale blue sky with all those clouds.

After a while, I became exhausted from trying to escape.

Then, someone was talking, but I couldn't understand the words. I heard the sound of a woman's voice. It seemed important that I listen to what she was saying, but the words were unclear. No matter how hard I strained to hear, I couldn't make out a single one. It was impossible to get closer to the voice because I couldn't leave the chair.

The voice kept talking, speaking with more emotion and growing louder, but despite the volume, it was still impossible to understand.

After straining to listen for quite a long time, I suddenly recognized the voice — my own. It was saying something very important, but I had no idea what that was.

As the voice…my voice…continued speaking, I saw the figurine of the kite flying the girl detach from the hook. Suddenly, it was overhead. Because the room was open to the sky, the kite was plunging from a great distance at incredible speed, the sharp point of the diamond aiming straight for my head.

The kite drove into my skull. I felt nothing except a softening of my brain.

Next, Dr. Wilcox uncrossed her legs and stood. The light moved away from her face. Then I saw that the skin had been peeled away. It lay in shreds around her neck and collarbone. All that was left was her skull and her eyeballs, staring at me, floating free inside the bone sockets. Her teeth and jaw, formed a giant grin, mocking me.

I screamed. And then, I was somewhere else I'd never been, a strange room, maybe. A lot of nonsense experiences followed, one after the other, none of them connected.

When I woke, I couldn't remember the surreal parts at the end. The last thing I remembered was that skull grinning at me.

I poured a glass of wine and sat in my living room, wearing nothing but the long T-shirt I'd been sleeping in. Even though I curled up and tucked my bent knees inside the shirt, it didn't make me feel more secure.

As the image of the skull faded, what really terrified me were the things I'd said that I couldn't make out.

10

Ann

People are fond of asking children what they want to be when they grow up. As a child, I was asked that constantly. As an adult, when I'm at a party that includes children of a certain age, I find myself asking the same question. It's instinctive.

Of course, one of the ways we identify our adult selves is by our occupations. And posing the question to a child is a way of carrying on a conversation with a small, partially-developed human being, a way to evoke more interest than mundane inquiries about their schoolwork or sports activities. It's a way of making them feel important. It's a way of bringing them up to an adult level.

I was never able to answer that question. I have a crisp memory of staring blankly up at my uncle when he asked me what I wanted to be when I grew up. The stare stretched from seconds to minutes. He laughed. "You must have some ideas? A nurse? A movie star? President of the United States?"

I studied his dark brown eyes, the muddy color of the iris almost indistinguishable from his dilated pupils. I was trying not to get too caught up in the rash along the left edge of his jaw. I didn't want to be any of those things he mentioned.

My uncle was a dentist. I couldn't imagine putting my hands in people's mouths, knowing they might bite down on me if I caused them pain. Even with rubber gloves, I didn't want to be touching saliva and blood and all the microorganisms growing inside that small, dark cavity.

"You might consider dentistry. It's an interesting, well-paying profession," he said. "Or if you don't want to go to school for so many years, you could become a hygienist."

Even the word — *hygiene* — good *hygiene,* but also poor *hygiene* — sounded awful to me. He didn't explain what a hygienist did, but I knew that wasn't anything I wanted to think about ever again.

"Ann, are you dense? By your age, you should have imagined yourself in any number of careers. Even if all you want is to be a mommy, that's okay. Girls have choices."

"I haven't decided."

"I'm not asking you to *decide*. Why are you so difficult?" He laughed. "I think I need to talk to your mother about your attitude." He grabbed my ear and pinched it lightly.

For a few days, his question, and my failure to find an answer troubled me. Finally, I decided he was weird. His profession sounded boring and disgusting. I didn't owe him a decision or even a list of things that interested me. My parents weren't concerned about it, so neither was I.

Adults continued to ask that ubiquitous question, but now I knew that a blank stare wouldn't be well-received. An immediate response was required. I gave them all the same answer — *I haven't decided yet.* Because it came without delay, they accepted my response and nodded as if they understood that I was wise beyond my years.

In my second year of high school, the only elective class

that fit my schedule was *An Introduction to Psychology*. The moment the teacher began to talk about how long human beings had worked to understand the makeup of their own minds, I was hooked. Addicted. I read my entire psychology textbook the first two weeks of class. When different chapters were assigned throughout the semester, I re-read them. I went to the school library and checked out books on psychology. I read online articles about Freud and Jung.

When I told my parents I'd made my decision, my father was pleased. My mother worried out loud that it meant two advanced degrees and it might be a stretch to pay for all that education. My father said, "It's easy. If she's passionate about this, she'll earn scholarships." As if his words were a prophecy, I did just that.

I'm not so different from Gemma Hughes. She said she wanted to do something that mattered. I also wanted to make a difference in the world. I didn't want a job where my contribution was swallowed up by a corporation or a university or a political party.

Every single day of my career is different from the days that came before. Every single moment. Although the human psyche has patterns and human behavior is often predictable, and one person's neurosis isn't all that unique compared with another, at the same time, the small varieties are infinite. I never know what someone will say. I never know what incidents from the past affected a patient and changed the course of her life. The story of my uncle, for example. What does it mean? Why do I remember it so clearly? I still haven't answered that question, but I will, someday.

I like being a listening ear. I like providing the petri dish, so to speak, for people to explore their own minds, to adjust the worldviews that don't serve them, to improve their lives.

Self-understanding affects your career, your friendships, your approach to growing older. It affects your family relationships and conflicts. Most of all, self-understanding affects your romantic partnerships and marriage and parenting. It's the key to a happy life. People who live blindly, who lack awareness of how their subconscious minds are directing them and controlling their behavior and influencing their moods often find happiness elusive.

Being a therapist allows me to profoundly influence the life of every patient I treat. There's nothing more satisfying than seeing my patients achieve the lives they deserve.

11

Gemma

Geoff sent a text — he hadn't heard from me since I started therapy. He wondered whether my brain had been picked apart and there was nothing left of me. Typing *LOL* in his next message didn't make me any more interested in telling him what was happening in therapy, not if he was going to make fun of me.

An hour later, he sent another text.

Geoff: *Sorry. I know it's important. Hope it's helping.*

Gemma: *Too soon to tell.*

Geoff: *I can offer some old-fashioned therapy.*

Gemma: *What's that?*

Geoff: *Tequila shots.*

I sent my own *LOL,* and we made plans to meet at an upscale Mexican restaurant in Palo Alto.

He was already seated at the bar when I arrived, dressed in his usual jeans and flip-flops. He wore a faded navy blue T-shirt stamped with the always-recognizable *Cal* logo in gold script, his alma mater where he'd received a degree in environmental studies.

Now, over ten years out of school, he hadn't found a job related in any way to the green industry. Knowing my brother's history, I doubted he'd done more than talk to people working in the industry, bought beers, gulped expensive coffee, and outlined his dreams and visions and plans.

Instead of a job, he blogged, making discretional spending money from affiliate clicks. Other than that, he relied on the endless nurturing of my mother and the detached shrug of my father — living in their large, nicely appointed Los Altos home. He had a dumb joke he repeated whenever he was asked about his background and career status — *Using the parents' green until I get situated in a green career.*

His willingness to live there like a child embarrassed me. If I could manage to live in Silicon Valley on a schoolteacher's salary, he could get his act together and support himself, but he didn't seem inclined. My mother welcomed his dependence, my father had given up years ago, tolerating whatever came his way.

Yes, my condo was small. My car was six years old, and not as worthy as the hybrid he drove, but it was paid for.

A shot of Patrón Silver sat on a napkin in front of the empty stool beside him. Another shot sat on the bar in front of him. He waved me over as if I wasn't capable of finding him, even though he was the only guy with wavy hair that fell past his broad shoulders among a crowd of well-trimmed tech workers.

I scooted onto the stool. We gave each other an awkward, prolonged one-armed hug, and downed our shots. Geoff had ordered a basket of tortilla chips and a selection of salsas and guacamole. We ordered another shot each. Without turning to face me, he said, "So what's it like, having your brain shrunk?"

"No one says *shrink* now."

"I do." He scooped up tomatillo sauce on a red tortilla

chip and ate the entire thing in one bite. "So how is it?"

"Weird."

"Weird, how?"

I shrugged. I took a sip of my second shot. "I'm not sure what I'm supposed to say to my therapist."

"Whatever's on your mind, right?"

"That's harder than it sounds. If someone asks a question, you might have two thoughts, and how do you know which one to share? Which one means something? Sometimes I have five or six thoughts at the same time."

He laughed. "Don't over-analyze it."

"That's what Dr. Wilcox said."

"To me, you'd be better off getting revenge on that asshole, instead of trying to talk out your feelings."

"Revenge wouldn't make my feelings go away."

"You might be surprised."

"I love him. Why can't you understand that?"

"*Loved*. You *did* love him."

"That's not true. I still do. That's why it's so…" I couldn't finish. I sipped my tequila. I wanted the buzz to grow slowly. I wanted to get pleasantly drunk, not ripped. I didn't want to barf or pass out. I just wanted everything wrapped in that fuzzy blanket that alcohol provides, taking the edge off the pain…until it comes back stronger than ever.

"How can you love someone who treats you like shit?"

"That's why I'm in therapy." I laughed, but it didn't feel very funny.

"I don't get it, Gem. He's a shit. I never even met the guy, and I know he's a shit. And I don't get how you can think he's the one and only after a few weeks."

"It was months, not weeks. And if you'd ever been in

love, you'd get it."

"I've been in love." He drawled the words and offered me a sappy smile.

"You've been in lust." I sipped my shot and nibbled on a chip with a thin smear of guacamole. "I thought you invited me out to make me feel better."

"I'm trying. Finish that, and we'll get another."

"Slow down. I don't want to get wasted."

"It's good for you. The sweet little schoolteacher steppin' out. Let Dr. Tequila pour some of that Latin passion into your blood. Rage. You need to turn all that unrequited love into something useful."

"Useful?"

"It's better than letting some asshole live inside your head. And he never gives you even a passing thought."

"You don't know that."

"I do know that. If he's gone, you're out of his head. Trust me. Now drink up."

I finished my shot, and he ordered more. We ordered street tacos and two Coronas to balance the tequila.

"I'm right, you know. Anger is good," he said.

"It's not healthy."

"Is that what the doc says?"

"She doesn't say much."

"Then how're you supposed to get better? Doesn't she give you advice?"

"No. It's not that kind of therapy. That's why I said it's weird. A little scary, to be honest. I do almost all the talking."

"Doesn't she tell you when you should be thinking differently, give you…I don't know…strategies?"

"Nope."

"Then how does it change anything?"

"I talk, and sometimes she asks questions. It's supposed to make me think about my answers and my thoughts differently, saying what I'm thinking helps me hear what's going on inside of me, and then I'm supposed to get my own insights. Her questions are to make me think about why I think the things I do."

"Okay. So psychoanalysis or something?"

"I guess. I'm not sure if psychoanalysis and therapy are the same. Maybe."

He pulled out his phone. "I'll look it up."

"Not now. I thought we were drinking."

"I'm drinking. You're moping."

"I'm not moping."

"You look so sad." He put his hand on my shoulder. "I could punch that guy. I really could. Pulverize his nose. I could get some friends, and we'll take him down. Just tell me where to find him."

I pushed off his hand. "No. That wouldn't help at all."

"I think it would."

The tacos arrived, and we picked up the soft tiny tortillas, folded them closed around the pork and onion, cilantro and salsa. We took simultaneous bites and chewed at the same pace. I was never sure if our tendency to chew at the same pace was the result of genetics, growing up in the same family, or a coincidence that might happen with anyone when you ordered the same meal. I'd never noticed it except when I ate with Geoff, which made me think it was genetics. Maybe that was simply wishful thinking, wanting to stay close to my brother, always aware of a faint, irrational fear that he'd disappear from my life one day.

We gobbled down our food, drank one more shot and two beers each, and stumbled outside to share an Uber. The driver dropped me off first and then doubled back up El Camino Real toward my parents' home in Los Altos.

Geoff's parting words were that I should tell the therapist to fast-track me. And that I should consider doing some damage to David. Geoff was absolutely sure it would make me feel better.

12

Dr. Ann Wilcox: Notes on Gemma Hughes

In the end, I didn't ask Gemma for explicit permission to make the initial contact with her parents. After she told me her dream, with its clear desire for suicide — her desire to open the door of an airplane and jump into the clouds — I decided to place the call.

New patients fill out a five-page form about their background, a brief medical history, and contact information for family and friends. I ask for three names. The excess information gathering is never questioned. Starting therapy makes them feel vulnerable, and they want to know that if they have an emotional breakdown, or whatever else they fear might happen under my care of their psyche, they have several options to make sure someone can assist them while they're in a fragile state.

Gemma listed her brother, both of her parents, and a college friend who was also an elementary school teacher.

I viewed this as implicit agreement that I could contact anyone on her list. Yes, it blurred the lines, possibly wiped them out entirely, but neither could I risk destabilizing her further by expressing concern over her suicidal thoughts.

I don't think she even realized that's what her dream was suggesting. Even more troubling to me than the obvious desire to toss her life out of an airplane was the subliminal intention to harm an entire plane full of others. The loss of cabin pressure would happen in microseconds, and the death would be horrific, not to mention collateral deaths from a plane barreling into a populated area below. She brushed casually past all of that. Yes, it was a dream, but a dream like that needs to be taken seriously.

When I asked her to tell me what she thought the dream meant, she focused on the god-like nature of the figure purported to represent me. She was obviously unfamiliar with the popular belief that all figures in a dream represent a facet of the dreamer. This is an extremely simplistic view of the function of dreams but widely agreed to in pop culture. She was almost exclusively upset by the voice that she couldn't decipher. She was certain the real meaning of the dream was contained in those words she couldn't comprehend.

I asked whether she had a guess as to what was being said. She claimed to have no idea, and when I suggested again that she make a guess as to what it might be, she snapped at me —

How would I know? I told you, I couldn't make out the words.

Concluding thoughts: Lack of self-insight evident in her focus on the dream figure representing me rather than on her own desires.

13

Ann

Instead of going directly home as I usually do after work, I went out for a light dinner at a lovely Italian restaurant where I enjoyed mushroom risotto and a glass of Zinfandel. I returned to my office and placed a call to Tamara and Rob Hughes.

I hoped Tamara would answer the phone, and I wasn't disappointed.

Women are more wary, more protective of their children's privacy, but men are less likely to listen to a stranger past the first few words. They're more abrupt, not always, but in general.

She answered on the second ring.

"Mrs. Hughes? Tamara?"

"Speaking. Who is this?"

"My name is Annie. I'm a friend of Gemma's." I'd taken this clearly unethical but necessary approach because I didn't want to alarm her. I needed insight, I didn't need her panicking that I believed her wounded daughter was suicidal, possibly intent on mass murder. There was no way of knowing how a parent might respond to that kind of information.

The response could be anything from a simple refusal to take me at my word, to a poorly timed and damaging confrontation with her daughter. To have a therapist call you with deep concerns about your daughter is not in the normal course of events. And despite listing them on the form, Gemma may not have told them she was in therapy. I couldn't break that confidence. Perhaps she freely listed those names because she assumed they would never be needed. She would glide through therapy and come out healthy and whole with only a few tears shed and no ripping apart and rebuilding of the self she thought she knew. I made a choice between two unethical approaches — lying about my identity versus breaking her confidence. Clearly, the lie was the better choice.

"*Who* are you?"

"Annie. I can't believe she hasn't mentioned me." I laughed. "That's kind of upsetting, a little hurtful, actually. But I forgive her." I laughed again, more softly. "I'm a teacher at Sequoia Elementary with Gemma. I teach third grade." My lies were compounding, but I had no choice. My concern was genuine.

"Maybe she has mentioned you. I…sometimes I can't keep her co-workers straight. I'm sorry. I feel terrible about it. I haven't met any of them, and it's hard to remember who's who."

I told her a few details about the school, brief anecdotes about Gemma's students that she'd mentioned. I referred to how long she'd worked there and where she'd gone to college. The details soothed Tamara's reticence. I think she believed my story.

I knew I was doing the right thing, despite the white lies. Gemma had more than enough resistance to me. If I'd mentioned my desire to talk to her parents, her lack of trust would deepen. The ethical lapse ate at me, but sometimes the end really does justify the means. Everyone knows this.

Tamara cleared her throat. "And what is this about?"

"I was wondering if we could meet for coffee."

"Why?"

"I'm worried about Gemma."

"Is there trouble with her job?"

"No. It's about her ex-boyfriend. David."

"Oh, him. Yes." She sighed.

"Have you met him?"

"No, but I never had a good feeling about him."

I was beyond curious to delve into her feelings, but I needed to keep focused on my objective. I needed to encourage her to agree to meet more than simply stating her bad feelings. Not having a *good feeling* could mean anything from not liking his profession to wanting her daughter to marry a family friend. It was hard to predict, and I needed to stick to a conversation I could control.

"Would you'd be willing to meet? I don't mean to go behind her back. I'm just…she seems a little depressed over him. I don't want to gossip about her with the other teachers. I would never do that. I love Gemma. But I need to get your take. I want to help her. She's one of my closest friends." It was a little much, but she didn't seem to react badly.

"That's very sweet," she said.

"It's tearing me apart, watching her suffer like this."

Tamara was silent. After a few seconds, I heard a sharp intake of breath and a slight sniffle. "She's taking it hard."

"Yes. So, coffee? I was thinking Peet's in Palo Alto…the one on University."

"That sounds nice."

It was a strange way to say it. We were talking about her daughter's mental health. No matter how you looked at it, the meeting wasn't a pleasant chat over cappuccinos. Politeness and convention ruled this woman's behavior. This might be easier than I'd expected. "Does eleven on Thursday morning work?"

"Don't you have school?"

I swallowed. "I have a doctor's appointment, so there's a sub covering my class that morning."

"Then, yes. That would be fine."

"Maybe don't mention it to your husband for now. Or your son. I don't mean to tell you what to do. But I already feel bad, talking to you without her knowing. I just feel like I have to talk to someone. It helps to have a shoulder to lean on."

"I understand. No, I wouldn't worry them unnecessarily. Should *I* be worried?"

"I don't think so? I hope not. I just want to be the best possible friend to her that I can be."

"You sound like a charming, caring person."

"Thank you."

We said goodbye after another confirmation of the day and time.

I made notes about the call in my personal diary. It wasn't something I wanted in Gemma's record. It would interrupt my overview of the flow of her progress because it wasn't something she'd initiated. It didn't come out of her own insight or growth. It was just something to help me guide her more effectively.

It's all about formulating the right questions, and I didn't yet have the right questions for Gemma, nothing that had the potential to peel back that thick surface covering the deepest parts of her mind. Her mother could help me with that.

14

David

Gemma was luscious. There's no other word for it. She was like a soft-serve ice-cream. I couldn't stop looking at her. She gave off an air of openness which made her seem almost innocent. Not naïve innocence, so maybe that's not the right way to describe her. She seemed like she had a positive, easy-going view of life, that she wasn't complicated. That's a lot to infer from watching a woman at the gym, but it was a strong feeling. She stood out.

I was using the elliptical machine. Those things take a fair amount of coordination and concentration. Not like the treadmill where you can read long-form journalism and still keep a steady pace. On the elliptical, it's easy to lose the rhythm if you're not paying attention. Maybe for a more athletic guy, a guy who's quick on his feet, someone who knows how to dance, it's easy, but not for me. The machine will trip you up as if it's programmed to do just that. The motion is unnatural. A treadmill allows you to walk or run with normal movements. On the elliptical, your legs are locked into what the machine dictates, sweeping through the atmosphere like alien appendages, lifted above the ground and propelled by an outside force.

Because the elliptical machines are located behind the treadmills, I had plenty of time to watch Gemma.

She wore those skin-tight pants women work out in. She had blonde hair tied in a ponytail and a pink sports bra that had straps woven across her lightly tanned skin like a work of art. Eight straps — I counted them, several times while she ran on the treadmill.

Watching her feet pound that rubber surface and the rhythmic movement of her body and the bouncing ponytail, I couldn't turn away. I could hardly blink. I thought about the view from the front, wishing I could see both at the same time. I wasn't lusting, just admiring.

After a while, I figured out her schedule and managed to be on the elliptical machine ten or fifteen minutes before she arrived. That way, I could watch her without her noticing.

I kept my head angled up toward the bank of TVs, but it was easy enough to let my gaze drop to the treadmills. My workouts started lasting longer, the intensity reduced because I disappeared into a fog of her body racing toward nothing, the movement of her legs and all that hair — long, incredibly thick, soft hair. I wanted to feel it draped across my skin.

It's not something a guy wants to admit, but I was lonely. Achingly lonely. I was lonely for sex, yes, but not just sex. Affection. I was lonely for a woman's body wrapped around mine at night, lonely for a kiss when I least expected it, lonely for a woman to notice me. I don't want to say how long I'd been celibate because that's a strong word, an exaggeration, but that's how it felt. It wasn't a shocking length of time — maybe a month or two, but I'm young, not even forty. Every few days is more to my liking.

Occasionally, after she finished her workout, she'd give me an easy smile as she walked by. I wasn't sure she really noticed me, or was even aware that she saw me every morning at the same time. It was more a general friendliness, smiling at anyone in her vicinity, anyone with whom she made casual eye contact.

She seemed like the kind of woman who kept things simple. Who was open and calm. She seemed like a woman who said what was on her mind without filtering it, and someone who didn't create drama. Not that you can know any of that by simply looking, but maybe you can.

I was lonely for a woman who would touch me. I wanted a woman to hold onto me as if she needed me. I'm a decent-looking guy. It's not like women were repelled by me. Far from it. But there I was, needing affection, needing sex, needing something I couldn't always define. It's hard to admit, but it's the truth. I wanted a woman who couldn't keep her hands off me. A woman who wanted me as much as I wanted her.

15

Gemma

It was hot outside, the kind of burning heat the Santa Clara Valley gets in the fall. Leaves are falling to the ground, crunching under your feet, and the mornings are cold. But the afternoons rise up and smack you with a dry fire that makes you loathe the leather boots and long-sleeved shirt you were foolish enough to wear. Your hair that looked so silky and smooth in the morning is now a thick blanket over a sweaty neck.

After living in the San Francisco Bay Area most of my adult life, I never understood why I somehow forgot about the heat of October afternoons. It felt like the weather god, if such a thing exists, wanted to torture me. The stores were filled with comfy sweaters and boots, leather jackets and wool dresses and all kinds of inspiration for layering. Pastel colored scarves were draped around the necks of mannequins. Some wore jewel-colored mittens or camel-colored kidskin gloves. Sandals and a sleeveless dress were more appropriate.

The previous day, the temperature had climbed to eighty-three, sweeping away the chill of air that had cooled to forty-three overnight. But I remembered. I did choose a sleeveless dress and sandals, topping it with a short leather jacket for the morning. After I finished grading spelling tests, I headed north to Palo Alto for therapy.

I was looking forward to therapy. It might have been the first thing I'd looked forward to in months. I couldn't wait to talk about David. I needed to talk about him. I missed him so terribly. The chilly mornings made me think about how good it would have felt to wake up with his arms wrapped around me, the heat of him filling the bed, making my body feel soft and welcoming.

We never got to share a cold morning. Our life together started in the middle of June, and he was gone before September was over. The brevity made me want to cry. Everything made me want to cry. It was impossible to understand what had gone wrong. I hoped Dr. Wilcox would help me figure that out. If I knew what went wrong, maybe there was still a chance. There had to be a chance. I was empty without him.

The minute my butt touched the cushion of my chair, Dr. Wilcox started to unroll her agenda. For someone who wanted me to figure out things for myself, who insisted therapy should take a natural course, she didn't seem interested in what I wanted to talk about. She didn't even ask how I was doing, didn't ask if I'd written in the journal, didn't ask anything about my day or even what I thought about the weather.

"I think it will be helpful to talk about your sexual relationship with David. I'd like you to talk about how you responded sexually with him."

Helpful? Helpful to me? I didn't mind talking about sex, not at all. At the same time, what we had was so amazing and so unique and so private, I didn't want to betray that. Once you talk about something, some of the magic evaporated. And if there was one thing I was certain had not gone wrong between us, it was sex. "How I responded?"

She nodded.

"I guess…it was so much more than sex. We were soul mates. That's what hurts so…" I gasped for air. "…badly. A piece of me is gone. Our sex was…it was perfect. Blissful. He loved it. The way he touched me, the way he felt…it proved he was my soul mate. I never doubted it."

"Let's put the *soul mate* construct aside for now. I think it would be helpful to focus solely on the physical relationship."

"Why?"

The smile she gave me wasn't that different from the way my smile felt when I was trying to explain something to one of my students, and they kept asking *why*. Did she consider my question childish? I thought it made absolute sense. She wanted to know about my sex life, and I had no idea how that would help this pain. She never talks about the pain, and I don't know what I'm supposed to do with it. I know that talking is supposed to give me insights and that will help me. She promised it would help, but so far, nothing.

"Sex is more visceral," she said.

I picked up the bottle of Fiji water from the table beside me. I opened it and took a sip. "I don't feel like any of this is helping. It hurts the same as always, almost worse. Some days it's hard to get out of bed. I feel like I drift off during class. I'm outside my body, watching me supervise the reading groups or line the children up for recess."

"I told you it takes time."

"I want the pain to stop." I swallowed more water. My voice rose until I sounded a little hysterical, but it just came out, even though I knew she wouldn't like it. "I want him back!"

"Would having him back make the pain go away?"

"Of course."

"What if you had him back, as you call it, and he wasn't fully yours? If you aren't the ideal person for him, but he stayed with you without loving you to the degree you desire, would that lessen the pain? Or make it worse?"

I started to cry.

She waited. Her pen sat on top of her leather notebook. She hadn't written anything yet, which made sense since I hadn't really said anything. But sometimes, she wrote in her notebook even when I hadn't spoken.

"Would that be more painful?"

"Yes. But it wouldn't happen." I pulled a tissue out of the box and held it to my nose. I wiped my left ring finger across my bottom lashes, and it came away smeared with mascara.

"Wouldn't it be better to explore yourself, to understand yourself? To love yourself without a possessive need for another person?"

"Will that make it stop hurting?"

"Do you think it would?"

I hated it when she asked questions after I asked a question. It was confusing. Maybe Geoff was right. Maybe getting drunk was the best therapy. But I couldn't spend my whole life drunk. I smiled into my tissue.

"You have to trust the process. Can you do that?"

I shrugged.

"Can you trust me?"

I shrugged again.

"Why don't you give this some more time. See what happens. Can you do that?"

"Okay."

After a slight, almost non-existent pause, she said —
"So tell me about sex with David."

"I told you, it was amazing. Like nothing I ever
experienced."

She waited for me to say more.

"It made me feel whole."

"What does that word mean to you — *whole?*"

"That I was where I was supposed to be. It made me
feel like I was connected to someone. It made me feel loved.
It made me feel like nothing was missing in my life."

"Before this relationship, did you feel something was
missing from your life?"

I crossed my legs. Even though I'd been sitting in her
office for fifteen or twenty minutes now, there was still sweat
behind my knees. When I crossed my legs, sweat smeared
across the top of my other leg, making me feel I couldn't sit
still because my legs were sliding all over the place. I tried to
put my slippery skin out of my mind. "I'm not explaining it
very well."

"That's okay. It's more important that you express what's
on your mind than how it comes across to me."

That made me feel slightly relieved. But what could I
say, really? I closed my eyes. I thought she would immediately
fire another question at me, but she didn't.

I remembered our first time…David unbuttoning my
blouse, his fingers surprisingly adept with the small, tight
buttons. The way he stared at me and moved so slowly as if
those buttons were the most fascinating objects he'd ever
seen. He unbuttoned my blouse down to the hem and then
moved the two sides apart. He traced the top edge of my bra

with his finger. My insides dissolved into warm, thick liquid. I felt like the most precious object in the world.

Time seemed to sink into itself as he continued with his soft, slow touches, gradually removing my blouse, then unhooking and taking off my bra. He sucked on my breasts for what felt like hours before he moved to the button on my jeans, and then the zipper.

When I was naked, he picked me up and placed me on the bed. He touched me all over, stroking my skin, exploring my body. It was so clear he wasn't just after sex, concerned with his own satisfaction. I would never say this to Dr. Wilcox, it's too precious, and it's almost embarrassing, but he worshipped me. There's no other word for it. I think I had two orgasms before he even took off his clothes.

There was no way I was telling her about that. It was too private. I wanted to hold it inside of my heart. It belonged to me, and I didn't need to talk about it to find my way through.

She wanted me to talk, so I talked. I talked about how I felt about him in general and what I liked about him. Her interest in sex seemed creepy, like she wanted to have some kind of vicarious experience through me. I know that's not true, but I couldn't stop thinking it. I didn't tell her that, either.

16

Dr. Ann Wilcox: Notes on Gemma Hughes

Once again I was caught off guard by Gemma's reluctance to reveal anything uncomfortable. My overall sense, after listening to her first try to avoid talking about the subject, and then dwelling mostly on her feelings with a fair amount of gushing over his good qualities, is that the relationship was primarily about sex. I believe that's why she emphasized at the outset that she was thrilled to meet a man who wanted more than sex.

I believe she's recast the story in her mind to make him into someone she wishes he were. First love? Pure fantasy, fed by the media? I'm not sure. The relationship was likely short-lived simply because it was purely physical. He became bored and moved on. She inflated it in her mind into something it was not.

Directing her thoughts to recognize and ultimately accept this reality is a long-term effort, and I hope she doesn't lose interest or become so resistant that we never reach that point. It's obvious her frustration is increasing. She verbalized some of that — said she didn't think therapy was helping. She's chosen to forget that I told her at the outset we were looking at a year, possibly more.

It's demoralizing to see her suffering. It's very obvious and painful to look at. Listening to her desire to steer the conversation to soul mates when it was definitely the polar opposite of something that deep is almost embarrassing. It shocks me. I shouldn't be filtering in so much of my opinion here, but that word isn't too strong — it's truly shocking to see how blind she is to the reality of her situation.

She's young, but not so young I would expect so much naïveté. In her early thirties, she's surely had other serious as well as casual relationships and should know the difference.

I'm considering prescribing something to help alleviate her depression, although she hasn't asked, so I don't want to rush to that.

Concluding thoughts: Strive to keep her off the fantasy of soul mates. Revisit her first love affair. Has she also mischaracterized that in her mind? Get a more complete history of her romantic and sexual relationships. Detailed, including one-night stands, if relevant. Consider methods for deepening her trust. The lack of trust is a significant inhibitor.

17

Ann

I was waiting in Peet's when Tamara Hughes arrived. I knew it was her because she had a strong resemblance to Gemma. Her identity was cemented as she stood just inside the door, looking around the room. I saw the realization cross her face that she had no idea who she was looking for. I hadn't provided a description.

I pushed back my chair and walked to where she stood. "Mrs. Hughes? Tamara?"

"Yes."

The large gray eyes she turned on me could have belonged to her daughter. In addition to the color, they had the same elaborate makeup as Gemma's, and a similarly vulnerable, slightly anxious look.

"I'm Annie."

"Oh. I didn't realize until I got here that I had no idea what you look like." She laughed.

"Thank you for meeting with me."

"You sound so formal." She laughed again. She had a beautiful laugh and none of the permanent grief that had etched itself into her daughter's face.

I led her to my table, asked what she wanted to drink, and went to the counter to place the order. A few minutes later I returned with two cappuccinos. I sat down and pulled my cup closer to me. "I'm not sure how to start," I said. "I don't want to upset you."

"Has he done something? Is he threatening her?"

This startled me. For a moment, I lost the thread of what I wanted to say. "Why would you think that?"

"Because you sound so worried."

"Oh. No, it's about her. I'm concerned she's more depressed than I suggested when we talked on the phone."

Tamara nodded. "She's very upset. She took the breakup hard."

"Yes."

"She doesn't spend all day in bed. She hasn't missed any work, that I know of. She keeps herself groomed…I think she's coping. She's upset, but not depressed, not really."

I resisted mentioning the sometimes contradictory symptoms of depression. The list flooded my mind and was about to slip through my lips. "I've heard…" I coughed softly. "Not everyone shuts down when they're depressed. And she seems…angry, almost. One contributing factor to depression is anger at oneself."

"Angry? Gemma doesn't have a temper."

"I'm not talking about temper. It's not that she's lashing out, it's her overall mood."

"Are you worried she'll hurt the children in her care? Because she would never do that. Never."

"Oh, of course not. I know that." I smiled. "I do think she might be angry with herself. Although I can't imagine why. He's the one who broke up with her."

"Maybe she's worried she pushed him away. She wanted too much. She always wanted things she couldn't have."

I nodded thoughtfully.

She lifted her coffee cup. She blew on the liquid and took a few tentative sips. "Why did you want to meet with me?"

"Because I'm worried about her."

"Yes, but I'm not sure there's anything I can do. You see her every day. I only see her a few times a month."

"True."

"I appreciate that you're looking out for her."

"Absolutely." I ran my finger around the rim of my cup. The rough spots of dried chocolate and coffee where the over-filled ceramic had been splashed when I carried the drinks to the table dragged at my skin. "I wonder if she's angry at men in general?"

"Why do you say that?"

I took a slow breath and waited a moment. "She talks a lot about her high school boyfriend."

"Really?"

I surged forward. "Yes. Aidan."

"I haven't heard her mention that name in years."

"I suppose there are some things you don't talk to your mother about."

She sighed.

"Has she seen him since high school?"

"Not that I'm aware of." She moved her chair away from the table and pushed her coffee cup toward me, as if she wanted to put all the space around herself that she could.

"It struck me as odd that she's still obsessing about a guy from high school."

"Obsessing?"

"I'm sorry. Poor choice of words. Although..."

"What?"

"I get the impression she didn't have closure with him."

Her face hardened, and her eyes shifted to a blank stare. "I'm not going to gossip about my daughter. Especially with a stranger."

I'd hoped I had gained a small amount of trust, but I let her assessment lie there without argument. "I'm sorry. I didn't mean to come off like I'm gossiping. As I said, I'm worried she's depressed. More than she lets on. I sense a lot of hostility, and I think I'm just worried. I'm flailing, looking for answers." I sighed deeply.

"I have no idea why she's thinking about the past. And I really don't want to discuss her relationships. She had all the closure she needed."

"Teenagers take those feelings very seriously. They can be devastating."

"Are you an expert in child psychology?"

"No, but I did study some aspects of psychology…for teacher training."

"I see."

For whatever reason, she didn't want to talk about it. Maybe she was being truthful, and it was a sense of guilt for talking about her daughter. Maybe I hadn't established enough trust after all. I was pushing too hard. Despite those factors, I was certain there was more to the story with Aidan. That fact was even more obvious in Tamara's behavior than it had been in Gemma's mannerisms and recounting of the story.

We sipped our coffee drinks in silence for several minutes.

"I didn't want to upset you," I said. "I think I have."

"I'm fine." She glanced at her watch. "I should get

going." She moved her chair farther from the table and lifted her purse strap off the back, slipping it over her shoulder.

I looked up at her as she stood. "We should keep in touch. Just to watch out for her, share any red flags, don't you think?"

"What kind of red flags?"

"Concerns, that's all. I didn't mean to make it into something…we both want her to be happy."

"Of course." Tamara's eyes filled with tears. She managed to keep them in check without excessive blinking or wiping at her eyes. "Thank you for caring so much."

I reached out and put my fingers on her wrist. It was thin, almost all bone. "Gemma and I have been friends forever. I want her to get past this."

"Well, you have my number."

"I do. Would you like mine?"

"I don't think that's necessary."

"But I can call you again, if I'm concerned?"

"Yes. Absolutely." She turned and walked quickly toward the door. She pushed it open and let it fall shut behind her, failing to notice the couple straining to grab the edge of the door, trying to enter the coffee shop.

Talking to her had gone about as I'd expected. I had no new insights, but I had an open door.

18

Gemma

With David, sex wasn't just sex. It was special. It meant something. It connected us on every level. After we made love, he was so quiet, almost sad, as if he thought it might be our last time. I should have seen that as a sign, maybe.

Still, he would always manage a sweet smile.

The very first time, I knew he would be different from other men, I knew the two of *us* would be different.

After he kissed me under the overhang outside the restaurant, he put his mouth close to my ear. His breath and voice were warm inside my head. "I think there's something happening between us."

I nodded, my throat swollen with desire. I wanted him so badly I would have let him take me right there, in the rain, with people watching from rain-spattered car windows. Not really, but it seemed possible. I was insane with craving his body. All those times we'd sat talking, over coffee and lunch, his eyes on me, his quiet presence as he let me talk on and on and never seemed bored, he'd been taking possession of my soul.

He touched my cheek. "I'd like to take you to dinner, beautiful woman."

My hands started to tremble. I put them in my pockets and hunched my shoulders to stop the quivering.

"And then...a hotel room, if you agree?" His voice grew rough. "My apartment's a mess. The cleaner comes Monday, but I can't wait that long. I need you so badly." He slipped his arm around my waist and rested his forehead on the top of my head. "Can you?"

I nodded, feeling both our heads move, heavy and filled with longing.

The next evening we drove to San Francisco. We ate dinner in the restaurant of a five-star hotel. I couldn't imagine what the meal cost. I added up the price of our entrees, but I didn't see the wine list. David had taken control of that. The wine was like burgundy-colored silk, obviously expensive.

And then, the room. I'd never stayed in a five-star hotel.

The room wasn't enormous. It wasn't like those Vegas hotel rooms where they think all you want is lots of extra space. There's more to a nice room than square footage.

The bed was king-sized and so high off the ground that I felt like a child when he lifted me onto it. There was a layer of feather-filled padding on top of a firm mattress. It was so heavenly, I wondered if that's what a baby feels like in its mother's womb. Safe. So quiet and comfy until she's shoved out into the world, cold and screaming and forced to fight her way through life, never sure what's really going on until she's several years old, if we're ever sure.

Dr. Wilcox seems sure.

I'm not.

I didn't want Dr. Wilcox coming into my head. She was spoiling my memory of that night...

David had called ahead and ordered a box of chocolates and a bottle of champagne that sat on the table near the floor-to-ceiling window. We had a view of San Francisco all the way to the Golden Gate Bridge. The setting sun drenched the sky with shades of purple and pink, and the bridge shimmering against that backdrop was truly golden.

Making love to him was so incredible it still turns my legs to jelly when I think of it. He seemed to know every single part of my body that wanted him. He brought sounds out of me that are almost embarrassing when I think back. I can't even recall the things I cried out. At the time, I felt proud of my utter release, as if I was screaming out to the entire universe. I think I made him feel quite fine as well.

We fell into a deep sleep. I hadn't slept like that since I was a little girl. When I woke, the sun was up. He'd opened the drapes enough to let in a slice of the morning light. After we made love again and I was wrapped in a white terrycloth robe, we ordered breakfast.

We ate Eggs Benedict and bacon, strawberries with cream, and buttered toast. We drank icy cold champagne and sipped steaming hot coffee. I was starving.

He sat back in his chair and watched me eat.

"What are you staring at?" I laughed, feeling a little self-conscious, which was ridiculous after the previous night.

"I love watching you eat. You're as passionate about your food as you are about other things." He grinned.

I grinned back. "What other things?"

"Me, apparently."

"Yes."

"My hot body."

"Yes. Definitely."

His grin lingered. I laughed again for no reason, and he refilled my champagne glass.

We showered together and spent the morning walking in

Golden Gate Park. We ate lunch in Chinatown and then headed home.

I told him absolutely everything. I couldn't stop talking, I felt so loved, things just poured out of me. He talked about his childhood and high school pranks, his college trips to play tennis with the men's team. We didn't get into past loves, but it was early for that.

Talking about the hurts of your past isn't something you want to do so early in a relationship. It brings a negative tone into things. It makes you start thinking about all the ways that love can get damaged and stifled and beaten down. We told stories that made us laugh.

He'd traveled a lot, so he told me about Germany and Italy, Japan and England. I didn't have much to share in that department, but I told him how much I wanted to travel. It's hard on a teacher's salary. I take a vacation every summer, but I usually visit places where I know people who are glad to have me stay with them. And often, I drive — to Arizona or Oregon and Washington, to LA and San Diego with a few day trips over the border to Mexico. That and Victoria Island in Canada were my only trips out of the country.

That night, I fell asleep holding my pillow, letting my thoughts drift back over every minute of the past twenty-four hours. I'd never met a man like David. He was classy and sweet. He gave off the aura of a man in charge, but he was hugely vulnerable in bed. I felt protected by him, and needed by him.

After Aidan and I broke up, I hadn't been with a guy for the rest of high school. It was the same for my first year of college. Since that time, I've had five or six boyfriends. I thought I loved all of them, and for a while, I did. I really believe that, even now. But I think it was a childish kind of love. It was spoiled by competition, by game-playing, and control. Theirs, and mine, if I'm honest. When each of those relationships ended, I felt lost for a while. In some cases I hurt, for a while, but I knew deep inside it was for the best. They weren't right for me.

With David, I felt different from the very start. From the moment he smiled at the unexpected peek at my breasts, to coffee with only a mild electricity between us, one of comfort more than full-out lust. And it grew slowly and organically from there.

I knew I'd met *the one*. Like the two halves of the apple, separated and searching the world for the half that completes them. We'd found each other.

19

Dr. Ann Wilcox: Notes on Gemma Hughes

At her last session, Gemma was eager to share another dream. She boasted for several minutes about writing the details of her dreams in the notebook I'd advised her to purchase. When I asked whether she'd written about our sessions, whether she'd uncovered any insights, she brushed the question aside. She actually interrupted me in her thrill to get back to describing the details of the dream.

There were so many specifics, I wonder if she's fabricating part of the story. I've seen patients recall some fairly detailed dreams, retaining every nuance for months, sometimes years. But Gemma's recollection seems even more specific.

Nevertheless, her dream was quite telling. And perhaps it's more telling if she did fabricate parts of it.

I don't think it's necessary to capture every single description of temperature and moonlight, every line of conversation, every emotion that passed through her body, because even without any of that, the meaning was blatantly clear to me.

In summary, she dreamt she was in a very large house, containing over forty rooms. Each room was decorated in a different phase of a woman's life. For example, the ground floor rooms were decorated like a nursery, a toddler's room, a preschooler's room, etc. It was easy to distinguish the ages of the occupant in the early years, more difficult in the rooms depicting the sleeping spaces of a teenager, a young adult.

In the dream, she'd spent time exploring each room with extreme *curiosity. She could not stop herself from opening drawers, sliding her arm between mattresses and box springs, and combing through boxes on closet shelves. She knew she was looking for particular items, but couldn't say what they were. As her dream self, this lack of knowing what she was looking for didn't trouble her.*

In the rooms for each year of a teenager's life, she looked through diaries and read notes on scraps of paper, folded messages from girlfriends written in lime green and turquoise ink.

The first room she saw that belonged to an adult woman was not a bedroom like the others. It was an office, and the wall was lined with framed diplomas, including a doctoral degree in psychology.

Gemma laughed when she told me this. She accurately guessed that the dream signified her desire to probe every area of my life, and the intense curiosity was the natural result of all the things she'd shared with me. She felt no shame that her dream self had read diaries and private notes.

In her view, all of this was natural.

—We have an unbalanced relationship, she declared.

She's bothered that she tells me her deepest secrets (not true) and I tell her absolutely nothing. When I explained that's the nature of therapy, she laughed. The laugh was rather manic sounding.

It's normal for patients to be curious about the life of their therapist. But the dream, the sheer number of rooms, the intensity of her desire to go over every inch, to leave nothing untouched or unread, borders on obsession.

This dream, and other things she's said lead me to believe Gemma is becoming obsessed with me. It's not unheard of, but I'm honestly not sure how to handle it.

Concluding thoughts: Choose a story from my past to share with Gemma. A difficult balancing act. It may feed her obsession, but at the same time, trust is critical, and she clearly lacks that. Follow-up on other dreams — try to ferret out tendency to embellish the truth, to interpret events in her life in a way that fits her view of herself.

20

David

Gemma offered something that had been missing in my life for too long — a woman who made the first move.

Men like being the aggressor. *I* like being the aggressor, without a doubt. We're born and bred to be aggressors, and we like pursuing a woman who captures our attention. I know I do, and I believe I speak for most men.

But sometimes, maybe after one too many rejections, maybe from the sheer effort of charming and luring and flirting and coming up with places to go and things to do, and putting desire out there, always the one needing more than the other, we get worn down. I know I have.

It's not only that. It's not as if I've faced relentless rejection.

Being pursued is just nice. It's flattering. It strokes the ever-needy ego. It feels good.

There's nothing like watching as a woman notices you, then makes a move to show you she wants you. The implication is that she's ignoring convention, convention that still exists in the twenty-first century, because she wants you that badly. Being pursued feels great on all levels, which makes it so much more powerful. It makes you feel like you look good, that a woman wants your body, and that she thinks you're interesting. She's so attracted, she's willing to put *her* ego on the line.

When Gemma leaned over to tie her shoe, which didn't look untied to me, it was a thrill. Because of my elevated line of sight, I saw farther than I should have. She sealed my fate when she looked up and saw me staring. I smiled, and she smiled right back, proving it was a deliberate act.

I didn't get a scowl for being inappropriate. I didn't get a sharp comment about fucking off or keeping my eyes to myself. I wasn't accused of treating her like an object. I wasn't given a lecture on male privilege, on men deluded into believing every woman was theirs for the taking. I didn't get the finger.

My friends and I have received all of those things at one time or another. We're decent guys, feminists all the way through, but hormones still assert their will. And we get chastised for being obvious in our interest.

All I got from Gemma was that warm smile, filled with the same desire I was feeling.

There was an instant sense of something happening. Maybe it wasn't so instant, since I'd been watching her all that time. And maybe she'd been watching me after all, but with such caution, I wasn't aware.

She made me feel like she wanted me as much as I wanted her. She made me feel she wanted me even *more* than I wanted her. She made me feel like I was twenty years old.

21

Gemma

The phone call from my mother caught me by surprise. Usually, I call her once a week, more or less. In between, she sends emails every other day, wondering why she hasn't heard from me, issuing dinner invitations, pining for family togetherness.

She was very direct in her phone call. There were no opening pleasantries. She got right to it — an invitation to go shopping with her at Stanford mall. She wanted to have a *nice* lunch out with me. She hadn't seen me, we didn't talk like we used to. She had no idea what was going on in my life.

This wasn't entirely true. She knew David had broken up with me. She knew how my job was going. Other than that, she knew as much as I wanted her to know. And I wasn't sure when this idyllic past where we'd shared our feelings had existed. Only in her mind, but she would never admit that.

I wasn't in the mood to tell my mother every heartbreaking detail of what was going on in my life. She knew the essential part — David was gone. Telling her all the things I was feeling didn't interest me. As much as I longed to talk about him, to re-live every moment we'd spent together, to try to figure out that point in time when things went wrong, I didn't need to talk to her. We didn't have that kind of relationship. That's why therapy was good, no matter how slowly it was moving.

None of the things I wanted to say would be palatable to my mother.

She hadn't approved of David. She'd never met him, but she didn't approve. In her view, he had *too much* money. I didn't even talk about money, but she took a few comments about places where we'd gone, combined that with her sketchy knowledge of the tech industry, and inferred he did quite well as a Vice President in a high tech company.

I knew what she really meant. It was there in her tone, in the things I'd heard for years about *how the world really works.* He was *out of my league.* He'd get tired of me, wouldn't feel I measured up. He was *using me for sex.* All those things, buried in a nonsensical phrase — *too much* money.

It wasn't as if my parents were middle class. Not any more. When my dad's parents died, quite a lot of money came their way. It's what bought my parents a sprawling, multi-million dollar classic ranch-style home in Los Altos, a place that still had a small-town feel, surrounded by the ambition and competition of Silicon Valley, and infused with its easily flowing money. It was a place where old money and new money co-existed peacefully, for the most part.

She also had the opinion that David moved *too fast.*

If two people fall for each other, what's *too fast?* It's not as if he suggested marriage after a few weeks together. It was the trip to Hawaii, the week after I told her I was seeing him. That was *too much, too soon.* It was *giving the impression he was serious about me, when most likely, he was not.* I shouldn't be *too easy,* I shouldn't *think it was love when it probably was not.*

Other women who grew up in the seventies didn't share my mother's views. I never understood why she tended toward views of the world that came straight from her own mother's generation. A woman *plays hard to get*. A woman doesn't *put out*, at least not easily. *Never let him have the milk for free*. A woman lets a man make the first move in each step of the relationship. In other words, a woman is passive.

That wasn't me.

22

Gemma

"What's the occasion?"

My mother laughed with a slight touch of hysteria. "Does there have to be an occasion for me to see my only daughter?"

"I guess not. You just sound very wound up about it. Like you have a plan."

She laughed again. "My plan is to enjoy a day with you, without the boys."

We arranged that I would drive to her house early Saturday morning and have a cup of coffee with her and my father because he was missing time with his only daughter as much as she was.

Then, she and I would head out — ten at the latest, to be sure we found a *good* parking spot. We'd browse, try on clothes, maybe do a bit of early Christmas shopping, and eat lunch at any restaurant I chose.

Sitting in their kitchen drinking coffee with both my parents made me feel like an only child. Geoff wasn't around. They sat across the table from me, clasping their mugs as if they expected them to slide off the table of their own volition.

"How's work?" My father smiled, his dark blue eyes boring into mine, his Saturday morning stubble, mostly gray now, shimmering in the sunlight that poured through the window.

"Good."

"Any progress on that class size reduction effort that was supposed to kick in this year?"

"Yes, it's great. I only have twenty-three students. I'm so much more connected to each child."

"Good." He nodded. "Good, good. I'm glad to hear that. Are they paying you any better?"

I sighed. "Nothing's changed. You know that."

"Well, it's an outrage. You're responsible for molding the next generation. First grade is crucial. If a child doesn't leave first grade with solid reading skills, their education is sabotaged. Teaching is one of the most important jobs there is. Teachers are undervalued, which proves that we undervalue human life."

"It's not about money, Rob," my mother said. "Gemma didn't become a school teacher for the money. Just like you. Not everything is about money."

"I didn't say it was."

My mother smiled gently, untroubled by thoughts of a woman's need to support herself and save for the future. "Do you feel the children respond to you?"

"Absolutely."

"And you have friends, among the other teachers?"

"Yes."

She smiled with more force.

"It's not a social club," my father said.

"Friendships are important." My mother brushed her hair off her face. It was still golden blonde, with the help of her hairdresser. She looked like she was only ten years older than me. I hoped I inherited her good genes, and could afford expert color enhancement in twenty years.

My father jumped in. "What are the politics like? With the administration?"

I swallowed some coffee. "What's with all the questions? We've talked about all of this before."

"Just wanted to get an update. We never see you," he said.

"That's not true."

"Not enough." He smiled, but he looked sad. He patted my mother's hand, which was gripping the edge of the table, her knuckles and the skin around her fingernails white from the pressure.

All I wanted was to go back to my condo and crawl into bed for a late morning nap. The only good thing was I hadn't thought about David until that moment. Maybe there was a reason for their questions — distraction.

As if I hadn't pointed out they already knew these things, the questions continued until my mother announced we needed to get going or we'd have to park *miles* from the mall. My father agreed and stood to collect our still half-full coffee mugs.

At the shopping center, we started in the shoe department at Bloomingdales. We tried on glitzy holiday shoes, already out even though holiday parties and the new year still seemed months away.

Trying on shoes and clothes, made me feel, for a few moments, like a kid again. Back-to-school shopping with my mother. An annual event that included lunch out — half a day without my brother's presence.

We browsed purses and jewelry. We walked slowly

through Pottery Barn, admiring all the things that look so perfect on display but for which there's no place in most homes.

The diversion was nice, but still, my shoes seemed filled with wet cement and my body ached all over as I dragged it after her from display to display, store to store.

A few minutes after noon, we headed toward the parking lot, having decided on a Tapas place for lunch. She began firing questions at me. *Was I happy? What did I do in the evenings? How often did I see my friends? Why didn't I come for Sunday dinner every week? It seemed as if I was abandoning my family.* When she began to wonder out loud, not really asking, but talking as if I'd brought it up, about whether I might be happier moving home, just for a while, I changed the subject firmly. I began telling her some of the cute things my students had said.

As we passed the Apple store, I glanced at the crowd inside. Standing at the center table, where people fondled the latest phones and tablets, was Dr. Wilcox. She wasn't even looking at the products on the table. Her hands were in her pockets and she was staring straight at me.

She didn't wave or nod, but I felt her eyes on me, her gaze burning into me. When I glanced back after we passed, she'd walked out of the store and was following slowly behind us, remaining several yards back.

Had she been following me all morning? I felt a chill run through my arms.

My mother saw me shiver and frowned. She patted my upper arm and we kept walking. I shivered again, but I didn't look behind me. I didn't need to. I could feel her there.

23

Dr. Ann Wilcox: Notes on Gemma Hughes

While I was shopping for a new phone, I glanced out the open storefront because something made me feel wary, a sixth sense of some kind. Just outside, standing perfectly still, a few feet from the entrance, was Gemma. She was staring directly at me.

She didn't look away, embarrassed for being intrusive. She didn't seem concerned that I'd caught her. Her eyes were fierce, yet somewhat blank.

Knowing she'd followed me to the mall was deeply unsettling. She must have been waiting near my office. I'd stopped by to remove two of my notebooks from the safe so I could work at home that evening.

I wanted to talk to her immediately, to get a read on her state of mind, but by the time I walked out of the store, she'd moved on. As I wove through the slow-moving, frequently-stopping crowd of shoppers, I had second thoughts.

The more time I've spent with her, the more I've realized she's deeply troubled. I'm certain it's more than the breakup that's drawn her to therapy. On some level, she knew she had more significant issues. An unrecognized part of her was crying out for help.

The obsession with me wasn't textbook transference, as far as I could tell, but there was something in her that needed to be near me, that needed me to consume her life. If I broke that protective shell she'd constructed, if I pointed out that her behavior was unhealthy or threatening to my privacy, she might suspend therapy.

Of course, obsession isn't as dangerous as the word sometimes suggests. It simply means a constant preoccupation that repeatedly intrudes on a person's mind. We all have obsessions, even I do. We're obsessed with trips we want to take, sports teams, television shows, and movies that have touched us deeply. Goals and dreams can become obsessive.

But obsession can turn into something unhealthy, into a recognized disorder, and in Gemma's case, I fear that's where this is headed. I don't think we've had a single session where she hasn't been more interested in me than in exploring her own thoughts, in pursuing her stated goal of relieving the pain of her breakup.

I should have recognized this earlier.

As I watched Gemma make her way to the parking lot, I wondered if she'd wanted me to see her.

Another interpretation is that she wants to exert power over me. It's possible she took satisfaction from knowing she'd unsettled me. She was clearly uncomfortable with the imbalance that she perceived in our relationship. Still, the most likely interpretation is she thought she could find out more about my life. The more sinister interpretation is that she wants to do something to disrupt my life.

It's happened to me before. Never anything violent or worth involving the police. I haven't been stalked by men who wanted to hurt me or patients with serious issues, but I have received anonymous emails, some outlining perverse sexual acts patients wanted to perform with me, some accusing me of revealing their secrets, some simply ranting about the problems they were facing and my failure to comprehend their emotional devastation.

Now, the risk of sharing a personal story to ease her concern that therapy is too one-sided is that it will only whet her appetite. I need to take that risk, but if it backfires, I need to come up with a few alternative strategies.

It also crossed my mind that she might be jealous of me. I can't think why, but the instinct felt solid. It could be career envy. I think she felt forced into her career path by her father's insistence she do something "serious", when what she really wanted was a career as a dancer. She's not so much jealous of the particular work I do, but that I love my work. She seems to enjoy teaching, but I don't sense any passion.

There was no way she could envy my marriage. She knows nothing about it.

When I'm in a therapy session, I don't wear my wedding rings. On the middle finger of my left hand, I wear a silver ring with a long turquoise stone. Patients tend to think a single woman has more empathy. Dealing with heartbreak and other emotional difficulties stirs up envy toward people who have the trappings of a happy life — wedding rings are definitely part of those trappings. For the same reason, there are no personal photographs in my office.

Therapy can be a dangerous business. There are so many people who are so fragile and so many who've experienced a splintering of their hold on reality. Therapy digs into the dark corners that have been shielded with coping mechanisms. The monsters, if you want to call it that, are released as patients try to sort through the layers of their lives and conditioning, the damage that childhood traumas and years of human interaction often inflict.

Concluding thoughts: I won't confront her about following me. I'll wait for her to volunteer the information. Or, more likely, I'll decide when I see how the session unfolds. There's plenty of time to course correct if it happens again, or if it becomes more serious.

24

Gemma

Dr. Wilcox opened the door to her office and gave me the same smile she'd given every week, as if she kept it in her drawer and had one specially designed for each patient. There wasn't a hint of acknowledgment that she'd followed me at Stanford mall. Surely that was considered breaking the rules of professional ethics?

Therapy is supposed to be about me opening up. I'm supposed to be in control. I'm supposed to be the one who reveals what I choose about my life. She is not supposed to follow me when I'm shopping with my mother. She's not supposed to spy on me.

You always hear that therapy is all about your childhood. It's about remembering your parents' mistakes, digging up ghosts from the past that messed up your current state of mind. So far, Dr. Wilcox hadn't asked much about my parents. She was more interested in Aidan. I'd summed up the first fifteen years of my life in less than ten sentences, and she never asked any more about it.

Was that normal? I had no one to ask. I suppose I could have gone online and tried to find a forum where people talk about their experiences in therapy. But forums can be weird. You don't really know who you're talking to. How would I know if they'd even had therapy? In a forum, how do you know if a woman is a woman? How do you know anything? It could all be crazy people that have fun pretending their lives are more interesting by making up stuff.

My parents were a mystery to Dr. Wilcox, and possibly, a mystery to me.

Those two god-like people who define your view of the world before you even know what's going on are the ones who implant neuroses in your brain. At least that's what everyone says. People even joke about it around little kids. If a woman licks her finger and wipes a smudge of chocolate off a child's lips in full view of other children, everyone laughs that the poor kid will be lying on the therapist's couch someday, talking about her mother's unsanitary and overly-familiar behavior.

Of course, I was seated in a chair, not lying on a couch. And my mother never used her saliva to wipe food off my face. Sitting in a chair was one of the ways therapy felt more like a conversation than a doctor and patient relationship. Maybe that's why it bothered me that Dr. Wilcox hadn't told me a single thing about herself. It really bugged me.

So why was she following me? And why didn't she apologize, or even acknowledge it?

She settled into her chair, that same smile still on her face. "How are you today?"

"Fine, I guess."

"You aren't sure?"

"I'm sure that not much has changed. I still can't stop thinking about David. I still cry at the smallest thing that makes me think of him. I still feel sad all the time. I still have this hurt in my heart that never gets better."

She made a note in her book. She laid down her pen and

looked at me. "I thought I saw you at Stanford mall last weekend."

I smiled. What was I supposed to say? Of course she saw me. She was staring right at me. Why did she make it sound as if she wasn't sure? "I guess so."

"You don't seem very certain of anything this afternoon. Any thoughts as to why that is?"

"I'm sure of a lot of things."

"Such as?"

"That I want David back. That I'm doing a good job at work even though I feel like I want to die."

"Can we explore that?"

"What?"

"Feelings of wanting to die."

I sighed. I wanted to talk about David. I suppose she would think that was morbid. "It's just an expression. It's a way to describe how terrible I feel. I'm not going to kill myself." I laughed. She was so serious sometimes. I suppose it was her job to be serious, but every word doesn't always have some kind of deeper interpretation.

"Often people say something that, on the surface, they think doesn't mean anything, but there's a reason you phrased it that way."

"Is there?"

She picked up her pen and wrote something in her book. She was quiet for a few seconds. She was looking at me but didn't seem to be focusing on my face. I wasn't sure she was thinking about me at all.

"I don't know anything about you," I said. "But I have to explain everything to you and tell you all about my life and all my thoughts, even if they're personal."

She smiled. "That's why you're here. To delve into your mind, to understand yourself on a deeper level. To find inner resources that will help you heal."

"Maybe I don't have inner resources."

"Everyone does."

"So why are you so secretive?"

"Do you perceive me as secretive?" Without looking down, she wrote something in the notebook. "I'm a professional. You should view me as your employee. You've hired me to help you work on the parts of your life you find dissatisfying."

"I guess."

She wrote that down. I was sure she was writing that I kept saying *I guess* instead of giving her firm answers. If everything was a guess, maybe I didn't know myself at all. I supposed that's what she'd written. I supposed I should have mentioned that insight to her. Instead, I'd write it down myself, later. I didn't want to get off track. It was almost a game, and I was going to win.

There was no professional rule that she couldn't tell me *anything* about herself. And obviously, she wasn't so worried about being a *professional* if she was going to follow me around the mall.

"Have you ever been married?" She didn't wear a gold band or a diamond on her left hand, just a turquoise ring on the middle finger, but that didn't mean anything.

She smiled. "Do you want to spend your time talking about my life or do you want to find a way past your grief? To learn more about yourself so you can enjoy your life more fully?"

I sighed. "I don't like talking about myself all the time.

It's self-centered."

"That's what therapy is. In the course of life, we don't get to talk about ourselves exclusively. This environment gives you the freedom to do that."

"So you won't tell me anything about your life?"

"We're not friends, Gemma. I'm your therapist."

"I know that." I folded my arms.

She twisted her pen so the tip sank back inside the casing. She placed it in the groove where the pages were secured into the binding. "Would it help you share more of your thoughts if you knew whether I've had similar experiences?"

"Yes. I think it would."

She put the notebook on the table beside her.

She started off talking about grad school. As if I could relate to grad school. The point seemed lost on her, and I wondered whether she was trying to piss me off. Finally, she wound her way around from how excited she'd been to be digging deep into subjects she cared about, from her academic achievements to her social life.

She'd met a guy in a seminar about how mental institutions had evolved in the twenty-first century. The two of them had an instant connection — intellectual, social, and physical. She assured me she understood how I must have felt, being completely consumed by a man who touched me on every level.

After they'd been together only four weeks, they moved into an apartment two blocks from campus. They did everything together. Studied, went to baseball games, took long hikes in the foothills. They cooked and had sex and drank wine and talked. They studied in bed and on the couch, their legs wrapped around each other. They never argued. They were never bored. Their sex life was *outstanding*.

Then, one day she came home from class and the apartment was empty. Stripped of every single thing that belonged to him. Just like that. She'd had no warning. There were no signs. Nothing. Amazing sex on Tuesday night, a nice dinner in front of the evening news on Wednesday, and then Thursday, while she was meeting with her academic advisor, he'd evaporated into thin air. He dropped out of school, and she never saw him again.

The only thing he'd left behind was an index card. He'd written — *I can't. Sorry.*

She had no idea what it meant. She had no idea what significant part of his past he'd left out that fed into this sudden and unbelievable change. She'd thought she known him inside and out.

"I didn't know him at all. You think you know a person, and you don't. Not if they want to conceal things. When something happens like this, an abrupt break, part of what you need to learn, and it's painful, but it's the truth — that this is not the right person for you."

I didn't like her saying that. I thought her job was to let me figure things out, not lecture me. She started off telling me a story as if we were equals, and suddenly she was making me feel like she knew all the answers and I had to listen to her. "How did you get over him?"

"Therapy." She smiled.

So it wasn't really sharing after all. It was a sales pitch about the benefit of therapy.

25

Ann

Telling Gemma about my relationship with Jon
Meadows had been more painful than I'd expected. It was so
long ago, it seemed almost irrelevant. But subsequent pain
has a way of building on what's gone before, and when the
details are recalled, it sharpens again as if it's been lying in
wait all that time.

When I first jotted down notes about what I might tell
Gemma to gain her confidence, I considered fabricating a
story. She would never know, and the point was to stop her
fixation on the circumstances of my life. It didn't matter what
I said, the details were unimportant. What mattered was that
she turn her attention from me to her own issues.

She has more trouble with this than any patient I've
encountered. Most people are far more interested in their
own experiences and thoughts and feelings. In addition to
their self-interest, they're somewhat conscious of the financial
cost of therapy. They want to get the most for their money,
they almost want to hurry the process, hoping they can
complete it before their insurance coverage runs out.

I think the basic issue in this situation is that Gemma
wants to re-start the relationship with her lover. She doesn't
want to heal. She doesn't want to do any work on herself or
learn how to be a whole person without a partner. As a result,

her subconscious is throwing up diversionary tactics. She's convinced herself that she can't move forward unless we're on equal footing. In her mind, that means equal exposure of personal history.

For this reason, I decided she needed a compelling story, and I decided it wouldn't affect me one way or the other if I told her the truth. But it did affect me.

Recounting the details of my time with Jon opened a deep well of memories. I loved graduate school, and I loved the intellectual life Jon and I shared. We talked about theories and case studies. It seemed as if the conversations would never end. We could stay up all night drinking wine and talking, every word weighted with fascination, every idea fresh and exciting.

When I recalled that day for Gemma — finding the apartment empty, I felt a sharp pain in my throat that was unexpected.

Jon's half of the bar in the closet held nothing but empty hangers. All of his dresser drawers were bare, not even a stray thread. The bathroom cabinet was emptied and wiped down. He'd taken the few wine glasses he brought to our shared living arrangement, the rice cooker, the coffee bean grinder, and his mug from the University of Michigan. His jacket, umbrella, every single book, even old paperback novels — gone. The photograph of him skiing in Colorado, framed and hanging over the armchair in the corner of the living room had been removed, the hook and nail eased out of the plaster.

I was too shocked to cry. I might have gasped because I remember feeling as if I couldn't breathe. I stared at the empty spaces, the silence like something tangible and so heavy my bones were pulled toward the ground. I felt as if everything had been sucked out of me and thick, goopy cement poured into the empty cavity of my body. I couldn't think. I couldn't eat or open a textbook or check my phone. Finally, I sent him a text. I received a message that the number had been removed from service.

For three nights, I lay in the dark, staring at a ceiling I couldn't see when the blinds were shut and every light in the apartment was turned off. The pain of him leaving me was unbearable, and it was compounded by the not-knowing. I had no idea what I'd done wrong. I hadn't known anything *was* wrong. We talked all the time. He told stories from his past, as did I. He shared his feelings about our classes. We talked about why we wanted to go into the mental health field.

We knew everything about each other, or at least, as much as it's possible to know about another human being.

I can't.

Sorry.

What does that mean? He can't *what*? He can't be in a relationship? He can't be in a relationship with me? He can't be close to anyone? He can't have sex anymore? Was he diagnosed with some horrid disease? Had he met someone else? Had he suddenly lost his desire for…for what?

The note made me feel as if he wanted to torture me. Was he too much of a coward to tell me to my face he didn't want to be together? Or was there something else? Was he afraid I'd see what was really happening? My brain twisted itself into knots trying to understand, trying to *know* what could not be known. There was no answer.

Unresolved loss does a trick on your mind. It can drive

you mad, the not-knowing, the constant questions circling endlessly, not stopping even when you're sleeping. You wake going over them again, trying to find a clue. Anything. Asking yourself first one question, then another, giving your own answers, changing the answers, analyzing the answers. Never knowing if one possible explanation or answer is close to the truth or utter imagination. It exhausts the brain, as if that soft tissue is physically turning itself over and inside out. It's worn down like any muscle in the arms or legs that's overused and becomes slack and quivering and incapable of doing anything after an intense workout.

When you've been hurt that badly, you have to find a way to put it behind you. To cut it out of your life. To remake yourself. That, or die.

In my case, I threw myself into my work. I completed my master's degree early, and I received top scores in my Ph.D. program. I received recognition for some articles I published. None of those kudos have value when you go to start your own practice, but they made me feel better about myself. It made me feel strong and in control of my destiny. Another part of controlling that destiny was that I lived a solitary life during those last years of school. Solitary as far as a romantic relationship. I had lots of friends, but I lived alone and kept my feelings to myself.

I lied to Gemma.

Therapy didn't ease the pain. The torment simply faded with time. I suppose that's why it's still there, why I felt it resurface when I told her the story.

And maybe that's all therapy does. It's very helpful in self-understanding, in becoming aware of who you are and what shaped you. But therapy won't end the pain or even lessen the severity. Therapy helps you look at pain from an altered perspective. Time does the same.

26

Gemma

When David and I had been together just a few weeks, he took me to Hawaii. It was my first visit to the islands. In the days before we left, I couldn't think of anything but floating in tropical water, bathing in soft air, and the scent of flowers. I was thrilled to go to a place known for lovers with a lover instead of with a group of girlfriends as I'd planned a few years earlier, before the trip was canceled due to an inability to agree on dates.

David made all the arrangements. We would fly to Kauai and spend the entire four days on that island. He said it was the most beautiful island and if I'd seen it, I'd seen Hawaii. Not that the other islands weren't worth spending time on, when more time was available, but for the best experience, the first time, it was Kauai, hands down.

Everything about the trip was perfect. First-class seats from San Francisco started us off in luxury and comfort. We enjoyed another five-star hotel, remarkable food, the beach, three swimming pools, naps, and sex that gave meaning to the word paradise.

There was only one rough spot, and I'm not sure why it turned into such a *thing*.

We were sitting on our balcony, sipping champagne, watching the sunset. The perfect romantic evening. It was our second night, so the sagging feeling of time slipping too fast through my fingers hadn't hit yet. We still had another entire day, a final glorious night.

"We've never talked about our past relationships." My words startled me. I hadn't planned to say it, and they seemed to arise out of a hidden crevice in my mind where I hadn't known they lurked so close to the surface.

David put his hand on my bare thigh, just below the hem of the floaty yellow sundress I'd put on after we came in from the beach, showered, made love, and showered again. I felt relaxed and floating myself, between the champagne and the warm, sweet-smelling air caressing my shoulders and face, and now the feel of his skin on mine.

"We don't need to talk about that," he said. "Everything is perfect. Right here, right now."

"It would help us know each other better...understand some of our vulnerable spots."

"I know you." He squeezed my leg.

"There are things in my past. I think I should tell you. And I'm sure you have the same." I turned toward him, trying to smile, but my facial muscles felt weak and uncertain. My lips couldn't hold the shape I was working to form.

"I know all I need to know when I'm inside of you." He smiled. He lifted his glass to his lips and took a sip of champagne.

We sat quietly for several minutes. The sun moved closer to the water. Strands of clouds on the horizon turned pink, and then the orange ball began to melt across the water, like a scoop of sherbet dissolving into a bowl of punch. "I don't feel like you know me completely if you don't know about my..." I couldn't find the right words. It wasn't like I wanted to give him a history of every guy I slept with. But I thought he should know about Aidan and everything that happened when I was in high school. It just felt like a big gap in him understanding who I was.

He stood and walked behind me. He put his hand on my shoulder. He set his champagne flute on the tiny table that sat between our chairs. He put his other hand on my opposite shoulder, bent over, and kissed the top of my head. "I don't like dredging up the past. I want to be here, now. The past is over. Whatever happened, let it go."

"That's easier said than done."

"Don't overdramatize." The pressure of his hands tightened on my shoulders. "Everyone has things in the past. Whatever it is, your situation isn't unique. You don't need to explain every little thing."

He laughed softly, trying, I think, to ease his harsh words.

It hurt. I didn't like being stereotyped. I didn't like that after the weeks of listening when he seemed eager to hear everything I wanted to say, he was suddenly disinterested. "Actually, it is kind of a big deal. And I'm not dramatizing things."

He laughed again, not as kindly this time. "Of course not."

I tried to move, to turn so I could look up at him, but the downward pressure of his hands was firm, holding me in place. Any other time, I would have loved the feel of his strength. Now, I felt pinned down. My voice was hoarse, almost a whisper. "Couples usually share their past loves. It's part of who we are."

"Are we a couple?"

"I…"

He squeezed his my shoulders. "I think it's negative to talk about things like that. What's the purpose? How will it change anything?"

"People you've been with in the past are a part of who you are now. And you learn from your mistakes, it makes future relationships better, don't you think?"

"I'm not sure about that. I am who I am. I might learn from mistakes, but that hasn't made any significant changes in who I am."

"I just want to know all about you."

"Drink your champagne. Let's enjoy the sunset."

I took a small sip. The bubbles seemed to shoot up my nose. I coughed and then sneezed. I put down the glass.

"Our reservation is at seven-thirty, we should get going," he said.

"I really wanted to talk."

"We are talking." He let go of my shoulders. He picked up his glass and finished his drink in a single swallow. "Let's go."

"But…"

"Don't spoil the evening. And the trip. I don't understand why you're obsessing over this." He picked up my glass and finished my champagne. He went into the room, leaving the screen door open as if to hurry me along.

I sat there for several minutes. I shouldn't have made an introductory statement. I had made too big a deal out of it. But I hadn't wanted to just blurt out my own story. And I wanted to hear about his past as well. I knew about his sports interests and school and his career. But I didn't know anything about his feelings. Not really. I suppose I knew his feelings about those things, but that wasn't at all the same as his feelings for other women. Knowing about the women he'd loved before would give me a peek inside of his feelings for me, his thoughts about love and relationships overall.

Was he hiding something from me? I'd thought that if I told him about Aidan, and everything that happened to me, he would open up.

27

Ann

Tamara answered the phone on the first ring. I wasn't sure whether it was because she recognized the number, or if she was worried about her daughter and every phone call had the potential for alarming news, so it must be grabbed with a sense of urgency.

In contrast, her tone of voice was calm, as if she hadn't snatched up the phone after half a ring. She spoke softly as if she was simply sitting in her garden watching butterflies and was happy for a pleasant conversation with whomever might be stepping into her day.

"Tamara. It's Annie, Gemma's friend."

"I thought I recognized your number. I was hoping you'd call."

"Were you?"

"Yes. I've given a lot of thought to your concerns. And after talking to Gemma, I'm more worried. I really appreciate that you reached out to me."

It was curious that she was glad to hear from me, that she'd recognized my number, which had likely been retained in her phone's memory, but that she hadn't called me. It confirmed my belief that she was somewhat passive. Her abrupt departure after coffee had added to my early assessment. Passive people often want to leave before conflict arises. They think it puts them in control.

"I'd like to take you to lunch," I said.

"That's not necessary."

"Gemma's one of my closest friends. I'm so worried about her, and I want to help. I felt a connection between you and me. To be honest, you made me think of my own mother."

"Oh, how sweet. Does your mother live in the area?"

"She passed away a few years ago."

"I'm so sorry. And you're so young. How old was she?"

"Sixty-four."

"How terrible for you."

"Thank you." I paused. "Do you like Joya? In Palo Alto?"

"I've never been there."

"It's very good. They serve Latin food. Should we meet there? Friday? I have some more medical appointments that morning, so I'm taking the day off."

"Nothing serious, I hope."

"No." I didn't like the number of lies coming out of my mouth. I'm not a liar. I'm known for being direct and honest. Each time I said something untruthful, I felt a surge of dislike for myself, as tangible as bile rising in my throat. At the same time, I hadn't altered my belief this was necessary. Telling Gemma my story hadn't helped. She remained closed off. I saw the hardness in her eyes, the tightening of her lips. The effect of my story had been the opposite of what I'd intended — her distrust had deepened.

Allowing her distrust to increase further would be devastating. Helping people get their lives in order means everything to me. I can't bear to see anyone battling undeserved mental or emotional suffering.

Joya is sleek and modern with lots of windows and a nice outdoor patio. It's mobbed in the evenings and crowded at lunch, but not impossible to get into as long as you have a reservation.

I was seated on the patio. The sun was warm on my left arm and the side of my face. I wore sunglasses to block the glare.

Tamara arrived at the same time as the ice-filled glasses of water with delicate slices of lemon suspended in the center. She took the chair across from me and immediately picked up her glass of water. After several swallows, she put the glass down and glanced at the menu without touching it. "This is so sweet. I haven't had a lunch out in a long time. Except for lunch with my daughter a week ago."

"Well, that's good."

"It didn't go well." She opened the menu.

I let her comment lie between us. I didn't want the interruption of ordering to alter the flow. It was better to get business out of the way first. After we'd ordered the classic paella and two glasses of Chardonnay, I leaned forward slightly. "Why are you worried?"

"I think I can trust you. I feel like I can...I'm not sure why."

I smiled. "Because you can."

"I really don't like talking about her...but I'm concerned, very concerned. And her father doesn't see what I do."

"What's that?"

"I thought she'd moved past that man she was seeing. But I realized she hasn't done that at all. She's shut herself off as if she's mourning a deceased husband. She refuses to allow us to be part of her life. I suddenly realized she's not trying to get past it. She's hoping he'll change his mind, that some romantic reunion will sweep her off her feet."

"Do you know why they broke up?"

"I don't. I don't know anything. She doesn't confide in me much. She never has…and…"

"Even when she was a child?"

"Yes, but not after that crush she had."

"Why?"

"I'd rather not get into that. I shouldn't have mentioned it.

"Okay. It's just that she also talks about him a lot."

"The point is…" She tucked soft, golden hair behind her ear. "The point is, she doesn't tell me much. I'm so glad she has a friend like you. But I'm worried. She seems adrift."

"Did something happen with Aidan that made her not want to confide in you?"

"It's ancient history."

"Why do you think she's talking about him now, after all this time?"

"I really have no idea. What did she say?"

The server placed our wine glasses on the table. Tamara took a sip, leaving a faint smear of pink lip gloss on the edge of her glass. "This is good."

I nodded. "She sees him as the most significant relationship of her life, until David."

Tamara smiled. "I've worried about her constantly, ever since high school. All those years, all the best years of her life, moving from one man to another after a few weeks or months, never attached to any of them."

"This is after Aidan?"

She shrugged.

"So what happened with him?"

She turned and looked across the patio. She swallowed. She spoke without looking at me. "It was an ugly breakup."

"Do you think her breakup with David stirred that up for her?"

"I don't know," she whispered. "But I'm not concerned about what happened more than fifteen years ago. I'm concerned that she's wishing for something that isn't going to happen. After I spoke with you, she and I spent the day together." She stabbed her fork into a scallop. The fork moved slowly to her mouth, and she chewed deliberately, almost cautiously. Her eyes filled with tears. "I feel so helpless."

"So do I."

"Then what's the point of our meeting? I appreciate lunch, but what is the point, really?"

"To be supportive. We just need to be sure she's safe," I said.

"Safe?"

"Yes. That she's not…that she doesn't become severely depressed."

She put down her fork and clasped her hands together. "Do you think she is?"

"I'm not sure."

"I don't know what to do."

"Tell me about Aidan." I felt I was pushing the line too hard. But I had to know about this guy. What was the big secret? Gemma didn't want to tell me the full story, her mother refused to address it. Yet, he loomed as a driving force in Gemma's life.

I didn't want to make too much of it, but the fact that Gemma had come to therapy to deal with the pain of her recent breakup and then talked with such intensity about someone else entirely convinced me there was a connection in her subconscious. "She seems so...I don't want her to do anything crazy."

"She's interested in her work. She cares for her students. Those are good signs."

I took a sip of wine, trying to think about how I wanted to respond.

"Is there a problem with the administration at school? Her job's not at risk, is it?"

"I don't think so. It's more that I'm afraid she might..." I sipped my wine. I hadn't planned to go there. Saying that word would rattle her mother, it would rattle any mother.

She spoke in a whisper, closing her eyes for a moment. "Suicide?" She put her hand to her mouth, pressing her fingers against her lips. Her body swayed ever-so-slightly, and for a moment, I thought she might fall off her chair.

My fear of anything I said upsetting her was unfounded. Her thoughts had already gone there. "It's too awful to think about," I said. "I can't believe..."

She opened her eyes and pushed her plate away, most of the clams and calamari still there. When the server asked if she wanted a takeout container, she gave a single shake of her head. She picked up her wineglass and sipped it steadily until I was finished eating. We left things unresolved. I don't think either one of us had any idea what step to take next.

28

Gemma

Suddenly, I decided I liked therapy. The realization shocked me. No matter what my back and forth feelings were on Dr. Wilcox, it was honestly nice to have someone who was required to listen to me. There was no one else who allowed me to talk about David. My mother changed the subject if I even spoke his name. Geoff wouldn't stop urging me to punish him in some way. Neither of them would care to discuss what went wrong, why I'd lost him, or how I might get him back. Of course, Dr. Wilcox didn't want to discuss that either, but she might, over time.

None of my friends at work wanted to hear about him.

They told me to *take back my power.*

They said I should have a one-night stand to prove to myself I was strong and desirable and in control. They said he was a jerk who didn't deserve space in my head. They said I should find a counselor since I obviously couldn't get him out of my system and I needed to find out why. They had all kinds of advice, but not a single one had been in love the way I was.

None of them knew I'd already chosen therapy, although not to get him out of my system. Not really. How can you remove someone you love from your heart? It's not possible. Why would you want to?

Psychotherapy, which is different from just seeing a counselor, wasn't something I wanted to share with my friends. Especially as an elementary school teacher. Our insurance offered coverage for sixteen therapy sessions a year, so there wasn't supposed to be a stigma around it, but there was. People get nervous about protecting young children, concerned about the *kind of people* who are caring for their fragile bodies, who are influencing their malleable little brains.

People might say there's no stigma, that mental health should be treated like any other ailment. But even the words — mental health — sound extreme. In my case, it wasn't as if I was insane — the cancer of the mental health continuum. I had the flu of the mental health spectrum, possibly pneumonia. But even without the stigma, there's a hesitation to accept it in the same way. A physical problem is viewed as something outside of your control. A problem requiring therapy is at least partially your fault — you should be stronger, you should get a grip, you should shake it off. There's a worry that you aren't what you seem. Unstable. Unpredictable. Dangerous. There's a fear you'll damage the children, emotionally if not physically.

I'd made the choice to uncover the hidden parts of my mind, why not enjoy the process more? Maybe all my frustration with Dr. Wilcox, followed now by my sudden love of figuring out my own brain, was part of the healing process after all. I was interested in what was going on deep inside my brain. Despite the ways she irritated me, Dr. Wilcox seemed to have cracked something open. I wanted to understand myself. I wanted to know myself and feel comfortable in my own skin.

It was a bitchy thing to do, but for now, I didn't feel like telling Dr. Wilcox what I'd discovered. She thought quite well of herself, she didn't need more food for her ego. Maybe her story, the advertisement for therapy aside, had made me feel better — knowing that she'd also experienced the void left by a man who simply disappeared. Her experience meant I wasn't a freak. And it meant I might be able to recover. Maybe.

Of course, I still didn't want to get *better*, whatever that meant. I didn't want closure. I wanted him back. But if I couldn't figure out how to get him back, there might still be hope for me. If I became a person as calm and pulled together as Dr. Wilcox, I could meet someone else. Someone as amazing as David, but who would stay with me. Who wouldn't decide I was inadequate. But if I became as strong and centered as she was, David would want me back.

I finished writing these things in my journal and put down my pen. I stared out the window, watching a plane move slowly across the cloudless sky. It seemed to be drifting, and yet, a moment later, it was no longer visible. It was funny to me that a plane can appear to be moving slowly as it rockets across the country or around the world. I know it's not inching forward as it appears, but your eyes tell you it's doing just that.

My phone buzzed with a text message. I closed my journal and glanced at my phone. A text from Geoff. I tapped the screen to read it.

Geoff: *Can I come over? I could help with any repairs you need around the place.*

Gemma: *Repairs?*

Geoff: *Yes.*

Gemma: *Why?*

Geoff: *Because I want to.*

Gemma: *Well there's nothing to REPAIR.*

Geoff: *Can I still come over?*

Gemma: *Sure. I'll put a bottle of wine in the fridge.*

I changed into a clean pair of jeans, a loose black top that hung to the middle of my thighs, and sandals. I put away my notebook and brushed my hair, weaving it into a loose braid.

It would be great to see him, but the invite was bizarre. As far as I could remember, he'd never invited himself over to my place, certainly not to do repairs. I wanted to laugh, but it was also a little confusing in a way that made me wonder whether he was okay.

29

Gemma

Forty minutes later, Geoff knocked on the door. He never wanted to ring the bell. Ringing a doorbell was *too suburban*, he said. He liked knocking. It was more friendly, more natural, more everything. Doorbells were unnecessary, and their tone gave him the creeps. He never seemed to consider what might happen if no-one was nearby when he knocked and didn't hear the sound of knuckles on solid wood. He might be standing there for a very long time, and wind up with bruised knuckles.

He settled on my couch. "I'm ready for that glass of wine you offered."

"Sure." I went to the kitchen and poured two glasses.

When I returned to the living room, he'd kicked off his flip-flops. His heels were propped on my glass coffee table, his back curved into a C as he slumped against the back of the couch. He looked out of place on the dark blue fabric with its large white and pink flowers. It was too formal for his bare feet, T-shirt with holes from too many washings, and his long, tangled hair. He accepted the wine glass and took a sip. "How are things?"

"Fine." I sat on the matching love seat across from him. "What made you think I needed repair work done?"

"You never know."

"Well, there's nothing to do."

"Doesn't really matter. I wanted to see my sis. Check in on her."

"Why are you speaking in third person?"

He shrugged, causing wine to sweep up the side of his glass. "Don't know."

"We just saw each other. For drinking therapy."

"We don't see each other enough."

"We see each other more than any siblings I know of."

He shoved his hair away from his face. "You don't miss me?"

I did miss him, but it seemed healthier to spend less time together, not more. I was closer to him than to any of my girlfriends. I wasn't always sure that was a good thing. He'd pouted the entire time David and I were together, whining that I never had time for him. I was pretty sure he was happy David had walked out of my life.

He raised his glass toward me. "To siblings."

"Sure," I said.

He took his feet off the table. He leaned forward and put his glass down. He rested his elbows on his knees and cupped his chin in the palm of one hand. "I care about you. A lot. I hope you know that."

I laughed. "Of course I know that."

"It's not funny."

"Why so serious?" I tucked my feet up beside me, bending my knees so they pressed against the arm of the love seat. "You're making me nervous."

"Why?"

"Because you never get sentimental."

"What's wrong with saying how I feel? It should have

been said sooner. Years ago."

I shrugged.

"Lots of people care about you."

"What's going on?"

"Nothing."

"It feels like you're here to cheer me up."

"People should say how they feel more than they do."

"Some people talk way too much about how they feel."

"I mean about each other. We all bullshit about our feelings about politics and our jobs and sports and all this other shit that doesn't really matter in the end."

I sipped my wine and studied his face. His hair was tucked behind his ears, and his skin was scrunched up from the way he was pushing his hand against his chin. His eyes looked anxious as if he was worried I didn't believe him. "Well thanks for telling me."

"You're important. You need to know that."

"God, Geoff. Stop. What's up with you? You're acting as if one of us is going to die."

He sat up. "No one's dying. We're young. We have a lot to live for."

"Good to know."

"You need to get out and enjoy life while you're young."

"I'm enjoying my life just fine."

"You're happy?"

"More or less." I spit out the words, thinking that would end things.

"*More or less?* That's not good."

"I'm not walking on clouds all the time. I just lost the most amazing man I've ever known."

"The *most* amazing?" He laughed. "Forget him. He

didn't deserve you."

"I guess he agreed with you."

"He's an asshole."

"You never even met him."

"Proof he's an asshole."

"How is that proof?"

"He wanted to cut you off from your family. Classic control freak."

"Where did that come from?"

"My gut."

"Your gut is wrong."

"Maybe so. But why talk about an…"

"Stop calling him that."

"We shouldn't be talking about him at all. I just wanted you to know how great you are. A million guys would kill to have a girl like you."

"A girl *like* me, or me?"

"You. Definitely you."

"Not that it does me much good, when the man I love would not kill for a girl like me."

He sat back and picked up his wineglass. He took a sip of wine. "We should do something fun. Maybe take a class together."

"A class?"

"Learn to sail."

"I have no interest in sailing. Unless there's a crew and I can lie in the sun while they throw ropes around and keep the boat moving."

"We could go whale watching. Or take a pottery class."

I put down my glass. "Do you want something to eat?"

"Don't change the subject."

I stood. "Peanuts?"

"Sure. Whatever. But you aren't going to change the subject back to that…loser. And you and me are gonna do something fun. Something we've never done."

"Are you bored? I'm your project now?"

"Not at all. I just…"

"You just what?" I crossed my arms. "Tell me what's going on."

"I'm worried about you, okay? People love you, and I want to be sure you know that. You're a good person. And a fun person. Everyone thinks so."

"Who is everyone?"

"Dad. Mom. They…" Something shifted in his eyes.

"Dad? Dad doesn't notice anyone unless they've been dead for a hundred years."

"True enough."

"Did Mom send you over here? *Make sure she stops moping over that creep.* Is that it?"

He sighed.

"Don't play games. Give me that much respect."

"She's worried about you."

I didn't have to ask why.

"She thinks you're depressed."

"I am depressed. I think I'm allowed."

"But how depressed? You wouldn't…"

"Oh come on. I'm not going to kill myself, if that's what you think."

"I don't."

"Then who? Mom?" I laughed. "Of course. Mom thinks I'm suicidal. She was suspicious of David, like she's suspicious of everyone, and she sent you over to make sure

I'm not despondent over a guy she deemed unworthy."

"Not exactly," he said.

"Why did you let her get inside your head?"

"Because that's what she does best. She's a pro. It's not so easy to stop her."

"I'm not going to kill myself." I sat down without getting the peanuts. I picked up my glass and took a sip of wine. I didn't think I would kill myself. At least being pissed off had taken away the sadness. I didn't think I was the suicidal type. But who really knows? Apparently, I was still in the very early stages of dissecting my subconscious.

"Just one more thing," he said. "If you're feeling violent. Try directing that at him, not yourself."

I took another sip of wine and said nothing. I laughed gently and saw his face relax.

He truly did care about me, and that felt good.

30

Dr. Ann Wilcox: Notes on Gemma Hughes

The more I consider Gemma's behavior in therapy, the things she avoids saying as much as the things she chooses to share, the more I'm concerned about her desire to harm herself. To lash out...at someone.

She exhibits a flat affect at times. She has a tendency to stare at me as if looking past me or through me or at something else entirely, not really seeing me. There's her refusal to tell me the whole story about her first love affair. It's a high school romance. No one holds back the details of something that happened so long ago, something so insignificant when placed beside the events of their adult life.

Yes, teenagers can be devastated by so-called puppy love, but once they get solidly into their twenties — and Gemma is in her early thirties — they've put it behind them. Most can laugh at their dramatic adolescent selves and their wild emotions, their desire to be Juliet or Catherine or any other tragic romantic figure.

Usually, when strong concerns arise about a patient's potential for self-harm, I would share my assessment with a peer, but something is holding me back this time. I have to trust my gut that there's a reason for it.

Once she's completed three more sessions, I'll reassess and decide whether she might require a few days of inpatient care. It's a big step, and would be problematic because of her job, but caring for her is the priority. A job is just a job, at the end of the day.

This probably doesn't belong in Gemma's profile, but it's on my mind...SP is the only other patient I've had who could be labeled suicidal. I managed to navigate her through that, so I'm confident in my instincts. SP was similar in her resistance to therapy, her tendency to keep secrets. I was finally able to crack that shell. She had a moderate breakdown but recovered nicely with only two weeks in a hospital.

However, I need also to leave open the possibility that I'm reading it wrong. Instincts aren't perfect.

Concluding thoughts: I want, rather, I need to keep an open mind. I've thought asking her outright if she's considered suicide. Some respond well to that kind of directness, but that's another area where I lack certainty with Gemma. It's better to take it slowly.

31

Gemma

I walked slowly to my designated chair and slumped down on it. Before Dr. Wilcox could settle across from me, I let loose with my desire to shock her. "My mother hated every single guy I loved."

She smiled and nodded thoughtfully. "She told you this?"

"Not in so many words."

"Why don't we start with Aidan."

She sure had his name at her fingertips. I smiled. "I'm here to talk about David. I was just giving you the background."

"Why do you think she hated every man you loved?"

"Because she doesn't want me to have more than she does. Because she doesn't like that I'm loved more than she is, or something. I don't know. Maybe she just hates me."

"Is that what you really think? Or are you trying to get a reaction from me?"

"I'm saying what I think. Isn't that what I'm supposed to do?"

"Yes. Of course."

"She hated them, that's for sure. She doesn't care that David left me and she doesn't want me to get back with him. She doesn't want me to have my own life."

"You think she wants a lot of things, but you don't seem to have any proof."

"You can tell. Can't you tell what your mother is thinking?"

"That's a popular belief, that we have an instinctive connection that allows us to know our mother's thoughts. But why don't you try looking at that from a different perspective?"

"Like what?"

"Can you actually know what another person is thinking?"

I shrugged. Of course I didn't *actually* know, not for sure. But when your mother tells you what she thinks non-stop for the first eighteen years of your life, you have a pretty good idea of what's on her mind. You know what topics recycle themselves. You know what she thinks of you — your flaws and the things you've done wrong.

"There are a lot of topics on the table here. What do you want to address first? All the men you've loved? Your recent breakup? Your mother's implied hatred of the men you've loved? Or your ability to read your mother's thoughts?"

"Are you making fun of me?"

"Absolutely not. I want you to listen to what you say and decide why you think those things, then try to determine whether or not they're truthful. We say a lot of things to ourselves, and often, until we explore our motives through therapy, those statements are layered with half-truths and untruth."

There it was. Another advertisement for therapy slipped into her advice to me. So much for the rule of *no advice*.

Again. I imagined ninety-seven percent of the world managed to make it through life just fine, even live happy lives, without therapy.

Why did she irritate me so much? Two days earlier, I was loving therapy and the freedom to talk about whatever I wanted. But now that I was sitting across from her, I felt…I wasn't sure what I felt. I wanted David. I wanted to be with him, not sitting in this blue chair in this blue room with its painted clouds trying to figure out where every single thought came from. My head ached from trying to figure out what I was really thinking. Sometimes I felt like I said things just to say them and I didn't believe those things at all.

"Do you want to talk about why you believe I'm making fun of you?"

"No."

"Why don't we start over." She recrossed her legs, smoothing her skirt over her thighs. "So. Your mother hated every man you loved."

"Yes."

"Why does this matter to you?"

That stopped me. I had no idea. It almost felt like a habit, being mad at her for not liking Aidan or David. A man she never even met. "I feel like she wants to get back at me."

"For what?"

I bit my lip, just a tiny piece of flesh inside my mouth where Dr. Wilcox couldn't see what I was doing. "It runs in our family." I laughed.

"What does?"

"Revenge."

"That sounds dramatic."

"My mother wants revenge on me. My brother can't

stop talking about revenge. He wants me to get back at David. Punish him, or something."

"That's a natural feeling."

"Is it?"

"We all have feelings of revenge. When we've been hurt or rejected or betrayed…when someone has caused damage to our career or some other part of our lives. Especially when our hearts are broken."

"I thought wanting revenge was bad. Unhealthy or self-destructive."

"My point is, it's a natural response. It's self-protective in many ways."

I shrugged.

"Do you think you're making yourself important by asserting that taking revenge runs in your family?"

"How does that make me important?"

"That's a question for you to answer."

"It doesn't make me important at all. I'm not the one who wants revenge. I said it runs in the family, but it doesn't affect me."

"Good. Are you satisfied with that response? You believe you're telling yourself the truth?"

"Yes."

"Then what do you want to address? Your mother's dislike of the men you've loved?"

"I said that because it's true. Understanding why she hates them isn't going to help me. I'm not going to pick a guy based on what she wants. I'm the one who has to live with him."

"Assuming for a moment that's true, that your mother doesn't like the men…"

"Hates. She hates them."

"Okay. Hates the men you care about…can you allow her animosity to exist and not affect you?"

I shrugged.

"Can you allow her to dislike them while you carry on with your life."

"I have a question for you…why do you avoid the word *hate*? It seems like you can't say it. But it's true. It's not something polite such as *dislike*. It's pure hatred."

"I see."

"So how does this help me?"

"What do you mean?"

"How is this helping me with David?"

"You brought up the subject of your mother. Mentioning it suggested it was an area you wanted to explore. I can't answer how it helps you with David. Only you can do that, but your subconscious surfaced it for a reason."

I picked up the water bottle and broke the seal on the cap. I took a long swallow. Dr. Wilcox was twisting the things I said. I didn't want to explore my mother at all. She is what she is. "I just don't get it. There's nothing to explore."

"Do you think you pick men she won't like?"

I laughed. "No. She doesn't enter into it."

Dr. Wilcox made a note in her book. "Do you think her opinion carries too much weight in your life?"

That was a very good question. My mother controlled everything in our family. Until I moved out of the house, she chose our clothes, even my father's, and every morsel of food that went into our mouths. She dictated the color of the paint on every wall and the trees and flowers planted in our yard, and how we spent our free time. She arranged our social lives and pre-selected our friends. From the beginning, she'd wanted to get rid of Aidan. And now she wanted Geoff over-involved in my life so she could keep me from David. She brought up all that stuff about suicide to scare Geoff. She figured if he were spending all his free time with me, then I wouldn't have time to think about David, to figure out how to get him back.

Dr. Wilcox smiled. I smiled back.

Slowly, our smiles relaxed, sagging off our faces. At least hers sagged, and I felt as if mine was doing the same. Neither of us spoke. It was my turn. I did not think my mother's opinion carried too much weight in my life. Not any more. Dr. Wilcox was wrong. This was not my subconscious. All I did was make a comment about revenge running in the family, and Dr. Wilcox had yanked the whole thing in a different direction.

Most of the time when I sat across from her, my brain resembled a snarled spool of thread. She kept asking questions that pushed me this way and that. She said she wasn't there to tell me how to think, but her questions molded my thinking as surely as if she were shaping a lump of clay, using those long, thin fingers with their short nails. I sipped more water and waited for the next question.

"Why do you think you're so resistant to talking about your mother?"

"Am I?"

The rest of the session was a circular conversation, both of us trying to win the game of who was in control.

32

Dr. Ann Wilcox: Notes on Gemma Hughes

Gemma showed up at my house.

It was after eleven at night. I was sitting in the window seat upstairs, drinking a glass of wine and reading a book. I looked out and saw a woman across the street, staring up at my window. She wore nondescript jeans and a hoodie.

How on earth had she found where I lived? Had she been following me, watching me all evening? She must have waited outside my office, followed me to yoga, and then home. Had she followed me home before and I hadn't noticed?

After the initial ripple of cold down my arms and legs, my whole body began shaking, thinking of her out there, watching me while I read my book, while I relaxed my body in what I'd thought was complete privacy. I'd sunk into the freedom that comes from an evening alone in your room, not thinking of any other human being except the ones living in the pages of the novel you're reading.

This was more than the obsession that arose out of curiosity over her therapist and a desire to level the playing field. What did she want from me?

I debated whether I should phone right then and confront her. That would have allowed me to observe how she reacted, whether she ignored the vibrating, or saw my name and declined the call, or answered. And what would she say? First, what would I say? Would I let on that I'd seen her, or wait to see how the conversation played out? Waiting is the best course in most situations. *Waiting offers options. Waiting gives me control. All of therapy is wrapped around waiting...for a patient to respond to questions, to uncover her own motives, to recognize her authentic self.*

Waiting would be best. If I called, I made it about me, not her.

It was imperative that I tamp down my anger at her invading my space, unwind the thread of fear to focus on the therapeutic process.

Her willingness to expose her obsession to me so blatantly, along with the effort she put into following me and standing for hours outside my window has me deeply concerned.

An obsession that reveals itself in conversation is one thing. Her repeated interest in steering our discussions toward me, her apparent dissatisfaction with the concept of therapy period — that it's about exploring her life and thoughts, not an equal sharing of our lives — is one thing. Taking overt action, twice, is another thing entirely.

First, she made the choice to follow me. She put time and effort into waiting outside my office and considered thought into concealing her presence. She planned how she would stay close to me, yet far enough away to not be seen. She showed continued patience and deliberate action waiting outside my yoga studio for more than ninety minutes. Presumably, she went without dinner in order to stay close to me. And then she remained in the cold, standing for hours, unable to see much more than my profile framed in the window and my slow turning of the pages in my book, the occasional sip from my wine glass.

In all, she invested over six hours in her project.

And to what end? She wasn't able to watch the yoga class. She saw very little at my home. If she'd hoped to see me having sex, it wasn't possible to see my bed from the street, even with the drapes fully opened.

So what was she after? Did she achieve some kind of comfort being close to me? I don't think that's it because she wasn't involved enough. Does she need to know that I have a life outside of therapy?

Does she need to assure herself that I'm trustworthy, having invented a set of criteria for herself about what she expects my life and habits to consist of? Or is it leading to something else?

Is it possible she wants to harm me? She's so interested in trying to make us equals as if she feels inadequate for needing therapy. As if she perceives me as superior to her because I'm the one asking questions and she's the one exposing herself. I've seen it happen before, so it's a definite possibility to consider.

But my gut is whispering something else.

I don't think this is the end of it. And I do think it will escalate because it already has. This episode was more invasive, more threatening than her following me at the mall.

It's possible she might want to vandalize my home in an attempt to make me feel as vulnerable as she does. I don't know yet if she wants to cause physical harm to me, but I can't dismiss the idea. It happens. It happens more than people might realize. I can't minimize it just because I haven't personally experienced it.

I'm convinced, even though I can't say why, that the answer lies in her broken relationship with Aidan. It's my gut, from years of uncovering significant blocks in patients' emotional growth. I've noted before — there's no reason to keep the details of that teenaged relationship out of her therapy sessions. It was too long ago to be causing her such distress at this point in time.

Concluding thoughts: The next course of action is to push harder with her mother to find out what happened with that boy. Of course, this is far afield from the pain she's experiencing from her recent breakup, but these things have a way of compounding, and if she never healed from that first heartbreak, it's a definite possibility the residual effects are at play now. I'll delve more into that situation before I confront her about following me.

33

Gemma

My mother doesn't see herself as controlling. She sees herself as loving and nurturing. She's devoted her life to her family, especially her children. When Geoff and I were small, she was consumed with creating an idyllic world for us. Nothing ugly intruded into our lives — even a bird that fell from the nest was whisked away. I was told it was nothing, everything was okay. The light feathers ruffled by the breeze were pieces of fluff. I was imagining the tiny beak and the fragile, unmoving legs.

In her eyes, the colors of the walls in our home weren't of her choosing because she was controlling — she'd done research into the meaning of color and how various colors influence mood and perception of the world. Both of our bedrooms were painted yellow to give us feelings of happiness and youthfulness. Our thoughts on the matter were irrelevant.

The food we ate was playful, far beyond the usual pancakes with smiling faces. Our mashed potatoes were shaped like stars, and our hot dogs cut to look like rocket ships.

My brother and I attended a pre-school that emphasized the care of the whole child. The school had a whimsical philosophy that included lots of make-believe play. We were read fairy tales and drew pictures of magical places and animals. There was no concern with teaching counting and shapes. *Pressuring* a child to read at the tender age of four was forbidden. The school had no electronic equipment for watching movies or educational shows. Screens in any form were all destructive to the dream-like mind of a pre-schooler.

My mother spent hours on the phone with mothers of our friends and classmates, discussing child-rearing philosophies and methods for keeping children from growing up too fast, from being damaged by bullying or peer pressure. It became suffocating and embarrassing as we got older.

As our ages climbed to double digits, it took an ugly turn.

I was horrified and ashamed on my brother's behalf when my mother caught him masturbating at the age of ten and turned it into a family crisis. First, she took him to the doctor for a physical assessment. The doctor assured her it was early but within the range of normal. She violently disagreed with him, to the point of shouting him down in the examination room. When we passed through the waiting area, my face burned as people stared at us, mouths gaping, their shock over-riding their instinct to pretend they hadn't heard it was *not normal for her baby boy to be thinking about naked women while he stroked himself like a pervert.*

She was doubly repulsed by the semen on his sheets. In hushed tones, she discussed with her friends whether it was detrimental to have him change his own sheets, stiff with creamy, rank-smelling smears. Would that make him stop? Or did it shame him? She wasn't sure, and she needed input from her friends, all equally self-proclaimed devotees of keeping their children from being *overly sexualized* at an early age by a *sex-saturated* media and culture.

Her devotion to keeping us innocent and theoretically pure was one way for a mother to reach the pinnacle of her career. All this drive for maternal perfection came from my mother's college classmates who'd chosen to build successful careers alongside raising their children. Women who chose to stay home with their children had to prove themselves in their chosen profession of motherhood. They needed something to show for their hard work. This was my father's opinion, spoken in a very off-hand way when I was nineteen.

My brother seemed unaware of her conversations about his sexual exploration, but I couldn't believe he didn't overhear and absorb her comments deep inside, even if he never let on that he was listening. Maybe he was too ashamed to let any of us know he heard every single word and did indeed feel shame over perfectly natural behavior.

The consensus among my mother's friends was that making Geoff strip the sheets and put them into the washing machine, add the detergent, and set the machine for hot wash and rinse, as well as extra soil cleaning, would shame him.

The best approach was to downplay the incidents. And so she did. And of course, he continued. He probably would have anyway. What did she expect?

My father was humiliated in his own way — by my mother's fixation on the issue. He dove into a multi-year, in-depth study of Russian history as the washing machine hummed and throbbed down the hall. Except for his physical presence at meals and milestone events, he disappeared from our lives. He never returned.

While all this was going on, I was progressing with my ballet, learning to dance on point. I'd been taking lessons since I was four. It was a beautiful thing for a girl to do. My mother basked in my fresh face, made more prominent by hair yanked into a tidy bun, my pale pink leotard and frothy skirts that were the essence of a sweet little girl. But by applauding my success at ballet, she filled my head with dreams that were later deemed unrealistic, not practical for making a living, a set-up for disappointment.

I wanted to be a professional ballerina. I dreamed of performing at Lincoln Center in New York City.

My father emerged from his cave periodically to insist I needed a respectable and satisfying career, with the capability of supporting myself. My mother wanted her beautiful little princess. It was too soon to think about *careers*. We were children! She couldn't see past her efforts, to actually notice me as a person who needed to become a functioning adult rather than a specimen that was evidence of her superior nurturing. Those might seem like the same thing, but they're very different.

She never seemed to give a thought to the fact that eventually, we would grow up, no matter how she tried to keep us young and naïve and dependent on her, needing her. She didn't seem to foresee the day when Geoff and I would be outside her sphere of influence. She didn't think about how we would develop into adults, into human beings who were separate from her. She seemed to think she could stop that from happening. Because if it did, her career, her life, would be over.

34

Gemma

I finally gave up. I would talk with Dr. Wilcox about my mother. I was tired of the long silences, sitting in our armchairs, staring each other down. Her gaze and her silence made me feel forced into talking. Recently, she refused to ask a single question that didn't circle back to my mother. Once I answered the first one, she began firing questions at me. She wondered about my childhood experiences, wondered whether I'd had my own private self-analyzed in my mother's lengthy phone conversations with her friends, wondered how I might have acted out, either deliberately or subconsciously.

After taking in my vague answers without a lot of comments, she sat back in her chair. She held her palm facing up and balanced her fancy pen on her fingers. Looking at the pen, she took a breath. "Did you ever want to kill your mother?"

I laughed. "Of course. All teenage girls do."

"It's a serious question," she said.

"So is my answer."

She eyed me, not accepting that I was telling the truth. "Not all teenage girls."

I shrugged.

"What did she do to cause that desire?"

I couldn't make sense of my thoughts. Everything I said

prompted three more questions. The conversation never took a logical path. Each question opened up new areas, spreading out like a rapidly expanding cluster of cancerous cells. I felt I was frantically dancing across the pieces of my life, as if I were on a frozen pond where the ice was breaking apart, and the only hard surfaces were free-floating chunks of ice. I was straining to reach every foothold, my legs stretched awkwardly, constantly off balance and in danger of plunging into the water.

Dr. Wilcox remained calm, a gentle smile on her face. Her dark hair against her pale skin gave her a serene quality, like milk with dark chocolate. Or was I imagining that, drawing connections where none existed — between hair color and candy, skin tone and comfort food? In her mind, *everything* was connected. In *my* mind, all the fragments were completely disconnected. "I hated that she talked about my brother. That she shared something so personal and embarrassing with all her friends."

"And that made you want to kill her?"

I shrugged. "Sort of."

"Did you actually contemplate killing her?"

I laughed "Do you mean make a plan of how I would do it?"

"Is that what you think I mean?"

"I don't know what you mean. I don't fucking know anything. I'm confused. And none of this is helping me feel any better about David!"

"I've explained that you need to give it time. Exploring your past will help you put that relationship in context."

"I have given it time."

"Not enough."

I picked up my *free* bottle of water and took a long swallow.

"You felt defensive of your brother."

"Yes."

"Did you have...*do* you have maternal feelings for him?"

"I don't know. Maybe."

"Do you still have that protective relationship with him?"

"He's more protective of *me*."

She wrote that down. Or she wrote something down, who knew what it actually was. Maybe she was making a note for something she needed to pick up at the grocery store.

"And you wanted to kill your mother to defend him, or rather to get retribution?"

"I hated that she talked about him like that. She had no right."

"He was her child. She was..."

"I know he's her child. I'm just saying. She treated us like projects, not human beings. And he wasn't a little kid. He should have had privacy!"

"Does she still treat you like projects?"

"Maybe. Sometimes."

"Have you wanted to kill her recently?"

She seemed very fixated on the idea of killing my mother. Maybe it was her training. Something Freudian. Hadn't he gone on all the time about children wanting to murder their same-sex parent? It seemed as if Dr. Wilcox also wanted to make a project out of me.

"What are you thinking about, Gemma?"

"I don't know."

"Yes you do."

I shrugged.

"Are you thinking about killing your mother? Anything you want to say here is safe…I promise."

I believed her, until she said *I promise*. If she had to promise, that meant she wasn't sure. "Can we talk about David?"

"What would you like to talk about?"

"I don't understand how I can be so in love and he can't love me. It doesn't make sense. Love goes both ways."

"Do you believe life, and relationships, should make sense?"

"Most of the time."

"So not always?"

"Of course lots of things don't make sense. War. Starvation. Cancer…" She had me off the subject again. My head ached. Not like a normal headache from muscle tension, but a deep pain inside, as if my brain tissue itself were twisting around the questions. "He did love me. And then he didn't. I don't understand." Tears filled my eyes and spilled out, running down my cheeks.

Dr. Wilcox reached under her side table and pulled the tissues out of the cubby below. She handed the box to me. I suddenly realized that I didn't like that the tissues were so far away. By handing them to me each time I cried, she had to make a point of helping me get control of myself, had to be the one offering something to make me feel better. I was crying, she was not. I was a mess, she was not. "Why can't I keep the tissues beside me?"

"Is that what you'd like?"

"I just said I'd like it."

"You asked why, you didn't state a preference."

I wanted to throw my water bottle at her. If there was someone I wanted to kill right now, it was her. I smiled.

In return, she gave me a look that I couldn't interpret.

35

Ann

Once again, Tamara Hughes was not only willing, she seemed eager to meet with me. Now that I knew how she'd spent over twenty years of her life — discussing her children with other overly-invested women, I saw why it had been so easy to earn her confidence. In fact, I had no doubt that after a lifetime spent dissecting her children with others, there was no reason to believe she'd stopped that habit when they became adults. She barely recognized that they were adults.

"I feel like we're becoming friends," she said.

We were seated in the outdoor patio of a restaurant in Menlo Park. It was a balmy evening, and the place was filled with high tech workers unwinding with a glass of wine or beer after long hours creating whatever it was they were working on at that moment in history. They'd changed the world with computers and the internet and smartphones, and now, I suppose it's artificial intelligence research giving them get-rich-quick stock grants and astronomical salaries.

My job is one that can't be learned by a machine. A machine could ask therapeutic questions, and it might be effective at getting patients to open up, giving them a false sense of anonymity. Maybe even more effective because they wouldn't have to overcome the hurdle of obsessing over what another human being thought of the darkest parts of their lives. But they would have to face a much bigger hurdle — the fear that their deepest secrets would be stored in the cloud, easily exposed to the people they loved and hated by a hacker simply playing around.

A machine might learn to ask the right questions, might learn alongside the patient where to focus. A machine would not be able to comfort a patient or give assurance that she was becoming healthy. I strongly doubted a machine would ever learn to read body language or pick up on subtle changes in tone of voice or words designed to mislead.

On the table in front of Tamara and me were two glasses of Chardonnay. We'd both ordered the beet salad. Tamara took a slice of bread from the basket and smeared butter across the face of it in swirls that made it look as if she were spreading fresh paint on the interior walls of a new home. Cheerful, barely yellow paint.

She took a small bite of her bread and chewed it carefully. She placed the slice of bread on the plate and fingered the stem of her wineglass. "I honestly do feel like we're friends."

I smiled and gave her a tiny nod.

"It's so much harder when your children are older," she said. "I used to lean on my friends when Gemma and Geoff were young. I needed them, and they needed me. We shared our strategies and even our horror stories." She laughed.

"We discussed the parenting books we read. There was so much information to share, I could describe every detail of what I was facing and be confident I would get solid advice. Now, I don't even know what's going on in my children's lives. And my friends don't want to talk about their children except for superficial aspects — where they work, where they vacation. They think talking about them is violating their privacy."

She laughed, more shrilly this time. "But once a mother, always a mother. That maternal instinct doesn't die out just because your babies get older. At least it didn't for me. You have no idea how much I appreciate you telling me what Gemma's going through. It means so much." She took a sip of wine. "I said I didn't want to talk about her behind her back, but really, it's a relief to have someone to share my feelings with." She gave me a shy smile, lowering her head and looking up at me through her lashes.

"I'm glad."

Our salads arrived, and we picked up our forks. I stabbed a yellow beet and put it in my mouth. I let the sweet, tangy vinaigrette saturate my tongue, then chewed the meaty vegetable quickly.

"How is she doing? She hardly ever talks to me," Tamara said. "I'm worried that she's going to destroy her life, such as it is."

"That sounds extreme."

"From what I can get out of her brother, she's still in love with this man who treated her so horribly. I seem to have raised a daughter who's drawn to the wrong kind of man. Every time."

"How were the other men wrong?"

She began eating her salad. She kept her attention on her plate, barely pausing between forkfuls to thoroughly chew her food.

"I know you don't want to tell me about this Aidan," I said, "But I think I could be more helpful to her if I knew what the situation was with him."

"Geoff said her obsession is David, not her teenage mistakes."

"Not from my perspective."

She nodded. She took a sip of wine and resumed eating her salad.

I decided to try another angle. "Why do you think she avoids talking to you?"

"She doesn't like what I have to say."

"Does she get angry?"

"Why do you ask that?"

"I think I mentioned...she seems angry."

"I'm not aware."

"I don't know how concerned I should be."

"I get very upset when I talk about that situation." Her voice grew thin and strained. I expected her to start crying, but she managed to recover. Suddenly, she put down her fork. "She's been angry at me since she was seventeen. Non-stop. Since I separated her from...that boy." Her face wrinkled with distaste.

"How did you separate them?"

"I told my husband we needed to move far enough away that the boy couldn't easily get to her. We had to put her in a new school. Change the scenery, everything about our lives." She put her hand to her mouth. "They were having sex. I knew they were. It wasn't right. So..."

"She didn't try to run away?"

"No."

"I'm surprised. I would have when I was her age."

"We were quite firm. *Quite* firm. And we moved a considerable distance..." She picked up her glass and nearly gulped her wine. "And Gemma was not defiant back then.

Now, it's another story."

"Well, she's an adult. I'm not sure you should call it defiance any more."

"Yes, but she behaves like a teenager. Her attitude toward this recent man is rather teenage-like. Very giddy and giggly. Obsessed."

"And he wasn't right for her either?"

"Definitely not."

"Did she lash out at you? Regarding Aidan?"

"What do you mean?"

"I'm not criticizing you, I totally understand where you're coming from. You know that, right?" I reached across the table and placed my hand on her wrist. She froze, then I felt her arm relax beneath mine. "Doing something like that to a teenager…most of them wouldn't take it without an extreme reaction."

"She was *very* upset."

"What did she do?"

Tamara shrugged. The movement was a mirror image of Gemma's.

"Was she ever…" I lowered my voice. "…violent?"

"Why would you think that? Of course not."

"I just wondered. Because she's so angry. And because of how teenagers are. They're very physical with their emotions."

"No."

"Even now, there's an undercurrent of anger," I said.

"You keep saying that. I don't know. I'll ask Geoff."

"Maybe not. You don't want him to get upset. Brothers can be so protective, can't they?"

She sighed and turned her gaze away from mine.

"Do you think she could be violent now?"

"About a boy she had a crush on more than ten years ago? Of course not."

"And she wasn't then?"

"No."

"I just...I feel something. I feel this rage coming from her, and her body seems pent up, very tense. I worry she might try to hurt someone."

"I can't imagine her ever doing anything like that."

"She's never threatened to harm you?"

She gasped. She covered her mouth and nose with her hand. Again, I expected tears, but there were none. I wondered what that meant.

36

Dr. Ann Wilcox: Notes on Gemma Hughes

Killing one's mother is classic Electra Complex. Of course, Gemma was long past that infantile desire to be rid of her mother so she could possess her father, but sometimes, often, people become stuck in those early stages of development. From what Gemma had described, her childhood experiences were not normal. They weren't abusive or extreme, but they were distorted enough to cause deep-rooted issues.

Hers is a very perplexing case. A small part of me continues to debate with myself whether I should consult with a colleague, or refer her to someone else, someone who can do a better job gaining her trust. But then I think of how she's bonded with me, however dysfunctionally. I think of how she's broken down on multiple occasions, suggesting that the breaking down of the wall she's built around herself is coming soon.

So far, she only hints at doing something violent to herself, or another person. But neither has she admitted to stalking me, or others. It's entirely possible I'm not the only one.

Is she capable of violence? Has she been violent in the past? Is she capable, god forbid, of killing?

I honestly don't know, but I can't rule it out. When I see how casually human beings kill, I sometimes wonder if it's easier to cross that line than people let on.

How does a person, even a skilled therapist, know if another has that rare, deviant gene that puts murder on the table? How do you know if someone is planning it? There's nothing in a person's face to show that kind of intent. But once it's done, it's too late, and I can't always be driven by caution — I can't be responsible for an innocent's death.

Perhaps this is the root of her obsession with me. I'm a mother figure, and she wants to see my life unravel just as she'd like to see the same for her mother. Aside from the mother-daughter issues in her life, it's a common human desire to see the downfall of the presumably perfect. Gemma sees the veneer of my life and has deemed it perfect. She wants to shatter that.

Although I gave a mild warning to her mother, I still believe I'm the one who's in more danger. And I'm not sure what to do about it. Telling a colleague would thwart the process.

Concluding thoughts: It's not that I'm unconcerned or willing to casually put my life in danger, but at the same time, I'd feel a great sense of accomplishment and satisfaction if I'm able to help her.

37

Gemma

The first six weeks David and I were together, were perfection. I told people that being with David was an ice cream sundae with a cherry on top. I was in heaven. Literally. I was having the best sex of my life, and David said the same. I couldn't think about anything or anyone else. I couldn't talk about anything but David. My friends said I was infatuated. Geoff said I was nauseating. My mother said I was being foolish.

He took me to fantastic hotels where we ordered lavish dinners from room service. We cuddled in bed and made love in between eating popcorn and drinking wine and watching movies.

The subject of our past loves didn't come up again. Of course not, because I didn't bring it up. I thought that talking about Aidan and all the things that happened might show David the importance of opening up to each other. Once he knew me better, he'd want to do the same. But somehow, the time was never right.

When we lay in each other's arms, my head on his shoulder, our naked legs wrapped around each other, it seemed wrong to talk about having sex with other men. I certainly didn't want to hear about David making love with someone else. Thinking about that made me cling to him more tightly, shoving my curiosity to the background.

With a delicate glass vase holding a single red rosebud and a tea light candle and a bottle of wine between us on a thick white tablecloth, it was silly to bring up memories of high school. It was childish. It felt irrelevant. There was no good time when talking about other loves didn't threaten to spoil what we had. The more I thought about the fact that I'd been barely out of childhood when I loved Aidan, the more I wondered whether David was right. The past was over.

Still. I couldn't stop looking for a chance to bring it up. I wanted to tell him everything. I *needed* to tell him what happened. I was certain he had a *right* to know. Why was he making such a big thing out of ignoring the past? Every couple talks about their previous relationships, don't they? Dr. Wilcox said those conversations were normal, as long as it didn't become morbid or saturated with jealousy. I didn't think I was being morbid.

I wanted him to know all the parts of my life, and I wanted to know everything about his. I wanted to know him inside and out, and I wanted to understand his feelings. I wanted to know if he'd had his heart broken. I wanted to know if there were other girls he'd almost married. If I was honest with myself, I was curious about how many others he'd slept with. I wanted to know what his first time was like and I wanted to know what the other women looked like.

Comparing my body to girls from his past was not healthy. I knew that. But I was so curious. I didn't doubt that I looked pretty good. I was proud of my body, so I didn't think I'd feel jealous or insecure. I just wanted to *know*.

Not knowing made me imagine they were gorgeous. He was so good looking, of course, they had to be also. It was possible they were smarter and funnier than I was. There were so many possible points of comparison. His refusal to talk about it made me worry his heart had been broken and hadn't healed. Maybe he still loved someone else, even if it was just a little bit. I didn't want to be a rebound or someone he was settling for.

The other thing that was a tiny thorn in the softest part of my foot was that he didn't want to meet my family. I wasn't too concerned yet about my parents. I had a love-hate thing with my mother anyway, but Geoff was a huge part of my life. He was a huge part of *me*. He was there from my earliest memories, and we stuck together when we were kids. We played our imaginary games together, told each other scary stories, pranked other kids in our neighborhood, and talked about our dreams — the waking and the sleeping ones. Even though we didn't see each other as much as we wanted as adults, we texted constantly. And talked on the phone. And joked on Facebook.

At first, David didn't refuse to meet them, but he made excuses.

It should have been a warning, maybe. One of those red flags they talk about. If he loved me as much as I loved him, he would be dying to meet my family. I was dying to meet his. I never would, of course. His parents were both dead, and his brother lived in Singapore. Eventually, I would probably meet him, but not in the foreseeable future.

David said he was too busy with work to meet my family, which was sort of true. He said he wanted to be alone with me. He didn't want to share me. It was too soon. All of this made me feel cherished.

He said it would happen at the right time.

After a while, he said I made it sound like a chore. An obligation.

There was a shift in his tone when he said it was a chore. I felt I'd become a pest.

He suggested I had an unhealthy attachment to my family. He said I lived too close to them and hadn't developed my own sense of self. He thought it was actually a little pathetic that I still spent all my holidays with my mom and dad and brother.

When he said those things, even though I felt a pinch of pain with each refusal or criticism, I didn't see the truth. Now, I understood — if a man loved me as much as I loved him, he would be eager to meet my family.

And if he didn't love me enough to want to know my family, to be in every part of my life, did he really love me? With all of this, I should have seen what was coming. I should have seen that, like every single guy I've loved, he didn't love me back. Not the way I wanted. And then he left.

With all of the other guys after Aidan it was the same — first, they adored me. Their love was a solid thing I could touch. After a while I saw the look in their eyes, gazing at something else, not really listening to what I was saying, wanting someone else, I suppose. Soon after that, they left. I was never what anyone wanted.

It didn't make sense, and maybe it wasn't fair, but in some ways, I blamed my mother for David leaving.

She drove Aidan out of my life, literally. She dropped Geoff at his friend's house so he could finish high school without the disruption of a transfer. She put me in the front seat of her Camry, while my father drove the truck loaded with our furniture and dishes and bedding. My backpack and the breakable knickknacks from my bedroom were wrapped in paper and stuffed in boxes crowded around my feet.

She pulled away from the curb and drove me out of San Jose, all the way to Fresno where we lived until I went away to college at San Diego State. Once I was out of the house, they took my father's inheritance and bought that nice home in Los Altos.

She physically drove me out of Aidan's life, and trying to talk to David about what happened back then drove a wedge between David and me. In the end, maybe I did want to kill my mother, in the back corners of my subconscious mind. But I would never kill someone. I still loved her in a weird way, I just couldn't forgive her. Ever.

38

Dr. Ann Wilcox: Notes on Gemma Hughes

At our last session, I finally had an opportunity to ask Gemma for a detailed account of her sexual history. My sessions with her have been challenging. She's all over the map. She can't seem to focus on a single topic for more than a few minutes, jumping back and forth from her mother to her current ex to the heartbreak of her childhood. These leaps from one topic to another are laced with mild attacks on me and incessant curiosity about my life.

Before providing even a sketchy, high-level overview of her sexual history, she argued with me, of course. She didn't see how that had anything to do with David. Their relationship was special. It transcended anything she'd experienced prior to him, and therefore, her other sexual experiences were irrelevant. Sex was personal, and she didn't feel comfortable talking about her lovers in that way.

When I reminded her that our discussions were private and completely confidential, she didn't seem to grasp what that should mean for her. Instead, she seemed to believe the very act of talking about these experiences was a betrayal of the men involved. "David even said so."

I asked her what she meant by that statement.

She told me he'd said, and apparently persuaded her to believe, that her past relationships were in the past and there was nothing to be gained by dragging those experiences into a current relationship. There was no connection.

I told her I disagreed. I explained it was the opposite — painful experiences are re-imagined and re-lived in many different scenarios. I told her that without understanding this dynamic, the things that go wrong in one relationship are bound to be repeated with future partners. She gave me a chastising stare, calling me on my own rule — that I'm not there to share my thoughts and opinions.

After a word-tussle, she gave me an outline of what can only be described as slutty behavior.

I don't like using labels, but I was so shocked, I wrote the word before thinking.

Following the breakup with Aidan, she dated between five and twenty men a year. All were very short relationships, a number of them one-night stands or passionate weekend hookups. She seemed to believe these relationships were all grounded in love that died quickly, but it was clear from the few details she did provide that they were primarily based in physical attraction. I can't determine whether she's extremely naive, or constructing a fantasy of who she is and what her life looks like.

She talked a bit more about Aidan, but there's still information being withheld. She told me how her mother ended the relationship in a rather dramatic and final fashion. She admitted to continuing to love him for several years, which explained, in her mind, why her subsequent relationships were so brief.

She absolutely does not see that these men she's being "loyal" to were interested only in sex.

Concluding thoughts: Explore her fear of betraying men who have betrayed her. Request that she journal and choose a topic for the next three sessions? What will she do when she confronts the buried truth of all of her relationships, even David? Nothing but sex and not the soulmate she believes in so passionately? Violence?

39

Gemma

Browsing new cars was not the best way to have a conversation, and it was a far cry from his desire to learn how to sail or go whale watching, but Geoff was certain we'd have a great time test-driving cool cars. He assured me there was plenty of time for me to come up with other things to do with each other. This was his contribution. He punctuated his text message with a string of emojis, including a sailboat and a whale.

He insisted it would be fun. We could try out cars we couldn't afford. It didn't matter whether a salesperson was in the car with us, we could talk about whatever we wanted. We'd laugh about it later.

I had nothing else to do on Saturday afternoon, so I agreed.

What he didn't count on was the hoard of other casual car shoppers. There were easily thirty or forty people with the same idea on a windy Saturday afternoon. It was desert hot and dry when the wind died back, and too cold to be outdoors in my sleeveless top the minute it picked up again.

We stood under the wide overhang in front of the Nissan dealership. Wind whipped along the front of the building, blowing my hair across my face, gluing it to my makeup.

He leaned against the concrete post that supported the overhang. "Did I tell you how great you look today?"

I peeled strands of hair off my lips.

"I'm glad you're not letting yourself go," he said.

"Is that supposed to be a compliment?"

"Absolutely. You look awesome."

"Then why do I feel like I don't really look all that great?"

"I just said you did."

"But it sounds like you're shocked. You think I'm a basket case who can barely comb her hair."

"How did you come up with that interpretation? That's not at all what I said."

"Okay." I moved away from him, walking across the wide sidewalk so I was in the sun. The wind settled, and the heat on the top of my head felt calming, although I knew in a few minutes, I'd be too warm again.

He moved closer. "Are you doing better?"

"What does that mean?"

"Don't be so defensive."

"I'm not sure this is going to be as fun as you thought it would. I bet we'll be standing here for an hour before a car is freed up for a test drive. And I'm not sure they'll let us take a hundred-thousand-dollar GT-R on the freeway at all, not to mention that all these other people might want to try it out."

Geoff turned and walked toward the corner of the building where a bench was embedded in the concrete, the back of it in the shade, the front edge in the sun. He sat down and stretched his arms along the back. "Have a seat."

"I'd rather go inside. It's either freezing or too hot out here."

He stood. "Should we get some coffee and a snack? They have peanut butter cookies."

Inside, we went to the coffee kiosk, an immovable stand built to look like a sidewalk vending cart. I ordered a non-fat latte, and Geoff asked for a cappuccino and a cookie. We sat on a leather couch facing a fish tank built into a wall. The wall formed one side of a room where there were computers for customers to use while they waited. For what, I had no idea. I couldn't imagine spending so much time waiting for your car purchase or your service work to be completed that you felt the need to work on a computer.

"How's therapy going?" Geoff took a sip of his cappuccino. "This isn't too bad." He bit into his cookie.

I sipped my latte and agreed.

"So? How is it?"

"It's okay."

"When are you done?"

"Not for a long time."

He leaned forward and turned to face me directly, widening his eyes as he stared into mine. "You seem more depressed since you started it."

"I'm not."

"Are you sure?" He took a sip of his drink.

I shrugged.

"Do you feel any better at *all?*"

"I feel like my brain is breaking into a hundred pieces."

"That's why they call them shrinks. They mess with your head and shrink it into nothing. Might as well have a lobotomy."

"No, my brain is not shrinking. There are too *many* pieces, I feel like it's exploding. It's hard to describe."

"Try."

"My head hurts all the time. I'm not sure what I'm supposed to be talking about or how I should think."

"Is there a way people are *supposed* to think?"

"I don't know."

"Maybe she's not very good at her job. If she was, wouldn't you be feeling better by now?"

"She said it takes time."

"Wouldn't it be easier to fall for someone else? That would take your mind off it."

"It's not like I want just any guy. I want David."

"Well, you can't have David."

I pressed my lips together. "I'm aware, Geoff."

"You need to forget him."

"So you've said."

"You're making it too hard. I don't mean to be harsh, but I think you need some truth-telling. I care about you, and I hate seeing you like this."

"Thanks. But you don't get it."

"Help me get it."

"I love him. I can't just turn that off."

"People turn off their feelings all the time. Look at me, for example."

"I'm not you. I'm not other people."

"Well, what is she actually doing for you?"

"She helps me think about things."

"What things?"

"My past. How things were with David."

"And then what?"

"I'm not sure."

He stared at me for several minutes. "You look so

fucking sad." He took a few sips of his cappuccino. "Where did you find this person?"

"What person?"

"The therapist. The counselor. Whatever. Is she a doctor?"

I nodded.

"With a degree?"

"Yes. Of course."

"Can she prescribe drugs?"

"I think so."

"Maybe you need an anti-depressant."

"She hasn't said anything about that."

"Well if you think you do, ask for it. You're in charge."

"Right."

"Where did you find her? A referral from your regular doc?"

"A Facebook ad."

He stared at me. "Are you fucking kidding me?"

"There's nothing wrong with that. There are thousands of legitimate ads on Facebook."

"And there are *tens* of thousands of illegitimate ones."

"She has a couple of degrees."

"Oh, well that's good. She has *degrees*. Did you check they're legit?"

"They're hanging on the wall."

"How do you know they're real?"

"One's from Stanford."

"Anyone can print documents that look real. Did you *call* to check on her?"

"No. She has a really nice office, and she's…"

"I'm a little worried about you."

"She's fine. She's good at what she does."

"How would you even know? You've never had therapy before."

"So?"

"You have no idea what's good. What if she's fucking up your head? It sounds to me like she is. You can't let any random person crawl around inside your brain."

"It's helping. Okay? It just takes *time*."

He narrowed his eyes. I wondered what he was thinking, but he didn't say any more, and I didn't ask.

In the end, I was right. They didn't let us drive the GT-R or the SUV. They offered their electric model. Geoff said no thanks. We took some brochures and left. We went to PF Changs and sat at the bar. We ordered pot stickers and deep fried green beans with spicy dipping sauce. Geoff had a beer, and I had a cosmo. Then we had a second round. After our third round, we ordered egg rolls and another plate of potstickers to soak up some of the alcohol. Then he drove me home.

"I meant what I said last time." He pressed the button to unlock the doors. "You should do some different things. Get out of your rut, out of your head. Meet other people. And fuck therapy. It just keeps you trapped inside your own claustrophobic skull. You don't need a trip down memory lane." He grinned.

I went inside my condo. I filled a glass with filtered water. I took the Advil bottle out of the cabinet beside the microwave. I tapped three capsules into my hand and swallowed all of them at once.

As I passed by the living room, I thought about taking a nap, and then I decided sleeping on the couch wasn't really what I wanted. I climbed the stairs, took off my clothes, and slipped between the sheets.

I closed my eyes and thought about David. I cried, and then I fell asleep.

40

Ann

I was sitting in the cocktail lounge at the Four Seasons hotel in Palo Alto. I shouldn't have included personal thoughts in the notes regarding Gemma Hughes's therapy, but I needed to get something off my mind, to think it out on paper, and it did tie directly to her therapy.

I took a sip of Pinot Noir. I really didn't care if it took me two glasses of wine to write all of it out. I was scared, and I needed to calm down, and I needed to sort out what I was going to do. I guess I'm just so stubborn, I refused to give up on Gemma. I wanted to see things through to a satisfying outcome. I took another long, fortifying sip of wine.

This is what happened.

It was late when I got home from dinner with two friends from college. Undergrad friends, women in other professions, which is always refreshing. I like talking about career challenges that don't have to do with a dysfunctional sex life or childhood trauma or overbearing mothers and cold fathers. It gets me outside of my own head, and outside the heads of my patients, outside of that small room that I've tried to make tranquil and comforting. The truth is, it sometimes feels confining as it fills up with the fears and secrets and regrets that spill out of patients' mouths, grateful at last for someone who is listening.

41

Dr. Ann Wilcox: Notes on Gemma Hughes

The moment my front door swung open, my key still in the lock, I knew Gemma had been inside my home. The scent of the apple shampoo she uses penetrated every molecule of the air.

I told myself not to overdramatize the situation, not to imagine the worst possible scenario. I urged myself not to assume she was hiding somewhere, holding a knife, ready to end my life in an extreme acting out — stabbing the woman who had come to represent the mother she wanted to kill. But those thoughts wouldn't leave me. The other alternative scenario that tickled the back of my brain was that she'd taken her own life in my house.

Gemma presents herself as a calm, slightly naïve woman, acting younger than her years, and from what I'd learned about her so far, that somewhat deliberate effort to project a certain image wasn't completely off the mark. But I still needed to be aware of what I'd observed beneath that well-crafted exterior — controlled anger. An anger that was possibly influencing her behavior, even though there was no hint she'd actually done something violent. She'd never touched me. She'd never surged out of her chair as some patients have done — lunging at me or grabbing an object as if to throw it at me. She'd never lashed out with verbal rage.

I closed the front door and put my keys on the entryway table. The alarm wasn't set. I rarely miss that part of my morning routine, but from time to time, it does happen. I opened the closet door and hung up my jacket. I clutched my purse to my ribs as I walked through the first doorway on the right, into the kitchen. I flicked on the overhead light.

I wasn't sure why I was clutching my purse like a comfort pillow. Did my body have an instinctive response to protect my chest and stomach from a knife? A bullet? I didn't know. It was a gesture I'd never made before, and when I reached the kitchen counter, I found myself reluctant to let go of the soft leather, stuffed full of objects that would act as a barrier.

Finally, I placed it on one of the bar stools. The kitchen was just as it had been that morning. There wasn't a single coffee cup or fork to mar the unbroken gloss of gray and white granite. Nothing on the counter looked as if it had been moved. The coffee maker and grinder, the blender, and the knife rack were all in their proper places. All the knives were in their appropriate slots.

I walked through to the dining room. It too was empty. I didn't turn on the lights, relying on what bled out from the kitchen to see that all the chairs were in their correct places. The vase of dried flowers in the center of the smooth, satiny oak was unmoved. I walked back through the kitchen, across the hall, and into the living room.

That space also was devoid of life, everything unmoved.

The scent of apples was stronger. I went to the couch, crouched slightly, and put my nose to the back cushion. It smelled of fabric and wood and something I couldn't identify, possibly human flesh, but not unpleasant.

I returned to the entryway, walked down the hall and through the small TV room at the back and even checked the sunroom which was dark and gave me the shivers — nothing but a screen door between it and the long, black arc of the backyard. It was an easy place for someone to gain partial access, although of course the doors from the porch into the house were locked with a deadbolt.

It seemed highly unlikely Gemma would be able to get inside of *my house, although not completely outside the realm of probability. And that scent. It did not belong to me or anyone who had been invited inside.*

I returned to the kitchen and grabbed a small steak knife. I had no plans to stab anyone, no matter what I ran into, but even a small knife would give me some leverage, a slight defense. Unless I faced a gun.

After slipping off my shoes, I began climbing the stairs. I went softly. Each time I placed my foot on a new step, I slowly followed with the full weight of my body, hoping to avoid creaks.

If anyone was inside, she, or he, must have heard the front door, had heard me unlock, and open and close the back doors. So far, there hadn't been a sound except that of my own movements and my own breath flowing in and out of my lungs. And that smell, which seemed to grow heavier as I climbed the stairs.

Halfway up, I paused and realized I should call the police. I stood with my hand on the railing, the other clutching the knife, feeling foolish. Why hadn't I thought of it immediately? Did that mean some unrecognized instinct was telling me the house was empty? Had she been here, gone through my things, and left?

After all, she was more curious about me than anything. But still. That desire to kill her mother. A desire that was accompanied by a hard, almost vacant stare. And her hostility. Much of that is directed toward the therapeutic process, but I'm the one guiding her through that process, and she is definitely hostile toward me.

I did not call the police. I lowered my hand and held the knife loosely, confident it wasn't really required. After searching it twice, including the closets and under the beds, I determined the second floor was empty.

Downstairs, I returned the knife to its holder. I opened the window over the sink and one of the living room windows, hoping the night air would suck that odor out of the house and fill it with something fresh and impersonal.

I poured a glass of Chardonnay and sat on the living room couch, waiting to regain possession of my home, eradicating her smell.

Concluding thoughts: I've never been so uncertain about the right course of action. I'm a decisive person. When I feel threatened, I take action. But something is keeping me from seeking help with Gemma. For now. I do believe she's unstable, but I've yet to make a complete diagnosis.

42

Gemma

I had a craving, aching need to re-live those incredible three months that David and I had together. I wanted to feel him inside of me, consuming every cell in my body. I wanted to feel the happiness that flooded my heart for eighty-nine short days. Love never dies, it lasts for eternity, and I had all the time in the world to get him back.

In the exact same moment that I wanted to tell Dr. Wilcox everything about my life, I didn't want to talk at all. I didn't want her to know what I'd done. I wasn't sure *why* I wanted to keep bad things from her. She wasn't there to judge me, she'd said that over and over. But no matter what she said, there were things I couldn't say.

I was learning enough about therapy to recognize that if I told her there were things I didn't want her to know, she would ask me why that was. She would ask me if I was ashamed and if it was my own self, not her, making me feel ashamed. She would tell me I was projecting feelings I had toward myself onto her.

When David took me to that beautiful hotel in San Francisco, I felt more special than I ever had in my life. I felt like he'd gone out of his way to show me how serious he was about making the start of our sex life important and magical. After that, he suggested we meet at a hotel in Palo Alto. I felt he adored me because he was willing to spend so much money to give us luxurious nights together.

I felt cherished, all the way up until we came home from Hawaii.

When we returned, he told me he'd reserved our usual room for the following Tuesday. I told him I'd rather go to his place. Or have him come to mine. He said no, the hotel was better.

It was so obvious, later, but it still took a few more weeks for me to face the truth.

He *couldn't* invite me to his place. He would never invite me to his place.

He was married.

When this thought appeared in my mind, coming out of nowhere just as I was punching the buttons to slow the speed of the treadmill, I felt guilty. Sick-to-my-stomach-guilty. Not about falling in love with a married man, but for thinking he was married, for thinking he would lie to me. I felt ungrateful for turning those beautiful, romantic hotel rooms into a cause for suspicion. But the thought wouldn't leave me.

Everything about our relationship changed color. I felt as if a long, cold shadow had fallen over every moment we'd spent together. I thought about how he refused to tell me about his previous relationships. I re-lived all those nights in the hotel room. I thought about our trip out of state, rather than a long weekend at a nearby resort. I thought about how he refused to meet my family.

He was married, and he was hiding me from everyone in his life, refusing to be part of mine. That was why we ate our elegant dinners in the hotel room and why he never drove me anywhere in his car. It was why, when I thought about it, the main thing we did together was make love. We didn't have a relationship where we spent weekends just hanging out, doing anything normal like grocery shopping or going to a baseball game.

I was his mistress. I was the other woman to his wife.

If I told Dr. Wilcox about this, she would ask me why I lacked self-respect. She would tell me I should be glad he'd ended it. She would tell me it was the best thing for me, a relationship like we had was a dead end, and even if he left his wife for me, did I want to be with a man who would turn around and do the same exact thing to me a few years down the road?

Maybe she wouldn't say all those things. She wasn't supposed to give her opinions or tell me what to do. I was supposed to reach those conclusions on my own. And maybe I had. Maybe knowing what she would say meant I knew those things deep inside. The thoughts were all there, the embarrassment and the shame of what I'd done were right there in my head all the time. Alongside it was the shame of how stupid I was. Why hadn't I seen it?

The minute I woke in the morning, after those first few seconds when my conscious mind was coming back to life, it rushed in like water from a broken pipe, spraying all over the place, soaking the carpet and furniture and staining the walls.

The next thought, always, was that my mother had suspected all along. She'd said she didn't like him because he had *too much money*. She'd taken the money to mean that he had a well-established life, and why would a man like that be single?

If I wouldn't tell Dr. Wilcox all about high school, and I couldn't tell her David was married, how on earth was she supposed to help me? Why was I even in therapy? Everything about me was make-believe. I wanted her to take away the pain, but she didn't know everything that was making me hurt so badly.

Yes, there was the pain of him dumping me. The pain of not having him in my life, the pain of loving him and not being loved back. But there was also the pain of knowing I couldn't fix it. Not really. I hoped I could get him back, but I *knew*, deep inside, I could never have him. He belonged to someone else. He might even have kids.

I needed to be honest. I needed to tell her everything. My life would never change if I didn't tell her all about myself. It was the only way to find out whether or not she could help me.

I remember that Monday morning when I knew for sure — I'd woken at six, as always. By one minute past, I felt a smile move across my face as I remembered the previous Friday night with David. That night, I wondered if I'd been wrong about him being married. We didn't go to a hotel. Instead, we spent the evening walking on the beach. We found a secluded place where we ate sandwiches and drank wine and made love on a blanket. The foggy air made it romantic, and I was kept warm by the heat of his skin on mine.

I realized my suspicions had grown out of control. I'd put a bad light on everything. We had a chance after all. He was hiding parts of his life because he'd been deeply hurt by someone he'd loved, not because he was lying to me. I knew how that was. Hurt makes you pull into yourself, sucking yourself into the smallest shape possible, like a sea anemone when it's poked with a stick.

I stepped out of the shower on that Monday morning and saw there was a text message from David. I tapped my phone to read it.

David: *Haven't been straight with you. I'm married. I need to stop this. Wishing you a nice life, you deserve it.*

The pain was like an iron rod held into fire, turned into a glowing stick that burns through you, searing your insides, leaving the area around the wound bloody and raw.

43

David

I live in fear of running into Gemma. I hate that. I don't like being afraid of anything or anyone. I'm not used to being afraid. I don't like knowing she has power over my mood, my life. I hate that anyone can influence how I go about my day. But it's there, all the time. A small, faint whisper of unease. I have a knee-jerk tendency to scope out people in restaurants with more attention to detail than I have in the past. Most days, as I cross the parking lot toward my office, I find myself watching for her — standing in the shadows of the redwood trees a few yards from the building entrance.

The odds of seeing her are slim, but Silicon Valley can be a small place. She lives in Santa Clara, and even though I'm fifteen miles away in Palo Alto, the suburban sprawl from Gilroy in south county all the way up the west side of the bay to San Francisco is an unbroken chain of intermingled cities, their boundaries blurred along expressways and freeways.

Without a second thought, residents regularly cross over town limits. People in Santa Clara shop at malls in San Jose and Palo Alto. Those who live in tony Los Altos and Menlo Park often commute south for work. It was a definite possibility that Gemma could come my direction looking to purchase a new pair of shoes, to visit the dentist, or to eat at one of hundreds of fantastic restaurants.

Getting involved with her had been a stupendous mistake. It's not too strong to call it the biggest mistake of my life.

I was stunned when I thought back over each small step, seemingly minor, unimportant. Then, I'd suddenly created a situation I couldn't control — both physically and in the way she wedged herself into my life.

Talking to her at all had been a blind step down a slippery slope. Deciding to get naked with her was the first really bad mistake. I suggested the trip to Hawaii in the throes of an orgasm that was so incredible I couldn't recall the last time I'd experienced something that powerful. But of course, it only seemed powerful because it had followed a drought. It had nothing to do with Gemma herself.

The night I suggested Hawaii, I'd collapsed on top of her, struggling to catch my breath. My heart pounded with such ferocity I thought my ribs would crack. It followed that brief moment when I always come close to losing consciousness. My mind was nothing but a blank cavern, not thinking and hardly aware of the words formed by my lips and tongue, expelled with the sound of my voice. *We should go away.*

All I could think in that moment was that I had to have more. I longed to feel like that every single day. She cried and kissed me so deeply, I knew immediately the trip was a mistake, but the plane was taxiing down the runway, so to speak. I reluctantly suggested Hawaii because it was so close, but so far away from anyone who knew me.

It was easy enough to fake a business trip. But when we were there, I began to recognize how badly I'd fucked up. She wouldn't let up with her need to talk about previous relationships. There's nothing like that sort of conversation to wake you up, smack your face, and tell you that this woman thinks you're forming a bond that's headed toward marriage. She was so wrong. It was supposed to be weekly or semi-weekly fantastic sex, shoring up for the lean times. It was nothing more than that.

After Hawaii, I was more conflicted. I felt like a piece of shit most of my waking hours. But every time I put my mouth on hers, or saw her naked, or unbuckled my belt, I wanted her so badly I could hardly think. I became stupid with wanting nothing but fucking. Then, when I resurfaced, I knew I didn't really want her at all. I needed to get out.

The realization slowly emerged — I was sure to be caught. Even if I wasn't caught, I had my hands full with a woman who had misread the entire situation. It started with a casual pickup at the gym...the way she'd bent over right in front of me, flashing her tits, giving me that coy smile. I thought we were on the same page. How had it become so much more in her mind?

I was also a shit when I ended it. But I had to have a quick, clean break. We were participating in two different relationships. I was having great sex while she was planning a wedding. I could see it in her eyes, and hear it in her voice with the constant requests — *Let's go here...Let's do this...When can I see your place?...You need to meet my brother, my parents, my friends. Let's go back to Hawaii.*

After it was over, I kept thinking she was going to pop up when I least expected it. I worried she'd dig around online and find my employer, worried she'd show up at my office. I worried that I'd have this mistake hanging off the back of my neck for the rest of my life, like a tick that had bored its way into my skin and required a pair of tweezers to pinch it and twist it out, bursting the swollen body, blood oozing onto me.

It was all me. I knew that. There was nothing wrong with her that made her want so much from me. It was natural.

But I'd fucked up. Big time.

I'm not even sure what went wrong in my life. How could a marriage that had started with incredible sex itself, marriage to a woman who had truly been, and still was, my soul mate, have withered into a dried out husk?

I no longer knew what I wanted. I didn't want that husk, but neither did I want Gemma. Not really. Breaking up by text is the worst thing you can do to a woman. I knew that. But I needed it cold and final. Still, I'm not sure it was.

It would not have surprised me at all if I'd walked into my office and seen her sitting at my desk, wanting to talk. I knew that one day I'd take a seat at my favorite bar and glance to my left. She'd be sitting on a stool, those curvy legs crossed, her skirt pulled up mid-thigh. She would smile and raise her glass toward me. Then, she would slide off the stool and start walking in my direction.

44

Dr. Ann Wilcox: Notes on Gemma Hughes

In Gemma's last therapy session, I noted a significant change in her demeanor and the content of her conversation. I saw it the moment I opened the door. Usually, she was sitting on the sofa in the waiting area. This time, she stood a few feet from the door.

Instead of wearing her semi-exotic make-up, her face was scrubbed bare. And it definitely looked scrubbed — the skin was slightly red and had a shiny, raw quality to it. Her eyes were bloodshot, and her hair was wet, combed straight back into a ponytail and then braided, as if she wanted to remove it from her life to the greatest extent possible.

She wore black leggings, ankle boots, and a ragged peach-colored sweater that was stretched out of shape. The sleeves covered half of her hands, and it hung unevenly around her body, making her appear thinner than ever. Under the sweater was a soiled-looking camisole, the top edge exposed by the V-neck of the sweater.

She pushed past me into the office and went to her chair. She flopped down as if she was exhausted and I'd left her standing for hours.

As I took my seat, I asked how she was doing. She glared at me. After a few moments, she rubbed her eyes. She blinked several times and rubbed them again.

A few minutes of silence passed, and then she sat up straighter. In a loud voice, she accused me of messing with her head. She said therapy hadn't helped at all. I'd misled her, and now she felt worse than ever. She didn't know what to do with herself. She was afraid of losing it (she didn't elaborate on what "it" entailed). She was worried her erratic moods were jeopardizing her job.

She'd come to see that her mother had ruined her life by banishing the one man who ever loved her. She'd also realized that I was exactly like her mother — thinking I'm better than her, thinking I always know what's best, trying to tell her how to live her life. She wasn't going to let me take away the one man she loved. That had happened once before, and she would not allow it to happen again.

There was a tinge of madness, and I don't use that word lightly, to her tone and mannerisms and especially the things she was saying. They were almost nonsensical.

Then she switched gears. Her life was ruined. She would never have happiness. She deserved to be happy, but it had been ripped out of her hands, and now she had nothing left to live for. Her mother should be punished, I should be punished. She didn't understand why she was the one being punished when she'd done nothing wrong. Ever. In her entire life, she'd never done a single thing that could be considered wrong or a mistake.

She'd been good. She'd been faithful. She'd been a good daughter. Her only "sin" was falling in love when she was a teenager, but her mother had refused to allow her daughter to find her own happiness. That boy had been in her heart for years. She could never forget him. And finally, after all that time, she was given a chance at happiness with David, but that had also been taken away.

She railed about the unfairness — every person in the world was loved but her. She railed at me for looking at her with expressions of pity, suggesting she wasn't lovable. She cried and banged her fists on the arms of the chair. At one point, she even kicked her feet, slamming her heels into the chair legs and stomping them on the floor.

When I tried to interject a thoughtful question, she screamed at me to shut up and to stop acting like a know-it-all. When I asked her to *calm herself, she cursed at me, spitting with the vehemence of her rage.*

She said she knew where I lived, and then she thrust herself out of the chair, rushed to the door, and flung it open. A moment later, I heard the waiting room door slam shut. She'd left the door to my office open. I wondered whether she would return. I let the door stand open and remained in my chair for about twenty minutes. She never came back.

Concluding thoughts: Need to decide soon, very soon, whether to show my notes to a colleague. Go directly to the police? Or…? They're private notes, confidential, but I told Gemma at the start, if a violent crime is threatened, my duty to the safety of others takes precedence. Her threat was vague, but it was absolutely a threat. A passive threat, in keeping with her tendency toward passivity. Warn Tamara?

45

Gemma

Dr. Wilcox was completely still. She sat facing me, both feet flat on the floor. She wore ballet slipper shoes made of soft, supple leather and black tights.

Her skin looked more pale than usual and her smile impossible to interpret, as always. The notebook for my therapy sessions was closed, lying on the table beside her, the pen on top, the tip retracted. Her forearms rested on the chair arms. She looked like she could be dead. For a moment, I thought she hadn't blinked or shown any signs of breathing for several minutes.

"What are you thinking about, Gemma?"

"Nothing."

"We're always thinking. It's the nature of the human mind. Even if you were making a mental lesson plan for your students, it's helpful to note that. Your thoughts are important."

I smiled.

"You're feeling calmer this week?"

"About the same as always."

"And you look better. You took care with your appearance again."

I shrugged.

"That was quite a display last week."

"What do you mean?"

"Your extreme agitation."

"I wouldn't call it extreme. I'm not sure I'd even say I was agitated."

Dr. Wilcox smiled. Her hands remained still. She seemed to have lost interest in writing down what I was saying. Maybe my thoughts weren't so important after all.

"Do you not remember how you lashed out at me?"

"I didn't lash out."

"You did. You threatened me. You said you know where I live." She paused for nearly a full minute. "You said it in a way that implied you wanted to hurt me. It sounded like a threat."

I felt myself squint, as if narrowing my eyes would help me figure out what the heck she was talking about.

"You don't remember?"

"I never said I knew where you lived."

She nodded, a single lowering of her chin. "All of your thoughts are acceptable for sharing. I've told you that. You can't know yourself if you don't allow yourself to speak what's on your mind. This is a safe place."

"So you said."

"We all have thoughts of wanting to hurt another human being from time to time. It doesn't make you a bad person."

"I don't want to hurt anyone."

"You said you wanted to kill your mother."

"When I was a kid. And I didn't mean it. I just had the feeling."

"You threatened me."

"I did not."

"It's possible your heightened emotion made you lose consciousness for a moment. You don't remember."

"I would remember. I never said anything like that."

"Why do you insist you never said it?"

"Because I didn't."

She picked up her pen and held it. She twisted it so the tip emerged, then twisted it back. She did this three more times without saying anything.

"Why won't you tell me about Aidan?"

"It's not important."

"I think it is."

"Don't I get to decide what's important?"

"Your refusal to tell me everything about him highlights his significance in your life. If he weren't important, you wouldn't care."

I thought about this. I picked up my water, twisted off the cap, and took a sip. I took another sip. I replaced the cap and put the bottle on the table. She had a point. Why was I refusing to tell her? I was so confused. I didn't know why I did or didn't say anything. My thoughts seemed critically important and completely lame all at the same time.

I loved being in therapy. I did feel safe in her office, like she kept saying, over and over. But it was so hard to tell her the parts of my life that I was ashamed of. What my mother had done. What I did. That David was married and I was too stupid to see it.

"What are you thinking, Gemma?"

"Nothing."

"It's not helpful to lie to me."

"I know." Saying those words, I felt like she'd won the game we were both secretly playing. By admitting I was lying,

I conceded two points to her. Of course, it wasn't really lying, rather it was not saying everything, and that's not the same as lying. A small, sharp pain appeared behind my left ear. I rubbed the bone behind my ear, but the pain seemed deeper inside, deeper than nerves and muscle, a place where I couldn't touch, and so the rubbing didn't do any good.

I still couldn't tell her. I knew I would, eventually, but right then, it was too hard. I think it would be hard for anyone to tell another person, even a doctor who wanted to help, that she's done stupid things. That she'd let people manipulate and control her, that she was thirty-four years old and too stupid to realize the man she loved wanted nothing but sex.

When I'd told Dr. Wilcox that David was my soul mate, she made a face that was half disgust and half something else. But I couldn't figure out what the other half was. All I could think was that she was laughing at me, realizing how incredibly naïve I was. I felt her pity and her arrogance — she thought she was better than me.

David was everything to me, and I had no doubt he'd felt I was his soul mate. The things he said to me when we made love made my heart explode. He said he wanted me so badly it was difficult to breathe. He sat there in the coffee shop and listened to every word I said, even the unimportant ones. He gazed into my eyes as if he saw, and loved, my very soul. I thought he wanted to know every single moment of my life.

Some women would allow their love to turn to hate if a man acted as if he was in love and then dumped them. They would seek revenge, even if it were petty. But I couldn't hate him. All I remembered were his eyes, the warmth and ecstasy of his hands on my body, and how good I felt when we talked about life.

"What are you thinking, Gemma?"

I didn't answer. Dr. Wilcox kept asking the same question, using my name. It felt as if the words were meant to hypnotize me, as I heard them the same way, spoken with the same deadly calm over and over, every few minutes. Maybe that's what she was trying to do. Or maybe she was just trying to make me feel calm.

Instead, I felt like I was losing my mind. Maybe I was dreaming all of it, even sitting in the chair that very minute. I'd had lots of dreams about therapy. It was almost all I dreamed about now. I wanted to dream about David, but instead, I was always sitting in that chair, looking at her while she looked at me. In one dream, she scribbled a few words in the notebook. Before she realized what I was doing, I jumped out of my chair and grabbed the notebook. But I couldn't read her writing. It was a bunch of scribbles, the ink smeared where she'd written actual words. I tore the pages out and scattered them across the floor. All she did was give me that inscrutable smile.

Part of me wanted to tell her I was done with therapy. But it was a very tiny part. Most of me felt like I would be all alone in the world if I quit now. I'd have no one to talk to, no one that understood. No one who could help me.

"What are you thinking, Gemma?"

"I'm thinking, why do you keep asking me that?"

"You're here to share your thoughts. If you continue censoring them, therapy won't be very useful to you. If you have thoughts of wanting to hurt someone, to hurt yourself, it's better to talk about those. Talking will help you more than you realize."

"It hasn't so far."

"You told me it had helped you a lot. Was that a lie?"

Had I told her that? I think I told Geoff. Or maybe not. I did tell him it was hard to think, that my brain hurt. My thoughts were getting more and more confused. I wasn't sure what I'd said and what I'd thought. I wasn't even sure which thoughts were true, which ones belonged to me and which ones she'd suggested. Or was that the point? She suggested thoughts so I would think differently? I wondered if therapy was like this for everyone. I wondered whether I truly was losing my mind.

46

Ann

There are only a few perfect patients in a therapist's career. Gemma was one of mine. The only one, really. I'd crafted my ad to appeal to a woman with a broken heart, and she responded, due to some precise targeting on Facebook.

Despite the thoughts I'd recorded in my notes regarding her therapy, I had no intention of discussing her condition with a colleague. I could manage every aspect of her needs without assistance, for now. There was really only one viable outcome for her, and I'd known what it was from the start.

Gemma couldn't let go of David, she felt the pain with undue intensity because she believed in the concept of a soul mate. Actually, so do I.

A true belief in soul mates is the notion that each person has only one perfect mate on this planet.

A great many people discount that idea. They believe love is a blend of proximity, timing, and similar backgrounds. They firmly believe, as if it were a religious philosophy, that the possibility of only a single person out of seven billion meeting your needs and capturing your affection is absurd. They believe more people would travel the world looking for their mate if that were true. It was impossible to think your soul mate simply happened to share your country of origin, your socioeconomic class, and just happened to be acquainted with people you already knew, or chose the school you attended, or worked for the same employer.

They laugh at the belief that two people, and only those two, can find each other out of billions, and that those two will find bliss that can't be had anywhere else.

I had no idea how Gemma had come to this belief about David. To hear her talk, Aidan had captured her heart and soul at a very young age. If he wasn't her soul mate, why was she still thinking about him, remembering him with such regret, so furious at her mother for managing to remove him from her life? That too was a contradiction in Gemma's story. If she truly loved him, and he her, if they were indeed soul mates, nothing and no one could have kept them apart.

And then she became convinced that David was her soul mate.

You can't have two. She was oblivious to this discrepancy in her belief system.

Gemma was a perfect patient because she needed what I had to offer. It's likely…no, it's certain…providing a listening ear for her will be the epitome of my career as a therapist.

Although I still didn't know the missing pieces in her story with Aidan, I had no doubt that her relationship with him significantly shaped her future. Eventually, the shell around her would crack, and the truth would seep out. I just had to be patient. Until she gave me that piece of the story, I wasn't sure I could move forward.

And so we continued this dance of resistance and desire. Her fear of telling me everything, exposing the darkest and most tender parts of herself, battling her desire to pour out her heart to someone who's really listening.

Despite the things I'd written, I had no fear that she

would harm me. I was completely safe. I slept well at night. I was confident. I felt in control of the situation and honestly, quite proud of my skills.

As much as she wanted to talk about David, yet resisted sharing anything important, I wanted to talk about him more. So much more. I wanted to hear every detail of their relationship. And I had the time and the patience to peel off each layer, elicit each scrap of information until I had the entire story. It was important to get the entire story before her therapy could be completed.

She could fight me all she wanted, but I would win. I was smarter, and more careful. I knew what she needed more than she would ever comprehend. Part of my job was to wear down that resistance. The sheer force of my quiet waiting would bring her to the breaking point.

People want to talk. Deep inside, they want every part of themselves to be known. Patience forces that desire to the surface and eventually, people are unable to stop themselves from talking.

Gemma was the perfect patient for me because I'd written the ad for her.

Only for her.

I knew how to touch the raw spots in her, and I knew how to target the ad in a narrow enough circle that she was certain to read it. I knew all this because I'm a good listener. That's why I'm a good therapist.

The outcome of Gemma's therapy will be commitment to a mental health facility, one where she's unable to leave for a significant period of time. Even if she manages to heal enough to be released, it will be the end of her career. No elementary school will hire someone with a history of making violent threats.

I'm determined to see my patients get the lives they deserve. And Gemma will get what she deserves — punishment. She thinks she's already been punished, but she's so wrong.

Gemma is the perfect patient because I know her. I know how much she loves David because I love him too.

David Graves is my soul mate. And by definition, a soul mate only has one partner. For life.

47

Gemma

It was rare for my family to have a formal dinner together except on holidays. My mother liked me home for dinner every Sunday — a casual family dinner around the kitchen table. *Like it used to be.*

Sometimes I complied, many times, most times, I didn't. When I didn't, Geoff sulked and pestered me with text messages. My mother whimpered that she wanted her babies together in her house where she could make sure we ate properly. She wanted to know what was going on in our lives. She wanted to comfort us and smile at our stories. She worried we were all drifting apart. *You can hardly call us a family anymore.*

Her recent invitation involved roast pork. She emphasized that she was making a nice meal. She'd already purchased an expensive cut of meat. I hadn't been there in weeks, and she would not accept *no* for an answer. *Wear something nice*, she'd said. It sounded like a holiday dinner.

Holidays with my family had an air of phoniness. I suppose because holidays put a structure around the day that felt programmed. The way we interacted, the food we ate, the entire atmosphere was based on what had been done repeatedly in the past. There was no room for anything too upsetting or unpredictable. No overwrought emotions.

Take Christmas. The music was pre-ordained — a blend of classic chorals followed by folksy songs about winter characters and fantasies. The decorations on the tree dominated the first minutes of conversation. No one said anything that hadn't been said before, and the chit-chat provided continuity. A safe topic and a safe opening to the evening. Every single year we remarked on our favorite ornaments, told the stories of how they'd come to be part of the family tree, and had friendly arguments over which bauble was the most cherished.

We opened gifts — something to do as we sat around the living room drinking eggnog with brandy and eating pretzels, which my mother seemed to feel were the perfect complement to eggnog. Possibly the dry crunch made her think of toast. The eggy, creamy drink put her in a breakfast frame of mind despite the brandy.

Christmas dinner never varied. The center of the meal was turkey with stuffing, surrounded by cranberries, green beans, glazed carrots, mashed potatoes and homemade bread. Dessert was a plate of Christmas cookies served with coffee, to which my father and brother added whiskey.

Whiskey in coffee was a concoction designed to prompt nausea — the heat intensifying the heavy taste of whiskey as well as its effect on the brain. My mother and I chose to linger over our wine, letting the coffee grow cold in our cups.

Traditions are a good thing. Knowing what's expected, having the memories enhanced each year, adding layers and layers to the same core provides a sense of security.

So an invitation to dinner in early November seemed strange. It was too far from Thanksgiving to be considered an alternate celebration to that day. My mother said I'd missed too many Sunday dinners. She longed to have us all together again. Geoff said I needed to be kinder, to stop challenging every single thing she did. Geoff said my suspicion over what prompted the invitation was calculating and cold.

It turned out, my suspicion was not calculating at all, it was correct.

When I entered, the aroma of roast pork filled the house. Small white potatoes were roasting alongside the pork, and three-bean salad was marinating in the fridge. There was time before dinner, and she thought...

I interrupted her. "A glass of wine would be nice."

Geoff appeared in the entryway. "We thought a game of croquet would be fun."

"It's too cold. It's getting dark."

"Cold sparks your appetite," he said.

My father called from the living room, agreeing it was too cold. We would play a quick game of monopoly instead. I sighed. "That game is never quick."

Geoff went to the hall closet, got out the game, and we set it up on the coffee table.

As we shuffled money and tiny houses, chance cards and property deeds, our conversation focused on the mechanics of the game. I sipped my wine. The others drank sparkling water. I wondered at their sudden abstinence, but didn't ask.

Despite the diversion of the game, I was grateful for the soothing effect of a bit of wine floating through my veins. There was a brittle quality to the air as if we were waiting for something, and it wasn't the roast pork.

My glass was nearly empty, and all the property had been sold and bartered. I'd ended up with a meager collection consisting of the four railroads and the utilities, nothing on which to build homes and hotels, but I didn't really care. I wasn't a fan of the game. Geoff had loved it all his life.

Thoughts of David simmered in the back of my mind, filling my imagination with fantasies of spending a cold fall afternoon and evening playing a board game and eating a home-cooked meal. If he'd been there, the game would have taken on a whole new meaning. It would have felt interesting simply because we were together, doing something common, our hands brushing against each other as we moved pieces around the board. But he wasn't. And the game was dull and pointless. I finished my wine. I pushed myself away from the table, ready to head to the kitchen for a small refill.

The moment my father rolled the dice, my mother grabbed them off the board. "The pork is done. We can finish this after dinner." She gave my father a look that said, *don't argue with me*.

After the flurry of putting food into serving dishes and arranging the meat platter on the table, we were seated. My white wine glass had been replaced with a red wine glass, filled with Zinfandel. The others now had wine as well.

My father lifted his glass. "To family — always here for each other. No matter what."

My mother gave him a look. She put down her glass without taking a drink. We passed our plates to her, and she placed pieces of pork with a thick bone on each one. We scooped up potatoes and bean salad and buttered our bread.

"You heard your father's toast." My mother turned to me. She gave me a wide, stiff smile. "You do know we're here for you, don't you Gemma?" She held her glass out in front of her, the wine still untouched.

"What does that mean?"

"We have concerns. We want to help you," she said.

"Tamara."

She gave my father a vague stare, not really looking at him. "We said we would…"

"Don't." My father's voice was louder than intended, I think. His skin reddened. He picked up his water and took several sips. He moved the glass in a circular motion over his plate, forcing the ice to rattle against the sides.

I put down my fork. "What's going on?"

"Nothing," my mother said.

"It's all about timing," my father said.

"What is?" I looked from one to the other. All three of them held their forks poised over their plates, staring at me. The only thing I could read on their faces was discomfort. "Why are you all behaving like there's some sort of purpose here that I haven't been briefed on?" I thought about the holiday regimen, the expectations and the sameness. I longed for it now. I longed to go back in time, to refuse the game of monopoly which had made me feel like I was shrinking into my fifteen-year-old self.

"It's too late now," Geoff said. "She knows something's up."

"Don't talk about me as if I'm not here." I cut a piece of pork and stabbed it. I put it in my mouth and broke off a small section of potato which I added to the pork in my mouth. The combination was comforting and savory. I wanted to eat the entire meal as quickly as possible and get out of there. I wouldn't return until Thanksgiving.

"We think you should stop seeing this counselor, or whatever she is," my father said.

I looked at him. I looked at Geoff. At least my brother

had the decency to turn his attention to his plate. He peeled a piece of skin off his potato and ate it.

"You told them?"

He continued looking at his plate. "Sorry. It just came up."

"How did it *just come up?*"

Talking over Geoff, who wasn't saying anything coherent, my mother tried to make her voice louder, more commanding. "We're concerned. Geoff mentioned this counselor…"

"Therapist," I said. "She's a doctor. A medical professional."

"That's nice," my father said. "I'm glad to hear that."

My mother talked over him now. "Nevertheless, we're concerned. Geoff said…"

I gave my brother a hard stare. "Why did you tell them?"

"As I said, we're concerned." My mother's voice grew louder with each repeated statement. "I don't think counseling, or therapy, whatever you want to call it…"

"I'm not calling it anything. That's what it is."

"I don't think it's healthy," she said. "That's for people who have serious issues."

"You don't need mental help," my father said. "You need a new man in your life."

"Good riddance to that one," my mother said.

"You don't even know him."

"I know enough. But there's no need to sit around with a *therapist* rehashing what's done. You need to move on. You shouldn't be moping about someone who treated you so badly."

"He didn't, you didn't…"

"It's time to snap out of it," my mother said.

"Snap out of it?" I picked up my glass and took a long, soothing swallow of wine. I pushed my plate away from me. "I'm not hungry. I need to get going."

"Don't be like that," Geoff said. "Please. We're trying to help."

"Why did you tell them?"

Geoff spoke softly. I almost couldn't hear, but I deciphered his words because he'd said them repeatedly. "I think the doctor is messing with your head. And not in a good way."

"This is not the answer," my mother said. "Talking about him, pining over someone you're better off without isn't going to help you put this behind you."

I took another slug of wine. "You have no right to give input on my relationships."

Her eyes were glassy. "We just…"

"Therapy is helping me. I'm learning a lot of things about myself, and her insights are very helpful."

"You'll be much happier if you meet another man. Are there any teachers at your school who are single? There must be. Or you could take some classes," my father said. "Maybe in subjects that attract males."

"I committed to therapy, and I need to work through this. I don't need classes. And I don't need help from my family."

"We love you," my father said. "We want what's best for you."

"I don't think you do." I shoved my chair away from the table, still holding my glass. I took another long swallow, emptying the glass.

"Don't go off in a huff," my mother said. "You're spoiling our nice dinner."

I laughed. My tone sounded slightly unbalanced. Maybe I was.

48

Ann

The unraveling of the cords that bound David's heart to mine happened in a dark place, hidden from my attention. It didn't begin with any deliberate act of his, or mine. Without noticing what was happening, over time, we'd slowly retreated into the private worlds inside of our heads.

We still talked. We talked about everything — work, politics, books, movies, our plans for the weekend, or trips away. We laughed together over social media memes, and we sat close when we read or watched TV in the evenings. We cuddled in bed before drifting to sleep. We made love, although not as often. We were busy. We loved our jobs. It's not like sex disappeared altogether, but it was definitely slipping into the background. Routine. I believed it was temporary. A short season of our lives. It meant nothing.

Our lives had all the indicators of an idyllic marriage. We displayed the outward signs of satisfying intimacy. But beneath the surface, something was breaking apart. It turned out that David was aware of this, even though he didn't understand it or fully realize that's what was taking place.

I saw nothing at all.

I believed, as I did the day we were married, that I'd found my soul mate. I thought...I *knew*, that David and I were special. I was secretly proud of the fact that we were better than other couples — happier, more intimately connected. We shared more, we knew each other inside and out. We loved the same things and laughed at the same things. We didn't have secrets, and we didn't have to filter anything we said to each other.

We cooked meals together, and we cleaned up the kitchen together. We discussed our investments and made plans for our future as if our minds were a single organism. This didn't mean we never disagreed or even that we didn't retain our differences of opinion. It's just that a lot of our views and thoughts had a natural harmony. We were made for each other. Mutual respect was the cornerstone of our relationship. We both supported the other's career. We were best friends and lovers.

When I saw him having coffee with Gemma Hughes, before I knew her name, there was nothing about that scene to make me suspicious. They sat across from each other. He leaned back in his chair, a casual, slightly disinterested expression on his face as she chattered on, her ponytail moving in time with the animation of the rest of her body. He smiled in a friendly way, and there wasn't the slightest suggestion of desire on his face.

Neither of them saw me. It wasn't that he was so absorbed by her that he didn't notice my presence. I was outside the window, a blur with other pedestrians, passing by on a mid-morning errand. Of course, Gemma didn't know who I was.

I didn't have the impression he was trying to hide the coffee date from me, or from anyone else. They were just two people — work colleagues or old acquaintances — who happened to be talking and drinking coffee.

What shattered me was that he never told me about it. Not that evening and not the next day. Over the following days, there was no sudden recollection of an insignificant meet-up. The slow realization that he was withholding something, that the withholding meant it was not casual at all, pierced me with a wound that was sudden and overwhelming.

When a relationship is as intricately woven as ours, when two people are so in tune they sense the other's thoughts and smile in shared acknowledgement of the same reaction when they're in a social situation, the shock of knowing a cup of coffee was deliberately kept secret is as painful as catching your partner naked with another man or woman.

I felt I'd been buried in an avalanche of boulders, the pain so crushing and pervasive, I couldn't speak. I wanted to buy a handgun and shoot someone, watching the bullet penetrate skull, blood pouring out, bone and flesh tearing apart. I didn't know who I wanted to shoot. I just wanted to inflict irreparable damage. I'd never in my life thought of owning a gun. The desire disgusted and captivated and shamed me.

I certainly didn't want to shoot David. I loved him. I wanted to hurt him, badly. I wanted him to feel the pain I was experiencing. At the same time, I didn't want to lose him.

I'm an organized and methodical person. Despite my violent desire to inflict sudden pain, I moved slowly and cautiously. The hurt was with me constantly, but I kept it hidden. I woke every morning and felt the knowledge sear my heart with a fresh wound. I couldn't focus at work. I was distant with David, but he didn't seem to notice. If he did, he said nothing.

Because he hadn't told me about his meeting with this

young, pretty blonde woman, I knew that despite his disinterested posture and expression as he sat across from her, something was happening between them. It might not have happened yet, but if the encounter were innocent, he would have told me. We told each other absolutely everything. At least I did. We were that way from the start.

I looked at his phone while he was in the shower. My hands shook as I entered his passcode and scrolled through text messages. There was nothing, of course. Although we shared our passcodes, his company provided him with a second smartphone that he used for work only. There hadn't been any reason to share that passcode with me. He never offered, and I never asked. It didn't seem important.

When he left the house to go to the gym, I searched his laptop. There was nothing. He left his email open and unprotected, and of course, it was all business all the time.

There was nothing left to do but follow him. It wasn't difficult.

In films, people are typically aware when they're being followed. But in the real world, for the average person, it's not something that's on their radar. They go about life and hardly even notice what cars are parked nearby. No one is watching for a car lingering behind, turning the same corners, holding back, turning again. Most people rarely look back when they're walking down a street or entering a building. Or a hotel.

Taking extra caution, I removed the front license plate from my car. But even knowing the color and make as well as he knew his own, he never noticed me. He was always looking forward while I followed, watching him.

The day he entered the Four Seasons hotel in Palo Alto,

and remained inside overnight, the day I thought he'd flown to LA for meetings and dinner, was the worst day of my life.

It was early evening. I'd been following him all day. It had been clear something wasn't right when he drove to his office instead of the airport that morning. It was a long, dull day sitting in my car on a side street leading into his company parking lot. I watched employees arrive throughout the morning, watched them leave for lunch, return, and then start the exodus home. At twenty minutes after five in the afternoon, David's silver Z3 pulled out of the parking lot and made a right turn.

He drove slowly, almost dreamily, to the Four Seasons. He parked his car and got out. He didn't glance around as he walked purposefully toward the lobby entrance.

Later, I checked and discovered he'd had a dinner reservation. I didn't need to check to see whether he'd booked a room because I remained in my car all night, never sleeping, until I saw him emerge the following morning.

During that long night, a plan began to evolve. I spent the entire night fully alert with aching, burning eyes and an even deeper ache in my heart, gazing at that sleek building holding my naked husband and a woman who wasn't me.

49

Gemma

Dr. Wilcox seemed different. I couldn't say how. Calmer, maybe. She didn't ask about my mother or about Aidan. If I was to describe it, I guess I would say she was disinterested. She still asked questions, but they weren't as pointed. They weren't as nosey. They seemed as if they'd come out of a therapy textbook — *Why do you think that? Do you know why you had that feeling? Why are you reluctant to talk about that? What themes have occurred consistently in your dreams?*

I felt she was bored with me.

Maybe I *am* boring.

How many women and men have dealt with broken hearts? Millions, billions, probably. Especially if the entire history of the human race is taken into account. Dr. Wilcox has probably cared for hundreds of patients who were trying to heal their shattered hearts. In fact, I know she has, because that's what her ad said. She had expertise in that area and could help anyone return to a place of wholeness. That promise had really appealed to me.

Despite her seeming boredom, I told her about my family's effort to get me to quit therapy. That was the first thing I'd said in two entire sessions that made her perk up.

Suddenly, she had a lot of non-textbook questions.

"What made you sense they had an agenda?"

"They didn't drink wine while we were playing Monopoly. They seemed tense. And before that, I think I already felt something was off because it was nothing like our usual dinners."

"And when you realized Geoff had betrayed your confidence, what was your reaction?"

"I was embarrassed, first. Then angry."

"That's an interesting response. Do you know why embarrassment was your immediate reaction?"

"My parents think we should keep our feelings in the family. My mother thinks Geoff and I should lean on her, come to her with our problems. We shouldn't need the crutches other people use."

"Have they ever said that?"

"Not in so many words."

"But you know it's true?"

I nodded.

"We should explore that, I think."

I shook my head. "It doesn't matter. I just know it."

"Okay. Then back to Geoff's betrayal — how did that feel?"

"Awful."

"Can you be more specific?"

"I feel like I can't trust him anymore."

"Had you asked him not to share the information?"

"No. But it should have been understood. He should have known. We've always had each other's backs. We both know how my mother is, what she thinks, what makes her want to interfere."

"And so he should have had your back?"

"Yes."

"Maybe he did. Maybe he's concerned about you."

"Then he should have said that to me. They made me feel like a child. They've…my mother…has treated me like a child my whole life. She's the expert, and I'm stupid. She knows how life is and I don't. She's right, and I'm wrong. She wants me to need her like I did when I was a kid."

"Do you hear the emotion in your voice when you describe those feelings?"

I nodded. I not only heard it, I felt it.

"Do you think Geoff is concerned about you?"

"Probably. But he's overreacting."

"How can he be overreacting…you've said you feel your heart was broken. That you're in constant pain. Maybe his reaction is appropriate."

"I don't know. Maybe. But he shouldn't have told them."

"What would you have liked him to do?"

"Talk to me."

"Didn't he already do that?"

"Yes, but…" She was twisting what I said. I wasn't sure whether she was pretending to be confused or she really was. Or, these were all questions to make me think about what was going on in my head. That's what they were supposed to be, but somehow they seemed to have turned into questions she needed the answers to.

She kept the same smile on her face, making me feel silly and kind of batty. I couldn't seem to keep my mind on track. I wasn't sure what I thought about anything. I hated feeling that the inside of my head was an endless maze, and I was wandering along poorly lit corridors. All of them looked identical and at the same time, completely unrecognizable.

Maybe there was something wrong with me. Maybe I

was unbalanced, and Geoff saw that. Was it possible Geoff truly did want to help me? Did I need help?

I closed my eyes and recalled their faces — looking at me, glancing at each other, exchanging looks that held secrets from their conversations behind my back. I'd assumed they were feeling pity. Maybe it wasn't that at all. Maybe they thought I was mentally ill and they were afraid of me.

Or was Dr. Wilcox trying to make me feel these things? Some of her questions were so random. I could answer each one five different ways. Did she want me to feel anxious and unsure so I would keep coming for therapy, so I would be completely dependent on her?

"What are you thinking about, Gemma?"

"My brother."

"You love him very much, don't you."

I nodded.

"What do you want from him?"

I shrugged.

"Do you want his love in return?"

"Of course."

"And didn't his intervention, as you like to call it, show a great deal of concern?"

"Yes."

"Doesn't that demonstrate love?"

I shrugged.

"Why do you wish your brother hadn't involved your parents?"

"Because they make me feel like a little kid. I already said that."

"Is it possible Geoff feels helpless? Like a little kid himself? And so he drew them into the problem?"

"I suppose."

"You don't sound very sure. Is Geoff feeling helpless a possibility or not?"

"It is." Now it seemed as if she was shoving me toward a certain answer. But she wasn't writing any of this down. Did that mean she didn't care? Did it mean... I put my head in my hands, pressing my fingers against my forehead, burying my nose in the gap where the sides of my palms touched each other.

"Are you okay?"

"Yes." The sound of my voice was trapped in my palms.

"What's bothering you?"

"I feel crazy. I can't think straight. Is it always like this?"

"Is what always like this?"

"Therapy."

"It's a complicated process."

"That's not an answer."

"It's the truth. It can make you pay more attention to your thoughts, question your patterns. Is that what's upsetting you? Do you feel like you're questioning assumptions you've held for a long time?"

I moved my hands away and sat up. "I don't know what I think."

"Our time is almost up. I don't do this often, but I have a homework assignment for you. I want you to use your journal to explore why concern from your family makes you feel like a child. Ask yourself the questions we've covered today. Explore why it's upsetting for you to have your family express concern for your well-being, why you're upset that your brother is trying to help."

She stood.

I wasn't ready to be finished. My throat was thick with mucous and tears and something else, as if my tongue had slipped and was partially sliding down my throat, clogging my windpipe.

50

David

Ann was the best thing that ever happened to me. That's a cliché, and I don't like phrasing it that way because she's not a *thing* at all. Nor is there anything clichéd about her. She's the best part of my life. She *is* my life. The way to put it is this — *Meeting* Ann was the best thing that ever happened to me.

My company hired her to give a lunchtime talk on stress management. It was terrific. Useful, actually.

I hadn't wanted to attend. BlueCloud had these lunchtime talks on a regular basis, and people at my level typically didn't bother to show up. Too busy. Execs don't take lunch breaks. The lectures were for the regular employees, designed to assist in their growth as all-around individuals, ultimately benefiting the company. Enrichment. A soft part of their benefits package.

During my semi-annual update with HR, they'd reminded me for the hundredth time that *leadership includes leading by doing*. Ignoring these talks sent the message that those at the management level considered employees less self-reliant, easily pacified by company efforts to *care* for them. By showing up, even occasionally, I sent the message that I knew I had things to learn, areas for growth, that I wasn't perfect or above them in some way.

So I showed up. I walked into the auditorium just as the

HR rep stepped to the side after introducing Ann.

Even from the back of the room, I was drawn in by her dark blue eyes and dark hair against her smooth, creamy pale skin. The color of her skin didn't give her an unhealthy complexion. Instead, she looked almost supernatural. She had an air of utter confidence, at home with who she was, and with her accomplishments and skills. She didn't brag about her credentials, and she seemed truly humbled by whatever the HR rep had said before I entered the room.

She wore a dark blue suit, nearly the color of her eyes, and a snug, light pink T-shirt. The skirt was short enough to show off her gorgeous long legs, but managed to avoid looking like she was working overtime to draw attention to them. The jacket had complicated looking pleats and buttons. It was open to reveal a long silver chain with a silver bar dangling from it.

Her smile made you feel she was looking directly at you. She didn't fiddle with her hair, constantly pushing it behind her ears like some women do. She had nice makeup but not so much that you wondered whether holding her close would leave a smear of flesh-colored cream across your shirt, as if her entire face had come off on your arm.

She spoke for nearly an hour and then answered questions, even though she'd encouraged interruptions for questions during her talk — an impressive demonstration of patience and grace. By the end, I no longer simply wanted to meet her, I *had* to meet her. It wasn't just her appearance that took possession of me, it was all of her. I couldn't let her walk out of the conference room and out of my life.

I made my way to the front of the room, feeling a bit like an awkward high school kid as I lined up behind ten or so other employees of BlueCloud. Most of them were women, wanting to discuss the more complex and varied stress that women face in the workplace. It had been a key piece of Ann's presentation, a bit of an eye-opener for me, to be honest. So maybe I needed those lunchtime talks more than I'd realized.

I stood there, hands in my pockets, listening to women talk about how they had to scrutinize every word before they spoke, navigate mansplaining and inappropriate aggression in every single meeting. This caused their stress levels to skyrocket beyond what their male colleagues experienced.

They were simply regurgitating what Ann had covered, but they seemed to need to keep talking, to tell their specific stories. They all commented that they appreciated her bringing these topics up in a forum with their male colleagues, although the audience had been about two-thirds female.

Each step forward brought a new anecdote. I watched her listen carefully, nodding in recognition. She didn't respond with platitudes or try to rush anyone off to the side so she could complete the informal greetings as efficiently as possible. She didn't look at the next person while one was speaking. I was sure she hadn't noticed me at all.

It was an awkward place to be. I was used to standing at the front of the room, responding to my own line of people with queries and comments after a presentation. I felt out of place, juvenile, almost. But I was not letting the chance to shake her hand slip away from me. I could have tracked down her contact information through HR, but I wanted to look into her eyes. I wanted her to see me. I wanted to touch her hand.

Finally, the others were gone. She looked at me and smiled.

"David Graves," I said. "VP of customer satisfaction. I don't usually attend these talks, but I'm glad I caught yours. Well worth my time."

She took my hand and held it for a moment, not in a formal handshake, but more as a clasping of hands to extend good wishes after a wedding or a funeral. I shook the unfortunate images from my mind as she released my hand.

When my arm was back at my side, I continued to feel the warmth of her touch. I imagined I still felt her blood pulsing beneath her skin.

As her eyes looked directly into mine, I'm sure I said a few other things. I'm sure she said one or two things herself. But those scraps of small talk sank into the past the moment I left the room.

I took a risk, hoping I didn't come across like a clueless male, turning her professional presence into something else, something to feed my needs. I'm aware of the issues women face. I try as much as I can to be a feminist kind of guy. "Can I get your contact information? I might have some follow-up questions," I said. Lied, to be honest.

Of course, I found out later she'd seen through me, but she didn't show it then.

She slid her fingers into her jacket pocket and pulled out a business card. She held the card between her thumb and index finger, pinned into place by fingertips with glossy red polish. Cherry red. Flamboyant and exciting and promising red. A color that suggested the navy blue suit and high heels and pink T-shirt didn't convey a fraction of what was inside of this woman. She smiled, and I felt her gaze penetrate my eyes, I felt her open up to me, I felt her interest.

I didn't think for a moment this was fantasy, that it was my ego interpreting casual friendliness as something more. There was definitely something more.

A week later, I acted on that belief. I sent her email inviting her to meet me for a drink. In her reply, she didn't ask whether there was a topic for our meeting. She simply wrote back, *Yes*.

51

Ann

When I first decided to lure Gemma into therapy through a targeted Facebook ad, all I wanted was to mess with her head. I had no plans yet for anything further. I would make her feel unstable and unbalanced. I wanted to shake her up. I wanted her to reconsider her life, to think about why she wanted a relationship with a married man and why she was so casual and almost malicious about the damage caused by that kind of behavior.

Of course, therapy never goes the way anyone plans — not the patient or the therapist.

When I realized during our first session that she was hiding something significant from her past, I became obsessed with finding out that secret, or secrets. It was a consuming challenge for me. It eased the masochistic pain of hearing about her infatuation with and seduction of my husband. Spending time trying to draw her out on those submerged pieces of her life quickly altered my plan. Watching her walk out of my office unsettled and unsure about who she was no longer seemed like enough. If I could uncover whatever she'd buried deep inside, I could go even further.

Targeting the ad at her was easier than I'd anticipated. I simply followed her when she left the hotel where she'd had sex with my husband. It wasn't long before I knew where she lived and where her parents' home was located. I knew her thirty-something brother still lived with mommy and daddy, which told me a few things about them. I knew she taught elementary school and I knew she had a cactus garden on the front porch of her condo.

I knew where she shopped and got her hair cut.

David never asked for details about where I was going when I went on my tracking excursions. Some of them were during the day, so it was easy enough to reschedule patients, giving me a free morning or afternoon. For the occasional nighttime or weekend afternoon excursion, I simply fabricated another engagement — lunch with a friend, shopping trips of my own, going for a run in the open space preserve.

The ad was targeted at females under forty in the city where Gemma lived and elementary school teachers. Thanks to a sticker on the back of her car, I was also able to target alumni of San Diego State. Those few fragments of her life almost guaranteed she'd see my ad. Everyone is on Facebook. It's like shooting fish in a barrel.

The mental focus on my project helped ease the relentless ache in my heart.

I wanted her out of his life. I wanted her inaccessible. I wanted her life damaged in the same irreparable way she'd damaged mine.

As she talked, I saw clearly what I could do. Having her committed to a mental hospital would take some doing, but it wasn't impossible for someone with my credentials. I just needed to take my time, meticulously plan every facet, and do my research. The first step was the collection of my notes from her therapy sessions.

Taking handwritten notes was my usual process. When I told Gemma that, I was telling the truth. Lying in my notes, creating an alternative persona for her, was interesting and actually rather challenging. That bit was a surprise.

During her first few sessions with me, I made notes as I usually do with my patients, writing down significant things she told me and my reactions. I wrote interpretive comments and noted areas for future exploration. After that, I began to embellish. I added obvious Freudian pieces about her desire to kill her mother, as well as thoughts of suicide. I invented a scenario where she was stalking me.

With each entry in the notebook, I increased the drama, making sure that I created a solid, believable picture of a woman who was a danger to herself at the very least, and potentially a threat to her family, and to me, the stand-in for her mother.

Now that the things I'm writing about her are nearly all lies, what actually happens in therapy doesn't much matter. Of course, I still want to know about Aidan, mostly to resolve my own curiosity, but the rest is really irrelevant. I just make up things to show her increasing instability and to begin demonstrating the need for twenty-four-hour supervision.

Once I'd recorded an escalation of disturbing behavior and threatening statements, mixed in with regular therapeutic comments and anecdotes from her life, I would have a tidy package of dangerous and unstable behavior to work with.

I sat in my office, alone. The sun was going down, and I was starting to get hungry, but I needed to review the notes so far. There were pages of them, too many to count. I guessed at least sixty or seventy pages of my small, neat cursive, intermingled with a few doodles and fancy question marks.

It was time to leave. I was meeting David for dinner at an Italian place just up the road. It was family-owned, and the food was absolutely fantastic, no heavy sauces that came out of bottles, a bit of sautéed garlic added to suggest they were home-cooked. Everything was made from scratch with fresh ingredients. You can tell the difference.

Recently, our dinners out were delicate affairs of mildly stiff conversation, punctuated with plenty of warm smiles and, at least on my side, a decent amount of inner turmoil as I tried to imagine what he was thinking about. Our dinner dates weren't unpleasant. Just awkward and different from what we'd known. I wondered often whether he found them awkward as well. As we tried to mend the broken places between us, I wondered whether the cracks would always remain visible.

The notebook, filled with pieces of Gemma's life, lay open on my lap. I'd started on the first page and slowly read everything I'd written. It was slightly more erratic than I'd envisioned. But I truly hadn't mapped anything out, and as I said, therapy is unpredictable. I never know from one minute to the next what any patient will say, what direction her thoughts will take, whether she'll reveal something petty or profound.

The quiet of the room filled me with a sense of tranquility. It was nice being alone in this blue space, a faint light coming through the sheer curtains. It was nice to relax in my chair and not have to think about composing the right question or trying to steer a patient back on course. I didn't have to listen to tears or self-pity or self-aggrandizement. For a few minutes at the end of the day, I liked the utter lack of surprise.

I finished reading the last page and closed the notebook without writing anything new. I needed to consider what should come next. I needed to make sure I had a solid thread of potential violence running through the narrative. That was the key. An unstable person, someone who is mildly depressed or neurotic doesn't need hospitalization. When a potential for violence enters the picture, there's a much stronger case.

It was difficult to look at Gemma and think of her as a person capable of violence. She was too sweet, and too mild. She was too gentle in her movements. There had to be a way to provoke her. And that's what I needed to put a lot of thought into. How might I provoke her to exhibit the latent violence that everyone possesses?

52

Gemma

The lock screen on my phone was filled with messages from Geoff. Since the so-called family dinner, he'd been texting me every day, several times a day, sometimes hourly. At first, his messages were simple and normal — asking me to *give him a call, just checking in* to see how I was doing. Then he began asking whether I was angry at him. I wondered whether he honestly didn't know. If he didn't, he was beyond dense. His tone became more anxious. He asked whether I was *okay*, and begged me to respond.

Brilliant question, was what I would have texted back, if I'd texted back. *Such a perceptive brother.*

Now, it had been nearly a week, and he was obviously frantic. *Let me know you're okay. I'm worried.*

I sat in the teacher's lounge, sipping the single afternoon cup of coffee I allowed myself on weekdays. The caffeine and heat hit my nervous system with a double injection of energy. The kids were at recess, and I wasn't on yard duty. I had an entire seventeen minutes to settle my thoughts and try to muster up the energy I needed for the final fifty minutes of the school day.

A small part of me felt sorry for Geoff. A very small part. It's terrible trying to work things out with someone who doesn't have the same desire to repair a rift. It's frustrating to leave voice mail that goes unanswered, send text messages that fly out into the atmosphere and dissolve.

I *was* angry at him. I didn't feel like sending tiny little messages about it, tapping out complicated feelings into a box designed for fragmented thoughts or simple questions.

If he wanted to apologize, he first needed to actually do that. So far, his messages had been focused on whether I was upset with *him* and how I'd misunderstood *him* and how I couldn't shut *him* out of my life. Once he gave an actual apology, I might consider answering the phone. But this was bullshit, and I wasn't going to cave. Besides, he knew I was at school. He knew I couldn't text or answer phone calls when I was teaching. But again, he was thinking about himself, not me and the world I lived in.

I swallowed some coffee and poured the remainder into the sink. I rinsed the basin and washed my mug, leaving it on the bamboo rack to dry.

Back in the classroom, I walked through the afternoon lesson on the metamorphosis of a caterpillar into a butterfly as if I were trying to claw my way out of my own cocoon. Instead of staying in the classroom to grade math tests, I stuffed everything into my book bag and stepped outside. I closed and locked the door.

I walked to the parking lot, trying not to recall how happy I'd felt during those first few short, gone-in-a-breath weeks of the school year. I'd been insanely happy when I left school every day. Knowing he loved me made everything seem more meaningful — the feel of the breeze, the clouds in the sky were more exquisite. I noticed every detail. I marveled at the world. Nothing bothered me. Bad drivers and traffic, a headache or a badly behaved student were all part of the wonderful chaos of life. My wonderful life of being loved.

During those weeks I was a better teacher. I had more enthusiasm for what I was teaching the children, more patience when they acted up, and a greater sense of purpose in how I was influencing their lives. I was giving something to the world that would last throughout their lives and in some small way, carry on to future generations.

As I drew closer to my car, I saw Geoff leaning against the driver's door. His arms were folded across his chest, the shoulders of his black suit jacket over a white shirt and jeans pulled tight, the fabric straining against the tension of his muscles.

When I was close enough to hear, he spoke. "You can't just cut me out of your life. We've been through too much together. We mean too much to each other."

"I'm not cutting you out of anything."

"You're ignoring my messages. It's passive-aggressive."

"So is blabbing my private life to Mom and Dad without telling me."

"I'm worried about you. So are they."

"Thanks to you." I pressed the remote to unlock my car. The alarm beeped. The clunk of the driver's door unlocking was distinct, but Geoff remained where he was, blocking my access.

"Where are you off to?"

"Home. Please move."

"I'll come with you. We can have coffee and talk."

"I don't drink coffee in the afternoon."

"Since when?"

"Since please move so I can get in my car."

"Come on Gem, don't be this way. It's not cool."

"Not cool? Neither is betraying me." I let out a harsh, brittle laugh. "So too bad. Now move."

"I want to help."

"My therapist is helping. I don't need your input."

"Please let me come over. I shouldn't have told them, you're right. Not without asking you first. I'm sorry, okay?"

I shrugged.

"Now can I come over?"

"I have to grade papers."

"I'll only stay for an hour."

He moved to the side. I opened the door and settled into my car.

Standing at the kitchen counter waiting for the kettle to boil the water, two tea bags resting inside their mugs, the strings and tags lying slack, I wondered if I should have stood my ground. At the same time, I was glad for his company. I hadn't thought about David or felt that unrelieved ache for nearly twenty minutes. The mere presence of another human being in my house softened the atmosphere.

When the tea was finished steeping, we took it into the living room and sat beside each other on the couch.

"I felt blindsided. And betrayed," I said.

"Is that what your therapist said?"

"That's what I said."

"Did you tell her about it?"

"Yes."

His voice was tight, almost breathless. "Do you tell her everything?"

"No."

"So you sit there every week and talk for an hour about a guy who dumped you?"

I felt my throat tighten. Every time I thought about losing David, my body reacted as if it was working independently of my mind, using its own will and memories as it strained to pull David back into my life. I put my mug on a coaster and leaned my head back on the couch to relax the muscles around my throat. "Actually…" I lifted my head. "I don't talk about him very much."

"What do you talk about?"

"My other relationships. Mom. How it was when we were kids."

"That's what I don't like about therapy. Going on about things that happened years ago. It's all about how your parents fucked up. Most parents aren't so awful. They do the best they can with what they have at the time."

I turned toward him. "Is that right? The *best*?"

He nodded. "Don't get caught up in blaming them. It won't help."

"Everything from a person's past affects their life, and their future relationships."

"Is that what she said?"

"No. I figured it out. It's about figuring things out myself."

"What else did you *figure out*?"

"That you wanted to help me. So that's why you betrayed me."

"If you know that, then why were you so cold?"

"I don't like how you did it. And I don't need your help."

"Did you complain about me to your shrink?"

"No."

"Do you talk about me?"

"It's not about you."

"Do you?"

"I told her a few things."

"Like what?"

"I told her about when you whacked off and how Mom talked to all her friends about it."

He stood and picked up his mug. He carried it into the kitchen. I heard tea splash into the sink and then the water running. He returned to the living room and grabbed his jacket off the back of the chair near the entrance. "It sounds like you know a lot more about betrayal than I do. That's none of her business."

"It's not about you. It's about me and how things affected my life."

"I don't like her stirring up all this shit from your past."

"It's part of the process."

"Yeah. Right. The *process*." He laughed, a loud, mocking sound.

I wondered if we were both angry. Dr. Wilcox kept saying that I was. Maybe he was too. "It's all confidential. You don't need to worry."

"You believe that? She's prying into all our lives. It sounds like she's trying to turn you against your parents who did nothing but love you and try their *best* to raise you right. And now they're getting older, and they don't need you accusing them of failure."

"It's not like that."

He laughed again. He shoved his arms into the sleeves of his jacket. "You wouldn't speak to me because I told them about your therapy. And now you go and barf up ancient history about me to a total stranger? You should think about how two-faced that is. Maybe you can explore that in therapy."

"She won't tell anyone. And it wasn't *about* you. It was about how it made me feel."

"How you felt about that is irrelevant."

He left without giving me a hug. All he said was *later*, and then the door closed behind him.

53

Ann

I was spending another evening alone in my office. This time, I wasn't meeting David for dinner. He was out of town for three days, and my schedule was entirely under my control. The minutes had disappeared as I lost myself in embellishing my notes about Gemma, adding fabricated comments in which she contradicted herself and evaded questions, more suggestions of her tendency toward violence.

I had to be careful with how I laid out a falsified history for her. While I wanted her to look dangerous to herself and others, I didn't want to be accused of waiting too long before seeking additional help for her.

I closed the notebook and secured it in the safe. I put on my coat, wrapped a white scarf around my neck, and picked up my purse. I turned out the lights and locked the office and waiting room doors. I took the stairs, my heels echoing in the stairwell.

The lobby was empty, the outer doors already locked for the night. I pressed the panic bar and went out. I turned right and walked toward the parking lot. My boot heels clacked on the pavement, the only sound of a human being outside of an occasional vehicle passing slowly, obeying the speed limit on the narrow street. The only other sounds were the occasional slam of a door or the beep of a car alarm.

It was a single block from my five-story building to the parking lot. I walked past a boutique home remodeling shop, a small clothing store, a store that carried nothing but athletic shoes, and a notary office, all of which were closed for the night. I glanced at my watch. Nine-ten.

Time had slipped by more than I'd realized. My last patient had been an evening appointment at seven, but I hadn't realized I'd become so immersed in filling out the blank spaces I'd left in my notes. I was surprised my stomach hadn't alerted me that it was so far past dinner time.

As I turned into the parking lot, another pair of footsteps echoed behind me. They didn't seem to be hurrying. They sounded confident, keeping pace with my own. I slowed to see whether my impression was correct. The sound of the other feet slowed as well. I wanted to turn, but that would signal fear. It was best to walk confidently to my car. My keys were in my coat pocket. I closed my fingers around them, running my thumb over the buttons on the fob.

The lot was mostly empty. I wove around the few remaining cars. The footsteps continued. When I opened my door, I'd have a moment to casually glance back. This was Palo Alto, after all. The chances of someone intent on hurting me were slim. Most of the crime here involved car break-ins, not muggings or assaults, certainly not murder.

I hit the button. My car beeped and the lights flashed. As I grabbed the handle, I turned to see who was behind me. The lot was empty of life. I turned the other way, knowing I should just get in the car and lock the door, not start searching for trouble, exposing myself as vulnerable and anxious.

I slid into the seat, closed the door, and pressed the

button that secured all four doors. I pushed the keyless start and heard the locks re-set as they were programmed to do when the car started.

With my fingers gripping the steering wheel, taking comfort from its solid presence, I looked out the left window. My headlights brightened everything nearby and made it more difficult to see other parts of the parking lot. I shifted the car into gear and moved forward over painted white lines. I turned and drove slowly toward the side of a two-story building that housed an enormous art supply store. There were a few cars parked up against the building. I slowed further, checking as far as I could see around each one to see whether someone was standing up close to the building, concealed by darkness.

At the end of the row, I turned and cut diagonally across the lot, barely touching the gas pedal. There was no one. As much as I could see inside the few parked cars, they were all empty.

Where had he gone? Or was it a she?

My hands began to shake, making it hard to keep the car moving steadily. The wheels of the car seemed to jitter beneath me.

The notes about Gemma stalking me were fiction. I had seen her at the mall, but it was a coincidence. Her standing outside, looking up at my bedroom, the scent of her shampoo in my house were lies, crafted to ensure I had strong documentation when I made the move to have her hospitalized without her consent.

I had an irrational and ridiculous fear that the things I'd manufactured had made an appearance in the physical realm. Even allowing that thought to pass through my mind made me feel foolish. There was no way a story I'd written in a notebook could turn into something real. I felt light-headed and disoriented.

There was an extremely slight possibility she might begin stalking me…but no one was there. Had I imagined the footsteps? Had reading the notes, reviewing the detail with which I'd described those incidents, somehow embedded the scenarios so firmly in my subconscious that I was hearing things?

I hadn't seen anyone. I hadn't felt that creeping tingle along my spine that sometimes occurs when you know another person is nearby but not in your line of sight. The only observation I had to go on was the sound of footsteps on pavement.

Possibly, the sound was simply an echo of my own boot heels. They were loud enough, and the street was empty enough, that maybe they'd caused some kind of delayed reverberation. That too sounded slightly foolish in my mind, but not as absurd as thinking my manufactured story had come to life to haunt me.

I drove out of the parking lot and turned toward Hamilton Avenue, headed home.

Inside my house, I exhaled deeply, feeling as if I'd been holding my breath for fifteen minutes. After that, I gulped in air, almost hyperventilating. I went into the kitchen and opened a bottle of Cabernet. I poured half a glass and took a sip without bothering to take off my coat and unwrap the scarf around my neck. I took another sip before placing the glass on the counter.

I hung up my coat and scarf, turned on the TV to provide human contact, such as it was, and returned to the kitchen. I cracked a hardboiled egg and chopped it up. I mixed in mayo and a bit of chopped green onion and celery, salt and pepper. I spread the creamy mixture on a slice of sourdough bread. I added the second slice and took a bite, standing over the sink.

It was a sorry way to eat dinner — drinking a decent Cab and eating egg salad so the part that oozed out could fall neatly into the sink while I stared into the darkness.

When the sandwich was gone, I refilled my wine glass and went into the TV room. I tugged off my boots and curled up on the love seat, placing a fleece blanket over my feet and lower legs. It was hard not to think there was someone outside, watching me move from room to room. It was hard not to think this was some kind of payback from my psyche for being so dishonest, unethical, really.

In the end, I polished off the entire bottle of wine and went to bed not recalling what I'd watched on TV, hoping for a dreamless sleep, and a renewed sense of purpose in the morning.

54

Gemma

Using the notebook Dr. Wilcox recommended had been hit-and-miss. I was surprised to discover I liked writing in it. I liked writing about therapy because it made me feel less crazy. Walking out of her office, I usually felt my mind was slipping loose from my skull. I couldn't recall what I'd said, what she'd said. I couldn't decide whether I believed the things I'd said or simply spouted words because they came into my brain and I felt that was what I was supposed to do.

After therapy, I often went home and took a bag of chips and a glass of wine upstairs. I stripped off my clothes and slid beneath the covers. I ate enough to take the edge off my hunger, drank a small glass of wine, and went to sleep. In the morning, I sometimes felt less crazy, sometimes more.

I never dreamed the night after a therapy session. But the next few nights? My sleeping brain was flooded with strange things. I couldn't recall dreaming so often over the past five years as I had during the past five or six weeks. When I woke from a dream and got up to take a few sips of water, I would return to bed, and another dream would start.

Some of my dreams were related to what had happened in therapy, but most of them were just plain crazy, the way dreams are. Our crazy selves come out to play in the moonlight. That inner demon can do and say whatever she pleases. She lives for a while in a world that makes no sense. People come and go without announcing their departure. They transform from one person into another. They refuse to speak, or they shout at you or do nothing but cry, seemingly for hours on end.

The last dream I'd had I wrote about in a single sentence. It was too vague, and I only remembered a single image — the kite flying the girl from Dr. Wilcox's office, except the girl was naked. Instead of her dress floating about her legs, there was a bloody umbilical cord. I was chasing the figure across a field, jumping up to grab hold of her. My fingertips brushed the tail of the kite, but it drifted out of my reach.

After that fleeting memory of my dream, there was an entry about what had happened in my last therapy session two days earlier. Dr. Wilcox and I had spent the entire session talking about suicide. Dr. Wilcox can say what she wants about me being obsessed with Aidan, but sometimes, she sounds awfully close to obsession herself. No matter what I said, she steered the conversation back to suicide. I started to wonder if someone close to her had taken her own life. It crossed my mind that she might be considering it herself.

Toward the end of my session, she veered off suicide and began asking about my so-called hidden desire to hurt other people. She wanted to know if it had happened in my dreams.

It had.

She wondered whether I'd written about it.

I had.

She wondered whether I wanted to share some of those dreams with her.

I did not.

She seemed irritated when I left her office, and I felt the same. Whenever I sensed her annoyance with me, I felt exactly the same toward her. It seemed that her annoyance stirred up my own. She had no right to be annoyed with me. She was supposed to help me. It's like our irritation was feeding the other's. It made me feel out of control of my own state of mind.

The dream from the night before had not been violent. It was really quite simple, not a constantly shifting mirage or full of complex situations that I couldn't quite figure out, either during the dream or after.

I'd been sitting in my usual chair, facing Dr. Wilcox. She wore a wedding gown and veil. She had the kind of veil that also covered her face, which made it difficult to hear what she was saying.

I was talking about David, overwhelmed with love for him. The pain of losing him was absent, making me think we were together. And yet on some level I suspected…no, I *knew* something was wrong between us.

I kept asking Dr. Wilcox why she was wearing a wedding gown. Her answers were too soft to decipher. No matter how often I asked her to speak up, she refused. I strained to hear, but couldn't.

Suddenly, she stood, flipped the veil off her face and pointed her finger at me. This time she spoke clearly. *You belong with David. What are you waiting for?*

I argued with her. I wanted to know why she thought that. I told her he didn't love me. I suggested it was for the best that things were over, even though a moment earlier I'd thought we were still together. She got increasingly angry, shouting that I was stupid, that I was giving up the only person who really loved me. She ordered me to stop letting other people determine the circumstances of my life. She said David's wife was deciding our future, tearing us apart.

The first thing I recalled when I woke was Dr. Wilcox in the wedding gown. I had no idea what that was supposed to mean. I drank coffee and tried to figure it out, but all it did was make my head hurt. The rest of the dream was a blur. Then, during my shower, it came rushing back.

As soon as I finished drying my hair, I grabbed my notebook and wrote down every detail I could remember. I described her lace-covered dress and the filmy veil. I described the pink dress and hot pink flip-flops I was wearing. I wrote down every word I remembered.

When I finished, I placed my pen across the words. I laced my fingers together and rested my chin on my joined hands. Dr. Wilcox said our dreams can provide guidance. There was only one question, written three blank lines below the details of the dream — *Was my subconscious telling me to fight for David?*

I believed it was.

55

Ann

Less than a week after David's *trip to LA* when I'd seen him enter The Four Seasons hotel, he told me he had to go to San Diego overnight. I gave him a tight smile and commented on the unusual nature of two trips to the same area in the span of three days. He laughed and said something about lack of planning and logistical screw-ups. His face was smooth and calm, without the slightest tremor of guilt, or sadness. His kiss good-bye caught the corner of my lips and landed with a splat on my cheek.

The next day, I followed him from our house to the same hotel. He used valet parking this time. I didn't hang around.

Following him to the room was too risky, so I hired someone to do it. For less than five hundred dollars, I found out what room he booked every week and what they ordered for breakfast. I found out he requested the same room every time. A few weeks later, when David had a *boys' night out*, after which he planned to *crash with one of the single guys who lives in the city rather than hunkering down in the back of an Uber too drunk to see where they were going*, I booked the room right next to his.

The day of his phony night out, I left the house before dawn. In order to check in so early, I'd had to book the previous night. It was a small price to pay to find out more. I was aware of the masochistic nature of what I was doing — staying in the room next to my husband and his lover, buying a device with a sensitive probe that would allow me to hear every sigh of pleasure and groan of release. I've always coveted information. *Information is power.* David repeated that cliché often, and I agreed.

Lounging around a five-star hotel room by myself was nice, when I wasn't thinking about why I was there. Of course, I couldn't use the restaurant or bar, the pool, the workout facility, or the spa services, but my room was large and featured sliding doors to a balcony as well as a small love seat and an ergonomic desk and chair. I could work, feeling the warm breeze through open doors. I could lie in a luxurious bed and read. I could order room service, and I could book a massage in my room.

As it turned out, I was unable to focus on work, given the circumstances. I watched a few movies. I booked a ninety-minute massage. The iron-firm fingers of the masseuse drew my thoughts into my tight muscles, where they were released by expert pressure, and my mind was pleasantly empty for a short while. My body followed suit, for a while.

I ate too much — starting with a breakfast of bacon and potatoes, a delicious omelette and an entire pot of coffee. This required forty minutes of yoga to try to calm my nerves that had had quite enough tension before slowly absorbing all that French roast.

After yoga, I showered and watched *The Bourne Identity* to take myself into a different world. Then I watched a violent thriller, still desperately needing to take my mind off where I was. The movies helped to harden my heart against the ache that gnawed at me through all of my pleasurable activities.

For lunch, I ordered a bottle of wine. I was careful to allocate a single glass for each hour — one glass with my croissant turkey sandwich, one glass with another movie, and one glass as evening approached and I knew my illicit neighbors would be arriving soon.

They entered the room at five-forty-seven. I was already sitting close to the wall, my device in hand, the probe touching the wall, listening to silence. I didn't want to miss a single word, the sound of hands moving across fabric, tongues crawling down throats, and the whisper of skin touching skin. Of course the device wasn't powerful enough to pick up any of those noises, but there was enough that I had a pretty good idea of what was happening each step of the way.

The first thing I heard after the door opened was a female voice exclaiming over champagne and chocolate-dipped strawberries. Both items showed an incredible lack of imagination. David might as well have looked up a list of *Five Things To Do When You Want To Fuck A Woman Just For Fun*. Because really, no matter what he said to her, this wasn't love. I had no doubts about that. My knowledge didn't ease the pain, but I was confident this had nothing to do with love.

Despite the commonplace nature of champagne and chocolate-dipped strawberries, it hurt. How long since David and I had toasted *anything* with a glass of champagne, much less our love, or the passion between us?

After a while, they became quite vocal. Gemma's name was revealed the moment she was naked.

Oh, Gemma. I knew your body was incredible. An awkward laugh from David. This was followed by an eager, flattered female laugh. Giggle is probably a better word.

On my side of the wall, I wanted to vomit. And sob. But I couldn't. Hysterical crying might be heard without the aid of a listening device.

Listening to them was one of the most painful things I've ever done. But I didn't shrink from it. I would be glad in the end. I couldn't sit back and allow my husband to destroy the magnificent thing we'd shared for over eight years. *Eight years.* Such a brief time, and at the same time, an eternity. Enough time that I had trouble recalling feelings or sensations from my life before he was in it, but short enough that I couldn't believe the beautiful thing we had was already damaged.

I listened to every breath, every sigh, every outburst of passion. I listened to the bed and the running water when the toilet was flushed and when they showered. As they fell asleep, I heard the silence. It was the kind of silence that speaks of bodies coiled around each other, rhythmic breathing. Not the silence of emptiness. The silence that filled the home where David and I lived at that very moment.

When it was over, I forgot every word that David spoke. Even the sounds of pleasure seemed distant and uncertain, part of a dream. It shows what the mind will do to protect itself.

She was another matter. I recalled every word as if I'd recorded it. I heard things that made me think about who this woman was. I heard things that brought up a multitude of questions I might ask her. Most important of all — who was Aidan and why did she cry out his name when she was having sex with my husband?

The final thing I learned about her was that she *knew*. She knew what she was doing. She knew she was hooking up with a married man. All her confused blinking over learning he was married was self-delusion. The knowledge of what she'd done was something else she'd buried neatly in her mind. Maybe she didn't know consciously, but a woman who's invited to meet a man in a hotel knows, on some level, that something isn't quite as it should be.

Tracking down her last name was easy enough. The names of the staff at the elementary school where she worked were published on the school website.

Once I knew her full name, locating her presence on Facebook and Instagram was easy. Both accounts were private, but Facebook less so. I could see her employer, which I already knew, and I saw enough photos to identify her brother and parents. I saw the change in her status — *In a relationship.*

Like hell she was. Not for long.

56

Gemma

The dream made it clear what I should do. I did not feel the need to analyze it with Dr. Wilcox.

Besides, as I wrote about the dream and my feelings around it, I came to an incredible realization — Dr. Wilcox absolutely would suggest I fight for David. Yes, she'd advertised that she could help me find wholeness without requiring a man to complete myself, but most of my therapy had focused on Aidan and my mother! Dr. Wilcox wanted me to break free of the things that weighed me down. The things that had pushed David away from me!

Why hadn't I seen that weeks ago?

That's why the progress of my therapy had been so confusing, the reason I felt crazy half the time. She was waiting for me to recognize where her questions were leading me. She was pulling apart the threads of my past and mending what was broken. Her ad was just the teaser to find people who needed mending! The reality was something else. She wanted me to be happy. She wanted me to be with my soul mate. What she knew, in the things she'd studied for her profession, was that to have a healthy relationship, the past needs to be dealt with.

Hadn't the first fracture between David and me come when I tried to dig into the past? He was right. It had nothing to do with us now, and if I'd dealt with my own past, if I'd put it to rest, moved on, as they say, I wouldn't have even thought about discussing those things. Aidan was a teenaged fantasy! David and I were adults. Whatever happened before was irrelevant.

I felt a rush of affection for Dr. Wilcox. She was my friend. She cared about me more than my mother ever had, more than most of my other friends. I now saw that her questions weren't irritating, they were gentle and kind. She didn't push hard. She'd taken my hand and was pulling me gently toward something she wanted me to see for myself.

Maybe it was time to tell her everything. About Aidan. About my mother.

But first, I needed to follow my heart. And the guidance was clear. I'd read somewhere that everyone in your dreams is you, a facet of your personality. So even though it was Dr. Wilcox telling me what to do, it was me in that beautiful ivory gown, ready for my marriage to David.

He'd said I was exquisite, that he needed me, that he thought about me constantly. He'd said so many things. Now I knew, he didn't truly want to go back to his wife. His love for her was dead, but the obligation, the *past*, made him feel as if he owed her something. But he did not owe her his happiness. I was sure he would agree now that he'd had time to think about it, time to miss me.

I dressed in jeans and dark brown leather boots. I wore a top that was fitted but wasn't trying too hard. I put on the long white sweater I'd worn on the flight to Hawaii. He loved that sweater. He said it made him think about how soft and sweet I was. Kind of silly, but it made me feel good.

By seven o'clock in the morning, I was waiting in the

parking lot outside the only exterior entrance to the buildings that housed David's company. The main building was three-stories tall, made of white concrete with green-tinted glass. It was one of a collection of buildings that were set at odd angles surrounding a park-like center with a fountain and grassy areas. The center area was protected by the buildings and adjoining concrete walls. There were lots of shaded benches for work conversations or quiet thought. It was possible to see straight through the lobby to this interior space where employees could stroll with perfect peace of mind since the single lobby door was locked and accessible only with a company-assigned badge, or guarded by a receptionist during business hours when the door was unlocked. It made me wonder why Garden Grove elementary school wasn't like that. There was nothing fortress- or prison-like about David's office complex. It looked completely safe and entirely welcoming.

I sat on a bench near the lobby entrance. The air was cool. Sitting in my car would have been nicer, but I needed to be close to the entrance so he didn't slip inside before I could reach him. I couldn't be running across the parking lot, calling his name, only to have the door slam closed.

He arrived at seven-forty. He looked thinner. The smile on his face was hiding something. He wasn't happy if he was losing weight, trying to cover up his deep sadness with a forced grin and a confident arrangement of his shoulders.

When he saw me, he stopped. His arms stiffened at his sides, and his shoulders clenched. Even his face seemed to freeze, keeping the smile, but hardening the shape of his lips into something garish and cold. I shivered.

He spoke in a low voice, even though there wasn't

anyone else nearby. "What are you doing here?"

"I need to see you."

"Don't do this."

"We need to talk."

"No, we don't."

"I made a mistake."

"So did I," he said.

That part surprised me. It wasn't what I'd expected him to say, although I don't know what I did expect.

It hurt.

What we had was beautiful and magical. I wouldn't allow him to call it a mistake. He didn't mean it. That was his wife talking. She'd twisted his thoughts to believe obligation and history were love. It was not. He'd forgotten what love was really like. He was thinking only of duty. A false sense of duty. "Let's go get coffee," I said.

"I'm at work."

"Not yet." I smiled.

He didn't return my smile. "You need to leave."

"It was a mistake to bring up the past. I can see that now."

"What are you talking about?"

"It damaged what we had, trying to tell you about my past, and focusing on yours. The past doesn't matter. It was just a high school crush. It's not important. I got pregnant, that's all. And I wanted you to know, but now I understand it's not important."

He took a few steps back. He gave the impression he was afraid of me! He hadn't even blinked when I said I was pregnant all those years ago. Something you don't forget. That seems important to tell your lover. It was good that he knew now, we could move forward.

He lifted his face toward the grayish sky, so I couldn't see his eyes. "Please don't do this."

"I love you. And I know you love me. You're just…"

"A little advice, Gemma. Don't be so needy. It's a turnoff."

I felt a flush of anger. He looked at me as if he was pitying me. I owned my own condo, I had a good job. I had friends and a close relationship with my brother. "I'm not needy."

"Yes, you are. It bleeds out of you." He took a few steps to the side, turned and walked quickly toward the lobby doors.

"Wait."

His voice sounded far away as he called back over his shoulder. "If you try to follow me inside, if you don't leave, I'll call security."

I stood there, feeling as if I wouldn't be able to move my feet ever again. For a moment, I hated him. And then I remembered my dream. I would not let go.

57

Ann

Tamara was eager to meet me for breakfast. I'd shaken off my fear that someone was stalking me. My focus had returned, and I was ready to finish building the walls around Gemma.

Soon, I needed to move toward letting Tamara know who I really was, but I was still waiting for the right time — that moment when she would be more concerned with her daughter's mental deterioration, her potential for violence or self-harm, than she was with my lies. She had to see my lie as one of concern for Gemma. She also needed to recognize that deep inside, she feared her daughter.

The situation between Tamara and I had grown stagnant, but I had a plan for that as well. I would push things forward more quickly.

This time, Tamara was waiting for me.

We ordered our food — oatmeal and fruit for both of us. It wasn't what I'd normally choose for a Saturday breakfast in a restaurant, but my stomach rebelled against the idea of eating at all, so I chose something gentle.

Tamara inserted her spoon into the cereal, puddles of milk drifting across the top like a marsh after heavy rain. She scooped from the far side of the bowl and then swept the spoon up and across the bowl, then up again to her mouth. It was an awkward way of eating, and I tried not to stare, tried not to get distracted by her movements or let them influence me into hyper-conscious gestures of my own.

I swallowed my spoonful of oatmeal and took a sip of coffee. "She told me about Aidan. Finally."

"Really?"

I nodded. "I'm not sure what the big deal was." I hoped my vague lies would carry me until she was eager to fill in the blanks, to correct my *misunderstandings*. I was confident, once she believed I knew, she would spill out the details. I wasn't sure why I hadn't used that tactic earlier, gone all-in on lying. I felt like a less-than-competent therapist. Not that therapists are trained to mislead patients, or their families, not that we're taught to pry when we should be waiting for others to know their own minds. Not at all.

Therapy requires a great deal of patience. It doesn't work unless the patient arrives at a destination under her own volition. Forcing an insight or pushing them to a course of action usually backfires. I'm a very patient person, but I was getting tense. I didn't want Gemma in David's life, or anywhere in the periphery. I wanted David to myself, to rebuild what we'd almost lost without the threat of her interference. I wanted him to forget her name forever.

Tamara put down her spoon. She swallowed. "What did she tell you?"

"How painful their breakup was."

"Obviously. What else did she say?"

I ate a spoonful of oatmeal and shook my head gently, trying to give her the impression I had a mouth full of food, and politeness prevented me from answering her question. I sipped my coffee, then pretended a seared tongue before speaking. "It's shocking that he would do something like that."

"He?"

"Aidan."

She nodded. "What exactly did Gemma tell you?"

"That you kept them apart." I held up my hand. "I'm not judging you. I totally understand. I don't have children, but my younger sister was pretty wild." I laughed sadly. "My parents had to work overtime to restrict her. So I get it."

She nodded.

"Gemma and Aidan were too young for sex," I said.

"Yes." She pressed her palms on the table on either side of her bowl. "And they proved it. By being so stupid."

I nodded, waiting for more, determined not to speak too soon.

"I didn't raise my children to be stupid. But I guess I failed." She clenched her hands into fists, then slowly drew them back to the edge of the table. "I did my best."

"She got pregnant." I held my breath, hoping it was the truth.

She nodded, avoiding my gaze.

I slowly released my breath. "I'm guessing the forced separation from him has made her unable to forget him. And the intensity of a pregnancy at that age..."

"She acted like they were Romeo and Juliet, tormented by her wicked, elitist family. I was the evil queen of fairy tales, of course. Her father refused to get involved. He wouldn't put his foot down. I had to do it all." She sighed. Her fists tightened.

"But you were smart to separate them."

"I shouldn't be telling you all of this. You're Gemma's

friend. As angry as I am at her, even now, sometimes. I hate to say that, but if I'm honest, I am. Still, I shouldn't be talking about her with her co-worker, her friend. I feel terrible." Her eyes filled with tears. "But I have to talk with someone."

"You needed to get it off your chest."

Behind me, a child began banging a piece of flatware on the table. It went on for several seconds. I tried not to turn as Tamara stared over my shoulder. A moment later, the banging stopped. A parent must have intervened.

"It's a parent's responsibility to place boundaries for their children, even when they're nearing the end of childhood, when they seem like adults, but they're still so far away from maturity. The last mile is the most difficult."

She nodded eagerly. Finally, her fingers uncurled, and she relaxed her hands onto the table. She picked up her spoon and began eating. The drumbeat of the flatware started up again. This time, Tamara didn't look past me to study the situation. It went on for several minutes while we ate and talked about other things.

When my bowl was only half empty, I pushed it to the side. "And why now? I keep asking myself that. Why now? She never mentioned him before in all the time I've known her. She's...do you see how she is? It's almost like she's grieving for a boy from high school."

She shook her head. "Sometimes talking to you scares me. I wonder if I should be doing something, not just talking."

"Like what?"

"I don't even know. She needs help. Maybe medication or something."

"It's possible."

"Do you think so? Do you think she's going to…" Her eyelids trembled, and her eyes grew glassy again.

"I don't want to scare you, but I've wondered the same."

"I'm shocked that she talks to you about him. I thought that was all in the past. Just like that other man ought to be." She shuddered.

"I guess ancient things can resurface and torment all of us."

"Do you think she needs medication? An anti-depressant, or something?"

I shrugged. "It's hard to know. I might ask her if she wants to have dinner together. I'll see what she says when we have more time to talk. I can let you know."

"Would you?"

"Yes. You and I are a team. We both want to help her. We're both worried about her."

She reached across the table and took my wrist. "Thank you."

I smiled, and she returned the warm look. Next time. The next time for sure, I'd tell her who I was.

58

Gemma

I sat in my blue chair and listened to the rain pound against the enormous window of Dr. Wilcox's office. It was raining sideways. Not at a ninety-degree angle, obviously, but rain was hitting the glass all the same. The sound made me feel relaxed, tranquil. It made me feel the world was folding in on itself, that everyone was tucked inside warm buildings and homes. I love rain. It makes me feel clean, not just standing in it, but watching it, listening to it. I like knowing all that water is washing away grit and grime and filth and stains, that there's so much power in it.

Rain makes me feel the world is taking care of itself, and it makes me feel as if everything will be alright. If rain can return every winter, it means the universe is in working order. It means things will turn out okay.

Maybe that's all silly fantasy.

I didn't mention these thoughts to Dr. Wilcox. Even if she didn't consider them silly, I wasn't interested in digging deeper into each one. I wasn't interested in discussing my philosophy of life or the meaning of rain — she would probably ask why I thought the world was dirty and want to know more about what things had not worked out okay.

Instead, I smiled at her.

I'd learned it was important to avoid bringing up new

subjects, or they would become the focus of a detailed exploration into something irrelevant. But this left me rather tongue-tied. I had no idea what I should say, where I wanted to start.

"What do you want to talk about today?"

"David."

"Okay. What about him?"

"I had a dream where you told me to go back to him. To fight for him."

"Why do you think you had that dream?"

"Because my subconscious is telling me not to give up so easily."

She smiled. "Understanding your dreams is not quite that simple."

"I didn't say it was. But I do know the feeling I had after was very clear."

"What feeling was that?"

"I knew I should go see him."

"How did you know?"

"Because you directed me to…in the dream. And I just knew I had to act on it. The feeling was overwhelming."

She made a note in her book. "What else?"

"That's all."

"Did you think immediately about what the dream meant?"

"Yes."

"And you're confident you have it right?"

"Yes."

"Were there any others in your dream?"

"No."

"Not your mother? Aidan?"

"I said no."

"Is it possible I represented your mother?"

"I don't think so."

"You seem very certain."

"It's the first thing I've been certain about in a long time."

"That's good."

I smiled, but she didn't.

"I went to see him."

She didn't blink. Had she expected that's what I would have done? Or did she just have a good poker face that always held its own no matter what one of her patients said or did? I supposed she had to.

"How did that turn out?"

"He was caught off guard. But I know I'm on the right track. He just needs time."

"Why do you think that?"

"Because I know him." I smiled. "I know he's not a talker and he doesn't blurt things out. Well, he did blurt out a few things, but I think he'll consider the things I said and see that he's making an awful mistake. Betraying his own feelings."

Dr. Wilcox nodded. "You seem very confident, again."

"I am."

"What will you do if he doesn't respond?"

"I can't think about that."

She wrote in her notebook, several words. Then she spent a few minutes looking at what she'd written. She underlined something. I almost got out of my chair and went over to look at it, but she would have covered it, so it wasn't worth the effort.

"I want to ask you more about the figure representing me in your dream. I think, knowing more about dreams than you do, that there are other angles to this that you might be missing."

She didn't look as condescending as she sounded, but I didn't disagree with her. "It didn't *represent* you, it *was* you."

"Often in dreams, all the figures represent yourself."

"I know. But not always."

"Is it possible that I represented all the people that you and I have talked about? Your mother? Aidan? Your brother? Father? Ex-lover?"

"David."

"Yes, David. Is that possible?"

"No."

"Just think about it for a minute."

"I thought I was supposed to come up with my own conclusions, not have you tell me what to do."

"But I'm here to guide you."

I waited. "I thought about it, and no."

"I feel like there's something you're not telling me. About Aidan."

"Why do you keep asking about him?"

"In your other sessions, it was clear that you have unfinished business there. But you consistently want to dodge the issue."

Suddenly it came back to me how I'd felt about Dr. Wilcox after the dream, how I'd realized she wanted to help me get better. In the turmoil of thinking about what David said to me, searching for ways to reconnect with him, I'd forgotten. I was feeling I didn't need her because once David returned, the pain would be gone. But I wasn't there yet, and maybe Dr. Wilcox could still help. She *wanted* to help.

"I want to talk about how I can get back together with David."

She stared at me as if I'd said I planned to commit murder. "I think you're off track, Gemma." She gave me a thin, tiny smile. "You came to therapy to get grounded in who you are, independent of any man."

"Then why do you keep bringing up Aidan?"

"That's the point. Because you find elaborate ways to avoid talking about him. You described him as a profound part of your early experience. But it's obvious you're keeping something back that's painful for you."

"What happened with Aidan has nothing to do with David."

"Are you sure?"

I wasn't.

"Is your goal to continue in a relationship with a married man? Is that all you think you're deserving of?"

"He doesn't love his wife."

"He told you this?"

"No, but..."

"Marriage is complicated."

"So?"

"What he tells you and the truth of his marriage may be two very different things."

I felt like my head was going to explode. My dream was so clear, and I felt so good knowing that Dr. Wilcox really wanted me to be happy, that deep inside I knew this and that knowledgeable part of me created the dream so that I wouldn't forget. But now I was confused. I didn't know how I was even going to contact David. I couldn't keep showing up outside his work.

It hurt worse than ever, knowing he was just a few miles away, so close. Remembering every word he whispered to me, the way he collapsed onto me and held me after we made love. I craved the heat and the weight of him, the emptying of himself into me. It was more than just sex. He gave his whole being to me, and I still had him.

Thinking about making love made my legs and hands tremble. I felt like an addict.

I didn't know what I thought, what I wanted to talk about, why I was sitting in that chair. I started to cry.

Dr. Wilcox got up and pulled a tissue out of the box, even though I could reach it. She handed it to me and looked away. "I'm wondering if I should prescribe something for you."

"No. I don't want drugs."

"Medication. Not drugs. It could help you calm down. Focus."

"I am focused!" I blew my nose hard and soaked the entire tissue. I put the wet, soggy thing on the table beside me, not caring if my snot got on the nice wood finish.

"From my perspective, you're all over the place. You seem splintered and…somewhat erratic."

"Because you keep asking me irrelevant questions. It's confusing. I don't know if I'm thinking what I think, or my thoughts are different because of what you say. Maybe they're your thoughts."

She picked up her pen and tapped it on the slightly bowed pages of the notebook where it made a hollow thud. "I'm trying to pursue areas of your life that have come up, but we haven't gone into with any depth."

"What happened with Aidan was I got pregnant. Okay?" I had no idea why I blurted that out, maybe just to shut her up, to prove it wasn't important. "My mother was furious. She acted as if I'd done it just to wreck her life, or something. She thought me being pregnant when I was still in high school was this horrible stain on our family. You'd think it was the 1800s the way she carried on. She made it all about her." I laughed.

"Is that funny to you?"

"No."

"You feel bitter about it?"

I could barely speak, so all that came out was a whisper that I didn't think she could hear. "Yes."

She nodded. She heard me after all. Her face filled with soft color, staining the usual milky white of her skin. She looked smug and happy, as if she'd finally won the final round, by making me say it.

So I told her the rest of the story. She had won.

59

Dr. Ann Wilcox: Notes on Gemma Hughes

My instinct that something had seriously impacted Gemma's life near the end of high school was absolutely correct. The story she told was shocking. Not that it's the first shocking story I've heard from a patient. Far from it. But this notebook belongs to Gemma, not my other patients, and based on the way she first presented herself, and the initial impressions I had of her family, I was shocked.

From what Gemma had told me prior to this, her mother seemed somewhat overbearing, but generally a devoted parent, a woman who cared deeply about her children. She may have humiliated her son as a child, but nothing too severe, and nothing that couldn't be overcome with therapy.

She'd filled Gemma's mind with a few fantasies, but nothing outside the realm of normal. The mother seemed to be overly disturbed by the absolutely normal sexual activity of a seventeen-year-old girl, but again, nothing that we couldn't address in therapy. There was no abuse, no extreme dysfunction, no obvious mental illness.

Unlike many women of her generation, Gemma's mother didn't seek to protect her reputation or keep the family stable by helping her daughter obtain an abortion. Gemma didn't have any insight into why that was the case. It's not a religious family, so that aspect remains a mystery.

When Mrs. Hughes discovered Gemma was pregnant, she took charge, in Gemma's words. In less than a week, the family's home was on the market. The father accepted a new teaching position at a high school in Fresno, and they found a recently constructed house, slightly larger than their previous home. With a decent-sized piece of land, it was easy for the family to keep to themselves. The brother remained behind, living with a friend while he finished his last year and a half of high school.

A tutor was hired, and Gemma was basically kept under house arrest for her entire pregnancy. She studied and did well, although there was a lot of fighting about her pregnancy, as well as Aidan and the abrupt end to that relationship.

It's not clear to me why Gemma didn't fight to see the boy. She refused to answer my questions in that regard.

Most seventeen-year-old girls would fight, to the point of running away. It's possible he'd lost interest, and Gemma never wanted to face that.

The other equally likely possibility was that he simply ran fast and far from the idea of fatherhood, relieved that Gemma's parents had intervened and removed his responsibility.

It's still surprising to me that she allowed her mother to take total control over her life, to the point of cutting her off from all social activity. She was isolated until she went away to college, where she was thrust suddenly into dorm life, partially unprepared following an extremely cloistered year, a critical year in her development as a young adult.

I can't help but wonder whether her failure to fight to see the father of her child, her failure to fight for her child at all, lies beneath her blind determination to fight for her ex-lover beyond all reason.

Is there some drive that comes from recognizing this past failure that's adding significant emotion and energy to her current desires?

It's perplexing that an educated, otherwise well-balanced woman would want to be in a relationship with a married man. Of course, she *insists he's in love with her, but that delusion is equally difficult to untangle.*

Gemma gave birth to her daughter at home. Her mother assisted.

Alone, her mother cut the cord, cleaned up the baby, and took the infant to the local fire station where she abandoned the child to caring hearts and hands.

Concluding thoughts: Focus on Gemma's unresolved, and mostly suppressed grief over losing her daughter.

60

Gemma

I called the school principal and told her I needed to take a week off. I told her there had been a sudden death in my family and I needed to travel to Florida. I had a good reputation at Garden Grove. Every year I received excellent feedback from parents. They heard about my teaching style and put in special requests to have me as their children's teacher. There were no issues in taking time away.

I wished I could travel to Florida. I wanted to get away from therapy and Geoff, my mother, and the cold, dry air of early November. I imagined myself in a bikini, lying on a lounge chair, sipping a piña colada and eating a healthy wrap or snacking on salted nuts. I would stare out past the frame of palm trees and soft white sand at the seamless, endless blue.

Instead, I put on yoga pants and a fleece sweatshirt, hunkered down in my condo with hot tea and too much wine, and tried to figure out what I was going to do. I wanted David. I also wanted my peace of mind, my sanity back. I was confused all the time. I was tired of talking about my life, things from the past that Dr. Wilcox was obsessed with. Of course, once I had David, peace of mind would follow right behind. I wouldn't need therapy.

The pressure of Dr. Wilcox's erratic questions was

making me so tired I couldn't think. I felt anxious and uncertain about every part of my life, past and present. Except the wanting David part. I found myself thinking, and having bizarre dreams about things I hadn't thought of for years. I dreamt about dancing and woke wondering why I'd given up the thing I loved the most.

Nothing had made me happier than moving my body with precise control across that polished wood floor, losing myself in beautiful music. Why hadn't I ignored my mother and pursued my dream of becoming a ballerina? Others did it.

I suppose getting pregnant, which put a sudden end to dance lessons, had a lot to do with it. But still. After my baby was gone...

Why had I told Dr. Wilcox about what my mother did? How she locked me in the house, and stole my baby? And I didn't do a thing about it. I sank into my bed, escaped into sleep for weeks. And then I did what she said — turned my attention toward college.

Of course, I didn't know what had happened to Audrey, but I didn't even try to find out. I was in a fog, I don't know what I was thinking. It's all a blur now. My mother had all the power, and I had to do what she said. It didn't seem to occur to me that I could try to find out. I should have looked for my baby. I should have told someone, anyone, what she'd done. Why hadn't I?

I wondered what kind of terrible human being I was. I failed to protect my baby.

Audrey.

That's what I called her. My mother said I wasn't allowed to name her. That privilege belonged to some faceless, nameless couple out there, longing for a baby, people who *deserved* a child. That privilege did not belong to me, a child myself.

But I called her Audrey in my mind.

I still do.

I'll never forget that single glimpse of her sweet, precious, beautiful little face. I never saw her eyes. They were closed.

Now, I closed my own eyes. I saw the kite girl from my dream with her bloody umbilical cord. I opened my eyes and took a sip of wine. I wasn't turning into a drunk, but I needed to escape my head, I needed my thoughts to stop spinning in circles. Drinking a bit of wine to escape was natural, and I didn't blame myself. I wanted to stop thinking. I wanted my brain to feel normal again. I was so tired. Tired of dreaming and talking, tired of trying to figure things out. Tired.

The only thing I was not confused about was David's love. He didn't turn away because of something in me. It was his wife. He still loved me! He belonged to me. Heart and soul. Or was it body and soul? Either way, he was mine.

Text messages from Geoff streamed across the screen of my phone, lighting it up every few minutes. This is what happened now whenever I didn't speak to him for a day or two. He demanded to know how I was, what I was doing, why I wasn't answering him.

My phone rang for the third time that evening. I finished my wine in a solid gulp, splashed a bit more into the glass, and answered the phone. "Why do you keep calling me?"

"This is important."

"I'm fine."

"It's not about you this time."

"Good. Then what is it?"

"I need to talk to you about Mom, and Dad…mostly Mom."

I took a sip of wine.

"Can I come over?"

"Just tell me."

"It would be easier…"

"Just tell me. Are they redecorating? Someone has cancer?"

"That's a fucked-up list."

"Then don't be so mysterious." I put my glass on the nightstand. I leaned forward and rearranged the pillows behind me, so there was a fatter cushion of fabric and feathers between me and the headboard.

"You sound so cold. You make it sound like you wouldn't care if one of them did have cancer. Is that what therapy does? You hate your parents now? You hate me?"

"I don't hate anyone."

"Then what?"

I sighed. "Just tell me what's going on. Quit trying to psychoanalyze me."

"I can't come over?"

"No. And my phone is at fourteen percent, so talk fast."

He was quiet for a moment. "I'm worried someone is setting Mom up for a con."

"Who?"

"I don't know who. These con men, or in this case, women, target older people and…"

"You make her sound ancient. Sixty-two isn't old and addled."

He talked over me. "This woman has made friends with Mom."

"So?"

"She's a lot younger. Late thirties, early forties at the most."

"Get to the point."

"Mom doesn't know much about her. Just her first name, I think. She refused to give me her full name. Annie is all I got out of her. They meet all the time for coffee or wine. They go out to lunch."

"What's wrong with that?"

"There's something off about it."

"Why?"

"She's vague about how they met. She can't seem to explain what they have in common."

"Maybe they both like eating lunch in restaurants."

"That's not the basis of a friendship."

"How do you know?"

"We need to do something. Try to find out more about her."

"I don't see how you'll do that without talking to Mom, and it sounds like she's doing fine. Having a perfectly good time."

"That therapist is turning you against them. You don't even care. I don't like it. That's what therapy does. They start picking apart your life and blaming your parents and siblings for every little thing."

"I thought you wanted to talk about Mom getting conned?"

"I do."

"Then tell me."

"I just did."

"So that's it? Mom has a new friend, and they go to lunch. You don't know her last name and Mom can't explain why they're friends. Can you explain your friends?"

"Actually, I can. People from college. People who like to hike and cycle."

"Well Mom didn't go to college, and she doesn't cycle."

"That's not what I mean. There's something off about it. Can't you trust my judgment for once in your life?"

"When did I not trust your judgment?"

"You just don't. And now, I need you to."

I took a sip of wine. I held up the glass and moved it gently, watching the red sway from side to side, smearing up the insides of the glass. "I doubt she's being conned by someone she goes to lunch with. And you should maybe mind your own business. How about that?"

"You should be concerned about your inheritance. This woman could bleed them dry."

"So you aren't worried about Mom, you're worried about you."

He didn't say anything.

"I'm really tired, so I'm hanging up now. Plus, my phone is dying." I ended the call before he could say more. He was upset, hurt maybe, but so was I. My mother's social life was the furthest thing from my mind.

61

Ann

I struck gold.

I could have carried everything to its conclusion without knowing anything about Gemma beyond her relationship with David. But this was so much better. Easier, and faster to get where I wanted to go.

Knowledge of the gaping wound in Gemma's life made it so much easier to complete my therapeutic mirage for her. Knowing that her mother kept Gemma out of circulation and then whisked her newborn out of her arms made it easier to nudge Tamara toward the place where I wanted her. All of this eased my mind about what I was doing.

If you dig deep enough into anyone's life, there are wounds, things that dramatically shaped their lives, and not for the good. There are parental missteps that are sometimes horrific, and other times magnified in the cobwebs of memory into something horrific by childish interpretation. There are after-effects of torment by siblings and peers, the bully down the street and the mean girls in the bathroom at school. Everyone has a psyche that's ruptured in spots, covered with scar tissue, easily broken open, if you know how.

Being wounded did not justify Gemma's decision to seduce and start a love affair with my husband.

Besides, she was delusional, at least in the casual sense of the word. David had not told her the things she imagined. His interest in her was purely physical, and she'd fantasized it into the status of eternal, transcendent love.

I was justified in what I was doing. I was simply taking what had been given to me and shaping it in a way that righted things. I don't like to see undeserved suffering. I was sorry she had to suffer when she was a teenager. It marked her terribly, but now, she deserved to suffer. She'd almost destroyed my marriage, and if I wasn't such a resourceful person, she might have succeeded. If I weren't so deeply, hopelessly in love with David, she would have finished us.

The gods of retribution were smiling on me.

Of course, there probably aren't any gods of retribution, but I don't know that for certain. Getting even feels good. It's considered wrong. Any therapist will tell you it's extremely unhealthy. It's so frowned upon that pithy sayings have been crafted to help people resist that temptation — *Living well is the best revenge.*

Is it?

I needed her out of his life. She had to be inaccessible. I needed to punish her. She should not have been falling in love with a married man. She had no right to call my husband her soul mate. She barely knew him.

I sat on the window seat in our bedroom, reading a novel, looking out at the quiet street below. The window seat is my favorite spot. Our bedroom is and has always been a sanctuary for both of us. I've decorated it beautifully in sage and white, with touches of charcoal. We have a walk-in closet with mirrors inside and cubbies and hangers and drawers for every article of clothing. There's a built-in jewelry storage case and pegs for scarves. The master bathroom has a jacuzzi tub and a shower large enough for two. We've shared it many times. Especially recently. Those daily intimacies slipped for a while, a long while when we were disconnected, drifting away from each other.

Now, we shower together most mornings, unless David is traveling.

I do trust him when he travels. He's proven to me over and over that Gemma was a mistake. She's nothing to him. He was vulnerable, and she exploited that.

We talk like we used to at the beginning. Our sex life is incredible. It feels like we just met.

I still have occasional tremors of sadness, but they'll fade, over time. Often, I need a glass or two of wine before we make love — something to blot out thoughts of her. But that too will fade. I haven't just learned that from therapy. Life has taught me that.

Our bed is the central feature of the room — king-sized and soft and welcoming with its sage green duvet, topped with sage and gray and white pillow shams, embraced by a white ash frame. The walls are sparsely decorated with photographs from trips we've taken together — all scenery, no selfies or posed shots. We're the ones looking at the breathtaking vistas. It's as if the photographs are windows and the two of us are looking back in time and remembering what we felt as we stood and looked out on the ocean or a valley, a forest or a magnificent and iconic man-made structure.

We have two armchairs in an alcove where we sometimes read, as well as the window seat. I love the window seat. It has lots of pillows so I can lean back comfortably. The windows open out in summer, without screens, so the fresh scent of commingled flowers and trees and grass drift to where I'm sitting. I like to sip a glass of wine and read a book, or sometimes, just think.

As I looked down into the darkness, the street was empty. Then, a figure moved near the curbside tree of the house next door. I sat up suddenly, splashing wine on the leg of my jeans. Fortunately, it was white.

I turned my attention to the window, wondering why I'd been more interested in the wine on my oldest pair of jeans than in someone watching my house. The scenario, if not the size and shape of the figure, was just as I'd described in Gemma's notes. The figure wore a dark hoodie that was too large, nondescript jeans, and dark shoes. It was impossible to tell whether it was a male or female.

I put my wine glass on the windowsill, shifted to the right, and pressed my back against the wall, out of sight from anyone looking up at the window.

The figure made no move toward the house, and there was no suggestion of a weapon, but I was still unreasonably frightened. I wished David were at home, there to reassure me I wasn't seeing things, first of all.

How incredibly preposterous was it for the scene I'd made up in my notes about Gemma to play out in my life? It made me feel off balance and very afraid. I wasn't reading a Stephen King novel at that moment, but I'd read enough to know that things in this world are often not at all what they seem. Terrible things can happen, if you believe in that sort of thing.

I don't believe in those sorts of possibilities, but I couldn't steady my heartbeat. That unruly muscle thudded against my breastbone, so heavy and deliberate, I wondered how it managed to keep going without my constant attention under normal circumstances. My breathing was shallow. I felt rough and weak and vulnerable.

Vulnerability is the worst. I despise that feeling, and I was well on my way to righting the thing that had made me the most vulnerable of all.

It could be Gemma down there, if the person were a female. But that was too bizarre to allow my mind to entertain the idea. Setting her up in my notes like that, giving her the characteristics of a stalker, and having it become true was the stuff of fantasy films and stories. Tales of the supernatural.

The other possibility was a patient who was no longer seeing me. There were several who ended treatment with chips on their shoulders. Greg Calhoun, who came to loathe me as he uncovered the things in his own behavior that had driven his children away from him. He couldn't accept that it was his own flaws destroying his relationships, and so he was angry with me for daring to pose the question. There was Teresa Green who was convinced she'd been unjustly let go from her job, and again, blamed me for asking questions that suggested she might be anything less than the brilliant, incredibly capable person she saw in the mirror. There were others.

But all of them were several months to years in the past. So why now?

62

Gemma

Showing up at David's office complex a second time was risky, but it was the only way to reach him. I'd thought about it constantly, and there was no other choice. He seemed to have quit the gym where we'd met. I didn't know his usual habits beyond work. His wife had blocked me on his cell phone. I could buy a burner phone and text him, but he might not respond. Especially if his wife was around.

Seeing me was better anyway. Seeing me would remind him of what he'd had. Only a person's physical presence can do that. Passion is physical. Love is physical. No matter how beautifully written or spoken, love can't be contained in words. I read that Nicole Kidman and Keith Urban never communicate electronically. They say it makes their marriage blissful. I can see that. Texting and email are cold. You forget the look and the feel, the dimensions and the sound of the human being you love. Even the smell of them, the energy. It's just words, and words can get mixed up and misunderstood and misinterpreted. Just like his final text message to me hadn't been what he meant to say at all. Those words had been dictated. I recognized that now.

This time, I wouldn't be quite as conservative in what I wore. When he saw me, and I touched him, and his flesh remembered me, he would wake up. Right now, he was walking in a permanent dream, thinking he wanted to save his marriage. But saving a marriage doesn't make sense if there's no bonding of two souls. He'd already fallen in love with me, he couldn't go into the past and fall back in love with her. That just doesn't happen.

People can say all they want about affairs and cheating, but those things happen because you meet the right person. Sometimes, lots of times, the first one you married was a mistake. Too young. Too quick. Too predictable. You don't see that until you're older, or until you grow apart. So many times, it wasn't real love to begin with.

I wore the turquoise dress that I'd worn our first night in Hawaii. He would remember the dress because he'd remarked on the color and how good it looked on me. He would remember undoing the three small buttons in front, lowering the zipper on the side, watching while I pulled it off slowly because he thought it was too complicated to be able to manage himself.

I wore the white sweater he loved and flat, ballet slipper shoes to emphasize his height so he'd feel powerful.

Seated in my car, parked close to the building entrance, I sipped my latte. I pinched small pieces off my scone and nibbled on them while I stared at the glass doors. The early sun hit them, preventing me from seeing into the lobby or the area beyond.

It was ten minutes to eight. I'd thought David was usually at his office by seven-thirty or so. The parking lot was slowly filling with cars, giving me the sensation of sitting in a series of time-lapse photographs. Each time I turned to scan the lot, more slots were occupied.

By eight-forty, there were hardly any vacancies. David

still hadn't arrived. At least not that I'd seen. I was annoyed with myself for getting the scone. Maybe I'd looked down more than I realized, maybe I'd taken an extra minute to check for crumbs and missed him.

I opened the car door and got out. The sky was clear, but there was a stiff wind. I'd noticed the branches of trees moving, but didn't realize how cold it was. I tugged my sweater around me and walked toward the building, trying not to hunch my shoulders. I stood a few feet from the lobby doors and scanned the parking lot for David's silver sports car.

There were so many silver cars. I turned toward the lobby. I took a few steps, trying to think what to do. It was possible he was traveling, but now that I'd been sitting there all that time and was all dressed up, it was a waste to assume that was the case and leave.

Talking to the security person at the lobby desk might be difficult. They wouldn't be inclined to help someone who wasn't there on business. I didn't think I could just give my name and expect them to call him to the lobby.

I turned back.

A woman was crossing the lot, passing by the charging posts for electric cars. She walked quickly, her scuffed black boots clacking the pavement, her wool coat moving around her as if it were assisting her forward momentum, like a superhero's cape. I giggled then straightened my face. I relaxed my body and uncrossed my arms.

When she was a few feet away, I smiled and said *hi*.

She said *hi* and kept walking.

I took a few steps toward her. "Excuse me. Can I ask a favor?"

She stopped. "Are you lost?"

"Not really. I…"

Her brow furrowed above her sunglasses. "Do you work here?"

"I'm looking for David Graves."

"Check with reception." She started to walk around me.

I grabbed the edge of her coat.

She stopped abruptly as if I'd yanked her back, but I hadn't. "Sorry," I said.

"What are you doing?"

"I need to see him."

"I'm not sure about that, because if he wanted to see you, I think you'd have his cell number."

"Do you know him?"

"What do you want?"

"I need to see him."

"For what?" She glanced at my dress, her gaze pausing on the low-cut top. Her eyes swept down my legs to my feet, goosebumps probably showing themselves through the sheer covering of my nylons.

"It's personal."

She moved away. "Either give him a call or check in with security in the lobby." She turned and walked quickly toward the lobby doors, flung one open, and disappeared inside.

I stood there, my mouth partially open, trying to understand why she'd been so rude to me. A moment later, a man in a uniform came out through the same door. He walked toward me with his hand resting on the gun at his hip.

A gun! Who did they think I was?

"Can I help you, ma'am?"

"I'm looking for David Graves."

"If you don't have an appointment with Mr. Graves, you need to phone or send email and arrange to meet him."

"Can't someone…"

He put his hand on my arm. "There's no loitering here."

I moved away. "Don't touch me."

"If you don't have an appointment or a meeting at BlueCloud, I'm going to ask you to leave."

I stared at him. He was acting as if I were a criminal. A stalker that was here to do something violent. Why did he have his hand on his gun? "I just…" As I moved to the side, he stepped in front of me.

"If you don't leave the property, I'm going to have you cited."

"For what?"

"Trespassing."

"It's public property."

"It's not. The parking lot is owned by the BlueCloud company."

"Well, I…" My mind was a blank. Wiped clean by Dr. Wilcox, probably.

The guard took my arm and began moving me across the sidewalk toward the curb. I shook myself away from him and went to my car.

I sat there until lunchtime, hoping to see David, but I never did. I felt lost and defeated and empty.

63

Ann

David's to-die-for meal was my mother's lasagna. It featured homemade tomato sauce and buffalo mozzarella, expensive, but unbeatable in taste and texture. It was also made with tiny meatballs instead of ground beef. I tossed a green salad with balsamic vinaigrette to serve on the side. Not very original, but tasty and a perfect complement. There's a reason you often see green salad paired with pasta dishes.

I'd also bought a nice bottle of Cabernet and a loaf of sourdough bread.

We ate in the dining room.

Slightly more formal dinners were part of my effort to re-build what we'd had, to make every night a celebration, to really look at each other, our features altered and enhanced by the flicker of candles. The dining room had a way of reminding us by the sheer force of its presence — large, luxurious oak table, chairs, and breakfront, the picture window looking down the sloped backyard, the thick carpet beneath the table, framed by hardwood flooring, the elaborate iron light fixture over the table and the glass bowl of roses in the center, that it wasn't a place to absent-mindedly pick up our phones.

David sat at the head in the captain's chair, and I sat to his left. Not like Judas Iscariot, although that thought passed through my mind. I would never betray David in the way he'd betrayed me. I knew he was eaten up by regret. I was done punishing him with an icy exterior. I loved him more than I could put into words. I wanted everything to be the same. Better than the same.

Knowing he'd had sex with another woman, that for a while he'd become obsessed with her, filled me with fear that we weren't soul mates after all. I was terrified that once a fracture like that happened, we could never be soul mates. But I refused to let that thought take root. If we were soul mates before, then we were now, and nothing could shatter that connection.

After listening to David and Gemma in the Four Seasons, I brooded for weeks, trying to decide how I would confront him. At first, I wanted to splash my vitriol all over him, like projectile vomiting that made him equally sick. It was what he deserved. I didn't want to wait, I couldn't bear the thought of him touching her one more time. Then what was I waiting for? I was scared, I think. Afraid of how badly things might break. Afraid, maybe, that he might choose her over me.

And then, he came to me. It's part of what makes me know there's hope. Coming to me means we still have, buried deep, the incredible love that made every facet of my life shimmer.

We'd been sitting on the back porch drinking martinis. It was hot inside the house and out. The ice-cold martinis helped ease the discomfort of bodies sticky with sweat. I took a sip of my drink. Like nothing else, a martini dulled the relentless pain, the indecision about how and when I should tell David I knew what he'd done.

Were our lives cracked beyond repair?

He picked up his drink. He cleared his throat. He took a long swallow and balanced the glass on the fingertips of both hands. "I have something to tell you."

My hands shook. The gin and vermouth wobbled in the glass as if an earthquake were rumbling through the fault line twenty miles from our home. I placed my glass on the table between us.

"I fucked up," he said. "Really bad. I'm so..." He inhaled sharply, "...sorry." His voice was low and rough. He kept his gaze fixed on the trees, their branches at eye level at the bottom of our sloped yard, lining the creek that had been nothing but an empty bed during six years of drought. After drought conditions eased, a narrow stream of water ran through the creek, even in summer. The sound of it was refreshing when the air was hot and still.

I can't remember the words he used that night. I've blotted them out. It's unnerving that I can't remember. I feel as if a small piece of brain matter was severed. Even knowing what he would tell me, hearing it was beyond painful. He lashed himself with his own words — *so stupid...almost destroyed the best thing that ever happened to him...* That part brought me up short. He seemed confident he'd only come close. It was comforting and infuriating in a single word. *Almost.*

Later, he would try to explain why. But not that night. I didn't ask, and he didn't offer.

He wept, which was the truest part of what he said. Until that day, I'd never seen a tear come out of his eyes.

Now, as we ate lasagna, he sipped his wine quickly, topping off the glass every five minutes. I didn't like it that he was racing through the bottle of expensive wine. Not that we couldn't afford it, but I wanted to savor it, I wanted to linger over it throughout the evening.

"Slow down," I said.

He nudged his glass away from his plate. "Something happened."

His tone caused a tremor to run through the center of my body. I ate a noodle wrapped around ricotta cheese and a single tiny meatball, chewing slowly.

"Gemma showed up at my office again."

I let out a slow breath and swallowed my food, tasting the hint of basil and the rich tomato flavor. "What did she want this time?" She wanted him, of course. But I was curious what she'd said. How he'd responded.

"I didn't see her."

I looked down at my plate, hiding my smile. He touched my hand, squeezing his warm fingers around my cold ones.

"She was harassing Karen Latimer. You know, the one in market analytics who works for…"

"Yes, I know who you mean."

"Karen asked the Security staff to talk to her."

"What did they do?"

"She was escorted to her car. Apparently, she sat there for a few hours before she finally left."

I stabbed another meatball. "I think you should get a restraining order."

"That's not necessary."

"Your call." I popped the meatball into my mouth.

He shifted in his chair and leaned across the table. He tucked my hair behind my ear. "I'm so sorry." He gently fingered my earlobe.

I leaned toward him and kissed him. He pulled my head closer and kissed me until I tasted the faint touch of salt in the tear that ran down his cheek.

We would be okay. I was sure of it. We needed time. Each word we spoke, each touch and kiss, and every night spent sleeping beside each other would bind us together again. All the shared experiences, even the unpleasant ones, would cement our bond. What we had would be rebuilt over hundreds of moments until nothing could ever break us apart.

Leonard Cohen, musician and poet, wrote — *There's a crack in everything, that's how the light gets in.*

I clung to that belief.

64

Gemma

Something about Dr. Wilcox's office felt different. I settled into my chair and took a deep breath. I couldn't pinpoint whether the temperature was lower or higher than usual, or there was an unfamiliar aroma just beneath the surface, or there was something in the doctor's mood that suggested a change.

She looked the same — dark hair combed smooth like a silk curtain, legs crossed at her ankles, expensive boots, a mid-calf-length flowing skirt the same dark brown as her boots. The skirt looked silky, yet thick and warm at the same time. A diamond rested on her skin and bone in the scooped out oval of her pale yellow cashmere sweater. I'd never seen her wear expensive jewelry, so maybe that was the difference. Maybe she carried herself differently because of the fragile chain and the obvious cost of the stone.

"I have a suggestion," she said.

I folded my hands in my lap, wondering whether her eager suggestion was the difference I sensed. I wanted to cross my arms, but that would communicate hostility or resistance, and she would call me on it and then we'd have to discuss why I had those feelings. There wasn't a single move I could make, not a word I could speak without second-guessing myself, wondering what it would lead to, in what new direction it would send her thoughts. In turn, her constantly moving thoughts would twist mine into a thick mass that threatened to choke out my life.

Sometimes I wondered whether she was trying to confuse me, deliberately changing the subject to make me unsure about what I was thinking. It might be a con to keep me in therapy longer. I knew that's what Geoff would say. Geoff thinks everything is a con. I smiled, thinking about him arguing with me, his eyes steely and unwavering.

"What are you smiling at?"

"Nothing." I adjusted my hands, lacing my fingers in the opposite pattern, my right thumb in front of my left.

"So, my suggestion...I think it would be a good idea for you to confront your parents about what happened with your daughter. About the whole situation."

"I don't know..."

"The reason your recent breakup was so disproportionately painful was because it compounded other losses in your life."

"I'm not sure that's true."

She nodded carefully, as if she were considering my words. She wasn't. I could see her brow, puzzling over how to move to the next thing she wanted to say. "David was a married man. On some level..."

"I didn't know that when we got together."

"On *some* level, you knew that, and you knew nothing would come of it. Yet, you poured your entire self into him. I suspect that unhealthy behavior had its beginning when Aidan was removed from your life, followed so soon by the loss of your daughter. Two extremely traumatic experiences for which you *believed* you had no recourse."

Obviously, it was traumatic, but if I agreed, it would sound as if I were agreeing with everything she'd said. Why was she talking so much? Telling me what to do? This wasn't the way it was supposed to work.

"Let's assume I'm correct. Work with me for a minute."

I sighed, deep inside where she couldn't see or hear.

"I believe you wanted to have a tragic end to your love affair. It's become a pattern for you."

That actually made sense in some messed up way. But it didn't make me stop loving David. And it didn't mean we weren't soul mates. That was the part she kept missing. This wasn't just any old love affair. It was different. Transcendent.

"Even if you question my assessment, I think it would be good to speak to your parents. This has affected all your relationships, especially your relationship with them and your brother, for your entire adult life."

"Will talking to them make the pain go away? We never talk about the pain. I've been seeing you all this time, and I still feel so..." My voice seemed to be sucked inside of me. I unclasped and fluttered my hands, trying to keep my composure.

"It will empower you. That's what you need more than anything. Empowerment will enable you to view emotional pain from a new perspective."

I rubbed my palms on my thighs. "Maybe."

"Maybe is not an empowering word." She smiled, and I wasn't sure whether that was a joke meant to lighten my mood or she seriously meant I shouldn't use that word if I wanted to be empowered.

"Your parents need to know what those events did to you. And you need to experience and express your grief. And yes, your rage. You've never done that as far as I can see."

I wondered whether telling my parents how much I'd suffered would actually help me with David. It didn't make sense…but she said I needed to heal myself. And David said I was needy. Maybe if I had the courage to tell them what they'd done, I would be a stronger person. David would feel my strength, he'd see it in the way I held myself, he'd hear it in my voice. I saw that in Dr. Wilcox. She was very strong, you could feel it even when she wasn't speaking.

"I'd like you to consider it part of your therapy. I think you'll be surprised about how affirming it is. Confrontation. Resolution."

I nodded. "Do I seem needy?"

"Why do you ask?"

"That's what David said." My throat spasmed as I spoke, but it felt good to be telling her. At the same time, her eyes grew cold. She was judging me. I sensed it as if she'd laughed right in my face.

She coughed softly. She took a drink of water and wrote something in her notebook. "You do give that impression. And I think resolving, or at least starting the process toward asking your parents to own what they did to you will help you gain strength. And thus, you'll be less needy."

I nodded. "I'll think about it."

"You'll feel stronger if you make a decision right now. The act of making that choice is empowering in itself." She pulled open the drawer in the table beside her. "I know it's not easy. And I know you're opposed to medication…" She pulled out a tiny clear plastic bag with a single blue capsule inside. "It's Valium, just a half dose. It will help you remain calm and clear-headed when you talk to them."

She stood and crossed the space between us. She picked up my hand. I felt my fingers uncurl with a will of their own. She placed the plastic bag on my palm and returned to her chair.

"I really hope you'll do this, Gemma. I think you'll be shocked at the impact it has on your life."

She smiled, and it felt genuine and non-judging.

65

Ann

The TV was playing nineties music videos while David and I sat beside each other on the sofa. He was reading a legal thriller, and I was reviewing notes from a patient who stopped therapy a year ago and had now decided to return. I was pleased he'd realized he'd run away in fear.

Glen was a man who had cared for both his ailing parents for close to five years. He battled intense resentment when their estate was split equally between him and his sister. The sister lived in the UK and hadn't visited for three years before their deaths and didn't return home for their funerals, which enraged him.

There were deeper issues. I felt that he'd wanted to show his sister up, that most of his life he'd wanted his parents to prefer him over her. That desire led to his willingness to be their caregiver. He harbored lifelong animosity toward his sister. He had an over-developed and infantile need for parental approval, even after their deaths.

David picked up the remote and lowered the volume on the music. "Hard to concentrate," he said.

I nodded. I preferred no music at all when I was reading for escape. David liked background sound at all times. He was almost anxious when confronted with a silent house. The only time he enjoyed complete silence was when we were hiking or lying on a beach.

I read two more pages.

As I turned the last page of notes from Glen's final session, there was a tap on the window, a pebble hitting glass. I closed the notebook, keeping my finger in the spot. I glanced at the side window, trying to figure out where the sound had come from.

David placed his tablet beside him on the couch. "Did you hear that?"

There was another tap on the glass, clearly coming from the side window.

He stood and crossed the room, reaching toward the drapes.

"Don't open them," I said.

He turned. "I need to check."

"I haven't told you…I've seen someone out there. Watching the house."

"When?"

"The last time you were in Chicago."

"Why didn't you tell me?"

"It seemed like nothing."

"What happened?"

"There was someone standing out there, looking up at the second floor. From the sidewalk near the Talese's plum tree."

He reached for the drapes again.

"Don't open them."

"I need to see what's going on."

"What if…"

"What if, what?" He parted the drapes a few inches. He peered through the gap, not moving for several seconds. "I don't see anyone."

"I suppose that's good."

"I should have checked right away. Was it a man or woman?"

"I couldn't tell. The person was wearing a hoodie and was kind of hunched over. Plus, I was upstairs looking down, so the angle made it difficult."

He let the drapes fall closed. "We need to make sure we don't forget to set the alarm."

I nodded. Knowing David had heard the sound made it better because I didn't feel I was imagining something. Or that other thought that wouldn't leave me alone — that my lies about Gemma's therapy had conjured up some shadow persona who was now stalking me.

This was the third time, which made it more real. The first time was easily explained away as an unusual echo. The second was more difficult, but not impossible to explain — a misreading of the intent, personalizing something random, innocent loitering. Now, there was no avoiding it.

Was this person out to frighten me, or did he want more? He? Or she? I noted how my brain easily slid into assuming the individual was male. Was that the effect of socialization that made my mind default to physical threats more often coming from men? Or had my subconscious identified the person as male, even though my conscious mind felt the figure had a lot of ambiguity?

Even with only one page left in my notes, I found I couldn't return to them. The words ran together on the page — a mass of unruly lines, making me think of nerves running through the brain, although those follow a pattern.

David remained by the window, his finger in the slit

between the panels of fabric, peering out every few minutes. So far, he hadn't indicated seeing anyone. Would he tell me? Was he stepping into the male protective stance, determined to keep me calm by keeping me ignorant?

"Can you see him? Or her?"

He shook his head.

"It was probably nothing," I said.

"Someone threw stones at our window, it wasn't nothing. I'm worried it's…"

"Come sit down," I said.

"In a minute. Go check the alarm."

"I doubt anyone wants to break in. They can see we're home."

"Just check it. You don't know. It's strange behavior for someone staking out a house for burglary. Those stones were meant to get our attention."

"Why?"

"I don't know."

I went into the hallway and re-entered the code to set the alarm. It beeped once. I went to the kitchen and mixed two martinis. When I returned to the living room, David was standing with his back to me, his face pressed against the glass as he peered out at our lifeless street. Except for the periodic neighbor coming home after a dinner out, or from a business trip, there was next to no traffic at night. He wouldn't see anything.

I placed the tray on the table and picked up my drink. I took a small sip. It was sharp — just what I needed. The strong, cold alcohol burned through my blood vessels and made everything untwist. I settled on the sofa.

A few minutes later, David joined me. We touched the

edges of our glasses together, but said nothing by way of a toast. He returned to his novel, and I sat staring at the unmoving drapes, wondering who was out there. I took a sip of my martini.

66

Gemma

Dr. Wilcox's phone call caught me at a bad time. I was
lying in bed at nine-thirty on Saturday morning. On Monday I
would have to return to teaching, everything in my life still
unresolved. The night before I'd consumed an entire bottle
of Chardonnay, drinking it with a slice from the small cheese
and onion pizza I'd had delivered.

When I saw Dr. Wilcox's name come up on the screen, I
sat up quickly. The move was so sudden, my vision clouded
for a moment and my brain seemed to float freely inside of
my skull. I pressed my fingers across the top of my scalp and
ran them through my hair in a poor imitation of combing it,
as if I expected her to see me when I answered the phone.
My fingers came away slightly oily and damp with
perspiration.

I pressed my moist thumb on the button. The screen
refused to respond. I pressed again and said *hello*.

"I'm calling with some encouragement for you," she
said.

There was no introduction, no mention of our last
session or what topic she was referring to, although I knew.

"I wanted to remind you what we talked about."

I almost laughed at the *we*. She'd done the talking. I'd
listened and tried to figure out how yelling at my parents for

something that happened over fifteen years ago was going to help me win back the man I loved. But I had nothing else to do. I had no other ideas. I'd lain awake until past one o'clock trying to think of a way to remind David of what we had, of how he felt about me. I came up with nothing.

How would talking to my parents help that? Yes, he might see me as stronger and more confident, less *needy*... how I hated that word. It was so pathetic. So...loser-like.

But I *still* had to *see* him for him to recognize that. I *still* had to find a way to make him pay attention to me.

If nothing else, talking to my parents would get me out of bed. It would force me to wash and style my hair. It would force me to not have two glasses of wine for lunch with my reheated pizza. It might make me feel better to purge all this gunk swimming around in my head.

And Dr. Wilcox would be proud of me. In fact, maybe she would give me ideas about David after I did what she'd told me to do. Or maybe talking to my parents would stir up my brain and I'd dream of an idea.

She broke in with a sharp, motherly-sounding tone. "Are you listening to me?"

"Yes."

"What are you thinking about?"

"I'm surprised you called."

"I want to see you get what you deserve." She laughed. "Baby steps, right?"

"Yes. It's a good idea. I'll drop by to see them today. Thanks for pushing me."

67

Gemma

Two hours later I'd showered and washed my hair with apple-scented shampoo and conditioned it with the aroma of almonds. I'd dried it to a silky drape and dressed in my best jeans and a V-neck sweater that showed a bit of cleavage. A subtle message to my mother that I was an adult woman!

I scrambled two egg whites with nothing but pepper for seasoning. I ate a piece of unbuttered whole grain toast and drank two cups of black coffee. I was still hungry, so I ate half an out-of-season peach that was too hard, but surprisingly sweet. I filled a small glass with water and swallowed the capsule Dr. Wilcox had given me. If it turned out to be stronger than she said, I had the coffee to counter any potential drowsiness.

I felt a tremor of shame that I couldn't face this without chemical support, but neither did I want to lose control and behave like a child. Calmness and clarity were my goals.

Geoff's car wasn't parked out front. He usually went cycling on Saturdays, but it was still a relief to see he hadn't changed his routine. I couldn't imagine this would go well if he began inserting opinions about therapists blaming parents for everything. I honestly didn't think that was true. Sure, therapy focuses on the past, but there's a good reason for that. Parents make mistakes and kids take those early experiences with unfiltered intensity from these god-like creatures ruling their lives. That's what Dr. Wilcox said.

And in my case, my parents really had screwed up. My mother had no right to cut Aidan out of my life. She was beyond cruel, taking my daughter the way she had, giving away my baby like she was dropping off a pair of out-of-style shoes at the thrift store. I felt sick thinking about it. Tears rushed to my eyes, and my throat closed as if it needed to do something drastic in order to keep all the bile in the pit of my stomach.

Feeling those things made me realize that Dr. Wilcox was right. I'd never really grieved. I'd never looked with clear eyes at the rage I felt. At the horrendous loss of someone I loved with all my heart. I buried it all and went off to college, pretending to be a normal girl. A part of my life, a huge part, was gone forever and there was nothing I could do about it. All the while, my mother acted as if she were helping me and I should be grateful! She acted as if it was nothing.

It was everything.

I got out of the car. The branches of the bare trees looked sharp — claws reaching into the sky. The sky itself was a flat sheet of gray, but at the same time, I felt as if I could see through the strands of vapor that had now taken on the appearance of distinct threads woven together. I giggled.

Then, I laughed out loud at my giggle.

Why was I giggling about a sky thick and damp with depressing cloud cover? Why was I giggling at all? This was serious. I was furious and hurt. I tried to remember how I'd felt just a few moments earlier, about my daughter, and my mother, but the feeling had shattered like glass. All I saw inside of me were tiny crystals, the pain and rage broken into a million pieces that were now melting like individual snowflakes.

I giggled again. I bit the inside of my cheek to make myself stop. I shoved my hands into my pockets and walked toward the house. When I reached the front porch, I stood there for a moment, unsure what I was supposed to do. How could I ring the bell with my hands in my pockets?! I laughed out loud at the perplexing problem.

I pulled out my hand and pounded on the door.

My father answered while I was still hammering. "What a nice surprise." He grinned and stepped back so I could enter. "I'll get your mother. She's making Geoff's bed."

I giggled.

He rolled his eyes, assuming that he and I were sharing a joke at their expense, but I had no idea why I was giggling. It wasn't about my mother treating Geoff like a child. I couldn't seem to stop the laughter. Maybe it was nerves. I was scared to confront them. I'd never done anything like that. Even as a thirty-four-year-old woman, I still behaved as if they were the grownups and I was the little girl. As a teenager, I'd thrown fits and cried, but I'd never talked to them rationally and made them see what they'd done to me.

They told me what was up, not vice versa.

We went into the living room, and I wedged myself into the corner of the couch.

"Do you want coffee? Or soda?"

My heart thumped too fast, slamming against my breastbone, reminding me of the two cups of caffeine I'd already had. "Just water."

He shrugged and left, calling my mother's name as he

moved toward the kitchen.

When the three of us were seated, I cleared my throat. My parents sipped their reheated coffee that stank like something had died, even though their mugs were far from where I sat, too far for me to truly smell the contents. I cleared my throat again. "I need to talk to you."

My mother pressed her hands together in front of her heart. "Oh no."

"Why do you say that?"

"You sound upset. I hope nothing worse has happened with that...man. I hope he hasn't done something to you."

I giggled. The colors of the room made my eyes hurt. The soft blues and grays were suddenly too bright. I closed my eyes. The smell of stale coffee filled my nasal passages as if the dead thing was decaying inside my sinuses. I opened my eyes. What was wrong with me? I'd never taken Valium, but surely half a dose...

My father looked worried. "Yes?"

"What?" My eyeballs jittered. I felt them moving like a doll's eyes, snapping between his face and hers, my lids clicking up and down as if they were made of plastic.

"You said we owe you an apology....?"

I didn't recall saying that, didn't recall speaking. I picked up my glass and took a few sips of water. I needed to blot out the strange colors and smells assaulting my brain. I needed to focus. I needed to tell them what I had to say before Geoff came home. I laughed.

My father leaned forward and put his mug on a coaster. "Are you all right, Gemma?"

"Are you?"

His forehead wrinkled.

I lurched to my feet. "You had no right to steal my baby and throw her away!" I picked up my glass of water and hurled it at my mother. It crashed against the wall to the left of her head, splashing water on the light gray paint.

"Gemma!" In a moment, my father was across the room. He grabbed my wrist. I tried to wrench away from him, but he wrapped both arms around me, pinning my arms to my sides. "What's wrong, honey?"

Someone was screaming. A loud cry, like the wail of a fatally wounded animal.

"Calm down. It's okay. Everything will be okay," he said.

The screaming continued. I wanted to put my fingers in my ears, but I couldn't move my arms. I wriggled inside his embrace, but he was much stronger.

"Shh. Shh," he said.

I looked at my mother. Her lips were pressed tightly together. Who was screaming?

I closed my eyes and saw a swirl of colors as if the scream had turned into vivid orange and red, a tornado of fire behind my eyelids. The horrific sound faded. I gasped for air.

My father's embrace remained solid. "What's the matter with you?"

"It's the therapy," my mother said. Her voice was loud as if she was standing right beside me. "This is what happens. It distorts your mind. The mind is very sensitive, and it's easy to cause a lot of damage."

"It's not the fucking therapy!" My voice was hard and cold, but I sounded calm, at least in my own ears. "Let go of me."

My father released his grip. "Can you get control of

yourself? I don't want any more displays like that," he said. "We're adults. We can discuss this like adults. Did we make some mistakes? Possibly, but…"

I flopped onto the couch. I stared at the wall beside my mother. A shard of glass was embedded in an oil painting depicting the grand canyon. Water dripped from the frame. The bottom of the glass sat on the floor, jagged edges pointing up.

"*Possibly? Mistakes?*" I laughed, the sound like something electronic and tinged with madness. "You cut me off from Aidan. You had no right to tear my life apart like that. You ripped my daughter out of my arms. I never got to hold her or love her or watch her grow up. I had no say in what happened to my baby. And I can never, ever…*Ever* get her back."

My voice was thin and high-pitched, but I was too tired to scream. Too empty. My muscles were limp and incapable of lifting my bones off the couch.

My father sat beside me and patted my shoulder. "It was an upsetting time for all of us. But the child is better off. We're all better off."

I watched as my parents' heads shrank to the size of peas. I heard sounds coming from them that were like the Munchkins in the Wizard of Oz, the voices produced by helium-filled lungs. Tears ran down my face. They grew hotter and thicker. Soon, they were so hot they were cutting crevices in my skin.

I pressed my hands against my face, but it didn't stop the liquid from slicing deeper, cutting my flesh. I jumped up and ran into the kitchen. I yanked open the freezer door and pressed my cheek against a frozen chicken.

A moment later, I felt my father's hands grasp my upper arms. He pulled me away from the comfort of the cold meat, and I felt myself collapse onto the floor.

68

Ann

I called Tamara on Saturday afternoon at four o'clock. By that time, I was fairly certain Gemma would have visited them. If Gemma had any trust in her therapist, she'd taken the blue capsule containing a small dose of LSD. Her parents didn't appear to have a lot of street smarts. It would never enter their minds that their daughter was under the influence of a controlled substance. No matter how she'd reacted to the drug, her behavior would have been significantly out of the ordinary. Whether she'd been incoherent and seemed disturbed, or she'd had laughing fits, or gone completely mad, I would be one step closer to maneuvering them toward the next phase.

Their help was required in getting Gemma committed to a mental health facility. It wasn't impossible for a therapist to do this without family support, but so much easier if I had it.

When Tamara answered the phone, I asked whether she could talk in private.

"I suppose. I don't know. It's been a rough day." Her voice broke.

"What's wrong?"

She spoke in a whisper, almost inaudible. "Gemma. I don't know...something's not right with her."

"Oh, no. What can I do to help?"

"Nothing, I don't think." She gasped. "I have no idea what to do."

"Is anyone listening to you now?"

"I don't know."

"Can you go somewhere private so we can talk?"

She sighed. "I need to lie down anyway."

Her voice became muffled. I heard her speak to someone...*going to lie down...don't feel well...too much.* There were a few minutes of silence. I heard a door close, followed by vague sounds of movement.

"I'm here," she said.

"What happened?"

"She..." Tamara groaned. "She threw a fit or had a breakdown...or something. Oh God, what's happening? I don't know what to do!"

"I might be able to help, if you'll let me."

"What can you do? We're all helpless here. She's coming apart. She's digging up all kinds of bad things from the past. I think it's her counseling. It's not helping her at all, but she refuses to listen. To me. To her brother...her father. We've tried."

"I have something to tell you. I hope you'll give me the benefit of the doubt. I hope you'll listen before you react."

She sighed. "What are you talking about? I'm just beside myself. I'm her mother. I should be able to make her feel better. It's my job to take care of her. This is so, so..."

"Tamara, can you listen to me for a minute?"

"What is it?"

"I haven't been completely honest with you. But..."

She started to speak.

I cut her off. "I felt I had to be careful, because of

ethical requirements."

"What are you talking about?"

"Let me finish...I didn't adhere perfectly to my ethics, but because I have so much concern for Gemma, as I've told you...I...I'm deeply concerned about her state of mind."

"So am I!"

"My name is Ann Wilcox. Dr. Ann Wilcox. I'm Gemma's therapist, and I..."

"What? What are you saying?"

"I'm trying to help her..."

"You aren't a schoolteacher?"

"No."

Her voice rose. "You lied to me? You're the one causing all of this!"

"Please don't let anyone hear you. Not until I explain. Please let me explain."

"Explain what? You misrepresented yourself. Why am I even talking to you?"

"Please. Don't hang up. You're an excellent mother. One of the best. I know how deeply you love her. You would do anything for your daughter, I know that. I can tell from the things Gemma has told me, you were...you *are* an amazing mother."

"Thank you. I don't feel like that right now."

"You are. She just needs help."

"Yes. She does. Why did you lie to me?"

"I didn't have her explicit permission to be in touch with you. But I've been so concerned that she'll try to hurt herself, or someone else, I felt I had to do what was right. The rules don't always conform to what's right, don't you agree?"

"I suppose...yes, sometimes that's true."

"I'm very dedicated to my patients. I have a great deal of affection for Gemma, and I want to help her get the care she deserves."

"What's wrong with her? Why is this happening? You weren't here. You didn't see how she was."

"Can you tell me about it?"

She described in detail the fit Gemma had thrown, screaming like a *maniac* about the *illegitimate* child she'd given birth to. I wondered how much was accurate and how much was embellished by Tamara's shock, and by her defensiveness, but I got the general picture. The LSD had performed admirably.

When she was finished speaking, I let silence linger between us. She didn't try to break it. I wondered what she was thinking about, but this wasn't a therapy session. I stifled my instinct, my habit, to ask.

After a moment, I coughed softly. "I think Gemma would benefit from being in a facility where she would get full-time therapy and care. Not permanently, but for some time. Several weeks, at least. We'd have to see…"

"What kind of facility? An asylum? A mental hospital?" She began to whimper. "That sounds horrible."

"It would be nice. Not what you're picturing. Not the gothic, horror-show image. Not a *mental* hospital. Don't even think that word. It would have a spa-like atmosphere. It would be lovely, I promise."

This wasn't entirely true, but once Tamara bought into the idea, it would be easier to paint the place I had in mind with a generous brush. It did have a beautiful lobby and very nice gardens, and the rooms, although utilitarian, were warm and, for the most part, not overly institutional.

"I don't want her locked up. Absolutely not."

"Tamara. Please listen to me. I'm very concerned about the possibility she might harm herself, or someone else. I'm speaking as a professional."

"I…"

"Why don't you talk to your husband," I said. "I'm sure he's equally concerned. He probably feels helpless. Men have more trouble when they feel helpless, so be gentle with him. Gentle, but firm."

"He's very upset."

"I can imagine."

"And her brother. Geoff."

"I don't think you need to bring him into it."

"He loves his sister. He won't…"

"Talk to your husband first. This is a decision for you and him, not your son. I don't mean to be harsh. I just think her parents are the best ones to decide what's in her interest. You won't let emotions cloud your thinking. What I mean is emotional baggage, overemphasis on Gemma's feelings. It's time for people who love her to be strong and do what's best for her, without being driven by emotion."

"Maybe you're right." She sighed. She sounded calm, resigned.

If I wasn't reading too much into it, if it wasn't wishful thinking, I believe her sigh sounded appreciative. She was glad to hand off the decision, the responsibility, to someone else. She was convincing herself that she was simply following medical guidance.

69

Gemma

When I woke, it was dark. I couldn't make out any shapes in the room where I lay under a thick comforter. I wore my jeans, but my belt had been removed. My feet were bare, and I was wearing the sweater I'd worn to my parents' on Saturday morning.

What day was it? I felt I'd been asleep for days. Strange images and memories flickered under a dense layer of fog... dreams that were long and complex, laced with horror, but impossible for me to see clearly.

I certainly wasn't in my own bed. I moved my hand from under the pillow and slid it to the side of the mattress. It was a single, not my own queen-sized bed.

I pulled myself up to a sitting position and felt around for a bedside table. I took a deep breath. The smell of the room was familiar, but I couldn't place it, the familiarity on the edge of my mind, just out of reach. I'd been here before. Maybe a long time ago. For half a second, I hoped I was in the hotel with David, but then I remembered the single bed.

My hand found a table and the base of a lamp. My fingers crept up until I found a switch and turned it on.

The guest room at my parents' home. A single bed. As if my mother never expected me to be married, or have a man in my life at all. She never thought I would sleep beside a man in this room that she'd decorated when they moved into this house while I was away at college.

I threw back the covers and sat up, placing my feet on the floor. I felt light-headed and very cold. Under the covers I'd been perspiring, but now a chill ran through me in spite of my comfortable clothes. My lips were like putty. My eyes were so dry I felt my eyelids scrape across my eyeballs. I was exhausted, even though I thought I'd slept for an entire day, maybe more.

I laid back down, hoping the dizziness would fade. After a few minutes, thirst overcame the lightheadedness. I got up slowly and went to the door. I opened it and put my hand on the doorframe to steady myself. I stepped into the hallway. The house was utterly dark and silent.

I made my way to the kitchen. The counters were spotless, the sink polished. It smelled faintly of garlic and something else. Tomato sauce, maybe. The clock on the microwave read twelve-fifteen. I filled a glass with water. As I stood near the door and looked out onto the dark backyard, events from the previous morning began to surface in my mind. There were vague images of me crying, shouting, laughed like I'd lost my mind. The images were more like a dream than something I'd actually experienced, and yet, I had the impression they were real.

What had happened to me? I supposed it was a subject for therapy. Dr. Wilcox would explain that repressed grief had caused some kind of temporary fracture in my brain. It seemed like more than that, but I was too tired and too disoriented to think about it.

I walked back down the hall and stopped outside of Geoff's bedroom. I tapped my fingernails on the door. A grunt came from inside the room. I turned the knob and went in. A nightlight glowed from the corner near his closet door.

He lay on his back in his twin bed.

I closed the door softly behind me. "Are you awake?"

"Mmf. I am now. What's up?"

"What happened?" I took a sip of water and went to his bed. I sat down near his knees.

Geoff pulled himself into a sitting position. He reached to turn on the light.

"No," I said. "The nightlight's enough. It's kind of cute. I'm surprised it's not a choo-choo train." I laughed softly.

"I don't like the dark. Lots of people use nightlights."

I wasn't sure about that, but I said nothing. "What happened? I've been asleep for ages. It feels like days."

"It sounds like you threw a fit about something. Then you passed out."

"Did they tell you that?"

"You mean Mom and Dad? Yes."

I sipped more water. Geoff never knew about my baby. When we moved to Fresno, Geoff stayed behind to finish high school. I didn't see him for over six months. My parents went to visit him and left me at home. At some point, he and I must have discussed what was going on, we talked about everything, but for whatever reason, I have no recollection of talking to him at all from the time we moved to Fresno until just before I went away to college. You'd think a guy that age would figure out something was up, but I suppose he was lost in his own world.

During the months she had me isolated from everyone I knew, my mother fed me a constant diet of chastisement for my slutty behavior, for the terrible thing I'd done creating a child no one wanted. She assured me that my choices were to stay home and do as she said, or find myself on the street. During those last months, she only allowed my father into my room once. He patted my hand, couldn't look me in the eye, and mumbled a bunch of nonsense about how he should have done better. My mother brought meals to my room on a tray. It's not too dramatic to say I felt like her prisoner.

Geoff leaned up on his elbow. "Mom was holed up in her room again, talking on the phone to her *friend*." He spoke softly to mimic the volume of her voice. "Whispering, actually."

"Don't get off on that again. Please."

"I really think she's being conned, a long con. And I really think you should be more worried."

After what I'd been through, I cared even less. My mother could take care of herself. She was a tough lady. If she couldn't, it wasn't my problem.

"I'm really upset about it," he said.

"Because she whispers on the phone? Maybe she wants to keep her life private from her thirty-three-year-old son who's still living at home like a little kid. Turning on his nightlight every night, letting mommy make his bed and wash his undies."

"Stop it. That's not how it is."

"It sure looks like that to me."

"If she gets taken by a con, if both of them do, we'll have to pick up the pieces. Do you want them living with you?"

"You're paranoid. That's not what's going on. She has a friend. That's all."

"Then why is she whispering?"

"I just told you."

"It's more than that."

"Maybe you're reading into it because you're finally remembering how she whispered about you on the phone. You were embarrassed that she told everyone she knew how worried she was about your *perversion*. You blocked it out, and now Mom talking on the phone sends you into a subconscious frenzy of shame and panic."

"Don't spout that psychology bullshit at me."

"Psychology isn't bullshit. And what I said makes sense."

"No it doesn't." He punched his pillow and pulled it lower behind his back. "I'm tired. Did you want something?"

I stood and drank the rest of my water. I placed the glass on his dresser and went to the door.

"Take your glass."

"You can carry a glass to the kitchen and put it in the dishwasher like a big boy." I giggled. The sound of my laughter carried me back to that morning. The constant giggle that had erupted out of nowhere.

I opened the door and went out.

"Take your damn glass."

I closed the door and returned to the guest room. I crawled into bed and pulled the covers up to my neck. I closed my eyes and thought about our childhood.

What my mother wanted were children that remained in her care, needing her forever. She wanted me to take ballet lessons and perform in recitals where she could apply makeup to my soft, young face, and comb my hair and twist it into a tidy bun. She wanted to clap for me and take photographs, some with her in them, some with me and my brother, me and both my parents. But she didn't want me to be an adult performer. She did not want me living in New York City or somewhere in Europe, outside of her control, doing things she knew nothing about. She didn't want me working myself hard, taking the beating that a career in ballet gives to a woman's body.

She definitely did not want Geoff masturbating. The horror in her voice when she talked to her friends was palpable. He might become a man. He would not be her baby boy. With him, she'd won, in a way. Achieved her dream. He lived under her roof and ate her food. She sorted his soiled clothes and dusted his bedroom. He needed her. He wrote his blogs and felt like he worked, deluding himself that the situation was temporary.

She wanted children forever so she could be a mother forever. A woman with grown children isn't needed any longer. She becomes a caricature, the butt of jokes about overbearing women who fuss over their adult children's physical and emotional needs.

My father pretended not to notice. He was lost in his history books and websites, emerging every so often to push us into getting an education, getting jobs, becoming self-reliant. It didn't matter what those jobs were, as long as we could care for ourselves. But why would we do that, when our mother was happy to be Mommy for the rest of our lives? If we'd let her.

70

Ann

It was still dark when I went for a run. It's impossible to run at the end of November and not face darkness, whether I went before work or after. For some reason, I felt safer in the morning darkness. There were more people out on the streets, getting into cars, backing out of driveways. They were normal people headed to work and school and off to the airport for business trips. At night, the people who were out on the streets might be up to anything.

I felt only minor apprehension over the person who had been watching our house, if it was even that. He or she had only been there at night.

As time passed, my concern lessened. Was it even the same person? Why throw pebbles to attract attention? When I'd seen the person the first time, I felt the intention was to keep hidden, to watch without me becoming aware. Why go out of one's way to risk being caught, the police called? It made no sense. And what was the point? Gravel at our window?

I tied my shoes and did some stretches. I went out and locked the door behind me. It was only five-thirty, but David had already left the house. He had meetings in San Francisco all day, starting with a seven o'clock breakfast.

I turned right and started jogging slowly. My running

never went much beyond jogging. It wasn't as if I had the style of a gazelle, flying with smooth, beautiful strides, graceful and light on my feet. Instead, my feet thudded on the pavement, and I was usually breathing deeply after one mile. I'm in decent shape, but I'm not an athlete. There's a difference.

Still, I like running.

My thoughts were scattered, thinking about the stalker, or stalkers, and irritation with David. Racing thoughts drowned out the techno music drilling into my brain through my earbuds.

I didn't like David's refusal to get a restraining order against Gemma. It wasn't a lack of trust on my part, it was his lack of desire to do absolutely everything in his power to return our lives to normal, to make our lives solely our own, to put me at the center of his world, no matter what it took.

I paused to look for cars before jogging across the street and turning right again, passing by a row of newly built condos. They were painted desert colors, difficult to distinguish in the dark. Mature Queen Palm trees had been planted in the tiny yards surrounded by iron fencing. As I slowed to admire cactus in pots lining the front steps of one unit, I heard footsteps behind me, thudding hard as mine grew softer.

Glancing over my shoulder, I didn't see anyone. I stopped and looked across the street. Still no one. Normally, I would have brushed it off, but after the other incidents…I turned away from the cactus and took up at my usual pace. I shoved my fists into the pockets of my jacket, which for some reason made me feel more secure, more tightly bound, less vulnerable.

I imagined I looked strange, running with even less grace, my posture rigid because of my hands stuffed in my pockets. But who was out to see? Except the person behind me.

On the next block, I heard the footsteps again. The houses along this side of the street almost all had lights glowing through drapes and blinds. There was no reason to be afraid and nothing tangible to be afraid of, but my heart beat more furiously than it should have after such a short distance.

Forcing my thoughts back to the restraining order, I tried to think about why I was so annoyed. They're notoriously useless. And I already had a plan. A restraining order wasn't necessary to keep Gemma out of our lives. Although if this was Gemma following me now, maybe I was wrong. Maybe she wasn't just harassing David at work, maybe she was after me. Maybe she'd figured out we were a couple. Maybe she had an inkling I was gaslighting her.

I shivered. I needed to focus on the plan, not a list of *maybes*.

The footsteps seemed closer, definitely louder, echoing in the empty street. I stopped and turned. At the far end of the street on the opposite side, someone was running with an awkward gait, obviously not a practiced runner. Their head was turned in my direction. I couldn't make out any gender-specific features due to a large hoodie and baggie, ankle-length running pants. I wanted to walk back in that direction, demand an explanation, but my whole body began shaking.

I was being ridiculous. It wasn't a threat. It was just someone starting a jogging program. It meant nothing. Coincidence. Curiosity. The look of anyone watching the sole other human being on a deserted street.

I increased my pace, approaching a sprint, but before I reached the next corner, my breathing was so labored, I found myself gasping as if I'd just swum up from the bottom of a lake. A moment later, a pinch of pain appeared under my lower left rib. I pulled my hand out of my pocket and pressed it against my rib. The pressure did nothing to ease the pain. I slowed. When I did, I once again heard the sound of another pair of feet hitting the ground.

Turning to look would broadcast my fear. I couldn't look.

Pain or no pain, I needed to get out of there. I ran as fast as I could, breathing harder, sweat spreading across my back and under my arms, trickling from my scalp down my neck. I circled the block and ran back to my house. Without turning to see whether the jogger had kept up with me, I unlatched the gate and entered the side yard. It was faster than pausing to unlock the door.

I hurried around the side of the porch and climbed the stairs. The sound of the creek, rippling at the bottom of our property was no longer pleasant. It was too loud. It had taken on an ominous tone as I strained to hear any other sounds it might be masking.

The back door deadbolt resisted me as I tried to stab my key into the slot. After a few more scratches at the wood, the key was in place. I turned it stepped inside, heaved the door closed, and locked it. I disabled and re-set the alarm to recognize my presence. I went into the living room and collapsed on the sofa. I had no idea who this person was, and I still couldn't escape the irrational fear that I'd conjured up a stalker with my falsified notes on Gemma.

When I was breathing normally again, I went into the kitchen and made a pot of coffee. While it brewed, I forced my mind to discard the idea of conjuring up anything whatsoever. I returned my thoughts to David.

He'd explained my part in breaking things apart between us. I'd seen his point, but at the same time, I'd felt he was making excuses. I wasn't the one who went out and had sex with a stranger. Maybe I wasn't perfect, maybe I shut him out in some subtle but significant ways, but I hadn't done what he had. I hadn't betrayed him.

He should be eager to get a restraining order. He should care about nothing but my opinion on the matter, my sense of security. Instead, it felt like he didn't want to make Gemma feel bad. He didn't want to treat her like the predator she was, and I didn't like that. I needed things to move more quickly to their conclusion.

71

Gemma

I didn't want to tell Dr. Wilcox what happened with my parents. I wasn't completely sure in my own mind what had happened. I felt like my brain had turned inside out. I was giggling, I was screaming, and for more than a few minutes, I hadn't even realized I was the one screaming. I passed out, and I'm not sure why. My father said I ran to the kitchen and was rubbing my face on a frozen chicken. It was so ridiculous, I thought he was teasing me.

That made me want to start laughing all over again. Or crying.

I remembered the crying. I remember my tears changed into something surreal...too hot or too thick, like molten lava. It had the feel of a nightmare, where no image is clear, nothing makes sense, the people I recognized were not themselves, and life leaps abruptly from one scenario to another. You wake with uncertain memories, only knowing it was awful, trembling with fear that can't be described.

It was five minutes past the hour, and I was sitting in Dr. Wilcox's waiting room. I stared around at the colors working so hard to communicate tranquility. I felt worse than I had before I started seeing her. And yet I was almost addicted to her. When she made me angry, I still needed to see her, to explain why I was upset, to win our little game. I couldn't imagine ending therapy, as if canceling my future sessions would be as devastating as cutting my family out of my life.

Just like I felt toward my mother. I was furious with her. I almost hated her. Yet, I loved her. I felt like Dr. Wilcox believed I needed to express more anger, to have a more honest relationship with my mother, but I didn't want to shove her out of my life forever. I needed her in some way that I couldn't explain. Maybe simply because she'd always been there. My mother was the only other person I knew who had seen and held, if only for a moment, my beloved baby girl. Even though that woman was the reason I'd only seen my baby for a few seconds, and never been allowed to hold her.

The inner door to the office opened, and Dr. Wilcox gestured for me to come inside.

That was nervy of her after leaving me sitting for nearly five minutes. I remained in my chair. I turned another page in the magazine I was holding but not reading.

"I'm ready for you now," she said.

I nodded. I slowly closed the magazine. She was allowed to take her time, cutting into the minutes that belonged to me, but now I was supposed to hop to it.

I placed the magazine on the table beside me, face down. It was the latest issue of *People*. I had to give her that, she spent money instead of leaving magazines that were years out of date like most medical offices did. The magazines were there to pretend the medical staff was thoughtful of their patients' time when they obviously were not, as if patients needed to read analysis of a political crisis that was eighteen months past its shelf life.

I stood and followed her into the office. I left the door

standing open.

"Please close the door," she said.

I went to my chair and sat. I crossed my legs.

She stalked across the room and closed the door, rather hard.

She took her seat and opened her expensive journal, filled with stories of my life and her opinion of me. "How was your weekend?"

"Fine."

"How was the conversation with your parents?"

"I told them how I felt, but they didn't apologize. Not that it would have helped. I don't think telling them accomplished anything."

"Why don't you walk me through what happened?"

"I got upset. I cried. I yelled a bit, they acted like I was freaking out. Over-reacting."

"Were you?"

"How can you over-react to your baby being stolen?"

She closed the leather notebook and held it close to her chest. She tapped her finger on it, creating a strangely hollow sound. She turned her gaze toward the windows. "That's an interesting way of characterizing it."

"What do you mean?"

"You said she was stolen."

"She was."

"That word implies you weren't present. That you had no say in the matter."

Something thick and solid swelled inside my chest. I stared at her. I closed my eyes and imagined scraping my fingernails across her face. I wanted to sink my teeth into the flesh of her cheek — that soft, pale cheek with its delicate, smooth skin. I would leave bloody gashes, a scar that remained forever. I opened my eyes.

"You look upset."

I dug my fingers into the arms of my chair. "I am upset. You make it sound like I could have done something."

"Couldn't you?"

"Of course not! I was a kid."

"Almost eighteen. Maybe you didn't really want the baby. Maybe you were glad to relinquish responsibility to your mother."

"How dare you say that to me!"

"I know it's difficult to hear, but it's something to consider."

"Don't sit there all cold and icy and judging me!" I felt my voice rise to a shriek, but I couldn't stop it. "You're supposed to help me." She had no right to act as if it were my fault. My mother took my baby, and she disappeared with her, and I had no idea where she'd gone. What was I supposed to do? I hated Dr. Wilcox. If I had a gun, I would have shot her right there. Not even thinking about it.

"You look very angry."

"I am."

"You look like you want to kill me."

"No one has ever said such terrible things to me."

"I'm trying to help you pay attention to your honest feelings. It's okay to be angry at me."

"Don't tell me what's okay. I'll decide that."

"Good. Excellent."

"Stop it!"

She put the notebook on her lap, opened it, and made a note on a page that looked blank from where I was sitting. "I want you to try to remember what really happened. What you were feeling."

"I felt lost. I felt betrayed. I felt completely alone in the world. What do you think I felt?"

"Good. What else."

"Good?"

"Good that you're bringing all of this out."

"Don't treat me like this is some kind of therapy exercise. This is my life. She was my baby!"

"But you didn't want her."

I slammed my fists on the arms of the chair. "Don't say that. I wanted her. I loved her. I've loved her every single day of my life, and I still love her."

"But you didn't fight for her."

"I couldn't." My voice sounded strange and far away.

She closed the notebook and put it on the table. "Can you tell me more? Exactly what happened with your parents on Saturday?"

"I told you."

"Did you feel in control of your emotions?"

"No! I flipped out. Okay? I felt like I was going insane."

She nodded. She folded her hands on her lap and gave me a tiny smile.

I was afraid I would smack her face, or claw her skin into bloody shreds as I'd imagined. Instead, I stood, grabbed my purse, and walked out. I left the door open.

72

Dr. Ann Wilcox: Notes on Gemma Hughes

Just a few short notes — I've made the decision to talk with both of Gemma's parents immediately about her need for twenty-four-hour supervision.

At our last session, when I broached the topic of Gemma's responsibility in giving up her child, she lost control of her emotions. She became hysterical and disassociated, much like the behavior her mother had described. She verbalized fantasies of killing me.

Prior to this, I had asked her to describe the confrontation with her parents. She carefully avoided mentioning any aspect of the psychotic break her mother told me about. She characterized the encounter as an experience of intense emotions, but nothing more. She didn't say anything about passing out or her bizarre behavior leading up to it. She didn't mention the uncontrolled screaming, a sound that had horrified her mother, leaving her unable to function for the rest of the day.

It's past time for a meeting with both of them.

I'll present my thoughts clearly and directly. I'll provide literature from the institution I'm recommending.

I don't imagine it will be hard to persuade her mother, and once her father hears about what took place in my office, I believe her mother, along with those details of Gemma's last therapy session, will persuade him to do what I strongly believe is the most helpful for Gemma's mental health, not to mention the safety of her family.

When I suggested to Gemma that she hadn't wanted the child and had deliberately allowed her mother to take control, Gemma flew out of her chair. It's the only way to describe it.

She rushed at me, tearing the notebook out of my hand. She grabbed the pen and made an attempt to stab it into the back of my hand. Fortunately, I was able to move quickly and avoided serious injury.

I wrestled the pen away from her, but she grabbed at my sweater and twisted it into a knot, making it almost impossible for me to put distance between us. She spit in my face, then slapped me, hard. The force of her hand left a red mark that was still there in the evening.

My husband was extremely upset when he saw my face, very concerned that a patient had assaulted me. He wanted me to report it to the police. He didn't see why I would need, or want, to protect someone who was seriously unbalanced. I managed to calm him down.

The choice her parents have to make is between an arrest for assault, or commitment to an institution for a period of time. Of course, it's more difficult to call the police after the fact, so I'm not certain that option does exist at this point. I didn't think to take a photograph of my face, and by the following morning, the mark had faded. She would deteriorate further in a jail setting, associating with women who have criminal backgrounds, many of whom have more serious and undiagnosed mental illnesses.

I know Mr. and Mrs. Hughes will see the need for more in-depth care. They'll come to understand how serious this is. And I believe they'll be very upset that she assaulted me. I need to reassure them the threat and assault were simply a cry for help.

73

Ann

Tamara and Rob Hughes agreed to meet me at a posh wine bar. On one hand, it seemed mildly inappropriate to create a social atmosphere around a purportedly serious mental health issue. It seemed wrong to enjoy the celebratory mood that wine signifies, when they would be walking out of the bar knowing their beloved daughter was committed to an institution for the mentally ill.

At the same time, I needed a glass of wine to steady my nerves. This was the final step, the only necessary step, really, the step toward which I'd been working for months. I also hoped that a glass of wine might lower the Hughes' inhibitions enough to make them more agreeable, more trusting, more open to my opinions.

My sense was that Tamara was already where I needed her to be. She'd more or less agreed to my proposal, but the final act still had to be completed. She had to actually submit to an interview and sign her name. A significant hurdle. And I had no idea where Rob stood on the matter. I hoped she'd talked to him extensively and he was close to being ready. I hoped the threat of police involvement would push him in the direction I wanted him to go. I hoped that he had more concern for his wife's safety, for her life, than he did for his daughter's temporary discomfort. But that was a lot of hope with no guarantees.

If they agreed, *when* they agreed, I would feel like celebrating the absence of Gemma Hughes from David's life. He would never know what had happened to her. From his perspective, she would be wiped off the face of the earth for long enough that he and I could complete the healing process.

Once her parents showed up at court and appeared before a judge, we'd be close enough to the finish line that I could relax.

Fifteen minutes before we were due to meet, I was seated at a corner table. I needed to see them enter the bar, look for me, and approach the table. I needed to be settled and in charge. Five minutes before the appointed time, three glasses of Willamette Valley Pinot Noir were delivered to the table. I also had a board with two kinds of cheese and some flatbread.

The moment I saw them, it was clear Tamara had been crying. I hoped it was grief for her daughter and not the result of a fight with her husband over meeting with me, or with the things I'd said to her.

She introduced me to Rob. I gave him a warm handshake, and he seemed to return it. They pulled out their stools and sat down. They thanked me for the wine, and each took several small, nervous sips.

I did the same, although without the jittery movements of my facial muscles that they seemed unable to control. "I'm going to cut straight to the bottom line," I said. "Since I last spoke to you, Tamara, Gemma assaulted me. She threatened to kill me."

Tamara's face sagged like a Salvador Dali painting had

come to life. I watched as her collapsing facial muscles caused folds in her skin that deepened as I spoke those few words that became knives, piercing her heart.

Rob's face did the opposite. His jaw tightened and his gaze turned hard and glassy. He pushed his wine glass toward the center of the table and leaned back, folding his arms across his chest. His lips did a dance of sorts, first pursing, then drawing into narrow, straight lines, then turning down at the corners. They continued to move, the whole array of human emotion acted out in those two strips of flesh.

Finally, he spoke. "I can't believe it was a serious assault. She's emotional, very upset right now, but she's not violent."

"She hit me with enough force to leave a mark."

He squinted.

"It's faded now, of course. This was last week."

He held my gaze. "Why did you wait so long to be in touch?"

"I needed to think through the right course of action."

"Thinking took five days?"

"Yes, it did. I'm not trying to punish Gemma. Don't misinterpret this. She's a sweet girl, a very capable woman. But as you said, she's been emotional. And those emotions are getting control of her. Her situation is serious. She needs rest, time away from her responsibilities, and…"

"This would have a negative impact on her career," David said.

"…And more in-depth care than I can provide in weekly or even semi-weekly sessions." I finished my thought and left his comment hanging in the space between us.

As if he were employing the same tactic that I'd used, he went on to complete his thought while ignoring what I'd said.

"She loves her job. She's very good at it. I can't imagine the school would accept a teacher of small children who has mental health issues. An *alleged* history of..."

"If anyone found out, there are discrimination laws," I said. "She could fight any backlash, and I think she'd have solid legal footing."

"Do you? Are you an attorney?"

Tamara followed our exchange like a woman following a professional tennis game, her head moving back and forth, tracking our conversation.

"It's the best thing for Gemma." I wanted to pull Tamara into the conversation, but I suspected he might interpret that as trying to turn her against him. He would dig in his heels with more force.

"I don't agree," he said.

I placed my hands on the table, my palms flat against the silky finish of the wood. "To be honest, you don't have much of a choice." I softened my tone. "One of the reasons I spent several days considering the options is that I needed to decide whether I should file a police report."

Rob laughed. "Don't be absurd."

"I'm not. She assaulted me, sir."

"She gave you a little slap, don't exaggerate."

Tamara took a long swallow of wine. She eyed the cheese but left it neatly arranged on the board. She spoke without looking at her husband. "We don't want her doing something that could damage her life permanently. Look at how she was on Saturday. You've pushed it out of your mind now, but you were as scared as I was."

I nodded.

David put his arm around his wife's shoulders. "I

wonder if we should get a second opinion. That's what would be done for a physical diagnosis."

I gave him a sympathetic smile. "A second opinion won't matter in this case because she assaulted *me*. She threatened *me*. You might get a different opinion about what's causing her behavior. That's all."

I placed a slice of cheese on a fragment of flatbread. I ate it deliberately, followed by a sip of wine, hoping my calm exterior hid the churning inside of me. This had to work. I needed it to work *now*. I didn't want any more discussion. "I don't mean to be cruel, but you need to think this through. She threatened to kill me. I don't know how much you know about the therapeutic process, but there's something called transference…"

"Heard of it," he said.

"Gemma views me as a substitute for her mother. She's furious because she blames her mother for *stealing* her baby, as she puts it."

Rob and Tamara opened their mouths but didn't speak.

"However, I believe she didn't really want the child, and I believe she needs intense therapy to face this fact, to forgive her mother, and you. And most of all, herself. But the bottom line is, if I stop treating her, if that dynamic is broken, it's very possible your wife's life would be at risk."

"That's…" he paused. He picked up his wineglass and swallowed nearly half the contents. He put the glass down hard. Wine splashed up the sides. The droplets clung to the inside of the glass like blood spatter. He sighed heavily. "If Tamara thinks this is what Gemma needs, I'll support whatever she decides."

Tamara looked at me gratefully. There wasn't a trace of

guilt in her expression for what she'd done to her daughter. It was clear she was happy to put responsibility for the baby's abandonment onto her vulnerable teenaged daughter.

Either way, I'd gotten what I needed. I took a long, slow sip of wine, enjoying a silent, internal celebration.

74

Gemma

Geoff looked like a little kid, sitting on my front porch, his knees jutting up, so they were level with his shoulders as his body accommodated the low step. His hair fell across the side of his face, concealing one eye and his cheek with a tangle of curls. He had a pile of rubber bands beside him and was shooting them onto the path in front of him. When he glanced up at me, his mouth was formed into an exaggerated pout.

I cut across the small patch of grass which wasn't really mine. A gardening service watered it and trimmed it and gave it fertilizer when required. The tiny lawn spread in an unbroken carpet to the condo next door, so if I had owned it, I would not have had a precise spot where ownership passed out of my hands.

"We need to talk," Geoff said.

"I'm going to the gym."

"That can wait." He stood and stepped to the side so I could get to the door.

I slid the key into the lock. "What's up?"

"Mom. The con that's being run on her. And probably dad."

"What is it, exactly?"

"I'm not sure yet."

"You need to let it go."

Geoff's fantasy, no worse than the fantasies he'd had all his life, was not going to take center stage again. I needed to take care of me, focus on me. He was going to have to wait this time.

"You need to pay attention to someone besides yourself."

"Can't do that right now."

He grabbed my arm. "Listen. This is serious."

"Let go of me."

To his credit, he immediately released his grip. "I'm not making this up, or being paranoid. I confronted her about her new *friend*. I told her that unsavory people are hunting all the time for easy marks and she…"

"I bet she loved that."

"Actually, she didn't object. The problem is that she didn't seem concerned."

"She's fine. You need more things to occupy your time. Then you won't be obsessed and sidetracked by what other people might, or more likely, might *not* be doing." I unlocked the door and stepped inside. "Maybe think about getting a job."

He followed closely, one of his aggressive footsteps almost pulling off the heel of my left shoe. He loomed over me, smelling faintly of body odor despite the cool weather. He stayed close as I went into the kitchen.

I felt slightly threatened, a thought that startled me. I couldn't tell him that, but I felt it — a clear inner alarm that he could hurt me. All my life he'd been my best friend, my little brother, someone I needed to take care of even though he was only a year younger than me.

"Can you back off, please?"

"What's wrong?"

"You're crowding me."

He didn't move.

"I asked Mom what was going on with this so-called friend. Mom said she needed help with some *things,* and this person understood her feelings in a way no one else did."

"So?"

"That's a bad sign."

"Why? She made a friend, why do you keep trying to turn it into something sinister?"

"It's not what it seems. Haven't you read about some of these complex cons? They're very sophisticated."

"Then talk to Dad about it."

Geoff spoke over me. "These people are very, very good at pretending to be someone they're not, at gaining trust, at…"

"Geoff. Stop bothering me about it. Mom has a friend, and you're jealous that you're not included. Grow up."

"I don't understand why you're dismissing my instincts."

"Because they sound more like paranoia than instincts, like you're looking for trouble, like you just want your mommy all to yourself. There aren't any *instincts.*"

"I know what I'm talking about, and if we wait too long, this person will gain more of her trust than we have. When that happens, Mom won't listen to anything we have to say."

"Talk. To. Dad."

"He might be getting conned too."

"You don't know unless you talk to him."

He shuffled around in front of me, blocking me from putting my glass to the water dispenser on the fridge.

I smelled his breath — stale. The odor of his body was even stronger. "When did you last shower?" I looked at his hair, slightly limp, dark from being unwashed.

"This is more important. I need your help," he said.

"You don't."

"We have to do this as a team."

"I'm not getting involved. So either talk about something else or you need to leave."

"Why don't you care?" He danced beside me, hopping from one foot to the other. "Oh! Oh, I know..." He sounded like a kid waiting to be called on in class, shouting out and madly waving his hand, hoping to be chosen. "This is because of whatever happened Saturday. You're pissed. What did happen?"

"You've lived your whole life in the dark."

"No I haven't."

"And you kinda stink." I moved away from him. I put the still empty glass on the counter. I pulled a bottle of Zinfandel and two wine glasses out of the cabinet. I twisted off the cap and poured half a glass. "Want some?"

He nodded. "Why am I in the dark? Do you know what's going on with this new *friend?*"

We took our wine into the living room. "I don't feel like going into it, okay? So don't ask a bunch of questions."

"About what?"

"Remember Aidan?"

He stared at me.

"The guy I was with in high school."

"Oh. I don't know...I..."

"My boyfriend."

"I don't..." he took a sip of wine.

"I got pregnant when I was with him. That's why we moved to Fresno."

He stared at me. The room grew so quiet, I could hear his breathing as well as my own. He held the glass in front of him but didn't move. After a long time, he spoke softly. "Oh, fuck." He looked ill. He moved forward as if he thought there was a chance he might throw up and didn't want to damage my couch.

"I had the baby. The minute she was born, Mom ripped her out of my arms. She dropped her off at the fire station like a box full of canned green beans at a food bank."

"Oh. Fuck."

"Stop saying that."

"I…"

"I guess I buried it, my feelings about it. And because of therapy, it's coming up."

"I'm…I'm sorry." His eyes filled with tears. The tender lids beneath his eyes turned red as if he'd been crying for several minutes.

I took a sip of wine.

"So you are pissed. At her?"

"That doesn't begin to describe it."

He stood suddenly. He downed the entire glass of wine. "Okay. That's some bad shit, but it's the past. Long over. I don't mean to be cold, but if Mom's being conned, if Dad is part of it…eventually the house, and their money is going to be ours. So we can't just ignore what's going on."

"I have enough to deal with. You take care of it." I stood and went into the kitchen. I poured my wine down the drain and went upstairs to my bedroom without saying goodbye to Geoff.

I took off my clothes and got into bed. I closed my eyes and remembered the feel of David's hands and the weight of him on my body. I fell into a light sleep and dreamed of making a baby with David. Our lovemaking was like something divine. After, he rested his hand on my belly and told me he knew a part of him was now living inside of me, that we were connected forever.

75

Ann

The first thing I saw when I got out of my car was the narrow strip of exposed earth along the side of the house. Every single one of the fifteen cyclamen plants had been stepped on. Paper thin magenta and pale pink petals lay all over the dirt and the driveway. Petals from the white plants covered the soil like a soft blanket of snow.

I walked behind my car to the row of murdered plants. Even at dusk, it was obvious my stalker was determined to hurt me. Destroying innocent life. I shivered, thinking of a stalker, *my stalker*, as if this person belonged to me alone.

And then I saw the window.

It was the side living room window that looked across the driveway toward the house next door.

The glass was shattered — a big hole with jagged teeth surrounding it. The ground was covered with shards and splinters of glass, piled on top of pink and white petals.

I'd only run to the store for two bottles of wine and some deli sandwiches because I hadn't felt like cooking dinner. David was due home early, he'd promised. In fact, he ought to be turning into the street in the next ten minutes. We'd planned to eat our sandwiches, drink some wine, and turn on the gas fireplace. We'd sit in the semi-darkness, drink more wine, watch the flames dance, casting their light across the room, and talk.

But now…

My hands shook. I hadn't set the alarm because I was only gone fifteen minutes. Literally. I'd waited ten minutes for the sandwiches to be made, perusing wine labels and choosing something we hadn't tried before. *Fifteen minutes!*

The stalker must have been watching the house multiple times, intuited that we had an alarm. We didn't have those stickers on our windows that are supposed to be a partial deterrent. I've always viewed them as ugly ads for the alarm company. I don't want to see the back of a huge label every time I looked out.

Most of the people on our street were either still on their way home or starting dinner. No one notices a prowler at that time of the evening.

I turned and opened the passenger door. I removed the bag holding two wine bottles, looping the twine handles over my forearm. I picked up the bag of sandwiches and went to the back door. I unlocked it and stepped inside. Nothing felt right. It wasn't clear whether my mind was playing tricks on me because I already knew nothing was right, or if there was a tangible disruption in my home's atmosphere filling me with apprehension.

Was it possible Gemma was acting out what I'd written about her in my notes? Every time the thought occurred to me I had two equally balanced reactions — shame at my ridiculous imagination, and concern that she was truly dangerous and more clever than I'd realized. She'd suffered a lot of trauma when she was young. Losing a man you loved, and a child you wanted left deep, jagged scars. Had she somehow gotten her hands on my notes? It seemed impossible, but I couldn't think of another explanation.

My breath caught as I thought again about that child.

Now…the baby girl, Gemma's daughter, would be… seventeen? Eighteen? Was it possible…?

I dropped the sandwiches on the kitchen counter. I grabbed the wine opener out of the drawer by the fridge. I tore off the foil rather than trimming it carefully. I stabbed the point of the opener into the cork and twisted it down. The cork slid out easily. I poured a healthy glass, not caring that the romantic ritual of slowly opening a bottle, pouring rich, smooth wine, and toasting each other with elegant glasses had been spoiled. I swallowed some wine and carried my glass to the living room.

The window looked even more ugly from the inside. The gaping hole was surrounded by triangles of glass poised to slice a life-threatening gash in my arm if I reached through the opening. And yet, the urge to reach through overcame me. It was similar to the urge that many people feel, that I myself have felt, to step off a cliff or climb out the window of a high-rise building. It's the same as the desire to press my foot on the gas pedal and race my car through the low railing on a bridge that spans a canyon. It's simply a form of cognitive dissonance, but unnerving all the same.

I turned away and sipped more wine. Cold air gushed into the room, and I heard the rattling of the fronds on the three palms that grew between our house and the house next door.

It would ease my anxiety if I went into the garage and found a scrap of plywood, or even a flattened cardboard box to cover the window until the following day. But the thought of walking into a dark, cavernous room that was mildly creepy on a good day was equally disturbing.

I sipped my wine, hoping for the calming effect of alcohol, longing for the sight of David's headlights sweeping across the front of the house.

I walked to the window. My feet crunched on broken glass. There seemed to be more glass inside and out than what should have come from the window. There was glass everywhere. I yanked the cord, closing the drapes. It blocked some of the cold. At least the jagged remains would prevent anyone from entering the house.

I sat on the couch, afraid to turn on a bit of music to calm me. I needed to remain hyper-alert for the sound of someone approaching.

By the time David pulled into the driveway, my glass was empty. Instead of rushing to the front door to greet him, I returned to the kitchen and refilled my glass. My hand shook as I poured the wine.

I'd thought that once Gemma was locked up, I could return to a life that didn't involve constant checking over my shoulder. But I hadn't considered the daughter...with DNA tests available to the public, you could find anyone now. And it was possible, after all our therapy sessions, I didn't know Gemma at all. Thinking back, she'd dodged an awful lot of questions. She frequently sat in sullen silence. I'd been so focused on crafting my falsified history of her, I hadn't considered all that she might be hiding as thoroughly as I should have.

I certainly had no idea who her daughter might be or what irrational hatred had festered inside her for nearly two decades.

76

David

The shattered window disturbed me more than it did Ann. Maybe I had more to fear. I had a potentially unbalanced woman intent on destroying my marriage. I imagined Ann felt she didn't have a lot left to fear. The worst thing that could happen had already ravished her life, courtesy of the man who supposedly loved her with all his heart.

I did.

I do.

The simple words of the traditional wedding vow. The shortest phrase there is. Only three letters, two words that mean everything. And I broke that stupidly simple vow. When I made that promise, I meant it with my entire being. I never conceived of anything that would take me away from Ann, that would threaten what we had. We were unbreakable. We had an ironclad connection, a steel box that contained our joined hearts.

I loved her. I adored her.

And I do love her, more than ever. That she would stay married to me is almost impossible to comprehend. That she not only forgave me, but put every part of herself into making sure what lay ahead of us was even better than what lay behind was so much more than I deserved. I'd told her that was my intention — I wanted us to be amazing, but I still had to live with the tremors of pain that occasionally rippled across her face. Pain that I caused.

I would die for that woman. And I would probably die without her. Seriously. A shell of me might go on, for a while. But she lived inside of me, and she felt like part of me. And if she were gone, would I exist at all?

So why in god's name did I have sex, and not just once in a drunken stupor, but repeatedly kiss and sleep beside and fuck and tell lies to another woman? It makes no sense. Looking back, it makes no sense to me, and I was there. I did it. In some ways, it was a drunken stupor of my senses.

Why?

Ann asked me that a thousand times. I still wasn't sure she understood my answer.

It happened slowly, as so many massive disruptions do, and I didn't see what was going on.

Ann loves her career. She's obsessed with the work she does. She has a burning passion that I haven't seen in a lot of people. She knew what she wanted to do at a fairly young age and she pursued it as if she was preparing a trek to the summit of Mount Everest. Over-prepared. Single-minded. I love that about her.

She was loyal and dedicated and adhered to the ethics of her profession in a way that I'm sure was extreme. And I loved that about her too.

As a result, she refused to tell me a single word about the people she saw in therapy. I didn't know their names. I didn't know how frequently she saw particular individuals — daily? Twice a week? I had no idea. I didn't know how long they were in therapy with her — weeks, months, years, soon to be decades?

I didn't know what they looked like or what they wanted from her. I didn't know whether she prescribed medication or spent most of her effort on talk therapy.

Were any of them dangerous? Was she seeing men who had committed murder or rape? Was she alone in her office for an hour at a time listening to sexual fantasies and perversions that I couldn't begin to imagine? She might be looking into the eyes of the deranged…or men who simply lusted after her.

I'd heard of transference. Psychology is a scary thing — fucking around inside another person's head. Who knows what can happen.

It drove me mad.

That's the only way to describe my state of mind. It sounds like I'm blaming her, but I'm not. That's just how it was. I was completely shut out of her life. She lived in a separate world and had intimate relationships with dozens of people that I knew absolutely nothing about. They might pass me on the street, they might work down the hall from me. They might live next door. Hell, one of them could be my manager or the CEO of my company.

I did not know!

She could be talking about absolutely anything with absolutely anyone. I assumed her patients were people with mental issues ranging along a very broad scale — from shopaholics to the criminally insane. The men, mostly men, seen in police photographs. That extraordinarily pale skin, because they always seem to be white men…I'm not sure what that is, the pale skin, but it's my impression. They look as if they haven't seen a ray of sunlight in ten years. Hiding in basements with photographs of women they're stalking, polishing their implements of torture, fondling their voodoo dolls for all I know.

Even when I wasn't thinking about the insane, I thought about men she might be drawn to. They were pouring out their hearts, their most intimate secrets, and their vulnerabilities to her. She might find that attractive. Most women do.

After we'd been married a few years and that glow of finding the perfect person transformed into the new normal, I began to feel like I occupied a small sliver of her thoughts, a shrinking, fading part of her life.

And then it got worse.

She stopped coming on to me. When we first got together, she was all over me. I never had to ask, never had to even suggest it. Sex just happened. We'd be sitting in a restaurant, and she'd slip off her sandal. She would inch herself down in her chair and slide her bare foot along the inside of my thigh or up the leg of my pants as far as she could reach. We'd be working in the yard, and she'd come up behind me, wrap her arms around me, ease her hands inside the waistband of my shorts.

I'd wake in the morning, and she'd be sitting on top of me, naked, ready for me, smiling.

It happens to every couple, that feeling of routine. But we were different. We weren't like other couples. And this was worse. It seemed as if she forgot about sex. She'd get into bed and roll over with her back to me. She'd start making all her little nestling moves with the pillow, wrapping the comforter around her shoulders, sighing with more pleasure over the bedding than she did with me. In the winter, she'd come to bed wearing long underwear and thick socks.

She responded to me, most of the time. Other times, she'd yawn and make half-hearted gestures until I moved away and let her fall asleep. Maybe all her desire belonged to her patients. In the past, we'd talked about that — how sex is better when the mind is engaged, when there's a mental connection more powerful than two bodies.

Later, I learned from Ann that expressing desire is a two-way street, but she's the psychiatrist, not me.

So I did it. I nearly destroyed the best thing that ever happened to me, simply I wanted to be wanted, and a woman made the first move.

Incredibly, unbelievably, she still loves me. She wants to stay with me.

We have sex now when I least expect it. We talk as if we just met, thoughts pouring out of us when we sit together in the evenings.

Every so often, I look at her and wonder. I wonder if she's remembering, imagining. I wonder if it will ever be exactly the same. And of course, it can't be. I wonder if *better* is even possible when you already had perfection. I also wonder, deep inside, in the middle of the night, if she really does love me or if she's just biding her time.

I shove those thoughts away. It's all good.

I would do anything for her. Absolutely anything.

77

Gemma

When I arrived home from work, Geoff was sitting on my front step. Again. There were no rubber bands this time, but his hair was limp with grease, and his skin looked discolored from lack of soap and water.

He'd done this before...lost touch with himself, was the best way to describe it. There was always something. This time it was a woman trying to con my parents out of their life savings. In the past, there were obsessions about a college roommate putting laxatives in his sandwich when it was left untended in the dorm fridge. Once he believed my parents' neighbor had a device that allowed them to pick up every sound from inside our house. He thought they laughed when they saw him, knowing all that went on in the privacy of our home. There were others, but always something. In between, he was fine. An awesome brother and a fun guy. My best friend. I think we were close not only because we were born one year apart, but because we were separated for so long. After that, we clung to each other.

I tried to ignore his off times, ride them out.

The problem was, all of his obsessions contained a tiny thread of truth. My mother did have a mysterious friend. Our neighbors often gave us sideways looks that suggested they knew more about us than we wanted them to know. My mother had him evaluated by a psychiatrist when he was nineteen. It wasn't schizophrenia — that fearsome breakdown that targeted males in his age bracket. It wasn't anything. There was some mild paranoia, nothing serious. The psychiatrist infuriated my mother because she was accused of smothering him. I suppose that's why she didn't think highly of therapy.

When he went through these obsessions, he was exhausting.

Once again I saw my plans to go to the gym slipping through my fingers. The only good thing about Geoff, about my entire family, was they'd become so magnified in my life, I wasn't thinking as much about David. Maybe that was Dr. Wilcox's plan all along. She wanted me so wound up and emotional about the unexplored and unhealed parts of my past, I couldn't think about my current pain.

Or maybe it was true what they said after all — time heals.

But if time heals, why was I feeling such fresh pain over the loss of my baby? I felt as if it had happened only a few days earlier. Why was I as furious at my mother as I'd been when I was a teenager, slamming doors and sulking in my room, hating her for taking away my cell phone, my driver's license, anything that would allow me to contact Aidan? Despising her for ultimately taking away the most important part of my life?

I stopped a few feet from where Geoff sat. "What do you want? If this is about the *con*, I don't want to talk about it."

He stood. "You're the one who's conned me."

"What do you mean?"

He followed me into the house and into the kitchen. "No one tells me the truth. All my life. You lied to me. Why didn't I know you were pregnant? That you had a baby?"

"You knew."

"I didn't. How would I know?"

"Because…I don't know. It's simple — how could you not know?"

"Well, I didn't. I wasn't even there. I stayed with Gabe's family. Remember? So how would I know?"

An enormous, wrenching sob rose up from the bottom of my heart. It surged out as if it were some other being that had lived inside of me. My body convulsed. I wanted something to hold onto, terrified I was going to fall, crack the back of my skull on the tile, soft brain tissue spilling across the floor. But I couldn't move. I was frozen except for the heaving, gasping sobs. I wasn't even sure if there were tears. I didn't feel any tears.

Geoff stared at me. He looked terrified.

I stretched out my hand, trying to find something solid. Suddenly, he was holding me. The smell of him was gone as if his body had melted away and all I felt was the essence of him. His soul. He moved back and put his hands on the sides of my face. He held my head as I continued to heave, giving a sound to all the pain filling every cell of my body.

A moment later, the sobbing subsided into quiet whimpering, and now the tears were spilling out.

Geoff's grip on my head softened, and he moved his face closer. He touched his lips to mine, gently, comforting at first although something inside of me began to rebel.

Then, his tongue slid into my mouth, so firmly and so easily as if it had found its home, as if it was exploring familiar territory, as if it had been there many times before.

I wrenched away from him. "No! No. No. What are you doing?" I wrapped my arms around myself, trying to stop the cold that raced from my scalp, down my spine, winding its way through my core and into my legs.

"You don't remember." His voice was low. "I wondered if you didn't. How could you forget?"

I lurched toward the table. I grabbed the back of a chair, wrenched it away from the table, and collapsed into it. I tried to take a deep breath, but the air wouldn't flow. My lungs were empty, collapsing. My vision was growing dark at the edges.

"Breathe," he said.

I couldn't. "I…"

"Don't talk. Breathe."

I gasped in air as if I'd been underwater for several minutes. My mind was a white fury filled with things I couldn't name.

"There was no Aidan," he said. "Just me. You and me. Our fantasy names for each other — Aidan and Aurora. We've always been there for each other. I loved you. I do love you. I need you so much."

"Stop!"

His eyes filled with tears. "Why did you let her take our baby?"

I closed my eyes. Everyone blamed me. It wasn't my fault. I didn't *let* her. She just did, and now, it was clear why she had, but it didn't ease my loss. Not one tiny shred. In fact, my loss now seemed so enormous I didn't think my body or my mind could contain it.

I felt the heat of him, and a moment later, he was

kneeling beside me. I had the ridiculous, unimportant thought that the tile floor must be painful on his knees. He put his arms around me. I was repulsed. I wanted to push him away. And yet, the warmth of him felt so good. How long had it been since anyone held me? I knew the answer to that question.

Had anyone held my daughter? *Our*...my mind emptied for a moment. I leaned into him, resting my cheek on filthy hair that suddenly seemed sweet.

My mother hadn't held Audrey for anything except the business of cleaning her, wrapping her, and disposing of her. I certainly never cradled her in my arms. I wasn't allowed to kiss her sweet face, to touch her perfect ears and fingers. What happened when she was found? I knew now — some of the shadowy parts of my dreams had been about this. My little baby, crying, longing for the warmth of touch — her mother, human hands. I remembered the dream of searching through a house, looking at all the rooms with the possessions for each stage of a girl's life, a woman's life. It wasn't about Dr. Wilcox at all. I'd been looking for Audrey, I was always looking for Audrey, and I would never find her.

I would never, ever find her.

And maybe, I didn't want to. Because then I would have to tell her who her parents were.

Geoff and I were crying softly, holding each other. The solid presence of him touching me felt good, but I remained cold and empty inside, and I was sure he felt the same.

78

Ann

It was a strange day. Two of my regular Thursday
patients had ended therapy the week before. Because it was
pouring rain, the sky emptying barrels of water onto the
streets, rushing along gutters, spilling out of drains, my
patient who was battling severe depression related to her
empty nest had canceled. When she called, I'd encouraged her
to keep her appointment despite the weather. Getting out of
the house was important, and letting rain and wind stop her
was an obvious metaphor for allowing the natural forces of
life to defeat her.

She was firm. She would see me next week, as long as
the weather improved.

I made a note to set up a series of exercises to help her
recognize that getting outside of the place where she felt so
barren was the way to fill up her life and move forward.

She'd canceled at the last minute, so I sat alone in my
office, irrationally feeling as if I would be abandoning my
patients if I left. It was an inexplicable feeling. No one was
coming, I might as well settle in at home with a fire and a cup
of tea, or a glass of wine.

My nerves were on edge. In three days I had my
appointment at the courthouse to arrange Gemma's
commitment. I'd left dates off the entries in my notebook so

it would be easy to fit her escalating danger to the timeline set by the court. The fact that I'd already talked to her parents was the only thing that might trip me up. Typically, the court wanted evidence of an immediate danger. I was planning a final entry that would escalate her physical attacks on me. I would simply explain that after talking to her parents, I decided to conduct one more session with her before making the final decision for involuntary commitment. Also planned was Gemma's carefully *documented* cancellation of her appointment, leading to a somewhat lengthy delay.

Fitting the pieces together was a delicate balancing act. The anxiety of all those segments aligning at the right time was contributing to my edginess. But there was nothing to be done until I met with her for the final time. I could have manufactured that meeting entirely, but the closer I stuck to the truth, the more unstable she would look when she argued with the false parts of my version of events. It would also contribute to her doubt of her own experiences because she would know I was being truthful in so many other areas.

I went to the window and moved the curtains aside to allow more light into my office, what little there was of it. The sky was inky black, almost as if the sun had already gone down at three-thirty in the afternoon.

I returned to my chair and took Gemma's notebook off the table where I'd placed it earlier. I had no doubt I was well-prepared, yet I flipped through the pages, checking my work yet again.

Like many things, it came down to her word against mine. And I hadn't run my practice in a vacuum for the past decade. I had a strong network of colleagues who respected me. Relationships, even a number of friendships, that I'd established over the years. Those years where I demonstrated the highest ethical standards, invested hours in learning more about my field, and supporting my colleagues. My network included a staff member at the John Milton Behavioral Healthcare Facility, the pseudonym for a modern-day insane asylum.

We don't like to call these places insane asylums anymore. Insane is a negative label for mental illness. An insane asylum implies being locked up, losing autonomy. Even though the reason it was called an asylum was to convey exactly what the word means — providing shelter, protection, and support. Now, the prevailing goal is improved mental health and acclimation into society. But there are those who need to be locked up, no matter how we cringe at the thought.

I tucked the notebook into my bag, closed the curtains again, and put on my coat. I took my umbrella out of the plastic cylinder where I'd left it to dry, turned out the lights, and left.

The parking lot was less than half full, adding to the eerie, surreal sense of the day. Sluicing water, lack of light, and a handful of cars scattered across the lot gave the area a post-apocalyptic appearance. Others who had offices nearby and in my building had obviously decided to battle the slick roads and traffic and gusting wind while there was still a thin presence of daylight. Cars from the lunch crowd were long gone, although it wasn't likely many had made the trek to downtown Palo Alto simply to eat lunch in the midst of a violent storm.

A few feet before I reached my car, I pressed the fob to release the lock. I yanked the door open and turned to slide into the seat, holding the umbrella out to cover the space between the door and the interior of the car. Wind grabbed the fabric, tugging at the ribs, trying to yank it out of my hands. I tossed my bag onto the passenger seat.

The car door wobbled. An arm shot out, and a hand gripped the top of the door. Light colored hair on the finely shaped male hand was plastered to the skin. The fingernails were longish, two of them so ragged they looked torn.

"Get away from me." I spoke in a firm, authoritative voice.

"I need to talk to you."

He shoved himself closer, his head and torso now sharing the space under my misshapen umbrella.

Rain poured onto my coat and splattered my face. He was equally wet. His hair, pushed back from his face, was soaked, and his skin was slick with water. He glared at me, his pupils dilated more than they should have been, even in the dimming light. They were so large, I couldn't make out the color of his eyes.

"Stay away from my mother."

"Leave me alone right now, or I'll scream."

He laughed. "No one will hear you. Do you think there are people walking around in this weather?"

"What do you want?"

"I want you to stop contacting my mother."

"And who would that be?"

"Tamara Hughes."

I swallowed.

He seized on my discomfort, pushing his face close to mine. His skin gave off an odor that even the rain hadn't washed clean. When he spoke, I saw dark shreds of meat stuck between his left incisor and the tooth beside it.

"I don't know what your game is, but I'm watching out for her. You aren't going to con her."

"I'm not conning anyone."

"Stay away from her, from both of them."

"Tamara and I are friends."

"That's bullshit."

"Did she tell you to speak to me?"

"This is between you and me. Leave her out of it."

I was completely soaked. Water was creeping into the seams of my boots. My toes were slightly numb from the freezing dampness. "I'm getting soaked. Let go of my door and leave me alone."

"When you promise to stay away from her."

"I can't do that."

"You can do that, or I'll…"

"Or you'll, what?"

He shook the door violently.

Although it put me at a slight disadvantage, I slipped into the driver's seat. I grabbed the door handle and tried to pull it closed, but he was stronger and had the additional leverage of standing up.

"If you want to have a conversation, please contact me at my office."

"I don't even know your name. And I don't want a conversation. I want you to know that my parents aren't an easy mark. They have a family who cares. They have people looking out for them. If you try anything, I'll have your ass in jail. You're not going to bleed them dry."

I laughed.

"It's not funny."

"I don't care about their money. I'm friends with your mother, that's it. Why don't you ask her."

I closed my umbrella. Water cascaded down this side of his head. He eased his grip on the door as he moved his other hand to wipe the water off his face. I shoved the point of the umbrella at his stomach. He doubled over and stumbled back. I threw the umbrella on the ground and slammed and locked the door.

I sat for a moment, breathing hard before starting the car and pulling forward.

As I turned out of the lot, I glanced in the rearview mirror. He was waving his arms, still talking to me as if the car were right beside him.

79

Dr. Ann Wilcox: Notes on Gemma Hughes

Gemma was waiting for me in the parking lot during a violent rainstorm. She followed me to the car and grabbed the door, preventing me from leaving. She began ranting at me about her mother. She said her brother was going to have me arrested. It was unclear what connection she thought this had to anything we'd discussed in therapy.

She was unconcerned that her clothing was sopping wet. She didn't even have an umbrella, and she wasn't wearing a coat. She smelled as if she hadn't showered for several days. When I tried to get her to leave me alone, she grabbed my umbrella and stabbed me in the ribs.

It was only because her hands were slippery that I was able to get the umbrella away from her and close the car door. I meant to call the police, but by the time I pulled my phone out of my bag, she'd disappeared, and I didn't see where she'd gone.

80

Gemma

I'm finished with therapy. I don't need it anymore.

I looked in the mirror to see whether I was communicating a confident impression. It was hard to tell. I needed to look strong and in charge when I spoke those words to Dr. Wilcox.

From now on, Geoff and I would support each other. That's what family's for. He was right. He knew all about me, and I knew all about him. Together we'd figure out how to live our lives, how to find love.

Dr. Wilcox had made me feel I was crazy. Talking to her had *made* me crazy. She wanted to pry into our family secrets. She wanted to expose our mistakes to the whole world. She was not going to find out anything about *Aidan.*

Most of all, she was cruel. She was not going to make me feel like it was my fault that my daughter was lost to me. I would tell her how unprofessional she was, trying to make me feel bad. I would let her know that I wasn't going to take that kind of abuse. Geoff had convinced me of that.

We need to stand up for each other, he'd said. *We need to be a family. Maybe we messed up, but that's over. You and I need to stick together. Our parents messed up, but they're family, and we need to protect them.* He couldn't let go of that part, and just like he was right about me, he was probably right about that.

When Dr. Wilcox opened her office door, I was ready. I stood a few feet from the door instead of sitting there like I usually did, waiting for her convenience. I'd already knocked twice. As the door opened, I looked pointedly at my watch. She ushered me inside without saying anything.

I was wearing a power suit and high heels, very high heels, expensive high heels. At least as expensive as a girl can afford on a teacher's salary. Still, they were a splurge, and I loved them. They made my feet look elegant, and my legs look longer. I looked like a classy adult in those shoes, someone who didn't need to spill her guts about her sex life to a therapist. They made me feel fantastic. With those heels, I was two inches taller than Dr. Wilcox.

I sat in the armchair and crossed my legs, glancing at my foot as it arched casually in front of me. I didn't touch the free bottle of water.

"How are you today, Gemma?"

"There are some things we need to discuss," I said.

She smiled. "Good." She took the leather notebook off the table and opened it.

"You won't need to write anything down. In fact, I'll take that with me when I leave."

She smiled. "So what shall we talk about?"

"I'm finished with therapy."

She didn't look surprised. Maybe she knew she'd crossed a line. She said nothing, keeping that empty smile on her face.

"You had no right to suggest it was my fault my baby was taken away."

"Did I say that?"

"Yes, you did."

She glanced at her notebook. "I don't believe that's how

the conversation went."

"That's exactly what you said. I'm very clear on it because I've thought about it. A lot. Almost all the time, in fact."

"That's good. Any dreams?"

"This isn't a therapy session, I'm just telling you I think you were unprofessional. And you're trying to take advantage of the vulnerable spots in my life to make money."

"Is that what *you* think?" Her emphasis on the word *you* was soft, but clear.

"Yes." It had been Geoff's idea, but he was right. I didn't need to explain that to her. I didn't need to explain anything to her.

"You signed a release when you began therapy…"

"What release?"

"Let me finish."

I glared at her. Why was it so easy for her to get the upper hand?

"It allows me to contact your next of kin if I believe you're a danger to yourself. Or to others."

"I'm not a danger to anyone."

She pressed her lips together in a look of disapproval. "I'm trying to explain something. I'd appreciate you giving me the courtesy of letting me finish."

"I'm just correcting your mistake."

"It's my professional opinion that you *are* a danger. Certainly to others, possibly to yourself. And so I spoke with your mother…"

"What? You had…" I uncrossed my legs and stood. "You had no right to do that."

"I reminded you about the release."

"I don't remember that. Not at all. Show it to me."

"If you'd like, I'll get it out of your file, later."

"It should be right there." I nodded at the notebook.

"It's not. My files are in the closet. It's not appropriate to get them out now."

"Why the hell not?"

"Your mother is very worried about you."

"What did you tell her?"

"I expressed my concerns. I told her you assaulted me."

"I never assaulted you." I pressed my thumb and index finger against the bridge of my nose. How dare she talk to my mother. I wasn't a child who needed parental permission. Who did she think she was? Geoff was right...she was trying to take over my life. Had he said that? I wasn't sure. Someone did. But she was...trying to take over.

"I think you've blocked that out. You've blocked out many things."

"No, I haven't."

"You don't seem to recall the confrontation with your parents."

"I freaked out. Because of that pill you gave me."

"It wasn't the pill, Gemma. There's something seriously wrong with you. Do you have periods of time you can't recall?"

"No. You aren't going to muck around in my head anymore." I stepped toward her. "Give me that notebook. I'm done."

She reached into the drawer in her side table and pulled out a packet of pills. "I'd like you to take one of these."

"No. I said..."

"Gemma, you didn't want your baby."

"Stop saying that!" My voice was high-pitched, hysterical. Too loud. I didn't sound like a mature adult, in control of her emotions.

"Shh. Calm down. I know this is so very difficult for you." Her eyes filled with tears.

I wanted to pluck her eyes out of her head.

"Your mother said you didn't want the baby. She did the best she could, given how you…"

I was screaming now. Hysterical. In the midst of the scream filling my lungs, echoing in my ears, I thought of David. How had my life become so twisted around? I felt like I'd been turned inside out. I wanted him. But I wanted my baby too.

"We can talk about how you feel, but I need you to take this."

"No. I know what that pill you gave me last time did to my head." I started crying. I shrieked something at her, but I wasn't sure what I said. I did feel like I was losing my mind.

"It wasn't the pill."

I stared at the green and beige capsule lying on her palm. It was so small. I was gasping for air, I needed something to help me calm down. This wasn't what I'd planned. I'd practiced being in control. I wore my new shoes, I…What if she was right? Was she right? I had no idea what was right or true or…Maybe Geoff was wrong. Look at the secret he kept from me. He remembered everything, and I didn't. Was Dr. Wilcox right?

"You're very upset. This will help you sort out your thoughts. It will ease your anxiety without making you feel drugged. I promise. Then we can talk about what you want. I can let you read my notes, but you need to be calm." She opened the bottle of water and handed it to me. She took my hand, uncurled my fingers, and inserted the capsule between my thumb and forefinger.

I put the capsule in my mouth and swallowed. I drank half the bottle of water, choking and crying, trying to breathe. I slumped into the chair. After a few minutes, I began to breathe normally. My head felt clearer. My heart was no longer thudding in my ears, sounding as if it were ready to burst open, spilling out everything to her salacious ears.

Dr. Wilcox sat across from me, smiling.

The room was silent. Such thick silence. I felt better, dreamy. Floating. All the confusion in my head seemed to untwist. Nothing seemed so terrible. Why had I been so upset?

I smiled back at her.

81

David

Ann's car was in the driveway when I pulled in. Normally, unless she was going out again, she pulled into the garage toward the back of our property. I turned off the engine. I stared at the rear of her car. I glanced at the house. There wasn't a single light on. It was nearly seven, the living room light that ran on a varying timer should have come on. It was set to come on between six-fifteen and six-forty during late fall and winter.

I got out of the car and set the alarm. It seemed futile.

I went through the gate and around to the back of the house, thinking she might be watching the news. Light from that room didn't show at the front of the house. The TV room was also dark. I opened the door to the screened porch. When I put my key into the lock on the French doors, the door drifted open, the latch not fully engaged.

After the broken window, she would never leave a door unlocked, even for a moment.

Suddenly aware that I was entering a bad situation, I grabbed the long fork that hung from a hook on the side of the barbecue.

Nudging the door open wider, I stepped inside. I held the barbecue fork up high, feeling one part foolish, two parts utterly unprepared for what might be waiting. I walked past the TV room. The door to the hallway was wide open, but there wasn't a scrap of light coming from the other rooms on the first floor.

I kept to the side of the hallway, my feet close to the floorboards where the hardwood flooring was less prone to creaking. The house was silent, not even the hint of breathing or a whimper to suggest where Ann might be, or whether someone was in the house with her.

My money was on the living room. Every cell in my body refused to consider she might be dead, the intruder already gone.

As I approached the interior French doors that opened into the living room from the entryway, something flickered on the glass. A quick flash of light, the reflection off a phone screen or a watch face. I slowed and took a deep, soundless breath. A chair creaked.

She. The other.

I held in my sigh of relief.

Images flashed through my mind of him, or her, pressing a gun against the side of Ann's head, a knife blade at her throat, terrorizing her into suppressing even the slightest sound.

I needed light for my own element of surprise. One of the hallway switches operated the track lights in front of the fireplace. The problem was, the panel was past the open doors.

I retreated down the hallway, went around and entered the kitchen from the back hall. I exchanged my useless weapon for a slightly less inadequate butcher knife.

I crossed the room quickly and went into the entryway. I took a deep breath, tightened my grip on the knife, and pressed the switch.

A spray of light spilled into the hallway.

I heard a grunt.

I lunged into the living room, knife raised.

"David! Don't." Ann's words were quick and sure.

She sat on the couch, her hands in her lap, both feet flat on the floor. Behind the couch was a man with longish hair wearing a faded peach-colored T-shirt and blue jeans. He didn't look deranged or high, but he had a knife of his own. The blade rested against Ann's throat — hard, glinting silver beside soft, pale skin.

I was startled by the volume of my own voice. "What do you want? There's not a lot of cash in the house, but…"

"I don't want your fucking money," the man said.

"This is Geoff." Ann spoke as if she were making introductions at a dinner party, but forgetting to complete the second half of the ritual.

"A patient?"

"No. The brother of a patient," she said.

"Not just a patient, although I'm sure they're all the same to you — cash cows." He let his gaze travel pointedly around the living room. "I'm Gemma's brother. And Gemma is a person, a human being, an amazing woman, a woman who's been taken advantage of, not a *patient.*"

My arm went limp. The hand that held the knife fell to my side. The knife began to slip from my fingers, but I managed to hold on.

Geoff laughed bitterly. "A woman who was happy and kind and fun to be around until your wife started peeling her brain apart. Nice gig, getting paid to talk to people until they don't know what they're thinking and aren't sure what's real and what isn't. And then they have to keep seeing you, and paying you, to try to put it all back together, if that's even possible."

Ann spoke calmly. "I explained…"

"Shut up, *Doctor.*" Geoff repositioned his grip on her hair, tugging her head back slightly.

Her throat looked even more vulnerable than it had a moment earlier. The skin seemed almost transparent. I felt as if I could see the workings of her muscles and esophagus when she swallowed. That simple reflex appeared to take tremendous effort.

"You can put down the knife, buddy," Geoff said.

I kept hold of it. "What do you want?"

"I want my sister back the way she was."

"As you pointed out, I doubt that's possible," I said.

"No talking."

"Okay."

"I said, *no* talking! And put the knife away."

I placed it on the chair a few feet from where I stood.

"I said put it away. You people are so used to telling everyone else what to do, you seem to have lost the ability to follow directions." Geoff giggled.

The giggle scared me more than the knife. There was something off about him, and now, I was terrified.

I'd thought I could handle the situation easily. He was smaller and slighter than me, and if he really wanted to kill her, he would have done it before I came home. That's what I'd believed when I entered the room. Now, I had no idea what might happen.

82

Ann

David looked scared. It was an expression I hadn't seen on his face in all the years we'd been together. Except for the day he told me what he'd done. Seeing that fear again was difficult. This time, I wanted to comfort him, not pound him with my fists. I wanted to assure him we'd be okay. We'd made it this far. Geoff Hughes with his obsessively protective feelings for his sister and mother wasn't going to be what brought us down. I was sure about that.

The look on Geoff's face when he realized I wasn't conning his parents out of their money, that I'd conned them into committing his sister to a mental health facility, was an infantile terror of abandonment. He looked like he might cry the bellowing outrage of an infant, suddenly aware of his helplessness.

It was unfortunate that his mother had made the last-minute decision to bring him with her when she met me at the hospital. She and Rob had already filled out the paperwork and completed their interviews. I'd supplied my notebook, filled with the details of Gemma's troubling statements, her stalking, her threats, her assaults. I'd helpfully highlighted the relevant passages. The judge had made her ruling without requesting further analysis — Gemma would be kept under supervision for two weeks.

After that, my close friend on the staff of John Milton Behavioral Health Hospital, Dr. Frank Shimmer, was allowing me the courtesy of continuing as Gemma's therapist while she was a patient there.

Yes, I was happy to have Gemma out of my world, but I would remain in hers for as long as I could manage it, for as long as I felt the need. The pleasure of revenge is so much more delicious when it's savored over months, possibly years, rather than one quick slice to the throat, which seemed to be what Geoff was looking for.

Having Gemma taken into care had gone smoothly despite Geoff's unruly presence. Eventually, the security guards had to be called to escort him to the parking lot. I asked his mother to say her good-byes to Gemma quickly, such as they were, so she could get Geoff off the premises.

Gemma was so incoherent, there wasn't much of a good-bye. Neither did she put up any kind of fight. She simply had no idea where she was or what was happening. She smiled almost constantly and was docile enough that when they asked her to sit in a wheelchair, she settled in with relief. They wheeled her through the doors which looked standard enough but locked securely.

Two hours later, when I opened my car door, Geoff was suddenly beside me, pushing me toward the backyard, flashing his knife near my heart while I obeyed his command to move quickly out of sight.

With the point of the knife sharp on the back of my neck through my thin cotton scarf, I unlocked the back door, disarmed the security system, led him to the living room, and turned out all the lights.

Now, we were at a standoff. An unbalanced standoff

once David acquiesced and placed the butcher knife on the armchair.

I didn't think Geoff knew how to kill me, that he could even manage the mechanics of stabbing me. My sense was that he wasn't sure whether he wanted to do that or not. His desire to lash out made dragging the knife across my throat appealing. The desire to have his sister close at hand made him feel dependent on me, the key to her release. There was no more talk of a con. During his rambling before David arrived, Geoff had been fixated on how I'd turned Gemma's own mind against her.

David stood with his hands in his pocket. He was trying to look confident and in control, although he was neither. "Now what?"

"I told you to stop talking. I'm not saying it again," Geoff said.

We remained silent for several minutes. David stood in the center of the room. He pulled his hands out of his pockets and folded them across his chest. Alongside the fear, he looked helpless and angry. Every few seconds, his gaze darted toward one side of the room or the other, working out possible ways to get control of the situation.

Geoff craved the illusion of being in charge — telling us not to speak, but he didn't know what to do with that prolonged silence. And he didn't know what to do next. I don't think he really knew why he'd done any of the things he'd done — stalking me, trying to understand why I was friendly with his mother, and now this.

After the silence lingered too long for his comfort, he began talking in spite of himself. "You messed her up. You fucked with her head. She was fine, and now she doesn't care about anything, and she's crying all the time. She can't think about anything but her baby. And your answer was to lock her in a mental ward with a bunch of nut cases? That should be against the law. It *is* against the law, I'm pretty sure."

I waited for more. Soon, he would realize that it wasn't satisfying to carry on a monologue. He'd want me to speak so he could lash out further.

"She doesn't belong in a mental hospital. She's more sane than you are. There's nothing wrong with her. You shrinks are all the same. You think you know it all, and you think digging up the past is going to fix everything. It doesn't."

I spoke carefully, aware of the blade touching my throat. "Do you have things you want fixed?"

"Shut up."

"Why do you want me to shut up?"

"I could cut your throat."

"You could. But I don't think you want to, not yet. You want something from me."

"Don't try to shrink my head."

"What do you want from me?"

"My sister."

"This is for her own good. She needs help. The sister you get back, eventually, will be healthy."

"She doesn't need your help. I need more help than she does."

"Why do you think that?"

"Don't talk to me."

"Why do you think you need help, Geoff?"

The pressure of his hand softened on the top of my head. His other hand, obviously tired of holding the knife poised at my throat for close to forty minutes now, relaxed slightly. I felt the cool tip of the blade move to the upper edge of my collarbone. I let out a soft breath, feeling less frightened myself. I saw the same in David's eyes.

I spoke in a low, soothing voice. "Your mother was very upset when you masturbated, wasn't she."

"Don't talk about that. It's not…stop it!" His voice rose. He took his hand off my head and ran his fingers through his tangled hair. The knife remained pressed against my collarbone.

"She wants you to stay her little boy. Seeing that you were becoming a man was traumatic for her. She made you feel ashamed of being a man."

"Whatever. That's bullshit. It's all a long time ago."

"But it's festering inside of you. She won, didn't she? You're still her little boy, living in her house, letting her take care of you."

"Not true. Shut the fuck up."

"I'm just trying…"

"Shut! Up! Let me think."

"I can help you, Geoff."

He didn't respond.

There was something else going on here. This wasn't about me conning his mother, or being shamed by his mother all those years ago. "I can help you. Gemma told me everything."

"She wouldn't."

"Shame is a crippling thing. But you need to own your behavior before you can free yourself."

"She didn't tell you. And I'm not ashamed. There's nothing wrong with me. People…"

He grunted. The knife moved slightly.

"People, what?"

"People overreact."

"I agree. There's far too much shame. The spectrum of human behavior is broad."

Another grunt.

"Talk to me Geoff. It will make you feel better. I promise."

"It didn't make Gemma feel better."

"Is that what she said? My impression was, it did. She uncovered a lot of things about herself. She's ready to heal. She just needs more time. More intense therapy. Supervision."

"She doesn't."

"Tell me what's bothering you."

"You are. You're bothering me."

"That's good. You're being honest."

"Don't fucking shrink my brain."

"I'm just listening."

He let out another soft grunt, more of a groan this time. "It's not her fault. She wanted the baby. She would have been a good mother. A great mother. She's a very loving person. So kind. So good."

"Yes. Just confused."

"Yeah. We were confused. But my mother decided our baby was shameful. It wasn't because Gemma didn't want it. And you made her feel that she didn't. You lied to her."

I held my breath, trying to process what he'd just said. I didn't look at David, I couldn't have whatever was passing through his head make me react. There was still a knife blade an inch from my carotid artery.

He really didn't know what he wanted. Absolution,

maybe. A lot of patients do. Clarity. A fresh start. There could be a lot of things. And he knew it was my fault his sister was out of his reach. Now I understood why he cared for her so very much.

83

Ann

Geoff moved, letting the knife slip to the side, closer to my shoulder. He lifted his other hand to wipe the hair and perspiration off his face.

David lunged across the space between us. He leapt onto the coffee table, flung himself onto the couch, and tackled Geoff. His foot landed hard on my leg, making me cry out, but the force of him, and the angle in which he leaped, pushed Geoff away from me.

A moment later, I heard a guttural sound from Geoff. David was grunting and cursing. I huddled at the end of the couch only a few feet from them, but David's body blocked me seeing what was happening. I knew the knife was penetrating Geoff's body, David's arm moving with such ferocious energy it seemed the knife might go all the way through to the other side. He continued stabbing him. Repeatedly. Deeply. Large amounts of blood began spreading across our cream-colored couch, soaking into the fabric as if the couch were suffering from unquenchable thirst.

I smelled the blood. I'd never smelled it like that before. It was unmistakable, sickening.

I cried for David to stop, but he didn't seem to hear.

Did I mean it? I'm not sure. I didn't want to see a man murdered. I didn't want to see my husband do such a thing and I didn't want to contemplate how he was going to feel after it was over.

But there didn't seem to be an alternative. Even if Geoff backed down and didn't cut my throat, or stab me through the ribs when the knife slipped lower on my body as he grew tired of holding it, I couldn't have him knowing.

There was too much risk that he might find out I was more than just Gemma's therapist. If he talked to his mother about David, if I slipped up and spoke his name as I almost had when I'd introduced Geoff, if he returned to our house, rifled through our mail, talked to Gemma when he visited... there were a hundred ways he might find out.

The analytical line of my thinking shocked me. My husband was stabbing a man right before my eyes, and I was planning the next steps. Vague thoughts of cleaning up the mess, burying Geoff's body, flickered in my imagination. But I always am thinking of the next steps, always planning, always analyzing. It's how my mind works.

Despite his weakened condition, Geoff began to fight back. With a burst of adrenaline, he kneed David in the groin. The pain and sudden loss of breath caused David to fall to the floor, crashing between the table and couch.

Geoff sat up, clutching his chest, moving his hands around his body as if he thought he could stop the bleeding. "Help me! You said you wanted to help me. Make it stop. You're a doctor. Help me, god damn it!"

84

Ann

I wriggled along the couch until I was beside Geoff. I pulled him up against me and pressed a throw pillow against his chest. I didn't really want to stop the bleeding. I saw clearly where this had to go. But I pressed gently, to get him to calm down, to give the impression I was helping him.

Beside me on the floor, David groaned from the pain of Geoff's knee in his balls. I glanced down and saw his face, sickly white. Even his lips had lost their color. "It's okay," I said. "I've got this."

As Geoff settled back, collapsing into my body from loss of blood and fading consciousness, I eased the pressure of my hands on the pillow. Dark blood appeared almost black as it spread through the sage green pillow.

I adjusted Geoff's head so it rested on my collarbone. I stroked his hair, and a moment later, I let the pillow fall to the floor. I took soft, shallow breaths, listening for the movement of his breath…out…a pause, gasping…pause…in…a sigh. He made choking sounds as blood pooled inside of his throat as quickly as it spread across our couch and my clothing.

Finally, blood and bile foamed out of his lips. He choked, gasped once, and then he was no longer breathing.

He died in my arms while David lay on the floor beside me.

85

David

When I was finally able to get myself upright after the brutal pain of a knee in the balls, I looked at the mess.

Blood. Everywhere.

I couldn't get my head around all that blood. I knew the human body contains over a gallon of blood, but this looked like so much more. The couch was swampy with thick red ooze. The guy's entire shirt was red and sagging with the weight of it. Blood coated his face and arms. Ann had blood on her jaw and neck. Her clothes were almost as soggy as his.

I looked down and saw the blood on my own clothes. On my hands. I wiped them on my pants, fighting a wave of nausea. As I wiped, the blood smeared across my skin, seeming to grow thicker. It remained embedded beneath my fingernails and along my cuticles.

I closed my eyes and pictured a gallon of water. The consistency and the color of the blood made it so much worse. Knowing it was nearly impossible to be rid of made it worse still. And really, knowing what it was, where it had come from, made the quantity seem five times that amount.

Ann slid out from beneath Geoff's body. She looked up at me, her expression curious. Wondering, I suppose, what I was thinking, trying to guess what I'd say or do first.

I wasn't even sure myself. I knew I'd possibly saved her

life. For a moment, that knowledge overwhelmed me. There had also been a certain amount of desire to save my own ass. I had not wanted this guy to find out that I was the one who screwed and dumped his sister.

We needed to call the police. Self-defense. An intruder. Armed. Holding a knife to my wife's throat. But the connection to Ann, and my own association, troubled me. There was no doubt those details would emerge if the police were involved. "I…"

She nodded. "Yes. We can bury him in the yard. It will take a lot of work, digging deep enough, but it's the only solution."

"The couch…" Why the hell was I thinking about the couch? A man was dead in my living room. I was a killer. My wife was planning…I wasn't even sure what was going on with her.

She stood and began stripping off her clothes. Right there in the living room. I wasn't turned on. Thankfully. At her directive, we had to be sure we didn't track blood into another room. While she stripped, she told me what she'd done to Gemma. Before she was finished talking, we were both naked. I was light-headed, uncertain whether I was more shocked at my own act or her lengthy, intricate plan to punish the wrong person.

Gemma wasn't the one at fault here. She hadn't known I was married. Ann refused to accept that. We argued about it, talking around each other.

Ann was firm. "On some level, she knew."

"Even if she suspected, she didn't know at the beginning."

"None of that matters. She knows now, and she still

wants you. She needs psychiatric help. She truly does. She believes you're soul mates. It's completely delusional. And the baby…her relationship with her brother…it's all for the best. You have to see that."

I did see that she was troubled, but Ann set her up. I was the one to blame. "I'm the one who hurt you."

"But I love you. This is what love is. Loving no matter what the other person does. Love that overtakes you. Love that you can't put an end to, even if you wanted." She came toward me, she wrapped her arms around my waist and rested her head on my collarbone. "All I did, really, was expose the damage. It would have seeped into her life at some point. She is truly better off."

"You really believe that?"

"I do."

I stopped arguing. I loved her, and that was all. Ann was my heart. I'd believed I would do anything for her, for us. And now, it was clear that I *was* capable of doing absolutely anything for her.

We brought in a box of large black trash bags and stuffed our clothes inside. Ann pointed out we'd need to have the carpet replaced, the walls re-painted, maybe a softer color than the intense blue that currently covered the walls. We went upstairs and showered and dressed in the clothes we usually wore for gardening. Ann made grilled cheese sandwiches, and then we got to work.

It took most of the night to dig an adequate hole. We chose a spot just beyond the small circle of birch trees that ringed a Koi pond in the far corner of our yard, close to where the ground sloped to the creek. I used a pick to loosen the ground. Both of us released copious amounts of sweat as we drove shovels deep into the earth, spooning up clay-like soil and rocks. We spread a tarp on the living room floor and rolled the body onto it. The tarp allowed us to drag the corpse through the house and out to the yard without leaving smears of blood.

Sharp pains pierced my neck from constantly looking toward our neighbors on either side, checking for lights, trying to assess the angle of their views into our yard. I was pretty sure our eight-foot fences, the lush border of trees, prevented any line of sight, but the fear, knowing it wasn't impossible, made for an agonizing night mentally as well as physically.

The sky was growing light by the time we finished filling the hole and transplanting a few agapanthuses on top of the burial site. I scattered half a bag of ground cover material over the fresh dirt. The final task was to wrap the couch in trash bags and duct tape in preparation for taking it to the dump. We ran out of bags, and I had to make a run to an all-night store for three more boxes while Ann went online and booked a rental truck.

The entire time we worked, I silently marveled at my wife's cool, precise demeanor.

Exhausted, we returned to the kitchen. We scrubbed our hands clean with steaming water and anti-bacterial soap. Ann made mimosas. We sat on the back porch and drank an entire bottle of champagne mixed with orange juice. We didn't talk. We ate buttered toast and kept our thoughts to ourselves.

My thoughts were difficult to sort out, but the bottom line was — I loved her. I loved her so much I knew I couldn't carry on any sort of life without her. She was right. No matter what she'd done…I loved her.

It seemed as if the things we'd done were like pouring cement into all the crevices between us. Soon, it would harden, and we would be rock-solid. Forever.

86

Gemma

My mother had been to visit me every single day. During her two-to-three-hour visits, we didn't talk much. The silence was unbearable for my father, and he'd only accompanied her once. Or that was the reason he passed to me through my mother's lips. More likely, he was still mostly interested in people that had died years ago. Possibly he liked that he didn't have to actually interact with them, but he could still feel as if he had companions in his life.

During my father's single visit, they told me Geoff had gone missing. His car was found parked near the Golden Gate Bridge at the mouth of San Francisco Bay. There hadn't been any reports of a man jumping, but the location had convinced my mother he'd jumped and been torn apart by sharks.

Thinking of his brutal death gave her nightmares she said. She needed pills to sleep. The loss of her child was so painful she physically ached all the time. It was difficult to get up off the couch, she said. Difficult to swallow food. "You have no idea how deep and constant the pain is," she said.

I wasn't sure he'd jumped off of anything. But because of my medication, I found myself in a calm, drifting state of mind most of the time. I was upset, of course. I was concerned about what had happened to him. I even feared he was dead, somewhere, just not in the bay. But I wasn't hysterical. I didn't feel bereft without him.

It was as if my feelings floated along the horizon and I needed binoculars to catch sight of them. They were so small, so blurred, and so far away, they didn't seem to have anything to do with me.

When they told me I would be staying in the hospital for a few weeks, I didn't get upset at that either. I didn't care. Not really. What did it matter? David didn't love me. He was gone from my life. I would never find my daughter, and even if I did, what had they done to her? Would she even be like me, raised by someone else? She'd never felt her mother's arms around her. She'd spent her first weeks unloved and untouched. She would hate me, I was sure of it. And how did you find a missing child anyway? DNA tracking only works when other people submit theirs.

The pills kept everything soft and pleasant and dreamy. I felt I was moving and sitting and sleeping on beds of rose petals — silky smooth on my skin, smelling sweet, and so gentle and delicate. I spent most days in the courtyard watching birds and looking at flowers. I took long naps and slept ten or eleven hours at night. I watched a lot of TV, but didn't really care what show was tuned in.

Twice a week Dr. Wilcox came for therapy. That too, was dreamy and soft. Therapy involved the same long periods of silence I shared with my mother. The room was quiet while my mind drifted on a glassy, endless sea.

My mother liked to place her hand over mine. She smiled at me. She patted my wrist. She told me what she'd eaten for breakfast or lunch, and she talked about her book club. She cried softly when she talked about Geoff, about how unbearable it was to not even know where your child's body was.

"I'm sorry you have to be here," she said.

"It's fine."

"Do you like it? Are you making friends?"

I gazed into her eyes and smiled.

"Dr. Wilcox is so helpful, don't you think?"

I wasn't sure what Dr. Wilcox was helpful with, but it seemed like too much work to argue with my mother.

"You look happy," she said. Her eyes filled with tears. "You look exactly like you did in your third-grade picture, with your hair like that. And smiling so sweetly."

I nodded. "You liked having a little girl to dress up."

She nodded. "You're still my little girl." She squeezed the back of my hand, pressing the bones together. She turned her hand over and slid it beneath mine to hold on properly.

She never wanted us to grow up. And I supposed that now we wouldn't. Not really. I would be meek and sweet and vaguely happy with my pills and TV and the garden. Sometimes they made me do craft activities and exercises. I didn't mind.

Geoff…well maybe he *was* dead. Where else would he be? My mother said he hadn't updated his blog. None of his friends had received a text from him. His credit cards were unused. It made sense that he was dead. I couldn't imagine him going to the trouble of changing his identity or going off the grid, as they say. He'd grown up, but he would never grow old.

My mother and I sat holding hands. I hoped Dr. Wilcox had a plan that allowed me to stay in this place for a very long time. I was happy here, and that's all I ever wanted.

87

David

She sat at the end of the bar, out of range of the track lighting that cast glistening circles on the polished wood and made the bottles of alcohol glimmer like gems. To her left were couples and groups of friends crowding up, empty drink glasses pushed to the side faster than the bartender could clean them up.

Her dark hair fell to her shoulders, straight and shiny, swaying with the slightest movement of her head. Her skin was clear and looked soft, even from a distance. She studied her glass of wine and smiled, presumably at her own thoughts.

She was the most beautiful woman I'd ever seen.

She wore a white sweater that was cut to the edges of her shoulders, revealing a lot of skin but without flashing it around. The sweater reached just past her elbows. Her right wrist had several thin gold chains around it and on her left wrist was a bracelet-type watch with a tiny face. She wore a fitted black skirt and black high heels.

I was nearly fifteen minutes late, and I was impressed she'd ordered a drink rather than sitting there tense and irritated. She simply relaxed and took care of herself. She waited casually as if the enjoyment of her wine wouldn't be dampened even if I never showed.

The chair beside her was empty, waiting for me.

We began talking. She didn't flirt, and I followed her lead. We just talked. About our jobs. About travel, about movies we'd seen recently and long ago, movies we loved and hated. We talked about books and music. It might seem like we'd had far too much to drink during our conversation, but it was the opposite. We were so engrossed in learning about the other, we'd been sitting there for an hour before we ordered a second round.

And then the conversation turned to partners. Despite the intricate turquoise ring on the center finger of her left hand, it turned out she was married. So was I.

And that's how it started.

We had dinner together that night, and she came to my condo afterwards. When we made love, I felt that I could die in that moment and not regret the ending of my life. Being in her arms felt like being home. I was more myself than I'd been at any other moment in my life.

Neither of us started out intending to cheat on our spouses, although I suppose asking and agreeing to meet for a drink meant that possibility already existed somewhere in her subconscious mind, and mine. But the attraction was too intense. And it wasn't just physical, despite her beauty. There was something on a mental level that I'd felt when I heard her lecture, and when we spoke afterwards. She'd felt the same.

We fell in love. We were certain we would be the exception, the anomaly in the data that says men and women who cheat will cheat again. We wouldn't simply hook up and return to our spouses when the excitement cooled. This was real. This was different. *We* were different.

Over the course of two years, both of us were divorced.

We were married on the shore of Lake Tahoe with a small group of friends and our even smaller group of family members.

Ann Wilcox and David Graves. We were soul mates. One of those epic love stories that's the stuff of fiction.

88

Gemma

I think Dr. Wilcox had always known what was best for me.

There's nothing really wrong with me, but the world is too much. Everything I loved is gone.

Here, I can sleep. A lot. And I can dream. I dream about my baby girl — precious little Audrey. In my dream, she has blonde hair, the same color as mine, just as mine is the same shade as my mother's. She smiles at me all the time, and I hold her. The scent of her sweet skin fills my mind when my eyes are closed.

She never cries, unlike her mama. I spent most of my life crying, deep inside, even if it wasn't visible.

Dr. Wilcox had told me to buy a notebook and write down my thoughts about therapy. I no longer have any thoughts about it. She asks me questions, and I make up answers, whatever comes to mind. Other times, I say nothing. She says nothing, hoping she can make me uncomfortable enough that I'll fill the silence with my life. My secrets. But I won't do that. There are no more secrets, and if she wants to know what I'm feeling, she can wait forever.

When she told me to buy the notebook, she also told me to write down my dreams. Those dreams frightened me, and I stopped writing them down. I wanted to forget them. I wanted to sleep without dreams.

And then, one day while I was in the garden where I live now, it came to me. Instead of putting my thoughts and dreams into the notebook, the notebook could put those things into my head. I started writing down what I wanted to dream. I wrote the same stories over and over — stories of making love with David, stories of holding my baby, feeding my baby.

Soon, I started to have short, wispy dreams of her. I saw her face. I kissed her and held her.

I didn't write any dreams of her growing up. I wanted her in my arms forever. My sweet little Audrey, holding her close to my heart as we gaze into each other's eyes.

When I'm awake, I feel dead, as if I'm lying beside Geoff. When I dream, I feel alive, and very, very happy.

89

Ann

I had to blame her. I could never blame him because I love him too much. Sometimes, I blame myself for not noticing he needed me, and that he needed me to need him. But most of the time, I blame her.

I don't know why I love him the way I do. Love is inexplicable. He took the most intimate treasured part of himself and placed it inside another woman's body. A body he desired as much as mine. No...more than mine, for a while.

But I was beside him every night. Available. For *him* to reach for me.

I blame myself for not seeing what was happening. How can a person trained for years to observe the workings of the psyche miss the signs of loneliness right beside her in bed, across from her at the dinner table? Why did I stop reaching out to him? I have no idea. Maybe I was under the societal delusion that men don't need to feel loved in the same way that women do.

We are soul mates. That never changes. The idea of a soul mate is being connected in every way — not just bodies or the circumstances of life mating with each other, but *souls* finding one another and joining together, recognizing another who looks at the world in the same way.

Now, we're connected in every piece of our lives. We're joined in what he did to Geoff and what I did to Gemma. We can't go back, but what we have will be even better. Leonard Cohen's voice drifts through my mind again — *There's a crack in everything, that's how the light gets in.*

Love is inexplicable, so I won't try to explain.

All I know is that every night, David and I die in each other's arms.

La petite mort.

A Note from Cathryn

Thank you so much for choosing to read *She's Listening*. Your support is greatly appreciated, and I hope you enjoyed the book as much as I enjoyed writing it. If you enjoyed the book, I would be extremely grateful if you could take a few moments to leave a quick review. It's always great to hear what readers think and it can also help others discover my books. Any recommendations to friends and family are also very welcome! I love hearing from readers so please feel free to let me know what you thought via my Facebook page or Twitter. You can even contact me directly through my website. To make sure you don't miss out on my upcoming releases and more, you can sign up to my mailing list at my website: CathrynGrant.com

Thank you again for all your support – it is greatly appreciated.

Cathryn.